Each Hidden Passage

Garrett Hutson

Warfleigh Publishing first edition August 2022

Cover design by Stuart Bache

For more information, or to book an event, please contact the author at www.garretthutson.com

Each Hidden Passage, Published in the United States

ISBN 978-1-953846-05-1 (hardcover)

ISBN 978-1-953846-12-9 (paperback)

ISBN 978-1-953846-14-3 (eBook)

For my friends who have been like family.

Hutson

Part I

Hutson

1

Friday, January 30, 1942
Lyon, Unoccupied France

Oliver Carmichael's heart skipped a beat when he saw the postmark on the telegram. It was from Vichy. No good could come of a message from Vichy.

He tipped the delivery boy a half-franc. "Thank you, sir," the boy said, dipping his head before hurrying out the door.

Oliver glanced at the four-foot poster board on an easel by the club's front door. It shouted in big, bold black lettering:

Chez Oliver presents:
Cécile Fournier!
For two nights, Friday and Saturday, 30 and 31 January,
Lyonnais can hear the voice that charmed Paris audiences

The same poster had adorned walls all over the *Vieux Quartier* for two weeks. He was expecting a larger than usual crowd tonight.

The club was a flurry of activity, with waiters scurrying around preparing the tables, while the young bar-back swept the floors one more time. Oliver had a letter opener in the office, but the bar was closer, and he grabbed a knife to cut the telegram open. *She can't cancel last-minute.* Cécile was nothing if not the consummate professional.

It wasn't from Cécile, but the actual message sent a chill through his entire body.

> VISITING LYON TONIGHT STOP
> EAGER TO SEE YOUR CLUB STOP
> WILL BRING ITEMS YOU LEFT IN PARIS STOP
> JACQUES CHASTAIN

He leaned against the bar and stared at the telegram, open-mouthed. Jacques Chastain? That was Hélène's husband. Oliver didn't actually know him. He thought maybe they'd been introduced once, more than two years ago at *Le Chien Errant* in Paris, where he used to play trumpet. To his knowledge, Jacques Chastain had never known about him and Hélène.

Or maybe he had. Oliver wondered what that would mean if he did. What kind of reaction could Oliver expect from him this evening?

It's my club, I can throw him out. But surely that wouldn't be necessary. The Chastains were haute-bourgeois, and as such they would always maintain impeccable manners, no matter how enraged they might be.

"Will bring items you left in Paris," he mumbled aloud. Oliver's stomach sank when he realized this meant the steamer trunk he'd abandoned in the back of Jacques Chastain's car—which Oliver had stolen from their garage the night he escaped from Paris in October, but had to abandon near Saint Sulpice. He and Lisette—and Marcel—had ultimately made their escape from Saint Sulpice in Jean-Louis DuBois's car. They'd had little choice—the Gestapo were firing on them, and it was the closest.

Why would Jacques Chastain bring Oliver the things he'd left in his car when he stole it? It made no sense. He certainly wasn't doing that out of the kindness of his heart. So what did he want?

Oliver tried to remember what work Chastain did for the French government. He was a high-level bureaucrat of some sort, but Oliver would be damned if he could remember which ministry. He and Hélène had never discussed that in detail.

"Excuse me, Mr. Carmichael." The feminine voice, quiet but still forceful, broke him from his reverie. He turned to see Térèse, one of the club's waitresses, holding a heavy tray of glasses. She was tiny, barely five feet tall, and the tray seemed to dwarf her small frame.

"I'm sorry, Térèse," he said, hurrying to step aside. He knew better than to offer to take the heavy tray from her. That had earned him a firm but polite rebuke from the miniature young woman a month ago, when they first opened.

"It is ok, boss," she replied lightly, in heavily-accented English, a hint of impish smile curling up the corner of her lips.

Her eyes glanced at the open telegram on the bar as she passed. He refolded it and slipped it inside his white dinner jacket.

Oliver glanced at his gold watch—incidentally, the watch Hélène had given him for his birthday a year-and-a-half ago. It was five o'clock, one hour until they opened. His eyes scanned the room until he saw the imposing form of Dolph Hansen in his black tuxedo jacket, a chart in his big hands, giving instructions to a pair of waiters.

Oliver slipped up quietly to not disturb them and waited until the waiters—both strikingly handsome young men, of course, given Dolph's tastes—scurried away to do their manager's bidding.

"*Salut*, Oliver," Dolph said, turning toward him and giving the informal French greeting. He was one of the few people at Chez Oliver who called the owner by his first name. But they'd known each other for several years, and it would have felt strange for Dolph to call him "Mr. Carmichael."

Oliver returned the informal greeting. "A gentleman is coming this evening, an important government official from Paris." Wariness clouded Dolph's deep blue eyes, and Oliver put his hand on his friend's massive arm. "Nothing to worry about. He's coming to see me, and I'd like for you to have him sat at table twenty-two."

The table closest to the office, and Dolph's expression said that he understood. "Will he give his name when he arrives?"

Oliver had to smile at the professional demeanor, though he was sure the news had caused Dolph a firestorm of anxiety. He didn't let it show because employees were in earshot, and of course they were listening even though none of them so much as glanced at their bosses.

"Yes. I'm expecting Mr. Jacques Chastain. He didn't say what time, so let's keep table twenty-two open all night."

"Of course." Dolph gave Oliver a crisp Teutonic nod. "I will let you know when he arrives. Any special instructions?"

"No, that will be enough. Thank you, my friend." He patted Dolph's hard-as-steel arm, built from years of wielding a chisel and hammer to create works of art from slabs of stone, and headed back to the office.

The safe was open, and he found Lisette in front of it, counting out stacks of franc notes and making marks in a ledger. Two cash drawers sat on the desk beside the safe, and she sorted stacks of five, ten, twenty, and fifty-franc notes into the slots.

"I expect it's going to be busy this evening," he said, leaning down to kiss her cheek as she counted.

She nodded but continued to count for several more seconds. "Yes, I am putting extra in each drawer tonight," she said, closing the metal flaps over each stack in one of the drawers. "We will not run out of change."

She stood then, straightened his black bowtie, and put her arms around his neck. "Do not worry, Oliver." Her brown eyes were soft and warm as she stared into his. "Tonight will be a big success, and Chez Oliver will become the most popular cabaret in Lyon." She stood on her toes and kissed him.

There was a knock at the office door before it opened, and Dolph Hansen's head and shoulders appeared around the side. "Miss Fournier has arrived."

"Thank you, Dolph." Oliver glanced at the clock on the wall. Quarter past five. "Right on time."

"Did you expect anything different?" Lisette asked, one eyebrow arched. "You should not worry so much."

He didn't reply, just looked back at her with silent acknowledgement before walking out of the office.

Cécile Fournier Dryden—who still used the stage name Cécile Fournier—stood on the stage, adjusting the height of the large silver microphone in the center. She wore a shimmering gold-sequined evening gown, with a high slit up the right leg, and a moderately low back. A fur wrap was draped around her shoulders. The round bulge in front belied her six-month pregnancy, and Oliver was amazed that she could commission such an expensive and elegant evening gown in a maternity cut.

Oliver waved to her. She smiled in acknowledgement, but went back to work immediately, tapping the microphone, and then speaking a few words into it. Her voice, smooth as melted chocolate, filled the room.

"Is Frank with you?" Oliver asked when Cécile came gingerly down from the stage, and they kissed each other's cheeks, left then right.

"He is at the hotel. He'll be here before the performance," Cécile said, in English. Since marrying Frank Dryden ten months before, Cécile almost always spoke English now to the many Anglophones in her life. And Oliver had noticed her accent getting better.

"I'm so glad you agreed to do this for us," he said, switching to English.

She smiled at him, and briefly touched his cheek with her gloved hand. The touching gesture surprised him.

"It is I who should be thanking you, my dear," she said. "I have anticipated this for weeks. I am in the clouds since you asked me."

For twenty years, Cécile Fournier had been one of the biggest names in the Parisian nightclub scene. But all of that had come crashing down last March when the Gestapo had tried to strong-arm her into performing at a Hitler Youth award ceremony in Alsace. Frank Dryden had married her, and used his diplomatic immunity to get her over the Line of Demarcation into the Unoccupied Zone.

Oliver was certain Cécile missed the stage, no matter how happy her domestic life might be. "I know it's not easy to get here."

"*Bof*," she said with a puff of air, waving a hand in the air dismissively. "Two hours by train is not a hardship. I would move to Lyon in an instant, if Frank didn't have to stay in Vichy for his work."

Oliver nodded. Vichy was a sleepy resort town high in the rugged *Massif Central* plateau, and the presence of the far-right French government wouldn't have improved its appeal to a sophisticated Parisienne.

"Do you need to rehearse any of the songs I sent you?" Oliver asked, though he was pretty sure how she'd respond.

"If it would make you feel better. But it is not necessary. I am prepared. A little warm up before we open is all I need."

Victor, their pianist, arrived just then, and Oliver called him over. He made the introductions, and they discussed the sets. Then he hurried to find the bar-back, Armand, and told him to light the coal furnace.

"I will do that right away, boss," Armand said in his lilting Caribbean French accent, rubbing his brown hands together.

Lisette finished with the cash drawers and was slipping on her coat when she found Oliver giving last-minute instructions to the musicians in the band.

"I'm going home to feed the cat," she said, giving him a quick kiss on the mouth. Then her eyes grew concerned. "Are you alright, Oliver?"

He tried to smile, but knew immediately that it looked forced. He could tell she wasn't fooled. "I'm just nervous about tonight. It's nothing."

She squeezed his hand. "Everything will be fantastic, you'll see. I'll be back for the show." She gave him a quick peck on the cheek, and walked out the door.

Oliver took a deep breath, running his hand through the side of his hair. Then he cast a glance at the band to see if anyone had noticed the nervous gesture, but they were all busy tuning their instruments. He hurried to the office and locked the door.

He removed the folded telegram from his jacket pocket and reread it before tossing it into a drawer. What on Earth did Chastain want from him?

Hutson

2

Oliver was giving last-minute instructions to Simon, their spotlight operator, when Dolph touched his shoulder.

"Mr. Dryden has arrived."

"Thank you," Oliver said, and scanned the room until he saw Frank Dryden sitting in one of the tall chairs at the bar. He glanced at his watch. Four minutes to six. He had just enough time.

"Welcome, Mr. Dryden. I'm so glad you to see you," Oliver said, loudly enough to be overheard by the bartender, Fabien, who was setting a highball glass of whiskey in front of Dryden.

"Oliver! Good to see you. I have to say, I'm impressed." He gestured around the room.

"I couldn't have made this happen without you," Oliver said, his gratitude sincere. *Not without all the money you paid me.* Then he leaned a little closer, and said more quietly, "Can we talk in my office for a few minutes?"

"Absolutely." Dryden laid a two-franc coin on the bar and picked up his drink. "I appreciate that you aren't gouging the price of bourbon, like just about everyone else these days."

"That's the last case." Oliver closed the office door. "Bourbon's as scarce as Scotch now."

Dryden shook his head sadly. "German U-boats can target American merchant shipping now, so the distillers aren't shipping it to Lisbon anymore." He took a seat next to Oliver's desk. "What do we need to discuss in private?"

Oliver opened the desk drawer and handed the telegram to Dryden.

"Jacques Chastain," Dryden murmured. "I know that name. Who is he?"

"A French government bureaucrat, from Paris." Oliver hesitated a second, then made a little shrug and added, "He's married to my former lover, Hélène Chastain."

Dryden chuckled. "So you think he's coming to Lyon to confront you about sleeping with his wife? Not likely, you know."

Oliver had to agree. The difficulty of passing through the Line of Demarcation would dissuade most—but Jacques Chastain could probably get an *Ausweis* from the German Occupation Authority whenever he requested one, within reason.

"He's a government official, so I'm a little apprehensive."

Dryden's eyes narrowed. "What are these 'items you left in Paris?' Anything incriminating?"

Oliver shook his head. "Just personal items, mostly—clothes, photographs." He hesitated again. Dryden arched an eyebrow. Oliver sighed and added, "And about a thousand dollars in cash."

Dryden's mouth set in a thin line. "That's a lot of money, Oliver."

"You paid it to me."

"Yes, and we need to make sure that doesn't become widely known." Dryden stood and paced the room once. "What ministry is Chastain part of?"

"I don't know." Oliver's cheeks heated.

"Hmmm," Dryden said. "As long as he's not in the Justice Ministry, I think you're safe from arrest. The question is, will he try to use your involvement in Captain Allard's detainment as leverage to get you to do something for him. And if so, what?"

Oliver's insides went cold. Sweat broke out on the back of his neck. "What should I do?"

"Meet with him, as requested. He's coming here tonight—so I'll keep an eye from the bar. If you need my assistance, just give me a signal. Look at me, and then signal the waiter for a drink refill, whether Chastain needs one or not. I'll come right over and pretend to be a friendly regular."

Oliver nodded. "I need to get back to the club. The doors are opening."

Dryden patted Oliver's shoulder on the way out of the office. "Don't worry about a thing. Just let me know what he wants after he leaves, and we'll go from there. It's probably nothing to worry about."

Oliver hoped he was right.

**

It was seven-thirty when Jacques Chastain arrived. Oliver recognized him from *Le Chien Errant* two years before. Looking distinguished in a gray pin-striped suit with a red carnation in the buttonhole of his lapel, he was thinner now, but everyone was thinner these days.

Oliver pretended to be busy looking over papers at the bar, while watching Chastain from the corner of his eye. Claude, their maître'd, escorted him to table twenty-two, then whispered something to Dolph Hansen, who was busy near the kitchen door. Dolph nodded, left what he was doing immediately, and approached Oliver.

Oliver shook his head and waved him off, and Dolph retreated, looking a little confused. After making Chastain wait a moment, Oliver walked to table twenty-two. "Mr. Chastain?"

Chastain stood, his steely blue eyes staring hard at Oliver as he shook his hand. "You are Oliver Carmichael, formerly of the Rue La Grange in Paris." It wasn't a question.

"That's right." Oliver motioned for Chastain to retake his seat. He took the seat opposite, where he could see Frank Dryden at the bar from the corner of his eye. "What can I do for you?"

Chastain took a pull on his cigarette, held it a moment, and slowly exhaled a stream of smoke, all the while never breaking eye contact. "We met at a nightclub in the *Quartier Pigalle* in 1939, *Le Chien Errant*. You played in the band there."

Oliver nodded, but remained silent, waiting for Chastain to say what he wanted.

"Congratulations on opening this cabaret," Chastain said, waving his cigarette hand in the air.

"Thank you." Oliver's patience was wearing thin, but he kept his voice and expression calm.

"I have been interested in you since October, when you took my car from my garage in the middle of the night and drove it to the sixth arrondissement. The Gestapo awoke me and my wife that evening, to inform us of its theft. I was curious why the Gestapo should be interested in this, and not the Paris police. Of course, it is no use asking the Gestapo such questions." He made a typical Parisian tiny shrug and momentary frown, the combination a sort of non-verbal "*Bof.*"

"Of course," Oliver agreed, watching Chastain closely.

"When the Paris police discovered my car near Saint Sulpice, they found some abandoned belongings in the trunk. These things did not belong to my family."

"Yes, your telegram mentioned that you had items that belong to me," Oliver said, no longer able to completely keep the edge from his tone.

"I knew they belonged to you because of a photograph, which included you and a young woman. I remembered meeting you. I surmised that you were...acquainted with my wife. I made an inquiry the next morning to the Prefect of Police, and I learned that you are wanted for kidnapping a police captain at gunpoint and holding him hostage for several hours."

A chill coursed through Oliver's body. He tried to hold perfectly still, but his breath grew rapid and shallow. His mind raced and grasped onto a thin strand of logic.

"If I were a wanted man, how is it that the police here in Lyon have not come looking for me? Surely the Justice Ministry would broadcast an alert all over the country for an escaped fugitive."

A humorless smile came to Chastain's lips, and he stubbed out his cigarette. "You have me to thank for that. I called in a favor from an acquaintance at the Justice Ministry, and they suppressed the Alert to All Patrols. The Paris Police are the only ones looking for you—if indeed they still are." He shrugged. "I would not risk a visit to Paris if I were you, Mr. Carmichael."

Oliver's lips had tightened into a thin line. "The Gestapo are reason enough for me to not wish to return to Paris."

Chastain chuckled without humor. "Indeed."

And a visit to Paris was impossible, anyway—even if the Gestapo weren't interested in him. Since the declaration of war in December Americans couldn't venture into the Occupied Zone without becoming permanent guests of the Wehrmacht. But he didn't need to point that out.

Oliver took a deep breath, tried to steady his nerves. "What is it that you want from me, Mr. Chastain?"

Chastain was silent while he lit another cigarette, took a long pull and held it a moment, and then released the stream of smoke into the air. "A certain man will come here in the near future and will say he is an old acquaintance of yours from Paris. He will call himself Charles Forgeron. I want you to meet with him."

Oliver's guard flew up, and his eyes narrowed. *Charles Forgeron—Charles Smith.* Obviously a fake name. "Why? Who is he?"

Chastain took another drag on his cigarette, but blew it out immediately this time. "He has recently returned to France from England, and he brings news that a group of us in the bureaucracy are interested in."

Oliver's breath caught in his throat. "Free French?" he whispered.

Chastain didn't move, only stared at Oliver.

Oliver glanced around the club. There was a good crowd tonight—their best ever, no doubt in anticipation of hearing Cécile sing. But a good number of the guests were regulars, those who had been coming to Chez Oliver since they opened four weeks before.

From the start, the club had become a gathering place for political dissidents who opposed the Vichy regime. No doubt Dolph had a hand in that. Most were members of the local Socialist Underground—people like their old friends in Paris. But there were others as well—a handful from the center-right Gaullist Resistance, plus a trio of Bonapartists, and even a pair of Occitan Nationalists. The word had clearly gone out that anyone with a bone to pick against the regime could find a friendly place to meet and hold forbidden discussions.

And apparently word had travelled all the way to Jacques Chastain in Paris. Oliver's stomach dropped.

A waiter hurried over and set a snifter of brandy in front of Chastain. The look on Oliver's face must have intimidated him, for he made a quick bow and departed in a hurry.

"Why don't you meet with him yourself?" Oliver asked, suspicious. "You took the trouble of coming here tonight, why do you need an intermediary?"

"Mmmm," Chastain grunted, and took another drag on his cigarette. He stubbed it out and leaned back in his chair, looping an elbow over the back and folding his hands across his chest in a very casual and relaxed posture. "He is far too cautious for that, don't you think? How can he know that he can trust me?"

Oliver thought about that for a moment. "But he trusts you enough to bring you information from England?" That didn't make sense.

Chastain shrugged and didn't answer.

"Why me?"

Chastain chuckled and sat forward again. "I think you know why. I believe you have done this sort of thing before, have you not?"

Oliver's gut tightened, and his breath grew shallow again. *He doesn't know anything, it's only supposition.* He faked a laugh. "Why would you think such a thing? I'm just a musician."

Chastain's eyes narrowed and held Oliver's gaze. "A musician with almost one thousand American dollars in cash in a traveling trunk. Tell me, Mr. Carmichael—how does a simple musician accumulate such a sum? It would take decades to save that much, and you look quite young to me, sir."

"There are many ways to make money."

He saw a twinkle of amusement in Jacques Chastain's eyes. "Not that much money, not in American currency." He lifted his snifter and savored a sip of brandy.

Oliver glanced at Frank Dryden, saw him watching from the bar. Dryden raised one eyebrow in question, and at the last second Oliver shook his head almost imperceptibly and turned back to Chastain.

"If I do this for you, will you give me back my money and my belongings?"

"Oh, I can give you back your belongings this very evening. I have no need of them." Chastain waved a dismissive hand in the air. "As for the money—let us say that this is one way you can earn it back. Given the circumstances under which it came into my possession, I think you are in no position to make demands upon it. Wouldn't you agree?"

Oliver's mouth pursed into an angry line, and he exhaled hard. "I cannot argue with your reasoning, Mr. Chastain. So then, what do you want me to do?"

**

Oliver had to lead the next musical set right after he finished speaking with Chastain, so he hurried past Dryden without making eye contact. He glanced at Lisette, who had taken a seat at the bar next to Dryden, gave her a quick half-smile and wave, and ducked backstage.

The band was going to open the set before Cécile rejoined them five minutes in. Oliver led from in front and slightly to the side, in the more modern way, so as not to stand between the audience and the musicians. Midway through the first song, he lifted his trumpet from a stand in the shadow of the orchestra box and played a solo. Then he returned to directing the remainder of the song.

Over the last year, he'd turned into a prolific songwriter. It had been an unexpected development, and he credited Cécile for the idea. Perhaps more unexpected, his style had turned out to be rather more contemporary than he would have ever imagined—more influenced by Gershwin, Cole Porter, and Irving Berlin, rather than the "Hot Jazz" of a decade ago that they'd played at *Le Chien Errant*. He was loath to be a conformist to the conventions of Tin Pan Alley, but he couldn't disagree when his songs were compared to the popular American standards of fellow Hoosier Hoagy Carmichael— no relation, to his knowledge.

He was pleased at the level of applause after each number, from the first full crowd they'd had since opening four weeks before. Every time he announced the next song, he saw waiters scurrying around, delivering drinks. By the time they finished the second set at nine o'clock, the mood inside the club had turned quite merry, with lots of laughter and animated conversations.

He found Lisette still sitting at the bar with Frank Dryden when he came out from backstage, and after glancing at the receipts— which sent his heart racing with excitement—he went to them.

"Hello, darling," he said to Lisette, putting his hand on her back and kissing her cheek.

"It was a good show tonight." The excitement in her eyes told him she wasn't just saying that.

"The place is really hopping," Dryden said in English, looking around appreciatively. "That ought to boost Cécilie's mood." At Oliver's questioning glance, he added, "She's missed the stage a lot lately."

"It's boosted my mood as well. Can I have a word with you for a moment?"

"Of course," Dryden said, and the look in his eyes was immediately all business.

"We'll be just a moment, dear," Oliver said to Lisette in French, and then led Dryden to the office.

He locked the door.

"What did Chastain want?" Dryden asked, getting right to the point.

"I'm still a little shocked, to be honest. He wants me to meet with an agent from the Free French. He said a group of bureaucrats in Paris is interested in the news the man is going to bring from England." Oliver recounted the rest of the conversation.

When he'd finished, Dryden looked up in thought, stroking his chin. "That is a little unexpected."

"A little?"

Dryden looked back at him, and gave him a smile—the type that didn't extend to his eyes. The type that Oliver had come to recognize when Dryden had secrets he wasn't going to divulge, at least not entirely.

"There have been some whispers around the diplomatic community in Vichy. Rumors that some in the government want to keep their options open, no matter how the war goes."

"But I thought they were all dedicated to their 'National Revolution,'" Oliver said. "Systematically dismantling all of the liberalization of the last seventy years."

Dryden chuckled. "You're referring to the decision makers at Vichy—Pétain and his advisors. They're all confirmed reactionaries, without a doubt. But when they established their new French State after the armistice, they kept the structure of the government from the Third Republic in place, and all of the bureaucracy with it. They had to. They weren't prepared to rebuild the entire government from the ground up.

"The low-level staff, well, they're keeping their heads down like most everyone else in France—doing their jobs and not making waves. But the mid-level bureaucrats, those with some authority over the functions of their respective ministries, these men are starting to grow concerned with what might happen if there should be a 'reversal of fortune.' And they aren't idiots—they know the U.S. entry into the war changes everything. Suddenly, General De Gaulle goes from being *persona non grata*, a condemned traitor, to possibly being the savior of France."

Oliver nodded, following Dryden's logic. "So self-preservation is what's motivating them, is that it?"

"Exactly." Dryden raised his eyebrows slightly and gave Oliver a wry look. "I expect the Free French agent coming here knows the score. He's unlikely to tell them anything *too* sensitive."

Oliver frowned. "Then what's the point?"

"He's going to want to earn their trust, so he'll give them something—it just won't be the intelligence equivalent of the crown jewels or anything. And they'll respond in kind, I'm sure."

"You want me to go through with it, then?" Oliver asked, apprehensive.

"Yes, and we'll arrange for you to pass the information to me before you pass it along to Chastain." Dryden smiled, and patted Oliver's shoulder. "Don't worry, it won't be as dangerous as you think."

But you didn't say it would be safe, either. "And you'll pay me, I presume. My old rate?"

A brief frown crossed Dryden's mouth. "Of course I'll pay you. But I'm not sure it will be as much as before—that was highly prized military production data, very valuable. This, well...let's just see what it is, shall we? Then go from there?"

Oliver nodded. "Deal," he said, and shook Dryden's hand.

**

Light snow was falling when Oliver locked up the club at midnight. He took Lisette's arm, and she huddled close to him while they walked the few blocks to the centuries-old building where they each had an apartment.

"Cécile hasn't lost her touch," Lisette said. "She was fantastic tonight."

Oliver agreed. Then he fell silent, looking around at the thin blanket of snow that covered the cobblestone streets of the medieval Saint Jean Quarter. Tiny crescents of white coated the tops of the rough stones that made the walls of these 13th and 14th century buildings.

They approached a *traboule*—one of countless arched pass-throughs under the buildings, not much wider than a sidewalk, that connected parallel streets in the old quarters of Lyon—and went through its door. At this hour, there were no workmen or residents moving through the passageway, so Oliver paused long enough to shake the snow from his hat and the shoulders of his overcoat.

"You're awfully quiet tonight," Lisette murmured when they resumed walking, now sheltered from the weather. "Is something on your mind?"

"Mmmm," Oliver grunted, not wanting to get into it right then.

"That is not an answer." She sounded cross. When he didn't reply, she asked, "Is it something Mr. Dryden said? You asked to have a word with him in private. What did he say?"

"It wasn't anything Mr. Dryden said," Oliver replied, revealing only part of the truth.

"So then, it *is* something," she pronounced, with that tone of Gallic pride that could be so irritating to foreigners.

"I don't want to talk about it right now, Lisette." Oliver's tone was sharper than he would have liked.

"Oh, I see," she said, cold. She kept her arm through his, but her grip noticeably loosened, and a sliver of distance opened between them.

Fine. "We'll talk when we get indoors." His tone was still sharper than he'd intended, but he felt her relax a little, and slowly ease closer to him as they stepped out from the *traboule* onto the street where they lived. It was only a block to their building, and Oliver picked up their pace through the falling snow.

"OK, we are indoors," she said once they'd entered the spiral staircase at the corner of their building.

Oliver shook his head. "Not until we get to my apartment."

Her lips thinned, and she followed him up the three flights of stone stairs to the third floor. Her apartment was down the hall from his; the landlady wouldn't allow them to rent an apartment together, even though they'd told her they were engaged. But she had allowed them to live within a few steps of each other's door—a sort of wink and a nod to the reality of the situation.

Once inside his apartment, Oliver took Lisette's coat and hat, and then took his time hanging up his own overcoat and hat, giving him a moment to think about what he was going to say, before sitting with her on the couch and taking her hand.

"You know that most of our regulars are members of underground groups. The ones who distribute opposition literature around the city. I'm sure you've noticed this."

She nodded but didn't say anything. Her warm brown eyes held his.

"Well..." Oliver wasn't sure how to explain how Jacques Chastain knew of him. Bringing up Hélène was touchy, even if Lisette had had her own lover during that time. "A man came to see me today—"

"The one you were sitting with when I arrived." It wasn't a question, and she continued to hold his gaze. "You looked very intense, very focused—you did not even notice my arrival."

In my defense, I had my back to you. Though he had to admit he could have seen her sit next to Dryden, if he'd been paying attention.

"Yes, that's the man. He works for the French government, and he asked me to meet with another man in a day or two."

A hint of wariness came to her eyes, and she pulled back ever so slightly. "What sort of man? A secret meeting? Oliver, I thought we were finished with all of that!"

He gave her a half-hearted shrug. "So did I."

Her mouth had tightened into a thin line. "And so you had to tell Mr. Dryden."

"Of course," Oliver said, surprised that she would even question that.

"I bet he told you to take the secret meeting, and then have more secret meetings with him." She sounded cross all of a sudden, and her posture stiffened.

Oliver felt himself shrink at her words. "Yes, he did." It annoyed him how meek he sounded. He hadn't been given much choice.

"I don't like this." She turned away from him, folded her hands in her lap, and looked down. "It is dangerous. Vichy has eyes and ears in this city—it is not like the Gestapo, of course, but they are here, watching and listening. They know that Lyon is where all of the opposition groups have gathered."

Oliver had the feeling she'd been more perceptive than he had been the last four months.

He took her hand in his right one, and with his left he turned her chin toward him. He looked directly into her eyes. "Listen to me—we knew things would change after America entered the war. We talked about it. I'm surprised it's taken this long for Mr. Dryden to ask me to do this kind of work again. It matters now more than ever."

Her eyes grew wet, and she looked away. "I hoped it wouldn't change like this," she said, quietly.

"I know." Then he forced a smile for her benefit and added in as cheerful a tone as he could muster, "If I were in the States right now, I'd be drafted into the army, and sent off to fight for real. What Mr. Dryden asked me to do is much less dangerous than *that*."

A weak smile stretched her lips, and the look in her eyes was so sorrowful it broke his heart.

3

Saturday, January 31

Oliver found Frank Dryden waiting for him backstage after the first set the next night. Next to him stood a tall, middle-aged, red-haired man who looked awfully familiar.

Dryden wore one of those smiles that Oliver knew to mean he wanted something. "Oliver! Just who I was looking for. You remember Mr. Robert Murphy, don't you? He's the *Chargé d'Affaires* for our embassy in Vichy, since Ambassador Leahy left."

"We met last year, in Paris," Murphy said, shaking Oliver's hand quite firmly, almost forcefully. "I officiated Mr. Dryden's marriage to Cécile."

Now Oliver remembered meeting him. He was Dryden's boss. "Of course. Nice to see you again, Mr. Murphy. And welcome to Chez Oliver."

"Yes, congratulations on that," Murphy said, glancing around. His accent was flat but nasal—upper Midwestern for sure, probably Wisconsin. He looked back at Oliver, and said, "Let's go somewhere we can speak privately."

Oliver almost cringed at the thought of another private meeting. He hadn't even met yet with that Free French agent who was supposed to contact him soon. He forced a genial smile and motioned down the hall. "Let's go to my office."

After locking the door, he offered them both something to drink, but Murphy waved it off. Mercifully, he launched right into the purpose of the meeting.

"Mr. Dryden told me about the overture you received yesterday from that French bureaucrat, Jacques Chastain. I looked into him this morning—nothing out of the ordinary. The only piece of relevant information I dug up was that he belonged to the center-right Democratic Republican Alliance during the Republic, same as Charles de Gaulle. That could partly explain his willingness to cooperate with the Free French, now that the odds have shifted a little." He pulled a cigar from inside his jacket. "Mind if I light this?"

Oliver shook his head, and Murphy struck a match and puffed at the cigar until it lit.

"I want to echo what Mr. Dryden told you, about our interest in this matter. The Free French are our allies now, so naturally, we want to aid them in any way we can. But we're not at war with France, so we have to tread carefully."

Oliver nodded. "I understand, sir." He didn't fully understand where Murphy was going with this, but he left that unsaid.

"After I arrived in Lyon this evening, Mr. Dryden filled me in on the details of how you came to know Monsieur Chastain."

Oliver's cheeks flushed. He should have known Dryden wouldn't—couldn't—keep that confidential. The intensity of Robert Murphy's gaze almost made him squirm, but he resisted the temptation. He'd never felt shame about his relationship with Hélène—but something about an older American knowing, and probably judging him for it, made him uncomfortable in that old familiar way he'd left behind when he came to France six years before. Or thought he'd left behind.

Murphy smiled then, the sort of smile that never extended to the eyes, which Oliver was used to from Frank Dryden. "Don't worry, Chastain wouldn't try to blackmail you with that. It's unfortunate that he's threatening to denounce you for that incident in Paris, when you kidnapped a police captain—but in this case we want you to do what he's asking, so there's no harm. Small risk he'd actually go through with the denunciation, anyway. Doesn't gain him anything."

Oliver frowned. "What do you mean?"

Murphy blew a stream of cigar smoke into the air, holding Oliver's gaze for several seconds. "This establishment of yours, it's become welcome ground for local *résistants*, I hear."

"I didn't plan that," Oliver interrupted, stiffening.

Dryden laughed, leaned back, and folded his arms. Murphy chuckled. "I know, Oliver. May I call you Oliver?"

Oliver nodded. After all, he hadn't named the club Chez Carmichael.

"The sort of friends you kept in Paris, the same sort of friends you keep here in Lyon, made it inevitable that your club would become such a meeting place. You didn't have to plan it."

Oliver nodded slowly. Where was Murphy going with this?

"You know how important these groups are, Oliver," Dryden said. "That's how you and I first came to work together, if you remember."

"I remember." Of course he did; Dryden must have said that for Murphy's benefit.

"Now that we're in the war, I'm sure you realize how much *more* important they've become to us. Mr. Murphy and I don't have to tell you that."

Of course not. Oliver shook his head, but stayed silent, waiting.

Murphy stubbed out the end of his cigar and stood. "I'm going to tell you something, Oliver, but it cannot leave this room. Understand?"

Butterflies tumbled in Oliver's stomach, and an electric charge ran down his spine. He nodded.

"*I mean it.*" Murphy emphasized the words with a shake of his finger into the air between them. "Lives depend on this information not falling into the wrong hands."

Oliver swallowed and nodded. "I understand, sir."

Murphy took a deep breath, exhaled hard. "The first American troops landed in the U.K. earlier today. Several troop transports put in at Belfast, in Northern Ireland—about as far from the eyes of Luftwaffe pilots as we could manage. They'll continue to gather there for now, but eventually we're going to build up a large force in England."

Oliver cracked a grin, a genuine thrill running through him. "That's exciting news, sir!"

"Yes, it is," Murphy said, chuckling again. Oliver noticed Dryden was also grinning, and it looked genuine. Was this news to him, too?

"We don't know at this point what the War Department's plans are against Germany. Presumably at some point we're going to initiate the liberation of occupied Europe—and whenever that happens, we'll need forces behind the German lines acting to inhibit their operations. Sabotage, ambushes, bridge demolition, that sort of thing."

Oliver was starting to connect the dots—except for one pertinent detail. "But that would be in the Occupied Zone, wouldn't it?"

"Mostly," Murphy said. "The Unoccupied Zone still ships a quarter of their agricultural output to the Germans. Wehrmacht soldiers are the best-fed people in all of Europe, and that makes them more formidable."

Oliver's stomach dropped. "You want me to convince my customers—and my friends—to sabotage food shipments to Germany?" He couldn't help that his mouth hung open.

Murphy shook his head. "No—not yet, anyway."

Not yet. But no indication of when, Oliver had to note.

"Right now, we're more interested in what the general feeling in the various underground groups is. What their intentions are, long-term. Eventually, we might try to steer them in a certain direction, but for now we just want to know what we have to work with."

"You've done this before, Oliver," Dryden said. "We want you to replicate what you did in Paris. You're of like mind with them, after all. You can become a confidant. Or even a comrade. Use your judgement on what will work best."

Oliver sighed, resigned. Yes, he knew how to do this.

"You've heard of the *Deuxième Bureau*, Oliver?" Dryden asked.

"That's the French spy agency, isn't it?"

"French *Intelligence* agency," Murphy corrected.

"Sorry," Oliver muttered.

Dryden continued. "Contacts within *Deuxième Bureau* have passed along some information to us. There is a network of resistance chapters across the Unoccupied Zone, led by a former soldier whom they have not been able to positively identify, but whom they believe to be in Lyon. It was originally called *Mouvement de Libération Nationale*, but a couple of months ago the group's name changed to Combat. We're told they publish a clandestine newspaper by that name, and it's been distributed widely around the Unoccupied Zone."

Oliver's eyes narrowed. "You want me to find out if 'Combat' is being distributed in my club?"

Dryden glanced at Murphy, who didn't move; then Dryden shrugged and said, "If you can, we'd like to know that. But mostly we want you to find out if any of your regulars are members of Combat. *Deuxième Bureau* believes the group has Gaullist leanings…so this Free French agent who is supposed to contact you might be connected."

That made sense. But then a chill ran through Oliver. "Isn't *Deuxième Bureau* working for Vichy? Am I endangering that Free French agent?" His heart raced with mounting panic.

Dryden held up his hands and shook his head. "Intelligence bureaus are loyal to their country first, not to particular governments." He glanced toward Robert Murphy.

"We're not going to give anyone's identity to *Deuxième Bureau,* I assure you. It would be against our interests, as allies of the Free French. *Deuxième Bureau* provided us information because they're trying to remain friendly with the United States, so they can maintain contact with both sides. And since the Vichy regime cut off diplomatic relations with Britain in 1940, our entry into the war has upped the ante for them."

Oliver nodded, breathing easier. But then he saw the look in Robert Murphy's eyes and sensed that there was more. Much more.

"Lyon seems to be the center of anti-Vichy sentiment in the Unoccupied Zone," Murphy said, echoing what Lisette had told Oliver the night before. "But we've heard whispers about underground resistance in other southern cities—Marseille in particular, but also Montpelier, Toulouse, Avignon, Valence. Probably elsewhere as well."

Oliver knew where this was going a second before they voiced it.

"We'll need someone to go to these places and make overtures," Dryden said. "Someone with connections in Resistance circles, who can make introductions for them. It can't be one of us." He motioned between himself and Robert Murphy.

"But my club—" Oliver started to protest, raising his hand palm upward and motioning around the office.

"It seems well-run," Murphy said, gruff. "And these would be quick jaunts—two or three days apiece." He leaned forward, staring Oliver in the eye. "I'm sure we can interest you in a nice mid-winter trip to the sunny south, can't we, Oliver?"

4

Monday, February 2

Oliver met Dolph in front of the club shortly after the sun went down, while dusk was fading into a deep blue twilight, and the narrow streets lay in shadow. Chez Oliver was closed on Sundays and Mondays, so they had the night off.

"It is not far," Dolph said. "About a quarter kilometer, off Place du Change."

"Lead the way," Oliver said, and shoved his hands deep into the pockets of his overcoat.

They treaded carefully over the slick cobblestones of the narrow medieval streets. The day had been sunny and mild, and the snow had all melted; but darkness brought freezing temperatures, and an icy shimmer reflected the light from nearby windows. Oliver slipped twice, but Dolph's big arms caught him both times.

The bells of the nearby Cathedral of Saint Jean Baptiste—after which this quarter was named—rang six o'clock from the gothic spire visible over the red-roofed buildings to their right. To their left, high on the Fourvière hill above the Old City, the white façade of the Basilica of Notre Dame de Fourvière shone in the light of the nearly full moon.

After fifteen minutes walking slowly over the slippery stones of Rue Saint-Jean, and across the Place du Change, Dolph stopped at a recessed doorway on Rue de la Loge. While they waited for an answer to their knock, Oliver gazed at the Baroque building across the street, with its five enormous arched doorways.

"The Temple du Change," Dolph said. "The pastor there is friendly to the cause."

"Ah," Oliver said, nodding. Temple might mean synagogue in English, but in French it meant a Protestant church. He'd overheard talk about Protestant churches across the Unoccupied Zone organizing aid for Jewish refugees from the Occupied Zone. *One minority religion helping out another*.

The recessed door opened, and the diminutive form of Térèse Barrineau stood in the doorway. She greeted Dolph and they kissed cheeks; then she looked at Oliver with a touch of amusement. "Hello, Boss."

Oliver scolded himself for looking surprised. "Nice to see you this evening, Térèse."

"Come in," she said, stepping aside. "Welcome to the Underground."

A long hall led down the side of the town house, the rooms opening on the left. Oliver followed Dolph and Térèse past a parlor and a modest dining room, to a larger room in the back. About twenty people gathered there, standing in clusters in the corners, or sitting on a pair of couches and several chairs. Looking around, Oliver recognized the entire front staff of the club. He supposed he should have guessed that.

Térèse sauntered over to a cluster of them, touched Armand's elbow, and said something low. Armand looked over at Oliver standing in the doorway; he grinned and waved. "Welcome, Mr. Carmichael!" Fabien and Simon echoed the welcome. Claude nodded at Oliver, but kept his mouth shut.

Oliver started to approach them. But then his eyes locked on a different familiar face on the far side of the room.

Marcel's dark eyes stared back at him, and Oliver couldn't read the young man's expression.

He became aware that Dolph was watching him, and his cheeks flushed at the look of concern in the big German's deep-set blue eyes.

"I am sorry, Oliver. He asked me not to tell you."

Oliver nodded, though he wasn't sure why. He didn't understand why Marcel hadn't wanted him to know he would be here.

"You should talk to him now, before the meeting," Dolph said, his voice quiet and gentle.

Oliver didn't say anything, but when he turned back toward Marcel, he found the tall young man still watching him. He took a deep breath and crossed the room.

"Hello, Marcel." After an awkward second's hesitation, he leaned in, and they kissed cheeks. "It's really good to see you."

"Dolph told me this morning that you were going to come to our meeting," Marcel said. His expression was blank, but Oliver saw a flood of pain pass across his dark brown eyes.

"I want to help," Oliver said with a shrug. An awkward silence fell between them. Marcel stood still. Oliver shifted his feet.

"I've thought about you a lot," Oliver said, taking a tentative step closer, a more intimate distance. He was pleased that Marcel didn't move away, at least. "I've wondered how you were getting along, if you were still in Lyon. When I opened my club, I asked Dolph if he would hire you as a waiter. I'd hoped you'd come work there, and we could be friends again."

Marcel's lips tightened briefly, for just a second, and then his expression went blank again. "He did not tell me that."

Oliver could feel the moment slipping away. "He said it wasn't a good idea, that you wouldn't want to see me yet. That made me sad."

"I am not responsible for your sadness, Oliver."

A jolt of pain stabbed through Oliver's chest. The words sounded so cold, so indifferent. Marcel used to care. Didn't he anymore?

"If you are going to join this work, we will be compatriots. It is important work. Important for France." Marcel hesitated before adding, "It is important to me."

In other words, don't screw anything up. "It's important to me, too."

Marcel stared at him for a couple of seconds before nodding. "Good. Excuse me."

He stepped away, and Oliver watched him join a trio of young men in the corner, who all stood dangerously close together, arms almost touching. One young man's hand lingered on Marcel's back for a couple of seconds too long after they'd kissed cheeks—and a pang of jealousy ripped through Oliver.

He marched to the refreshment table on the other side of the room, and poured himself a glass of wine, a local '39 Hermitage.

"The meeting is about to start, Boss," Térèse said beside him. "You can sit with me, if that makes you more comfortable."

Oliver thanked her, and followed her to the couch, where there was an opening barely big enough for both of them to squeeze together next to two others.

A short, dark complected man in his mid-thirties stood and called them to order. He had thick, coarse dark hair that was unoiled and parted on the left. He wore dark blue trousers and a thick woolen sweater of the same color. He gave a dry account of the printing and distribution of their most recent broadside against the Vichy regime's rollback of worker protections.

"I have not had a day off work in three weeks!" a young man standing next to Marcel shouted, to grumbled agreement from around the room.

The standing man raised his hands, and the room fell silent. "Now we shall consider the proposal to join Mr. Frenay's network, Combat."

Oliver couldn't help but notice the looks that some members of the group exchanged, while others leaned forward in anticipation. Térèse was among the latter. Dolph was among the few who didn't visibly react, just listened intently while the standing man spoke.

"I met with Mr. Frenay in secret earlier this week, and we discussed the reasons for joining forces. Since his French Liberation Movement merged with the Liberty network last month, they are without doubt the largest resistance network in the Unoccupied Zone—perhaps in all of France. Mr. Frenay's underground newspaper, Truths, is distributed throughout the city. He has renamed it Combat, and plans to expand distribution to Marseilles, Montpellier, Toulouse, and Limoges within weeks."

A tingle ran up Oliver's spine. Frank Dryden and Robert Murphy had asked him to go to Montpellier in a week. Did they already know about Combat's expansion plans?

"But Combat is a Gaullist group!" the young man next to Marcel shouted. "They work for freedom and democracy, it is true—but they do not care for the welfare of the workers! If we merge with a larger network, it should be the Armée Secret. They work for Socialist ideals."

"Why do we have to merge at all?" another young man asked. "Why not maintain our independence?"

"The Armée Secret is focused on fighting the German occupation in the north," the standing man said. "They have no presence in Lyon."

Armée Secret. Oliver had heard the name whispered by his friends in Paris. He could only assume that was the network that Serge, Sébastien, and Adrienne had worked for. Acts of sabotage had grown to include assassinations of German officers.

"De Gaulle has no respect for the unions that Vichy abolished!" the young man next to Marcel shouted, continuing his tirade. "What good will it do to join a larger resistance movement, if it betrays our ideals?"

Dolph stood to address the group. "De Gaulle is not the savior that I would have chosen for France. I would have preferred someone from the left. But he is the one we have. He is supported by the Allies, so we should work with his supporters here. That is the only way forward."

There was more discussion, including more shouting by the young man next to Marcel. Oliver watched Marcel closely, but his expression gave away nothing. *Typical.* He could be so damned frustrating sometimes.

The leader called for a vote. Slips of paper were passed around. Oliver took the stack from Térèse and moved to pass it along without taking one, but she put her hand on his. "You should vote, too, boss."

He didn't feel entirely comfortable voting on such an existential question, being new to the group. But then, if he were going to work with them, he supposed he should have some say in their future direction. He wrote "Oui" and folded the paper.

Dolph helped the leader collect and count the votes—fourteen in favor, eight opposed. Térèse applauded, and several others joined her. Oliver was just relieved the motion hadn't passed by a single vote, and he relaxed against the back of the couch.

"I will meet with Mr. Frenay again this week, and he will be pleased to hear of our decision," the leader said, a slight smile on his lips. "We shall adjourn until next week, when I will have more information about our cooperation."

Térèse raised her hand to get everyone's attention. "One more thing before we depart. Everyone must be vigilant at all times, and we must be wary of the SOL watching. Just a couple of nights ago, a mysterious man, a first-time visitor to the club where I work, followed me home. He kept behind me by a large distance, so I am certain he did not intend to rob me or rape me—he was following me to keep a watch on me. He had a military bearing, and the short-cut hair that military men have, so it is quite possible that he is from the SOL. Be careful, everyone!"

A murmur rippled through the gathering while she spoke, and when she finished everyone thanked her vocally.

"What is the SOL?" Oliver asked when they got up from the couch.

"The Legionary Order Service," she explained. *Service d'ordre Legionnaire,* in French. "A Pro-Vichy and pro-Nazi militia reporting to Joseph Darnand, a known fascist."

A chill ran through him. This echoed what Lisette had said the other night. "I've never heard of Joseph Darnand."

Térèse made a face. "He was arrested a few years ago as part of a plot to overthrow the Republic. When the Germans invaded, the conspirators were released and drafted into the army. After the armistice, they remained free. Instead, Vichy arrested Dormoy, the Minister of the Interior who had ordered the conspirators' arrests. They confined him to his home in Montélimar. Then last summer Dormoy's house was bombed, and he was killed. It is obvious Darnand ordered the execution."

"How do you know Darnand ordered it?" Oliver asked, more curious than challenging.

Térèse exhaled a puff of air in that classic French show of exasperation. "He had already founded the SOL in Nice. They terrorized opponents all along the Côte d'Azur." She waved a dismissive hand in the air, as if that explanation was all that was needed, and turned away.

**

That night, Oliver lay awake, Lisette curled up beside him. The air inside his apartment was freezing cold—the coal shortages were just as bad in the Unoccupied Zone as they were in the Occupied Zone, leading landlords to shut off furnaces at night—and Lisette had the covers pulled up around her shoulders, and her back pressed firmly against him.

Oliver stared at the ceiling, trying to relax. Images filled his head of mysterious men following him through the streets, watching his every move. That didn't surprise him. But interspersed with those images were others that caught him off-guard—memories of Marcel's backside.

He tried thinking about anything else—music, business at the club—but his mind always returned to images of those mysterious men in dark corners of the club, staring at him; and then images of Marcel's naked body walking towards him in his office, or bent over his desk...

He threw the covers off, and a wave of frigid air stung his bare skin. He slipped on a robe over his boxer shorts, and goosebumps rose over his body as he walked to his little kitchen, poured a shot of gin into a highball glass, and added a splash of tonic from the icebox.

He took a deep swallow, felt the contrasting warmth and coldness slide down his throat, and his nerves calmed a little. He glanced at the half-empty bottle of gin and wondered how much longer he'd be able to find any. He'd spirited this one away from the club to make sure he always had some at home, since it was so difficult to come by these days, with the war blockades, and Vichy's stubborn refusal to have anything to do with anything British.

He shivered in the cold, so he downed the rest of the drink and hurried back to his bedroom. He slipped into bed as quietly as he could, tugged the covers up to his throat, and put his arm around Lisette to pull her tight against him.

She stirred. "Are you awake?" she whispered, sleepily.

"Yes." He kissed the back of her head. "I can't sleep."

"Close your eyes and count sheep."

"I got a drink, that might help."

"Count sheep. Good night, Oliver."

He started counting sheep. That had always worked when he was younger. Before the war. Somehow, he'd lost the habit.

Six...seven...eight... He noticed he was counting in English. *Neuf...dix...onze...* Then an image of Marcel, naked and carrying a shepherd's hook, appeared beside the fence that the sheep were jumping. Oliver lost count.

Frustrated, he buried his face into his pillow.

**

Tuesday, February 3

There was a knock at the front door of the club Tuesday afternoon, while Oliver was busy doing paperwork at the bar. Only a couple of employees were there, one taking the chairs off the tabletops while the other swept dust into a bin.

"Mr. Carmichael, it is for you," Armand called after answering the door.

Oliver set down his pen and pushed away from the bar. At the door stood a tan-complected man about his age, in a blue uniform like a mailroom clerk or a hotel bellhop.

"You are Mr. Oliver Carmichael?"

"Yes."

"A message for you, sir." He held out a small envelope, unmarked.

Oliver took it, broke the seal, and removed a folded slip of paper.

Two o'clock tomorrow, at the Gallo-Roman theater.

"Thank you," Oliver said, and fished a franc coin out of his pocket. Before he could hand it to the courier, the man struck a match and set fire to the piece of paper. Oliver dropped it before it burned his finger.

"Goodbye, sir," the man said, giving the front of his cap a quick tug, and hurried away.

5

Wednesday, February 4

It was a bright, sunny afternoon, without a cloud in the blue sky. The winter weather in Lyon might be only a little bit warmer than in Paris, but at least the sun shone two or three days a week, in sharp contrast to the persistent *grisaille* that shrouded Paris for eight or nine months of the year. Oliver was grateful for that.

He climbed the slope of the Fourvière hill where a path split from the Montée Saint-Barthélemy—one of a pair of streets that wound up the side of the hill from the Old City. The wooded hillside below had given way to a manicured park that stretched up to the edge of the amphitheater. The air was crisp despite the warm sunshine, and only a handful of people wandered around the ancient Roman ruins.

Skin tingling with apprehension, Oliver crossed the smooth stone of the stage, where he imagined actors in togas had once performed works by Seneca for the residents of Lugdunum, the Roman city on this site, from which governors had ruled all of Gaul.

In a semi-circle around him rose twenty-five rows of stone benches, divided by three stone staircases. Above these bench seats spread more than a dozen boxes where the wealthy would have sat on cushions; grass covered the floors of these boxes now, and the short stone walls between them had seen better days. A taller stone wall encircled the entire structure above those boxes, with an archway through it that disappeared into the hill. More ruined stonework climbed the hill above the amphitheater wall, reaching all

42

the way to the crest of this hill, mere feet from the walls of modern-looking suburban houses. It was a strange sight to behold.

Oliver looked around, but he was alone.

He looked back across the stage he had just crossed. Below him stretched a spectacular view of Lyon, and his breath caught in his throat for a second.

A tight cluster of red-tiled roofs carpeted the narrow stretch of flatland along the west bank of the Saône—the Old City, where he and Lisette lived—with a much larger stretch of the same red roofs on the other side of the river, reaching to the Rhône a half-mile farther.

Lyon still felt like a Latin city, twenty centuries later.

He glanced at his watch—almost ten minutes past two. The Free French agent was late. Oliver's nerves made his stomach tumble. He looked down at the Old City at the base of the hill, tried to pick out the roof of his building a block north of the cathedral. Then he focused on trying to identify the spot near the quay where the club was located. He could just about pinpoint it, but the stone buildings all looked the same from up here.

A man in a gray trench coat approached from the left, from the direction of the basilica, and almost caught Oliver by surprise. He was an ordinary looking fellow, thick brown hair parted on the side, gray fedora in his hand, dark trousers and black shoes visible below the overcoat. He passed a few feet in front of Oliver, made eye contact.

"It has been a long time, my friend. Since before the war, in Paris." When he shook Oliver's hand, he nodded upward almost imperceptibly, then muttered in English, "Sound travels from below."

Oliver nodded. He would have never thought of that. *I'm out of my depth*.

The man climbed the steps and took a seat ten rows up.

Oliver glanced around before following him up the stairs and taking a seat on the row above the man, a few feet from him.

"Mr. Carmichael, thank you for meeting me," the man said in heavily accented English. "I am Charles Forgeron. I apologize for keeping you waiting, I had to be certain you were alone."

"I understand," Oliver replied in French.

The man called Forgeron expelled a puff of air in that very French way. He continued in English. "When they told me I was meeting with an American, I was surprised. An American spy, who would have thought such a thing?" Amusement tugged up the corners of his mouth.

Oliver wondered what was so funny about that.

He thought of what Lisette had said, about Vichy having eyes and ears in many places, and he asked to see Forgeron's identification papers.

"Of course," Forgeron said, and removed his papers from inside his jacket. Oliver inspected them closely; the photo matched, of course, but he moved his eyes slowly over everything else, trying to detect anything out of place. It looked one hundred percent real— Charles Forgeron, age 34, from Vienne. *If they're forged, they're really good.*

"I'm sure that's not your real name," Oliver said in French, to which Forgeron merely shrugged. "Are you actually staying in Vienne?"

Forgeron hesitated, a veil seeming to fall over his face. "I am staying in Vienne at the moment, yes," he said slowly, in French. "I cannot say exactly where, you understand. Or how long I will be there."

Oliver nodded. "I was told you have a message from England, for a man I know."

"Yes. And let me assure you that I do not know the man's identity—only that he works for the government in Paris. The communications with our supporters here have been very cautious."

Oliver frowned. "So then, why aren't those supporters delivering this message? Why do you need me?"

Forgeron shrugged. "That, I do not know. It is not my place to question the cut-out that they choose."

Oliver snorted. "If that's true, how do you know I'm not an informant who will turn you in to the police?"

Forgeron looked amused again. "You are not. I observed you a long time before I approached you."

Oliver let that go. He wanted to get this over with as quickly as possible. He glanced around, nervous, and made sure that no one else was anywhere near them. "What is the message you want me to pass along?"

"This is from General de Gaulle himself," Forgeron said, scooting inches closer and lowering his voice. "To any patriots remaining in France, working for the government. All choices come at a cost, but the impulse to preserve France is paramount. Do you have that?"

Oliver nodded. He glanced around again, saw no one near, and repeated it back.

"That's it. See that it is shared with any bureaucrats who are sympathetic to the cause of freedom." Forgeron stood to leave, but paused. "I have a two-way radio hidden, and I receive messages from Free French headquarters in London. If you were a professional spy, and not an American, I would assume you know that already. But since you are new to this, I cannot assume, no?"

Oliver was ashamed that the man's lack of assumption had indeed been correct, but he kept that inside and said nothing.

"When I have information to give you, I will send a courier to your cabaret. What would you like for it to say?"

Oliver was unprepared for the question and had to think for several seconds. It should be something that would seem like club business if anyone should look over his shoulder, but still be unique enough for him to recognize it for what it was…

"Say that my order for candles is ready," Oliver said, proud of himself. "Then tell me where and when to pick it up."

"We must have code names for the locations," Forgeron said. "If we meet here, I will say to get the merchandise at the store. If I want to meet in Vienne instead, I will say to come to the warehouse. There is a Roman theater in the heart of Vienne that is much like this one. It will be a good place to come as well. It is not wise to have only one meeting place. Now I will leave. You remain here a few minutes, and don't watch me."

He put his hat on, touched the rim briefly, and walked away.

Oliver exhaled hard. He was filled with a strange mixture of relief that the task was over, and apprehension at what would come next.

And the times after that.

**

"This is good," Dryden said after Oliver told him the message. "I'll be interested to hear Chastain's reaction. When do you meet with him?"

"He's coming back on Friday."

"Then I will be here on Saturday."

Dryden stood and pulled a twenty dollar bill from inside his jacket, laying it on Oliver's desk. "For keeping us informed." That was more than a half-week's wages for most Americans. Oliver slipped the money into a drawer.

"Why did he seem so surprised to meet 'an American spy?'"

Dryden laughed. "Because they wouldn't expect one. Tell me, Oliver—did you ever read any fiction about spies, any cloak and dagger dime novels?"

Not since I was fifteen. He just nodded.

"Was the spy ever American in any of those stories?"

Oliver tried hard to think of one, but couldn't. He shook his head. "No, never."

"There's a reason for that. The United States has always considered espionage a European vice, something to be avoided. And everyone over here knows that." Dryden shrugged. "But during the last war, it became apparent we needed to know more about what the enemy was up to than what could be observed from scouts, or even the new airplane reconnaissance. So the State Department created a special division for signals intelligence. Do you know what that is?"

Oliver ventured a guess. "Signals—as in radio signals?"

"Yes, among other things. We hired code breakers and set them up in a secret office in New York. It was very effective, and helped the Allies immensely. You wouldn't call them *spies*, of course—at least, not like the spies you read about in novels, but the operation was top secret.

"After the war its budget was cut back. But it didn't go away—it became the Diplomatic Security Service. The isolationists who ran the American government through the twenties wanted desperately to restore 'normalcy.' And they wanted nothing to do with the 'European vice.' And then when Henry Stimson was Secretary of State during the Hoover Administration, he shut down signals intelligence altogether. He thought it unethical to snoop on other diplomats, regardless of the benefit.

"So you see, Oliver, the idea of an 'American spy' would seem preposterous to people over here—especially to those doing clandestine work. But we can use *that* to our advantage."

Oliver wasn't sure he liked the sound of that. He frowned. "What do you mean?"

"What I mean is, you won't be suspected. Vichy is looking for British spies, not American ones."

Oliver didn't share Dryden's confidence. For starters, he could never be certain that Jacques Chastain wouldn't sell him out at some point. In fact, he was certain Chastain would sell him out in a heartbeat if it served his purposes.

"But what if I *am* found out? What will we do?"

An odd expression came to Dryden's face, and he was silent for several seconds—which made Oliver even more anxious.

"You don't have diplomatic immunity, so you could be arrested and thrown in prison." Dryden's voice was flat and emotionless. "Mr. Murphy and I have diplomatic immunity—but Vichy could still expel us from the country if they had evidence we were running spies against them. It's not a position we would want to be put in. With a war going on, we can't afford to lose staff at the embassy here. You understand, don't you, Oliver?"

In other words, keep your mouth shut and take the fall. "Yes, I understand," he replied, not hiding the bitterness in his voice.

Dryden's expression softened a little, and he put a hand on Oliver's shoulder. Oliver flinched a little, but Dryden didn't appear to notice.

"We would hire you the best lawyer in France. We would do everything possible to get you cleared of the charges and returned to the United States as soon as possible. But that won't be possible if the mission is compromised—which means you can't admit to anything. Nothing at all. Is that clear?"

Oliver nodded slowly. "It's clear."

Dryden squeezed his shoulder. "You have to trust me, Oliver. I count you as a friend, and I will do everything I can to protect you. But these are dangerous times. You'll have to be vigilant."

******

Thursday, February 5
Seyssuel, Unoccupied France

The man known by the alias Charles Forgeron sat hunched over the rough wooden desk. The fog of his breath clouded the light of the single kerosene lamp, turned low. It provided the only illumination in the cold attic of the eighteenth century farmhouse on the edge of the little village three kilometers north of Vienne.

He opened his cipher book to the correct date, and carefully encoded his message on a piece of scrap paper the farmer—a grizzled old veteran of the last war—had provided him.

At one minute before eleven o'clock, he switched on the power to the two-way radio hidden in the open valise on the desk. The tubes hummed and glowed as they warmed up. He carefully tuned the dial to the correct frequency.

At precisely eleven o'clock, he tapped out the required greeting in Morse Code. He waited nervously for several seconds before the expected response came back.

He tapped out his code name, using today's cipher, and waited until the recipient replied with "Go Ahead," also in today's cipher. Then he tapped out his message, confirming he met yesterday with the agent of the bureaucrat code named Chestnut.

This took a couple of minutes, but he'd worked all evening to make the message as succinct as possible, to preserve precious airtime.

Free French agents trained endlessly on how to send and receive messages as quickly as possible—but under no circumstances to be on the air for fifteen minutes. That was the amount of time it would take for the Gestapo's triangulation centers to pinpoint a transmission's precise location. If possible, they were expected to be on the air for less than ten minutes.

He waited with increasing impatience for the confirmation that his message had been received and understood—but the receiver stayed silent. He kept checking his watch. His heart pounded in his chest, and his breath became short and quick. He ran his hands through his hair several times.

Ten minutes passed. The receiver remained silent. He cursed under his breath, stood and paced in little circles in front of the desk, the anxiety about to consume him. In another minute, he would have to disconnect, confirmation or not. If no confirmation, he'd have to resend the message tomorrow night, same time.

Then, just when he was sitting down to shut off the radio, the receiver buzzed into life.

For the next several seconds, the radio operator in London tapped out the confirmation code for today. Forgeron's finger followed along on the page in the cipher book, his heart racing. The second the last letter of the confirmation came across without error, he switched off the radio transmitter and closed the case.

He looked at his watch. Thirteen minutes past eleven o'clock.

"Shit!" he cursed. He released one long, angry breath, his hands lying flat on the top of the false valise.

Tomorrow, he would have to find another safe house. He could not stay at this one.

**

Brest, Occupied France

The Gestapo listening station at Brest picked up the signal first, coming from somewhere in Eastern France. Once they'd confirmed the frequency, they alerted the other two stations. Augsburg picked up the signal a moment later, followed by Hamburg a moment after that. The transmission was stopped soon after, but they listened for the periodic ping indicating the set was still on that frequency.

Within five minutes, they had determined with certainty that the transmission was coming from south of the Line of Demarcation—in the Unoccupied Zone.

By the time the connection ended after thirteen minutes, they had the location narrowed to a ten-kilometer radius, just south of the city of Lyon.

The cryptanalyst in Brest, as the first to pick up the signal, took the report to his colonel a short time later.

"You cannot determine what was communicated?" the Gestapo colonel said with a deep frown that formed an exaggerated upside-down U on his ridiculously long face.

"No, sir," the young corporal said. "We have not cracked their code, but we have determined that this is from a group of codes used by the Free French, and not by British agents. Their codes have a different signature."

"So, there is a Free French agent hiding near Lyon. In the *Unoccupied* Zone." The colonel said this last part with obvious disappointment. Then he thrust the report back to the cryptanalyst. "Notify the French Justice Ministry. They will deal with the traitor in their zone."

**

Friday, February 6
Vichy, Unoccupied France

When Gilles Alphonse Matous was summoned to Vichy that afternoon, he was provided no information other than what office to report to at the Justice Ministry. When he was ushered inside immediately upon providing his name to the secretary, his curiosity was piqued. And when the Deputy Minister of Justice entered the room a moment later with none other than Joseph Darnand himself, the head of the SOL, Matous was fully intrigued. He'd never met the SOL leader personally, though he'd heard him give a few speeches.

"Positive proof that a Gaullist traitor is operating just outside of Lyon," Darnand said without preamble, and tossed a file toward Matous before he'd even taken a seat.

Matous read the report from the Gestapo listening station at Brest, in Brittany. "They nearly had the precise location pinned down. A few minutes more, and we would have him."

"That's why you are here, Mr. Matous," the Deputy Minister said, taking a seat at the head of the table. "Mr. Darnand here tells me that you have been very effective at rooting out traitors in Provence."

The Deputy Minister didn't mention Matous's leadership in suppressing the Jewish underground in Marseille and Toulon, but that didn't surprise him. Many of the leadership in Vichy were squeamish about the SOL's methods, even while applauding the results.

Darnand, taller and more controlled in his movements, took the seat next to the Deputy Minister, across from Matous. "He is one of the best we have."

"You want me to go to Lyon?" Matous asked.

"Precisely," the Deputy Minister said. "Mr. Darnand nominated you for the assignment. We need for you to begin immediately."

Darnand sniffed. "Lyon is a cesspit of resistance, worse than Marseille. We have had men there since December, but they have been...ineffective."

The challenge thrilled Matous. And what an honor! He would dive into the task of cleaning up Lyon, of restoring order there, and he would do it with gusto.

Of course, he would need to cable his wife that he wouldn't be home for a while—indefinitely, even—but that was not an obstacle. "I accept the assignment, gentlemen, with gratitude. I will find and punish this traitor, and all who harbor him."

6

Lyon, Unoccupied France

Jacques Chastain frowned when Oliver gave him the message. They sat alone at the corner of the bar, an hour after Chez Oliver opened. Chastain stared at his tumbler of bourbon. "That is all?"

Oliver could hardly blame him for being disappointed. The message seemed more like a warning than anything else. "That's all. He said it was from General de Gaulle himself."

Chastain's lip pursed, and he exhaled hard through the nose. "Repeat, slowly."

"To all patriots in France, working for the government. All choices come at a cost, but the impulse to preserve France is paramount."

Chastain listened, still staring at his bourbon, not moving. Then a few seconds after Oliver finished, a hint of smile twerked one corner of his mouth. "He paraphrases Corneille." At Oliver's questioning look, he made one of those exaggerated frowns the French were so good at when they wanted to be condescending. "The famous seventeenth century tragedian. Better than your *William Shakespeare*." He mouthed the name with an extra note of disdain.

Oliver let that go. He wasn't a particular fan of Shakespeare, anyway. *Romeo and Juliet* had been sheer torture to read in high school. "Do you want to reply?"

Chastain made a tiny shrug. "I will consider it. When do you next meet him?"

Oliver wasn't sure what there was for Chastain to consider. "I don't know."

Chastain's frown grew. "You do not know? You let him leave without arranging the next meeting?"

A chill ran through Oliver, and he leaned away from Chastain. "He said he would contact me. We established a code to use."

"American amateur," Chastain muttered, and took a drink of bourbon. He drained it and set the glass down hard on the bar. "Tell him, 'Preservation of France requires the preservation of the patriots working in her government.' Now, I must go. I have plans for dinner with colleagues. I leave for Paris in the morning."

"When do you return?" Oliver wouldn't forget that lesson.

Another tiny shrug. "Impossible to say. The Germans are not generous with the *Ausweis*, no?"

"But can't you get one as a government official?"

A bigger shrug this time. "From time to time. Not often, or the Boche get suspicious. Best not to have the Gestapo watching any more closely than they already do." He stood. "I will have a colleague in Vichy contact you, until I can return in person."

He started to turn away, but paused, reached into his jacket, and laid a one-hundred-dollar bill on the bar between his glass and Oliver's. Then he strode to the door without looking back.

Oliver slipped the hundred dollars into his jacket pocket, every muscle in his body tensing with irritation. For the risk he had taken, he'd only earned back a tenth of what Chastain had found? It was *his* money, damn it!

He took a deep breath, reminding himself that a hundred dollars was what the average American worker made in a month. It was a good price for one secret job.

But it was still annoying that Chastain held his other nine hundred dollars.

More ominously, Chastain could always have the Justice Ministry put out an alert across the country for an escaped fugitive who kidnapped a Paris police captain. Oliver was on the hook, whether he liked it or not.

*

On the way back to his office, his eyes fixed on Lisette sitting in the shadows of a back booth. Watching him. He stopped, shifted direction toward her, and slid into the seat beside her.

"This will bring us trouble," she said under her breath.

He took her hand, and was surprised at the strength with which she squeezed it. He glanced at her face, noticed the lines of tension around her eyes.

"It will be fine," he whispered, and touched her cheek with his other hand. She leaned into it, closing her eyes. Then he added in his most cheerful tone, "And besides, it lets me earn back the money I lost when we left Paris."

She sighed, so deeply he could feel it. She opened her eyes, but looked down. "We have enough money, Oliver."

He pulled his hand back from her face and shrugged, stung for reasons he couldn't explain, and looked away. Then he tried another cheerful smile. "If I earn back the thousand dollars I lost, then someday soon we can return to Paris in style."

The sadness in her brown eyes told him she'd seen through the false cheer. They wouldn't be returning to Paris anytime soon. In style or otherwise.

**

Saturday, February 7

The club was filling up fast the next night when Oliver finally spotted Frank Dryden coming through the front door. He'd expected him sooner, and the nervous anticipation of their conversation made his fingertips tingle.

Oliver checked his watch; the band needed to start the first set in less than ten minutes. Dryden was approaching the bar, so Oliver nodded toward his office.

He sat alone at his desk for a full minute before a quiet knock at his door was followed by Dryden slipping inside. "You met with Chastain last night?"

Oliver nodded, and recounted their conversation. "Does that mean anything to you?"

"They're volleying right now," Dryden said. "Feeling each other out. The bureaucrats are being cautious. As we expected."

"But they didn't shoot him down, either."

Dryden chuckled. "That's right. If they see a possibility the Allies win the war, and the Free French return to France in triumph, then they hardly want to be on their bad side."

"Seems I'm taking an awfully big risk while they just 'feel each other out.'"

Dryden's expression turned stony. "That's the job, Oliver."

Oliver looked away. "The band goes on in a few minutes. I have to get back out there."

Dryden's hand clasped Oliver on the shoulder. "You must be patient in this line of work. I know the cloak and dagger novels make it seem dramatic, but it really isn't. This is how it's done. Like I said last week, Mr. Murphy and I believe the risk to you is minimal—but in the unlikely event you do get arrested, remember to say nothing at all. Understand?"

It felt like a vice clamping Oliver's chest. "I understand." He opened the door, then turned back and put on his host's genial smile. "If you'd like to have a seat at the bar, I'll have Fabien get you whatever you'd like to drink, on the house."

"Thank you, Oliver." Dryden stepped past him into the hall. Then he leaned close and whispered, "We'll talk more later about Combat."

**

Sunday, February 8

"Our friends would not like you speaking to Mr. Dryden about their activities," Lisette said when they'd returned to his apartment shortly after midnight. Her words were clipped, and there was a flash behind her dark eyes when she said it.

The familiar guilt returned, sinking into the pit of Oliver's stomach. *It's like Paris all over again*. He ignored her and went into the kitchen to pour himself a small measure of wine. At the last moment before returning to the living room, he thought to pour her one as well. He handed it to her without a word.

"Things did not go well for our friends the last time you tried to 'help' them." The bitterness in her tone surprised him.

"Serge made a foolish decision," he said, defensive. "His impulsiveness was the reason he got killed. I had nothing to do with that."

The rage that swept her face made him instantly regret saying that.

"So you blame Serge? It is cowardly to blame the dead for their own death."

"I'm not blaming him, Lisette! I blame Allard. *He* killed Serge. But we cannot ignore that Serge's own impulsive choice brought him there, when he should have gone into hiding. That had nothing to do with the rest of us."

She stared at him, eyes hard and narrow, but didn't utter a word. He half-turned away, averting his eyes from her hostile stare. He sipped his wine. Serge had been in Allard's crosshairs for a long time before that night. That was the whole reason Oliver had to... He closed his eyes to shut out the violent images.

Lisette snorted, and he turned back toward her. She was shaking her head at him. He stared back at her, not sure what to say.

She downed the wine and thrust the glass at him. "I want no part in this. If our friends turn on you when they learn you are telling the American government what they do, the problem is yours."

She marched from his apartment, leaving his door open to the cold.

7

Wednesday, February 11, 1942

Franz Lemiel hurried down the train's narrow corridor, toward the rear, his limp making his head bob. He wore the uniform of the SNCF—*Société Nationale des Chemins de fer Français*—the French national railroad. A number of its employees were members of the Resistance, which allowed them to carry out small acts of sabotage in the Occupied Zone. And within the Unoccupied Zone, they looked the other way when Franz brought contraband onboard at Geneva. He also had an SNCF employee to thank for his uniform.

The SNCF operated the Lyon-Geneva Railway, including the fifteen kilometers of it that passed through Swiss territory.

Franz ducked into the freight room near the rear. He had three crates of banned books and similar contraband, all labelled as SNCF supplies. The train had to stop at the French border, so that customs officials could inspect passengers' identification and luggage.

Nearly all of Switzerland's western border butted up against the Occupied Zone of France; but a narrow strip around Geneva touched the Unoccupied Zone, and it was in the middle of this little stretch of border that the Lyon-Geneva Railway crossed. That meant no Gestapo. After his last experience with the Gestapo, Franz was cautious to avoid them at all costs.

Not that Vichy's customs officials would be any more lenient if they found Franz smuggling banned materials into France. But they were less thorough. And not quite as brutal.

He busied himself pretending to do official work in the freight room. There were pages of official documents in clipboards that he could pretend to peruse, a pencil in his hand to make it look realistic.

It felt like an eternity before the customs official appeared in the door. "Papers, please," he said in a voice as stiff as his posture. He was probably about forty, with a dark mustache curled and waxed at the ends in a way that had gone out of style twenty years before. His dark eyes gazed at Franz coolly while Franz removed the forged identity papers from his uniform pocket.

The official gave them a cursory glance before handing them back. "Manifests, please."

Franz handed him the clipboard from his hand, plus another one sitting on a shelf nearby. The official flipped through the pages, mouth clenched in a tiny frown. Then he began to march around the room, checking the labels on each crate and running his finger down the manifest pages until he found the corresponding entry.

Franz stood by the door, silent. He hoped this customs official would only check a handful of crates against the manifests, and then leave. Sometimes they did.

Unfortunately, this one was more thorough. He moved slowly around the room, checking every single label on every single crate, and taking time to find each entry on the manifests.

Franz held his breath each time the man reviewed one of his crates, which had all been labeled as "Woolen Textiles."

Once he'd finally made his way around the room and had checked every piece of freight on the car, the official turned back to Franz and thrust the clipboards back at him. Franz tried not to stare at the man's ridiculous mustache and focused his eyes on the clipboards. "Good day, sir," the official said, and marched out to the corridor.

Franz exhaled in relief, but resumed pretending to work in case someone else came by.

Fifteen minutes later, the train moved again. From the window, Franz watched the border crossing slip behind them. A moment later, the track passed along the side of a mountain, and rocky outcroppings blocked his view to the north. To the south, a vista of bare trees greeted him, with little patches of snow scattered around the forest floor.

They would be in Lyon in two hours, and he would disappear into the city with his cargo.

**

Dolph Hansen met him in the freight yard outside of the train station. Dusk was falling, and the sky had clouded up. Another train sat on the tracks beside them, which was fortunate—they were hidden from view while they unloaded the crates onto a cart Dolph had quietly commandeered. Three SNCF workers helped them carry the crates off the train, and once they had been loaded onto the cart, two of them helped Franz push it to a gravel road several hundred meters away, where a delivery truck idled, the black charcoal exhaust belching into the cold air.

Franz thanked the two SNCF workers, and he and Dolph shook hands all around. Then Dolph climbed into the driver's seat, and Franz hurried around and climbed into the passenger seat.

"Did you have any trouble?" Dolph asked him quietly, in German.

"None," Franz replied in the same language. "Although the Customs official this trip was more thorough than most."

German was the mother tongue for both, so when no one else was around, that was what they spoke. Franz was from Basel, a German-speaking Swiss city wedged between the German state of Baden, and the disputed state of Alsace—which was now *de facto* Reich territory again, even if its *de jure* status was undetermined. He spoke French fluently, since everyone in Switzerland studied all three official languages—German, French, and Italian.

Dolph grunted. "Let's hope that was an idiosyncrasy, and not a trend."

Full-on darkness had fallen by the time they drove out of the freight yard. Dolph flashed a permit at the security guard manning the gate—a forged permit, of course, but it was never questioned—and they sped west toward the city center.

The truck's headlights shined off the snow piled at the sides of the narrow streets. There was no official black-out in the Unoccupied Zone, so the truck's headlights were undimmed. Unlike clandestine missions Franz had run inside Germany and Occupied France, where slitted covers dimmed headlights *almost* to the point of uselessness.

Dolph pulled into an alley behind a soot-covered brick warehouse near the Rhône, midway between the freight yard and the city center. A heavy door slid open from the rear of the warehouse, and Dolph killed the truck's engine. Four young men emerged from the darkened interior and met Dolph and Franz at the back of the truck.

"It is good to see you again, Emmentaler," one of the young men said in French, using Franz's code name. Few of the *résistants* in Lyon knew his real name. Dolph knew, as did Marcel Thibeault; and of course, the American Oliver Carmichael and his *Parisienne* girlfriend Lisette Rousseau, whom he had assisted in crossing into the Unoccupied Zone the previous fall.

"Greetings, compatriots," Franz said, shaking hands. The temperature was falling, and their breath crystallized in big clouds. "I come bearing gifts from Switzerland. I trust you will use them well."

Dolph unlocked the back of the truck and raised the door. They struggled with the weight of the crates, but got them loaded onto carts and hauled them inside the warehouse.

A lone kerosene lamp lit a corner of the cavernous room, near a work desk, and from beneath it one of the young men removed a pair of crowbars. Franz stood aside while they pried open the lids, and then threw handfuls of wood shavings onto the concrete floor.

There were murmurs of appreciation when they looked at the covers of the books inside. A rush of warmth spread through Franz, and he had to smile.

"I haven't seen anything by this author in two years," one of them said, turning the book over. "It is in good condition, too. I don't know how you do it, Emmentaler."

Franz chuckled. "I have many sources, in many places." Librarians and university professors across Switzerland kept him well-supplied with used books, and sometimes new ones.

"We will see that these get to where they are most needed," another of the young men said.

Franz knew that these *résistants* had many librarians around the region who were quietly eager for copies of banned books, to be stashed in secret back rooms from which they would cautiously lend them out to liberal-minded patrons.

"That is God's work," Franz's father Dieter had once said of his mission to bring as many banned books as he could into Germany and France. He knew his father worried about him making these trips; but it was not in Franz's nature to sit back and let others take risks for him. He was a man of action as well as of words.

In this way, Franz did what his father could not. Dieter Lemiel ran a left-leaning newspaper in Basel, but he was constricted by Swiss censors, who did not allow anyone to print anything that would offend their Axis neighbors. But Dieter's connections did help Franz in one important way.

"The small box there, the one labeled 'Linen Cloth,' is for Combat," Franz said. "Recent editions of American and British newspapers. You will see that they get to Mr. Frenay?"

Eyes widened at his use of the Resistance leader's real name. It was a closely guarded secret, and few outside the group Combat knew it. Franz hoped his use of it would cement their trust, since he knew these young men to be Frenay's trusted lieutenants. And perhaps he enjoyed impressing them just a little.

"He will have them before morning," one of the young men said. American and British newspapers suffered less censorship than French, or even Swiss, newspapers, and so they were the best sources of information for Frenay's clandestine paper.

"We must be going," Dolph said, glancing at his wristwatch. It was always best not to linger at these places.

Franz bid everyone goodbye and accompanied Dolph out the back door. The four *résistants* followed, and fastened a padlock to the door. They slipped away into the darkness.

Dolph backed the truck out of the alley and drove it to the city center. White or tan stone Beaux Arts buildings, a fairly uniform seven to nine stories tall, lined the smooth blacktop streets here. Pulling off into a narrow alley behind a bakery, he parked it beside their trash cans. They alighted onto the frosty cobblestones and walked along the wide streets through the center of the city—deserted at this hour—westward toward the Saône. They crossed at the Pont Exchange, into the medieval Saint-Alain Quarter.

Dolph pointed down the quay toward the Saint-Jean Quarter. "That is where the Chez Oliver cabaret is," he said, slowing a little from the hurried pace. "I will take you there tomorrow."

A moment later, they slipped through a *traboule* to the next street, and turned north. A few blocks later, Dolph let them into a six-story building, and they trudged up four flights of stairs. When they reached Dolph's floor, a thin figure emerged from the shadows of the last flight and hurried down to join them.

"Good evening, Franz," Marcel said, and they kissed each other's cheeks. Then he and Dolph kissed cheeks, and Dolph's fingers trailed across the younger man's shoulder.

Franz smiled to himself. He'd wondered how long it would take before that happened. "We have much to discuss," he said, quietly, pushing aside the alluring image of Dolph and Marcel *in flagrante delecto*. "Let us get inside, where we can talk privately."

This was without doubt the part of the visit he'd anticipated the most. The events of the preceding months—aside from his unfortunately night as a guest of the Gestapo in October—had given him unprecedented opportunities to advance the cause. Keeping silent about them was necessary, but the opportunity to convey them to comrades-in-arms who would benefit sent a thrill through him.

"What news do you bring?" Dolph asked once they were safely locked inside his small two-room apartment.

Franz broke into a grin. He couldn't help it, the excitement was too great. "I have acquired some useful contacts over the last several months. I have a friend in the American diplomatic service, and between us we have managed to find an informant in the German secret service."

The look of shock, followed by unbridled excitement, that crossed his friends' faces brought him pleasure. He'd been reluctant to reveal his American connections at first...but now that the United States had entered the war on the side of Britain, it was useful for his *résistant* friends in France to know. He ignored that he didn't have strict permission to reveal such information. He was not an American, he was an independent operator; he intended to remain that way.

Besides, Dolph and Marcel could be trusted to keep that information to themselves. And they would know to share the rest with their compatriots.

Franz grew serious again. "We have all heard the rumors that the Germans are rounding up Jews across Europe and sending them to concentration camps. And I have reported about the horrible conditions in the camps. But what is not widely known is that Vichy has offered to expel any Jews in the Unoccupied Zone who do not have French citizenship—and they are going to turn them over to the SS in the Occupied Zone."

Dolph turned grim, eyes heavy. Marcel's mouth set in a tight line, furious. "When will this happen?" Dolph asked.

"I do not have specifics—but soon," Franz said.

Marcel turned to Dolph, his expression blank again. "This will be useful for recruiting."

Dolph looked doubtful. "People will not believe it." He looked to Franz, "Has your contact provided any evidence that can be shared?"

Franz frowned. "Not to me. I believe there are documents that have been photographed, but I have not seen them personally."

Dolph and Marcel exchanged a look. "No one will believe it without evidence," Dolph repeated. "We can share this news with the others, so that we can all be watchful for signs, but in the short-term there is nothing we can do."

"We can tell the rabbi," Marcel said, his level gaze seeming to bore into Dolph. The big blond statue of a man looked away a moment later and nodded in silence.

Franz dropped his other piece of news. "I know a pastor in Basel who writes often to Protestant pastors in France. He said they have developed an elaborate code to exchange information in such a way that the censors in both countries will not know that it is not innocent personal news between friends. He told me last week that the Reformed Church in France is organizing escape routes into Geneva, and also into Spain. They are prepared to hide Jews inside their temples or homes, and spirit them out of the country before they can be turned over to the SS." He grinned. "Just as their ancestors hid their own faith, or spirited their compatriots out of France. That is how my family came to be in Switzerland."

A gleam of recognition appeared in Dolph's blue eyes. "The place where our group meets is provided to us by the pastor at the Temple du Change. I will speak with him about it."

Franz put one hand on each man's shoulder, in a brothers-in-arms sort of way. "I must be going. I am expected at a safe house, and they will be anxious if I do not show up soon. I will be in touch again tomorrow."

He touched his forehead, gave them a crooked grin, and let himself out into the darkness.

**

Back on the street, Franz waited in the shadow of the doorway for a couple of minutes, looking for any watcher or sentry. He scrutinized everyone who hurried down the cobblestones, until he was satisfied there was no threat.

Walking back toward the Pont Exchange, Franz kept his ears tuned for the sound of footsteps behind him.

Not until he had crossed the Saône into the city center did he begin to relax. Even so, he took a zig-zag route through the heart of the city. The foot traffic was heavier in this area, so it would be more difficult to identify a tail—but also easier to lose him in the crowds if needed.

Reaching the Croix Rouge Quarter north of the city center, he passed through the door to a familiar *traboule*. This Renaissance-era neighborhood shared this peculiarly Lyonais architectural feature with the medieval quarters across the river, with covered pass-throughs being the most common connections between parallel streets.

He only heard his own footsteps echoing in the stone enclosure. But still, when he reached the end of the passage, which opened onto a large courtyard between two buildings, he ducked into the shadow of a plane tree. He pressed his ear against the stone at the corner of the *traboule* and listened for the low thump of footfalls.

One could never be too cautious these days. Especially after an unfortunate encounter with the Gestapo in southern Germany in October, Franz took no chances. He would limp for the rest of his life, but it could have ended much worse.

After several minutes, he had almost convinced himself that the anxious feeling in his gut was a superstitious illusion. But then the outline of a human shadow inched forward from the *traboule*. Someone with a light step; the shadow moved, but there was no sound. Not a single footfall.

His hand gripped the handle of the knife in his pocket. He held his breath.

A face appeared at the edge of the faint light cast from the apartment windows above, looking around the corner.

As the eyes focused on Franz, he leapt at the unknown figure, tackling him. His left hand gripped the man's throat, while his right hand brought out his knife, and let it glint in the faint light from above.

"Who are you?"

"I live here," the man said through constrained breath. "I am on my way home. I don't have any money."

This man didn't think Franz was a thief any more than he thought he was Charles de Gaulle. Franz brought the knife to the man's throat. He moved his face to within inches of his stalker's, and repeated his question, slower, emphasizing each word. "Who are you?"

The man's eyes grew defiant, and his mouth curled into a sneer. "I do not owe an explanation to traitors."

That was all Franz needed to know. He pressed down and drew the knife across the man's throat. The blade sank deeper and slid more easily than it ever had on the wooden dummies he'd practiced on, and the act was finished in barely a second. Its brevity made Franz's skin prickle.

Gurgled breath came out for several seconds, and every muscle in the man's body stiffened, but then went limp. His eyes stared into the sky, unmoving. Dark liquid pooled around his head and began to run between the cobblestones.

Franz took a deep breath, and huffed it out. He hated having to do that. And having a body with its throat cut this close to the safe house was, well, inconvenient.

He wiped the blade of his knife in the square of dirt around the trunk of the plane tree—never on your own clothes, he'd learned—and folded it back up. He slipped it into his pocket, and then dragged the body about a meter, fully into the darkness of the *traboule*.

He hurried across the courtyard to another *traboule* at the opposite corner. About a third of the way down this passageway there was a hidden opening; he slipped inside it and mounted the stone steps of the spiral staircase two at a time. The faint silvery light of the crescent moon through tall, narrow openings onto the courtyard provided the only illumination.

He stopped at the third floor and moved as quietly as he could down the corridor to the penultimate door on the left. He knocked in sequence, quietly, and waited for the expected response from inside. When it came, he knocked two more times in rapid succession, and the door bolt slid open. The door opened only half a meter, and he slipped inside.

"Emmentaler, thank God," the woman said. "We expected you more than an hour ago."

"I am sorry, Mareille," he said, kissing her cheeks. She was about thirty, and her dark hair was shoulder-length and curled at the ends. Her house dress was faded with age. "I had to meet with a couple of compatriots, to pass on important news. And then I ran into some difficulty in your courtyard."

Mareille's mouth tightened into a thin line. "Lucien!" she called over her shoulder.

The man who appeared from the hallway was a few years older than Mareille, in dirty workmen's clothes, and he was wiping his hands on a rag. "Good evening, Emmentaler," he said in a rich baritone voice.

"The traboule into your courtyard from Rue de Chartreux was being watched," Franz said. "I took care of it, but your guests are no longer safe here."

"We have two right now," Mareille said, a hint of anxiety coming to her voice. "We can only move one at a time."

Franz shook his head. "There is no time. I will take one of them for you, but we must hurry. Where there is one watcher, others will soon come." He looked toward Lucien. "We need to do something with the body."

Lucien sighed, his face grim. "There is an old well, next courtyard over. It has not been used in decades, and it is very deep."

Franz nodded, deep in thought. That would do. But they had to somehow move the body along the street without being noticed. "We will need a thick blanket, and a cart. Can you get these things?"

Lucien sighed again, heavier this time. "The blanket, yes. The cart...I suppose I can steal the cart belonging to our concierge. He keeps it locked in a work room off the courtyard, in the *trabloule* below us." He came closer to Franz. "Can you pick the lock?"

"Of course." That was the easy part. "Get the blanket and come with me. Mareille, fill a bucket with water, and follow us."

She glanced down the hallway. "That will leave our guests alone. I don't like that."

Her instincts were correct, but Franz couldn't worry about that right now. "Tell them to hide in a closet. Hurry!"

Mareille and Lucien disappeared down the hallway. Lucien reappeared a few seconds later with a thick woolen blanket; Mareille a moment after, carrying a bucket. "There is a spigot in the courtyard."

"Come, quickly." Franz led them down the stairs and into the *traboule*.

He paused at the entrance to the courtyard and held up his hand for them to stop. He watched the courtyard for a moment—not as long as he would have liked, but time was of the essence. One of the building's residents coming home from having dinner out might stumble across the body at any moment.

He motioned them forward, and he dashed across the courtyard to the opposite corner. Lucien followed on his heels, but Mareille stopped in the middle and hung the bucket on the spigot, then turned the handle wheel to start the flow of water.

Franz pointed out the body, and Lucien helped him wrap it up.

By the time they had finished rolling the blanket around the corpse, in too many layers for blood to soak through all of them, Mareille came trudging up, the full bucket splashing drops of water in her wake.

Franz motioned toward the large pool of blood, looking black in the dim light. "No matter how many buckets it takes to do it, the stones must be completely clean. Not a trace." He looked back to Lucien. "Show me the workroom where your concierge keeps his cart."

"It is back the way we came," Lucien said, and Franz cringed. Perhaps they should have fetched it first. He glanced up at the dozens of windows above them, but saw no faces.

"Let's go, quickly." He and Lucien dashed back across the courtyard to the corner they had just left. There, inside the *traboule*, Lucien showed him a recessed door, with a padlock on the handle.

Franz took his knife from his pocket, and in five seconds he had the lock open. Lucien led him inside and pulled a cord. A single naked light bulb illuminated a cluttered space. They found a cart under folded tarps, and they tossed all but one of them aside.

"We can return this before your concierge discovers it missing," Franz said.

They pushed the cart across the courtyard as quickly as they dared, and Franz was conscious of the noise the cart's wheels made across the cobblestones. Mareille was tossing another bucketful of water across the area when they arrived, and the two men heaved the wrapped body into the cart, then covered it with the tarp.

"The well," Lucien whispered, nodding down the *traboule*. They each took a handle and pushed the cart toward the next street.

They had just reached the next traboule a block down, when they heard the roar of several cars barreling down the street toward them. These medieval streets were barely wide enough for a single car to pass through—not wide enough for a car and a cart.

"Hurry!" Lucien said, and they huffed as they tugged the cart through the door of the *traboule* before the cars reached them.

"Wait a moment," Franz whispered, and cracked the door, peeking out at the street. Six police cars sped past and came to a sudden halt in front of the *traboule* they had exited a few minutes before. Two dozen gendarmes and a pair of men in suits emerged from the cars, and disappeared down the *traboule*.

Going toward the safe house.

That watchman must have reported something suspicious, Franz reasoned. Otherwise, the police would not have come.

Unless there was a second watchman around somewhere, who had seen Franz attack and kill his colleague.

There was no time to worry about that now—not until they had disposed of the body.

"We're running out of time!" Franz hissed through clenched teeth. "Let's go, now."

It seemed to take forever to traverse the length of the covered passage, but they finally reached the edge of a small courtyard. Less than two meters away in the corner—barely half a meter underneath someone's window, and only a meter from their door—stood a quadrispherical stone well.

"Leave the cart here," Franz instructed. It would make too much noise and invite curious stares out the window. Instead, Franz and Lucien carried the wrapped body, and heaved it over the edge of the well. They stepped back into the shadows immediately. It was several seconds before Franz heard the splash.

The well was deep indeed. *Good, that's one lucky break, at least.*

They took the empty cart back to the entrance of the traboule, but then Franz held up his hand to stop. "If the police see us with the cart, they will ask what our business is. If we are just walking down the street together, they will assume we are friends coming home from a night at a tavern."

"But our concierge—" Lucien started to protest, but then clamped his mouth shut and nodded. They would have to deal with that later.

**

The courtyard was full of police when they emerged from the *traboule*. Mareille was nowhere in sight, but Franz noted with some relief that there was only water on the cobblestones, and no sign of blood. Still, Mareille might have been safer if she'd not already returned to the safe house.

"Stop!" one of the gendarmes called, and marched toward them. "Who are you?"

"I live in that building there," Lucien said, pointing at the opposite side of the courtyard. "My friend was coming home with me for dinner. My wife is expecting us."

"Papers, please."

Franz's heart skipped a beat. He had the details of his fake identity memorized, but he wondered what address was printed on the identification papers Lucien handed over. He barely breathed while the gendarme inspected them, and then shined a light in their faces.

"Alright, you may pass," the gendarme said, stiffly.

Franz and Lucien kept their eyes down while crossing the courtyard. When they neared the entrance to the spiral staircase, they heard heavy footsteps descending, and they stepped aside to wait. Nearly a dozen gendarmes passed them, along with two men in handcuffs. The two plain-clothed inspectors followed, looking smug, perhaps even haughty.

Franz and Lucien cast glances at them all as they passed, keeping their eyes mostly down to avoid drawing attention.

"Your two guests?" Franz whispered when they climbed the steps.

"Yes." Lucien's voice was grim.

They left the staircase at the second floor rather than the third. Franz followed Lucien down the dimly lit hall, and when they reached the end, Mareille stepped out of the shadows. Franz heard an audible sigh of relief from Lucien.

"I had just emptied my last bucketful when they arrived," she whispered. "If they had come any later, I would have been at home, and they would be taking me away, too."

"We must get far away from here, before they come back looking door-to-door for the two of you," Franz said. Another spiral staircase opened to their left, this one narrower than the one at the other end of the hall—easy for someone to hide and listen. He motioned with his head for them to follow, and they hurried down to the street.

"Where are we going?" Mareille asked in a hushed voice when they had gone several blocks at a brisk pace.

"To the Saint-Alain Quarter, in the Old City," Franz said.

They crossed the Saône at the Pont de la Feuillée. They wound through the narrow streets, up one *traboule* and down another to evade any tail, eventually heading south across the Place du Change onto Rue du Boeuf.

Franz had Lucien and Mareille hide in the shadows of the staircase while he knocked on Dolph's door in the code sequence.

Several agonizing seconds passed, and then Franz heard hurried footsteps inside the apartment. Dolph answered the door wearing only a pair of boxer shorts. His face looked worried. The sight brought an impish grin to the corner of Franz's mouth, but there was no time to enjoy the view.

"You may wish to put on more clothes, my friend," Franz said, stepping into the doorway so that he could whisper. "The safe house was raided tonight. The guests were captured, but the residents escaped. I have brought them here." He'd tell the full story later.

Dolph's cheeks flushed crimson, and seconds later the blush extended down his neck all the way to his collar bone. He turned away in a hurry, and two long strides of his massive legs took him to a half-open door into a darkened room. "We have company," he said in a low voice.

"Who?" the familiar voice inside the room sounded worried.

"It is only Franz right now," Dolph said. "But he is bringing two more in a moment."

Franz spotted clothes scattered on the floor, too many for Dolph alone.

Marcel appeared in the doorway, naked and holding a small pillow in front of his privates. He grabbed at articles of clothing, and then disappeared back into the dark room. The door closed behind him.

Dolph was already tugging on his trousers and buttoning up the fly. "You may bring them now, Franz," he said, looking down to grab his shirt, his cheeks still bright red.

**

A few minutes later, Mareille and Lucien were seated on the couch, while Franz sat in a chair facing them. Dolph and Marcel sat at the small table nearby.

"Tell me about your two guests who were taken by the police tonight," Franz said. "Were they English? Or French?"

Lucien cast a sideways glance at Dolph and Marcel. Franz held up a hand to calm him. "It is alright—they are trusted lieutenants."

Lucien nodded. "They were both English."

"They said they were RAF pilots," Mareille said, then after a second's hesitation she added, "But one of them had a two-way radio in a valise, so I don't think he was really a pilot."

An SOE operative. That made this whole thing more dangerous.

The British Special Operations Executive regularly sent spies and saboteurs into occupied countries, to fulfill Winston Churchill's directive to "set Europe ablaze." An SOE agent might well need to use their escape route and safe houses if his cover were blown, alongside the usual downed RAF pilots evading capture.

"What will happen to them?" Mareille asked, before answering her own question. "The police will turn them over to the Boche, won't they?"

Franz nodded. "The RAF pilot will go to a prisoner of war camp in Germany." He left unsaid what would happen to the SOE agent; he would be handed over to the Gestapo, who would torture information out of him. And then he would disappear. "But first, the police will try to get them to identify their helpers. You will need to go away for a while."

"Where will we go?" Lucien asked, his eyes filling with moisture. "Lyon is our home."

Franz's heart broke for them. "I know it will be difficult, but it is not forever. There is a village up in the hills, an hour's drive from here, where a Protestant pastor I know of will arrange a new life for you. The villagers are all anti-Vichy, and very... determined." He almost said "stubborn," but thought better of it.

"Is it nice there?" Mareille asked, her voice cracking a little.

Franz gave her his kindest smile. "Yes, very nice. The air is clean and clear, and the mountains nearby are very pretty. The people there will be kind to you, and will protect you." His smile broadened, and he added, "You may not ever want to return here."

The shell-shocked looks on their faces told him his light-hearted jest had not landed.

"My associates here will take care of you. And in a few days, after arrangements can be made, my lieutenant will take you to the place I mentioned." He motioned toward Dolph. "Leave everything to us. And best if I don't tell you the name of the village yet." *Just in case*.

Hutson

8

Thursday, February 12

Térèse's eyes widened when she approached the table against the back wall at Chez Oliver the next night. "Emmentaler, I wasn't expecting to see you," she said in a low voice, leaning over him to brush some imaginary lint off of the tablecloth. "What brings you here? Should I send over Mr. Hansen?"

Franz shook his head. "I am here to see your top boss, Mr. Carmichael. I'm sure Mr. Hansen has already told him of my arrival."

A gleam came to Térèse's dark eyes. "I did not realize that you knew Mr. Oliver," she said, using the more familiar term that staff and regulars had begun to use.

"We have been acquainted for about two years. We have many mutual friends, you see."

A sly smile spread across her lips. "Emmentaler, you are full of surprises."

Franz nodded in polite agreement, but kept his mouth shut.

"Are you going to order a drink?" Térèse said, cocking her hip and looking at him with an amused expression.

"A glass of the house red, thank you."

**

Oliver passed Térèse on her way to the bar. She gave him a mischievous smile, and it dawned on him that she knew who Franz was. *Of course she does*. Franz worked with so many groups. Oliver suspected the little waitress had developed a new appreciation for him after Monday's meeting of the Resistance; and now realizing that he knew a famous Resistance coordinator.

"It's good to see you again, Franz," Oliver said.

The scruffy Swiss man stood and shook his hand. "And you as well, my friend. I see you have made good use of the months since our last encounter." He motioned around the club with an appreciative look.

Oliver had to grin. "Thank you. I'm proud of the place." He took a seat next to Franz. "If one has to be anywhere but Paris, this makes it almost worthwhile."

"This is a convenient place for our friends to connect. Less dangerous than the regular meetings. And conducive to the passing of confidential messages."

Oliver understood. "You have a message for me, then?" he asked, quieter than before.

Franz leaned closer. "I heard that a Free French agent recently arrived in this area from London, and there is a rumor that he is meeting with an American. My contacts did not know, or would not say, what American." His eyes asked the question he didn't voice out-loud.

Oliver nodded without confirming vocally.

Franz took an audible breath through his nose. "The next time you meet him, be very cautious, my friend. Fascist elements are watching, even in the Unoccupied Zone. Just last night, one of our safe houses was raided. Our operatives escaped, but their English guests did not."

A chill ran through Oliver, and a cold sweat broke out on the back of his neck. He glanced around, then whispered, "What will happen to them?"

"Vichy's lapdogs will take them to the Occupied Zone and turn them over to the Gestapo."

Oliver's insides went cold. "That's what I was afraid you'd say."

Franz's hazel eyes held Oliver's in an intense stare. "They will do the same to any Free French agent they find. And to anyone who meets with them."

Sweat soaked the back of Oliver's shirt, and he was grateful it didn't show under his white dinner jacket. He dabbed a linen napkin on his forehead. "Thank you for the warning." He thought for a few seconds, and then said, "May I ask how you heard about my meeting?" It worried him that word had spread.

A faint smile crossed Franz's lips, an attempt at reassurance, perhaps. "The agent is guarded by members of the Resistance group known as Combat."

And you work with Combat, no doubt. Oliver should have guessed that from the start.

Franz continued. "They have received overtures from a bureaucrat in Paris, but have ignored them until now. I do not know how he learned of the Free French agent's arrival, but Combat is prepared to cooperate in order to not push this bureaucrat into informing on him."

"I know the bureaucrat, but I can't illuminate how he knows," Oliver said, wondering himself what Jacques Chastain's source of information was. "It seems you already know more than I do about it."

A guarded look came to Franz's eyes. "Just see that you are careful. Be vigilant. The fascists might be watching at any time. If they see you talking to a Free French agent, they will begin watching this club." He spread his hands to take in the crowded room. "Be suspicious of all new customers."

A cold dread sank into Oliver's stomach. "Thank you for the warning." He stood, and Franz stood after him. "I hope you enjoy your night at the club. Your drink is on the house. Good night."

**

Across the city, in a private colonnaded dining room, Gilles Matous looked over the dozen ex-soldiers seated around the U-shaped table. Matous was standing at his place in the center of the table, and he addressed them after the waiters had closed and locked the doors.

"Comrades in arms for the future of France, I have brought you here for a celebration. Yes, I said celebration—though we did not catch the Gaullist traitor we seek, we did make a fine catch for our allies. If any of you are fishermen, you know without me saying it that before you hook the prize catch of your life, you will hook many other fine fish. You will learn from them, take nourishment from them, and trust the Almighty that eventually He will guide your hook to the prize catch you've been waiting for.

"So it was for us last night. We took a British spy from his lair, and have handed him over to the Gestapo, like a fishmonger selling his catch at market. This has earned us praise from our leaders in Vichy, and praise from our allies in Berlin."

Matous paused a moment while the SOL men around the table congratulated themselves.

"Still, there are lessons to be learned from last night's catch. Not only did we not snare the Gaullist traitor, neither did we catch the traitors who were harboring the British spy and the fugitive British pilot—a pilot whose plane was shot down while trying to bomb French cities!"

Angry murmurs circulated around the room.

"We acted too quickly. We must remember to be patient, to wait for the perfect moment before striking."

He looked at the SOL man who had overseen last night's operation, and held his gaze for a few seconds, until the man had to look down at his plate.

"We must not let the rats scurry away before we can entrap them! Next time, we will know better.

"But for tonight, we celebrate a victory. And tomorrow we get back to work, so that we may earn the ultimate victory for France—purification from the socialist and Jewish cabal that would drag her down. *Vive la France!*"

He raised his glass. The others held their glasses aloft and shouted *"Vive la France!"*

9

Friday, February 13

Oliver tossed the note from Frank Dryden, along with the train tickets, onto his desk. He exhaled hard and rubbed his temples, trying to release the tension that had suddenly given him a splitting headache.

He got up, poured himself a measure of gin, and tossed it back. *For medicinal purposes*. He took a pair of deep breaths, went back to his desk, and re-read Dryden's note.

> My dear Mr. Carmichael,
>
> I apologize for the delay in responding to your last note. I have enclosed the round-trip train ticket to Montpellier that I am unable to use, which you graciously agreed to take off my hands. I hope you enjoy your stay.
>
> I can recommend the restaurant Maison Guilhem as an excellent place for dinner. The Côte de Boeuf is second to none. If you go there on Monday night, you won't have to wait for a table. Eight o'clock will give you plenty of time to savor your dinner.
>
> I am, most cordially yours,
>
> Frank Dryden

Oliver looked at the train tickets. Second class, leaving 9:15 Sunday night on the overnight train, arriving in Montpellier 7:05 on Monday morning. The return ticket left Tuesday morning, arriving back at Lyon late in the evening.

A perfect fit for the days the club was closed. Oliver sighed. *No day off for me.*

He had no idea how he was going to break the news to Lisette. She still wasn't happy about his involvement, though she hadn't said anything further about it. This trip would likely change that. He considered asking her to come along, but that would only set her off again.

There was a knock at his office door. "Come in."

Fabien, the bartender, poked his head inside. "I'm sorry to interrupt, boss, but we need you to make a decision. Will you come down to the cellar with me and look at the shipment?"

"Be right there," Oliver said. At least it gave him a distraction. For tonight at least, he would focus on his business.

But tomorrow he'd become a spy. Again.

**

Sunday, February 15

It took two hours for the southbound train to reach Valence, known across the south of France as the "Gateway to the Midi"—the "Midi" being the colloquial term for the far south, the land of the noon-day sun. Oliver had been told it was a well-earned moniker— south of Valence, the sun shone more than three hundred days every year.

Light snow fell for most of the trip, and Oliver watched it from the window of the dining car. It was a moonless night, but the blanket of snow across the rugged countryside of the Rhône valley reflected back a bluish hue.

By the time the train stopped at the Valence station, the snow had started to fall hard. This was about a hundred and five kilometers—about sixty-five miles—south of Lyon. Parisians and Lyonais alike spoke of the South of France as warm and pleasant. Oliver asked the conductor how often it snowed here.

"A few times a year," he said. Then, looking out the window at the blanket of white, and more of it falling heavy and hard, he shrugged. "Not usually this much. But do not worry, sir—it rarely snows in the Midi."

When the train began moving again a half-hour later, it didn't accelerate very fast. It felt sluggish to Oliver, even a bit lurching. They crept through Valence, where the lights of the small city reflected brightly on the snowy streets, but almost no one was outdoors.

The next stop was at Montélimar—a small lump formed in Oliver's throat when he remembered that was Serge's hometown. It was scheduled for forty-five minutes after leaving Valence, a distance of fifty kilometers, about thirty-one miles. And yet, it never felt as if the train got to full speed. Oliver stayed in the dining car, having another glass of wine, and watched as the snow continued to fall. Hard.

It took almost two hours to reach Montélimar, and several grumpy passengers got up from their seats and hurried out, muttering about the late hour. By then Oliver had finished his fourth glass of wine. A warm buzz had slowed down the tumultuous thoughts in his brain, and he'd relaxed into his seat. His eyelids were growing heavy, so he glanced at his watch again. Just past one AM. He supposed he should probably get to bed.

The conductor was passing by, so Oliver grinned and asked him if he were sure they were traveling south.

The conductor did not look amused. "Of course we are traveling south, sir. This is the train from Lyon to Montpellier, and that requires traveling south." He marched away with his nose elevated.

Apparently, weather-related humor didn't translate well.

Oliver walked down the corridor toward his sleeping berth, concentrating hard not to weave in the narrow space. The schedule posted on each car said that the next stop in Avignon would happen in ten minutes—but that was still eighty-five kilometers away, according to the chart. About fifty-two miles. Impossible. Oliver imagined angry passengers waiting at the Avignon station, staring down the empty tracks.

The train began to move again about the time he reached his sleeping car. That was a quick stop. *Making up for lost time, I suppose.* It was chilly inside the car—hardly the southern warmth he'd expected by this point, well into the Midi—and he could see his breath. In the limited space of his sleeping berth, Oliver changed into the flannel pajamas he'd brought, and tucked himself under the covers. He pulled the blankets to his chin and curled up in a tight ball until he stopped shivering.

The rocking of the train was slow and gentle when he fell asleep.

**

Monday, February 16

The sudden jolt awoke him, and then a harder lurch made his head hit the end of the berth, hurting. He put his hand on top of his head as he sat up, certain he already felt a lump.

Out in the corridor, he heard a mix of angry and frightened chatter in hushed French voices. Then a few seconds later the train slowed hard, pushing him against the wall of his berth, and the squeal of brakes pierced his ears.

What the hell?

The conversations around the car were no longer so hushed.

The train shuddered to a stop a moment later. Oliver had never experienced an earthquake before, but he imagined that to be what it felt like. He poked his head through the curtain of his berth; everyone in the car was sitting up in their bunks, looking at one another in confusion.

The conductor came through a few minutes later, and the voices around him grew into a cacophony of sound. Oliver couldn't make out what anyone was saying, and he almost felt sorry for the conductor. Almost.

The poor man raised his hands, shouting to the passengers to quiet down so he could speak. It took several shouts in ever-increasing volume before they complied. The French do not like to be bossed. Out of nowhere, Oliver mused about how unexpected it was that they were so acquiescent to the authoritarian rule of Vichy. He shook his head at himself and concentrated on the conductor.

"The train has made an unscheduled stop," the man said.

"Where are we?" an angry middle-aged woman with a head full of curlers demanded.

"We are eighteen kilometers north of Avignon," the conductor said. "Unfortunately—"

"Why did we stop?" an elderly man interrupted.

The conductor cast him an angry glare, silencing him. "Unfortunately, the snow has become impassible. We are unable to continue the trip at this moment. The engineer has radioed ahead to the Avignon station."

"Do you mean we're snowbound?" a young woman asked, clutching the collar of her nightgown around her throat.

"I am afraid so, Miss."

At the sudden explosion of frightened voices, the conductor raised his hands again and shouted for silence. "We are perfectly safe where we are," he said, once the car had fallen silent again. "We

will remain here to await rescue. You will all remain calm. Help will arrive in due time. Now please go back to sleep."
   Fat chance of that.

10

Monday morning

Montmartre, Paris, Occupied France

Sébastien Bonnet awoke to the clanging bell of the alarm clock, and groaned. He was quite comfortable where he was—spooned around Sophie Verlac's soft bare form, while her husband Alain's firm body spooned around Sébastien's. The warmth of their naked bodies pressed against both sides of him, cozy under the heavy blankets, was not something he was prepared to give up quite yet.

Alain shifted first, reaching around to shut off the alarm clock. He heaved himself up, throwing the covers back, sending a blast of frigid air against Sébastien's back. He smacked Sébastien's buttocks twice. "Time to get up, darling boy."

Sophie slipped out from under the covers and into a waiting silk robe, which she tugged around herself, and hugged her arms across her chest. As Sébastien stretched and yawned, she kissed him on the cheek. "You have one minute to go back to your room before I wake up the children."

"Yes, ma'am," Sébastien said, reluctantly rising from the comfortable—and warm—bed. He threw on his bathrobe and padded quietly down the hall to the bedroom they had let him use since October.

He'd been staying here since he had to abandon his own apartment in the 5th Arrondissement, after the incident with Captain Allard of the Paris Police—the incident that had sent Oliver, Lisette and Marcel fleeing to the Unoccupied Zone.

The incident that resulted in Serge's death.

The main reason Sébastien remained in Paris—apart from the fact that it was the only city he had ever called home—was the burning desire to someday wreck revenge upon Captain Allard for killing Serge.

He retrieved his leather bath kit from atop his dresser and walked to the bathroom. The Verlacs had a spacious apartment, with four bedrooms, and a full bath rather than just a water closet. He found Alain at one of the sinks, a towel wrapped around his waist, spreading shaving cream across his stubbled face.

"The water isn't hot yet," Alain said, and Sébastien grunted. Like everywhere else in Paris, the building's concierge only fired up the boiler for an hour or so every morning, to conserve the precious coal rations. Sébastien took the other sink, and stood next to Alain, preparing the shaving cream. He was more baby-faced, and had far less stubble than his friend, but now that he held a job he needed to shave every morning.

He'd known Alain and Sophie for seven years, since they were students at the Sorbonne. Sébastien studied art, never made much money, and stayed in the inexpensive housing of the *Quartier Latin*. Alain, a year older than he, became a lawyer like his father, and moved back to the Right Bank—but settling in Montmartre instead of the 16th Arrondissement was their enduring nod to their bohemian youth.

Like Sébastien's father, Alain's father had been active in the *Parti Radical*, the center-left political party during the last decades of the Third Republic. Sébastien and Alain had become friends after arguing on the same side of a particularly vocal impromptu debate with a gaggle of student Socialists during Sébastien's first term.

They remained friends after graduating, even though Alain became respectable and *haute bourgeois*, while Sébastien remained in the 5th and led the life of the poor artist. Last fall when Sébastien needed somewhere to disappear, he didn't hesitate to call on Alain Verlac; and Alain didn't hesitate to say yes.

Though Sébastien and Alain had experimented a few times as students, it had always seemed to Sébastien that his friend was mostly heterosexual—so the invitation in November to join Alain and Sophie in bed had been unexpected, but hardly unwelcome. Now, being pressed in between them two or three nights a week was one of the highlights of his existence.

Alain finished shaving and wiped the last of the cream from his face with a plush towel. Catching Sébastien's eyes in the mirror, a half-smile curled up one side of his mouth. "See you at breakfast."

After shaving, Sébastien got dressed and walked down the hall to the dining room, where Alain sat between his two small children, dapper in a crisply pressed suit, eating bread with jam, and a bowl of plain yogurt. Sébastien took a seat next to Gaston, the Verlacs' three-year-old son. He tore a piece of bread off the remnants of last night's baguette, and was spreading the jam on it when Sophie emerged from the kitchen carrying three steaming cups on a tray.

"Coffee," she said, setting a cup in front of both men.

Sébastien grunted and blew across his cup. Ersatz coffee, made from chicory, was hardly satisfying; but it was still hot, and better than nothing on a cold morning.

"Will I see you in court today?" he asked Alain, who was folding up the newspaper and handing it to Sébastien.

"Not today." Alain took one last sip of ersatz coffee and rose from the table. "My next trial starts on Wednesday. The picture on page four looks like one of yours."

"Gérard Lebrec?" Sébastien asked, arching an eyebrow.

"That's the one."

"Yes, I did that one."

Returning to his art studio in the 5th was out of the question, as was opening a new one here in Montmartre. Too obvious, too suspicious. So instead, using a false identity that Professor Trusnik provided, Sébastien had quietly asked his father to find him a job at Le Figaro.

Before the war, Sébastien's father had been managing editor of a center-left leaning newspaper, the Paris Moderne. But after the occupation began, it was shut down—by the Germans, or by Vichy, Sébastien was never sure. But a friend at the center-right Le Figaro arranged for the elder Mr. Bonnet to run the local crime desk.

And so Sébastien's father had hired him—under his alias—to make charcoal drawings of court cases at the Palace of Justice on the Île de la Cité. That was dangerously close to his old neighborhood in the 5th, so Sébastien cut his hair short, grew a mustache, and wore false eyeglasses. That, plus the professional suit he wore, with the fedora that replaced his flat cap, should make him unrecognizable to anyone who had known him before. It wouldn't fool his mother, of course, but a former acquaintance would look right past him and never notice him.

The newspaper's office stood in the busy heart of the city, on Boulevard Haussman in the 9th Arrondissement. It was an easy enough bicycle ride from Montmartre, if the streets going down the hill weren't icy. This morning they were, so Sébastien opted to ride the Metro. Plus, the underground station offered a few blessed moments of heat.

And the trains were usually devoid of German soldiers. They traveled by automobile.

He arrived at his desk before eight-thirty. The day's court schedule was already on the desk. He perused it for a moment, and then got up to get a cup of ersatz coffee.

One of the boys from the mailroom was pushing a cart along the outside of the newsroom, and when Sébastien passed him, the boy held out his hand and slipped a note to him.

Sébastien stepped into a supply closet, pulled the chord to light the overhead bulb, and closed the door. He tore open the half-sized envelope—lacking postage or postmark—and read the hand-written note inside.

The dog has run away, and we are seeking a replacement. Yours, ZL

Sébastien cursed under his breath. It meant that a safe house had been compromised. But at least no one in the network had been captured or killed—then the message would have been that the dog was stolen, or the dog had died, respectively.

The signature—"ZL"—meant it was somewhere in the *Zone Libre*, or the "Free Zone," as Vichy insisted on calling the Unoccupied Zone. Not that any *résistants* had illusions about France being free anywhere.

He would have to make sure everyone along the route knew that the chain had broken somewhere south of the Line of Demarcation. Any escapees in transit would have to be kept in place for a while. And couriers would need to be extra vigilant.

Taking his cup of ersatz coffee, he strode to his father's office. The door was open, and his father sat at a desk piled with scattered pages of copy for his review.

"Good morning, Jean-Claude," his father said, using his alias. Sébastien was just glad that Henri Bonnet could say the name now without even a hint of smile.

"Good morning, sir," Sébastien said, keeping up the appearance. "May we have a word, please?"

The elder Bonnet nodded, and Sébastien closed the door. "I need to take a trip for a few days, to Orléans, and then to Tours. Are there any assignments you can give me?"

His father scrutinized his face, staring him hard in the eye, and Sébastien resisted the urge to squirm like a teenager caught sneaking out of the house.

"Are you going to Orléans and Tours for a side business?" he asked, using the language they had agreed upon, in case his office were bugged by the police. Or the Gestapo.

"The reason is personal," Sébastien said, while also nodding.

His father stared at him for a couple seconds longer, and then sighed. He removed his glasses and rubbed his eyes. "Let me see what I can find," he said, putting his glasses back on. "Come see me this afternoon."

"I'll have drawings for you after court today," Sébastien said. "Thank you, sir."

**

Rhône valley, Unoccupied France

Oliver pulled the rim of his hat low over his eyes when he stepped off the train into the brisk morning air. There wasn't a cloud in the blue sky, and the sun shining off the blanket of snow was blinding.

Land of the noon-day sun. But it's only ten o'clock. Looking around the empty countryside, he hoped perhaps by noon the sun would have helped them out by melting some of this snow. It had better—he only had ten hours until his meeting; it was already three hours past when they should have arrived in Montpellier, and they were still more than a hundred kilometers away.

There was a well-worn path alongside the stopped train, where the snow had been firmly packed, but beside it Oliver could see the accumulation was at least two feet thick. The evergreens carpeting the nearby hills were covered in white.

It took a while to reach the front of the train, where Oliver joined the collection of men with coal shovels removing snow from the tracks, little by little. It seemed like trying to empty a bucket with a teaspoon, but he supposed it was better than just waiting around for rescuers to reach them.

He sank his shovel into the powdery white snow and tossed it to the side. Repeat. And repeat again.

It didn't take long for his shoulders and back to ache. He paused for a few seconds to catch his breath, noticing that his forehead was sweating despite the frigid temperature, and then went back to work.

**

The sun was dropping below the western hills when the rescue team finally reached them, working their way north up the track from Avignon. The passengers cheered, and Oliver clapped along with them, then glanced at his watch. He was due to meet someone at a restaurant in Montpellier in just over two hours. He wasn't sure he'd make it.

And he also wasn't sure what to do if he didn't.

**

It was dark when Oliver hurried across the square in the center of Montpellier. He was already a half-hour late, and he still had his suitcase with him. The cobblestones were wet from rain, and he jumped a few puddles on his way. Fortunately, the cool night meant that there weren't too many pedestrians to get in his way.

He found the restaurant a block down one of the side streets. The yellow glow of the overhead lights gave the interior a warm and inviting look.

A pair of elderly women sat at a table by the window, conversing quietly. The only other person was a rail-thin waiter in black pants and a white shirt leaning against the back wall, beside the kitchen door. He hurried forward, and Oliver requested the table in the back. He stowed his suitcase beneath the table, hidden under the long tablecloth.

He took a moment to catch his breath. Then he took a small votive candle from his suitcase and lit it with a match, as Frank Dryden had suggested. And he waited.

He had no information about his contact, or what he looked like. The entire arrangement was murky, created in the shadows he knew little about. All Mr. Dryden had said was that his contact in *Deuxième Bureau* knew someone in Montpellier who wanted to work with the Free French. And so Dryden and Murphy had sent Oliver to make contact.

It would have made more sense to pass this task along to Charles Forgeron, but Oliver had been overruled.

"This is our operation," Dryden had said. "Let's keep it under our control."

The waiter cast a glance at the votive and disappeared into the kitchen. Oliver could only imagine what he was thinking. Or was the waiter his contact? That seemed unlikely—he would hardly be able to have a secret conversation, not a real one, anyway, beyond perhaps passing or receiving a short message.

A moment later, a man in a business suit came from the kitchen and sat across from Oliver. He was about mid-forties, his dark hair graying at the temples. "You are the one known as Candle?" he asked, voice low, just more than a whisper.

That was the code. "Yes, that's me."

The man's eyes widened. "Are you English?" he whispered.

Oliver shook his head. "American."

The man visibly relaxed. "That is better. The English, they are hated ever since Mers-el-Kébir." He turned his palms up apologetically. "You will forgive me, I expected someone French."

"I understand."

Britain was the only country technically at war with Vichy France, after they attacked the French fleet at Mers-el-Kébir in July 1940 to keep it out of German hands—but aside from that initial attack, nothing had come of this state of war. Vichy continued to profess neutrality in the war between Germany and the Allies.

"You were late—did you encounter trouble?" His eyes looked heavy with worry.

"Only from the weather." Seeing the confused look on the man's face, Oliver added, "The train was snowed-in north of Avignon. It took all day to dig it free."

"Ah, that explains it." The man glanced around, though no one was seated anywhere near them. He leaned a little bit closer. "I was told that you have a line of communication to General de Gaulle."

Oliver frowned. "I don't know if that's true," he said, cautiously. "But my associates can communicate with the Free French in England."

"But then, if the information is good, it will get to General de Gaulle himself, no?"

Oliver shrugged. He had no insights into the functions of the Free French. "Perhaps so."

The man glanced around again, and whispered, "There are many in Montpellier who are prepared to support the Free French. Vichy is not legitimate, just as General de Gaulle has said. The people here have grown weary of the regime, and its collaboration with the *Boche*."

"Are you organized?"

The man nodded. "We meet, in many places. Different groups, all eager to help free the country. We only need direction on what to do."

Interesting. "How many do you have?"

"Hundreds. There are groups that meet at every temple in Montpellier—there are eight temples here, it used to be a Protestant city during the Wars of Religion—plus many others at the university."

Oliver nodded, impressed. "What sort of direction are you looking for?"

The man made one of those ridiculously exaggerated frowns that the French were so good at, to suggest something was plainly obvious. "For General de Gaulle to tell us how we can best help him. To prepare for his liberation of France."

Oliver pondered that for a few seconds. He would humor him. "What are you prepared to do for General de Gaulle?"

The man sat up straighter and raised his chin. "Anything that he deems necessary, we will gladly do."

"Anything?"

"Yes, anything," the man said, and thumped his chest.

A bit theatrical, but effective. He couldn't help the half-smile that curled the corners of his mouth. "That is good to know, sir. How many of the others—the hundreds that you spoke of—how many of them are also prepared to do absolutely anything the Free French direct?"

The man stiffened. "We are *all* prepared, sir."

Doubtful, but others would decide the veracity of that. Oliver nodded, trying to look conciliatory. "Of course. My apologies, sir."

The man looked mollified. He glanced around again, and leaned back in. "When can we expect to hear our instructions?"

Oliver took a deep breath, and considered how best to answer that. He had no idea, of course.

"I will return to Lyon tomorrow with what you have told me. I will arrange to meet with my associate—that may take a few days. Then he will radio to the Free French headquarters in London on a predetermined schedule—I do not know what night that will be. After that, I cannot say how long it might take for them to make a decision. They will radio their answer back to my associate, who will arrange to meet with me again." He shrugged and made the little puff of air from his lips that the French always used to indicate uncertainty. "So perhaps two weeks? Or maybe three weeks? Impossible to say precisely, you see."

He left out the step of having to clear everything with Frank Dryden before he contacted Charles Forgeron in Vienne.

The man looked a little disappointed—he was clearly eager. Oliver had to give him something else. And he knew just the thing.

"In the meantime, our organization can provide you with copies of our secret newspaper, *Combat*. It shares news that Vichy's censors won't allow in the legitimate newspapers."

The man's face lit up like the noonday sun. "That would be excellent, sir. We can distribute throughout the city."

"Should I have the delivery made here?" Oliver arched an eyebrow.

The man considered a moment. "If they can make it look like a food delivery, then yes."

Oliver allowed himself a faint smile. "Our next issue will be released at the end of the week. I will arrange for a delivery to you."

The man nodded resolutely and stood. He extended his hand, and Oliver shook it.

"Thank you, sir. I am grateful for your kind words about our establishment. Good evening." He nodded, and disappeared into the kitchen.

11

Wednesday, February 18
Tours, Occupied France

Adrienne Charbonneau finished wiping down the counter before removing the dirty apron and tossing it in a laundry bin. She opened the swinging door to the kitchen and shouted, "I'm leaving, Papa."

"You are coming for dinner?" her father asked, coming toward the door, covered in flour from head to foot.

"Not tonight, Papa," she said, and kissed him on the cheeks.

"Have you told your mother you won't be over?"

She smiled at him affectionately. "Yes, Papa. I told her this afternoon, before she left." She slipped her coat on over the heavy woolen sweater she wore, tugged on a wool hat, and wrapped a scarf around her neck. They wished each other a good evening, and she hurried out the door.

The walk from her parents' bakery to the little apartment she rented by herself was almost a kilometer. The streets had grown slushy during the day, and her feet were soaked before she'd gone half a block, leaving her muttering curses to this blasted winter. *Third year in a row that the winter has been atrocious.* It was also the second winter in a row with hardly any coal, making it even worse.

The building was still cold when she climbed the stairs to her third-floor apartment. She kept her coat and scarf on, but tossed the hat onto a little table beside the door.

A folded sheet of paper sat on the floor a meter in from the door, and she stooped to pick it up. Her first name was written on the outside, and she smiled when she recognized the handwriting.

Café Touronum, seven-thirty.

That didn't give her much time. And she was expecting a courier to deliver a guest at nine o'clock, at the rendezvous point near the river. But Sébastien would understand that. He ran this escape line.

She had a few minutes to rest, so she plopped down on the wooden chair, one of two around her little kitchen table. This apartment was sparsely furnished—she'd had to leave behind almost all of her belongings when she fled Paris in October. She'd only had time to pack her clothes and a few personal items.

Such as the stack of playbills sitting in the middle of her table like a centerpiece. Whenever circumstances had her down, she perused some of the old playbills that featured a photo of her dancing on stage, usually in elaborate costumes. She'd been a lead dancer in the Follies her last eighteen months in Paris; it had taken her five years in the chorus to work up to that. Leaving that behind galled her most of all. She still had a good ten years in her, damn it.

But it had all been for France. If she had it to do over, she'd make the same choice when Serge asked.

For three weeks after the incident with Captain Allard, she'd hidden in a barn outside Barbizon, being fed by strangers who were sympathetic to the cause. Once it was clear the Gestapo weren't looking for her, they moved her on to Orleans, but she only stayed in the Safe House there for a couple of nights before moving on to Tours—her home town.

Never in her life had she expected to end up back in Tours. She'd made a life for herself in Paris and had come to think of herself as a true Parisienne. But back here she was, and she needed to make the best of it. So after laying low for a week at a cheap hostel, using the last of her cash, she finally went to her parents' house.

Where they promptly put her to work in the bakery. Like when she was a teenager. To be back in the exact same circumstances she'd left eight years ago was too much to bear, so she'd at least insisted on finding her own place to live after a couple of nights in her old bedroom.

She sighed, tossed the playbill back on the stack in the middle of the table, and got up. Tugging the hat back on, over her ears, she braced herself to walk out into the cold night.

**

The interior of the café was warm, and the windows were fogged over so that she couldn't see through to the outside. She spotted Sébastien sitting at a table in the back, and he grinned as he rose to meet her. They kissed cheeks, and then embraced, laughing.

"It is fantastic to see you, my friend," she said.

"I have missed seeing you, as well," he said, his trademark crooked smile firmly ensconced, bringing out that oh-so-familiar dimple in his cheek beside the unfamiliar mustache.

"May I ask what brings you to Tours?" she asked, quietly.

His smile faded, and he shrugged. "There has been a breach," he said, barely audible.

Her stomach tightened, and her heart skipped a beat. "Here?"

He shook his head. She breathed a sigh of relief. No immediate danger, then. She forced an amiable smile, and resumed the friendly conversation, for the benefit of anyone who might be watching. "Tell me news of Paris." She sighed wistfully. "I miss it so."

He chuckled. "Paris is the same. We go to work, we eat small meals, we bundle up to keep warm with no coal, and we drink wine to forget."

She laughed. "You make it sound just like Tours! But I know there is more excitement to be had in Paris than there is here. Remember, I know both places well."

*

Sébastien decided to leave out the unexpected polyamorous affair with Alain and Sophie Verlac. That could only make Adrienne envious. "The Germans have outlawed excitement," was all he said.

She laughed again and nodded. "They have indeed."

They both ordered a glass of wine—better than ersatz coffee or watered-down beer—and relaxed into the familiarity of an old friendship.

"Have you been painting?" she asked after their wine arrived.

He shook his head. "It has not been possible. But I have been drawing, for Le Figaro."

Her eyes widened. "Le Figaro? Are you crazy?"

"There is no difference between left-wing and right-wing newspapers anymore. They all print only what the censors will allow."

"I suppose that's true." she sighed. "Still, it is...unexpected of you."

"Sometimes the safest place to hide is in plain sight," he whispered.

"Indeed," she said, her eyes saying more than that.

They finished the wine, and Sébastien laid some coins on the table. She did not take his arm, but allowed him to open the door for her. The cold night air smacked them in the face.

A squad of German soldiers marched past, leather jackboots smacking the pavement, and all the pedestrians lowered their eyes and hurried by.

"Alright then, what brings you to see me?" she said quietly when they were alone on the street.

"I received a message that one of the safe houses in the Unoccupied Zone has been compromised," he said, equally quietly. "I do not know anything more specific than that."

"What does this mean for us?"

"For the time being, until we can find out where the chain is broken, we must not send anyone across the Line of Demarcation. We cannot be certain they are not walking into a trap."

She was quiet a moment. "What is your next step?"

"I have to find out exactly where the break is, and if it has been repaired." He paused for a few seconds. "I expect it has been repaired, or they would have sent more specific information. But I must find out."

"How?"

He wasn't entirely sure, so he stuck with a simple answer. "I will get a message to Dolph in Lyon."

She saw through it. "But what if the break is between the Line of Demarcation and Lyon?"

He didn't answer for a long time, and they walked in silence for a couple of blocks. "I may have to slip across and see for myself," he said at last.

She stopped walking and grabbed his arm to turn him toward her. "Are you out of your mind?"

He shrugged. "We have sent dozens of others across. Why not me myself?"

"Because it's dangerous."

He shrugged again. "No more dangerous for me than it is for them. And it may be the only way."

"But you know too much if you are captured," Adrienne said, scowling deeply. "That is too big of a risk. We cannot take a risk that big, Sébastien."

"We might not have a choice," he said quietly, returning her gaze evenly, unblinking.

She exhaled hard in exasperation. "You will do what you want, of course." They resumed walking. Then she muttered with a sideways glance, "Just like Serge."

That hit home. He understood her implication. "Serge took an unnecessary risk that night," he said, scowling. "He was supposed to go immediately to the safe house in Montmartre. Instead, he took it upon himself to confront Allard. He was consumed with getting revenge, and it clouded his judgment."

"He was right to want revenge, for what that fascist pig did to him."

Sébastien sighed. "I understand his feeling. I have felt it, too. But it must not affect our thinking, or we are lost."

She was silent, but he could tell from her rigid posture and the set of her mouth that she was furious. She wouldn't let him have it in public, however.

"I will leave you at the next corner." He nodded toward the intersection a half-block in front of them.

"When will you decide?"

He shrugged. "Tonight. Or maybe tomorrow, after I return to Orleans."

"I take delivery of a new guest tonight," she said. "What am I to do with them if I cannot move the current guest on?"

"They will have to share lodgings for a while. We have no choice."

"It might make us more obvious," she whispered as they reached the corner. "More feet to make a sound on the ceiling of the apartment below. And less food to go around."

They stopped at the corner, and he stared at her hard. "We have no choice," he repeated. "You will do what you must. And I will see that it is temporary."

He nodded, touched the rim of his fedora, and turned away.

12

Thursday, February 19
Riom, Unoccupied France

Frank Dryden arrived in the courtroom early enough to secure a seat close to the defendants' table. It quickly filled up, and the room morphed from chilly to hot and stuffy. He took off his overcoat, and soon regretted the heavy sweater he wore over his dress shirt and tie. The multiple layers had seemed appropriate first thing this morning, when the temperature had plunged well below freezing, and his breath came in great clouds on his walk to the station from the *Hôtel des Ambassadeurs*. Now he was sweating, pressed tightly between curious spectators

People in Vichy complained that they had never known a colder winter; to Dryden it reminded him of his childhood in Michigan. Not in a pleasant way, however.

The little market town of Riom was a forty-five-minute train ride southwest from Vichy, through the rugged hills of Auvergne. The area was covered in snow, which made for a beautiful scene out the windows of the train, deceptively peaceful. But the atmosphere inside this courtroom was electric with tension.

All conversations fell silent when a pair of gendarmes escorted the seven defendants into the room. Only the clicking and popping of flash photography could be heard as the seven marched to the defendants tables: Léon Blum, former premier from the Socialist Party; Édouard Daladier, his successor as premier, from the center-left *Parti Radical*; Daladier's successor as premier, Paul Reynaud, of the center-right Democratic Republican Alliance; Maurice Gamelin, former commander-in-chief of the French Army; Guy La Chambre, former minister for the French Air Force; Robert Jacomet, former Controller-General of the Army Administration; and Georges Mandel, former Minister of the Interior.

Murmured conversations resumed after the seven had sat at the two long tables, with their legal representation. The prosecutor and his assistants came in next, shook hands with the defense attorneys, but studiously ignored the seven defendants.

A gendarme ordered the court to stand, the room fell silent, and the panel of justices filed in and took their seats behind the raised bench.

Then they all sat, and Dryden watched Chief Judge Caous read from the charges.

"The Supreme Court of Justice has been empowered by a decree of Premier Philippe Pétain to judge whether the former ministers, or their immediate subordinates, had betrayed the duties of their offices by way of acts which contributed to the transition from a state of peace to a state of war before September 1939, and which after that date worsened the consequences of the situation thus created."

Dryden's heart raced, in spite of the calm exterior he maintained. Vichy was trying its predecessors from the last four years of the Third Republic, for crimes that were retrospectively created. No free country retroactively applied penal law, ever. This trial was the first real proof to the wider world that Vichy was a dictatorship—and that excited Dryden.

Caous continued. *"By decree issued by Premier Philippe Pétain on 30th July, 1940, this court is empowered to judge: first, the ministers, the former ministers, civil and military, accused of having committed crimes and misdemeanors while carrying their duties or on the occasion thereof, or of having betrayed the duties of their offices;*

"Second, every person accused of having attacked the security of the State and of connected crimes or misdemeanors;

"Third, every co-perpetrator or accomplice of the persons targeted by the above paragraphs."

The language was legalistic, and Dryden had to concentrate hard to comprehend it in French, but fortunately he'd seen a written copy of the charges in this morning's newspaper.

The Chief Judge asked each of the defendants in turn if they understood the charges. Six of them answered with a single world *"Oui,"* while Gamelin stared at the judge with defiant silence.

Dryden saw several journalists exchange looks. The reporters from neutral countries—including, technically, the United States—would report the defiance, but French reporters would almost certainly not be allowed to.

And yet, Dryden knew that information would still get to the public through unofficial channels—within the Unoccupied Zone, at least. He knew this thanks to the information Oliver had provided, about sympathizers in Switzerland who sent American and British newspapers to the Resistance group Combat to use in their clandestine paper.

This trial was likely to last for weeks. Dryden only planned to be here for the opening day or two, unless something striking happened.

But watching the defense tear into the injustice of retroactive crimes, Dryden had to smile. Word would spread, public opinion was bound to shift. And with any luck, it would bring a sea change.

**

Lyon, Unoccupied France

The note from Dolph said to come to the club early to discuss an important matter, so Oliver arrived there after lunch. The lights were out, and only the daylight streaming through the front windows allowed him to see Dolph standing beside the bar. The chairs were still turned over on the tables, and the club was otherwise empty.

"I need to show you something in the cellar," Dolph said, and turned toward the back corridor before Oliver had even reached him. Oliver hurried to catch up. An interior wooden staircase led down to the cellar, where they stored the meat, cheese, and wine. The bare lightbulb was already lit, and Oliver's stomach tingled with nerves as they descended.

The slender figure standing next to the wine rack was someone he'd never thought he'd see again. At least not anytime soon.

"Sébastien?" Then he laughed out loud and rushed toward his friend. Sébastien grinned, and they threw their arms around one another, then kissed each other's cheeks. "You escaped!" Oliver said, taking a step back and beaming at his friend. "Are you going to stay in Lyon?"

Sébastien's crooked grin dimpled one cheek in that familiar expression, but he shook his head. "I return to Paris tonight. I have work to do there, and it can resume now that I am assured every link in the chain has been restored."

"We have a delivery truck taking him to Brinay," Dolph said. "That is by the Cher, and a *passeur* we know there will ferry him back to Vierzon."

"Back into the Occupied Zone," Oliver said.

Sébastien clasped Oliver's arm in a comradely sort of way. "It is necessary, so that others may continue to escape from the Boche."

Oliver had long believed Sébastien and Dolph were involved in one of the escape lines that were whispered about, slipping political dissidents and downed allied pilots out of France. It was Sébastien who had sent him to Saint Sulpice when he needed to flee Paris; from there he, Lisette, and Marcel had followed the pilgrim trail south, until Franz Lemiel met them at Vierzon, where he'd arranged a *passeur* to take them across the Cher to the Unoccupied Zone.

Oliver nodded. "I understand. I will pray for you, my friend."

Sébastien responded with an amused half-smile. Then he took Oliver by the shoulders and shook him, laughing. "Ah, it is good to see you, my dear friend!" He put one arm around Oliver's shoulders, and the other around Dolph's waist. "I have missed you both."

"Did Dolph tell you I am working with the Resistance again?" Oliver asked.

Sébastien nodded vigorously. "He did."

"After we joined with others in Lyon under Combat, I went to Montpellier and brought several groups there into the network. Soon we will reach all across France."

Sébastien's arm squeezed him tighter. "That is important work, my friend. Thank you."

"I wish you could stay and enjoy my club tonight," Oliver said, feeling suddenly wistful.

"I would enjoy that." Sébastien's warm brown eyes looking him down-and-up told Oliver he'd enjoy more than a night of cabaret. "But I have already been away too long. I have a job at a newspaper, and they were expecting me back today. If I do not return soon, they may report my absence to the Gestapo."

"Say you had the flu," Oliver said with a shrug.

Sébastien chuckled. "I plan to tell them I was ill—but that will only work for a day or two. I cannot remain here any longer. I am sorry. It has been wonderful to see you, though." He gave Oliver's shoulder one more squeeze, and then disentangled himself from Oliver and Dolph.

"The truck will be here any moment," Dolph said, and started toward the stairs.

"Stay safe, Sébastien," Oliver said.

As his friend disappeared into the back of a wine delivery truck, hidden under a tarp, twin pangs of sadness and fear swept through Oliver's belly.

**

Sunday, February 22
Vienne, Unoccupied France

The sun was warm on Oliver's face, in stark contrast to the icy breath of the gale-force north wind that assaulted him on his way to the Roman amphitheater. *Le Mistral*, someone on the train had called it—the infamous winter wind that occasionally whipped down the Rhône valley from the Alps.

It had been a ridiculously short train ride, barely twenty minutes to go twenty-five kilometers south from Lyon; a journey of just fifteen miles. Oliver felt a little silly buying the ticket. It didn't matter how many times he told himself it was perfectly normal in France.

He was surprised to find the Roman amphitheater here was as large as the one in Lyon. It was carved into the side of a low hill overlooking the red-roofed buildings of Vienne, stretching along the east bank of the Rhône. He was open to the powerful wind here, and it whistled across the ancient stones. He huddled his chin below the upturned collar of his overcoat, and kept his hands shoved as far into his pockets as they'd go. But at least the wind kept most of the tourists away, and the few who were there scurried around, focused on spending as little time in the open as possible.

"They can find shelter inside the Augustus and Livia Temple." The man called Charles Forgeron appeared next to Oliver.

"Vienne has a Roman temple?" It hardly seemed a big enough city.

Forgeron looked at the end of his cigarette, which had been snuffed by the wind, and tossed it aside with a frown. "When Lyon was Lugdunum, it was the capital of Roman Gaul. The elite of the province had their villas here in Vienne, a day's journey from the masses in Lugdunum. That is why this exists." His hand swept over the open space of the amphitheater.

"I have a reply for you from the Paris bureaucrat I know," Oliver said. "He said 'The preservation of France requires the preservation of the patriots working in her government.'"

Forgeron frowned again. "I will report that to London this week."

The clipped way he said it made Oliver think the Free French wouldn't be happy about Chastain's cautious response. "Will they have an answer for him?"

"Of course they will have an answer for him," Forgeron snapped. "We must cultivate support among those working in the government, and we cannot afford to ignore someone just because he is reluctant."

Oliver stiffened. "I will wait for your message, then."

Forgeron looked around. "We must part soon, before it looks suspicious. What other news do you have for London?"

"The resistance group Combat has expanded to Montpellier." While Frank Dryden had authorized him to pass on this update, Oliver chose to leave vague his personal role in that development. "The new chapters there seek instructions from General de Gaulle. In the meantime, they distribute the group's newspaper. More people in France will learn the truth that Vichy wants to keep from them."

Forgeron nodded. "That is good news. When the time comes, we will need an army of Frenchmen to rise up to liberate the country from Vichy and the Boche."

Oliver's heartrate quickened. "For the invasion?"

"It is too soon to talk of that," Forgeron said, the words tumbling out in a rush. "But yes, eventually." He looked around again. "I must go. Anything else? Quickly."

Oliver shook his head. "No, nothing else."

"I will be in touch."

13

Friday, March 6
Lyon, Unoccupied France

Oliver almost laughed at how many people he saw reading the easily recognizable one-page broadsheet known as *Combat*. In open daylight, no less.

It was a cool but sunny day, and the streets were crowded with pedestrians enjoying the first hints of spring. Oliver was on his way home from the weekly open-air market downtown, with a bag of produce in each arm, or he would have grabbed a copy for himself from one of the benches or café tables where they'd been left. He consoled himself that the employees would have one at the club this evening.

Demand for the clandestine newspaper had grown exponentially over the last two weeks, as the mainstream newspapers reported less and less of the Riom Trial. Meanwhile, *Combat* devoted entire issues to the proceedings, and the public was riveted.

The prosecution had called hundreds of witnesses, but the defense had largely shredded them, according to the illegal broadsheets. Soldiers testified that the French army was inadequately equipped to resist the German invasion in May 1940, and the prosecution argued this was due to the Blum government's imposition of the forty-hour work week and paid leave for workers in 1936, which reduced factory outputs.

In an unexpected twist that had the public waiting for updates, Léon Blum himself cross-examined witnesses. He had been a lawyer before becoming a socialist politician, and now he induced admissions from the witnesses that the reduction in military spending had occurred while Marshal Philippe Pétain and his current Prime Minister, Pierre Laval, had both held cabinet positions under Reynaud.

Reading the illegal news at the club every evening, Oliver, Lisette, and their friends hooted at the reversals.

Crossing the Saône at the Pont Exchange, Oliver saw a police gendarme marching toward a man engrossed in reading today's issue of *Combat*. Oliver was about to shout a warning, but hesitated out of fear of drawing attention to himself. In that second, the gendarme tore the paper from the man's hands, crumpled it, and shook the wad in the man's face.

"Where did you get this illegal garbage?" the gendarme shouted, red-faced. "Who gave it to you?"

"I found it on a bench in front of the Hôtel de Ville," the man stammered. "It was just left there, I don't know by whom."

The gendarme's fury only increased at the man's allegation that such dissident opposition was lying around in front of the city hall. "At the Hôtel de Ville? Impossible! Who would have the audacity to do such a thing?"

The man only shrugged, making the gendarme look almost comical in his fury. He stormed off toward central Lyon, the crumpled paper clenched in his fist. Oliver was relieved he hadn't struck the man. The man watched the gendarme go for a few seconds, and then continued on his way toward the Old City.

When Oliver arrived home ten minutes later, he found the landlady sitting on her front stoop in the sunshine, glasses on, reading—a copy of *Combat* in her hands. She was one of the last people he would have suspected.

In a bold move, he said as much after greeting her, but cloaked it in a tone of jest and a teasing smile.

Her cheeks colored. "That is true. I still say that Marshal Pétain is a hero who saved France, but... he has obviously made a terrible mistake with this trial. They are making him look like a tyrant persecuting a scapegoat."

No, he makes himself look like a tyrant. But Oliver didn't contradict the landlady. On his way up the stairs, he thought of Paul Reynaud and Georges Mandel. A few days into the trial, Marshal Pétain had withdrawn the charges against those two without explanation—but had them taken to a prison fortress at Pourtalet, in the Pyrenees, where they remained locked up without charges.

That action had only been reported in *Combat*, and the mainstream newspapers had ignored it entirely. The government's censors would never allow legitimate news agencies to report such a thing, and Oliver was still bitter that only a Resistance propaganda rag told the truth.

In the mail he found a letter from his parents, and he opened it after putting away the fruit and vegetables he'd bought.

And he was shocked to see that there was almost as much black marker on the page as there was his mother's handwriting. Easily forty percent of what she'd written had been blacked out.

His hands began to tremble. His mother wasn't a danger to anyone, and it was outrageous that some censor would think her words dangerous. After almost two years, he had no trouble understanding that censors read all the international mail, incoming and outgoing, and he had long seen little bits of black on the letters from home. But this was a level unseen before.

He read through the three-page letter with mounting frustration. So many sentences were partially blacked-out that it made it almost impossible to understand some of the paragraphs. An entire section about his brother Paul and his family was reduced to virtual gibberish, without sufficient context. *Why on Earth?*

Then the thought jolted him that perhaps Paul had joined the army. But why would he do that, and leave his wife and kids alone? No, Oliver couldn't imagine that being true. There must have been something else the censor didn't want communicated.

About the only section that was—mostly—intact was the news from his father's church. The part Oliver always found the least interesting. *Figures*. Even that had little bits blacked out, but by now he could only shake his head in befuddlement.

He stomped into his kitchen and poured himself a glass of wine. He took a large quaff, breathed deeply as the warmth of it spread down through his chest, and then took another sip. He would have to write back to his parents and let them know that hardly anything Mother had written made sense after censoring. He could only imagine what kind of shock that would be to them.

Or would the censor black that out before it reached them? He huffed in frustration.

He briefly wondered if he should try to call them on the telephone. Sure, the line ran through the Occupied Zone, and so a Gestapo thug would inevitably be listening in, but what in the hell was he going to do if he didn't like it? Oliver was outside of their reach here; the most they could do would be to cut the line.

But he put the thought out of his mind. He only ever spoke to his parents on the telephone once a year, on Christmas day. The trans-Atlantic calls were horribly expensive, and so they only ever talked for about six minutes, three minutes being not quite enough time.

He checked his watch. Lisette would still be at work in the flower shop down the street. She'd be back shortly before they had to leave for the club. He downed the last of the wine in his glass, and dressed for the night.

******

Armand, the barback, was waiting at the front door of the club when Oliver and Lisette arrived at five o'clock. The slender biracial boy greeted them with a friendly smile. Oliver unlocked the door and stood aside for Lisette to enter. Then as Armand came in behind him, Oliver stopped beside the light switch and asked him quietly, "Did you happen to bring a copy of today's *Combat* with you?"

Armand grinned. "Yes, boss. I've got two copies." He patted his coat, and Oliver heard the crinkle of paper inside.

"I'll take one," Oliver said, and as Armand reached into his coat, Oliver added, "But don't tell me where you leave the other one, I don't want to be an accomplice if the police come poking around." For some reason he couldn't articulate, he suspected they might.

A curious expression crossed Armand's youthful face. "Alright, boss." He handed one folded page to Oliver, and then hurried toward the storeroom, tugging off his coat.

Oliver leaned against the bar instead of going back to his office, and read through the paper. Lisette came out a few minutes later, an eyebrow arched in what looked almost like irritation.

"I need to open the safe," she said, and then sidled up next to him to read over his shoulder. "I didn't realize you had a copy."

"Have you seen it yet?"

"Yes—but I haven't read it." Her tone sounded a touch cross, perhaps because he'd started reading without her. "One of the customers in the store had a copy in his hand, hidden between business reports from his office—but I could see part of the banner sticking out, so I knew what it was."

Oliver held the page between them. He was a little bit ahead of her, and he hadn't realized he'd audibly gasped until she looked up at him and asked, "What is it?"

He pointed to a paragraph in the middle.

Former Minister for the Air Force, Guy La Chambre, testified that on the day of the surrender in June 1940, the military still had more than two thousand serviceable airplanes, and that one thousand of these fighter planes had already been moved to safety in North Africa.

"The French military was perfectly capable of continuing the fight against the invaders, from North Africa, just as General de Gaulle argued to Marshal Pétain," he stated.

A gasp arose from the observers in the courtroom at the mention of General de Gaulle's name, and Chief Judge Caous had to call for order.

Lisette shook her head in wonder, mouth open.

"It was a bold move, citing de Gaulle," Oliver said, smiling. "Perhaps suicidal, but bold nonetheless."

"It's incredible." Lisette looked up at him, a hint of smile tugging up the corner of her mouth. "Everyone has been afraid to say his name outloud for so long." She shook her head. "Incredible."

"Do you think this will encourage others to talk about de Gaulle openly?"

She shrugged, but then shook her head. "I don't think so. Everyone fears arrest if they speak of him. La Chambre has already been arrested, so what has he to fear now?"

"Good point. Still, it's a start, isn't it?"

She shrugged again, half-heartedly, and continued reading in silence for a moment. When she came to the end of the paper, she exhaled hard. "Wow."

"I agree," Oliver said, smiling.

She nodded toward the office. "Come open the safe for me."

**

Dolph knocked on the office door ten minutes later, while Lisette was counting cash, distributing it to the drawers and marking the ledger. Oliver looked up from the order forms he'd been filing out.

"*Salut*, Dolph," he said, using the informal greeting. "What's up?"

"Térèse called a moment ago," Dolph said. "She is ill with the flu and cannot work tonight. Her fever is thirty-eight degrees."

Oliver still had to do the math in his head to convert Celsius to Fahrenheit, but he could do it quickly now. That was a hundred and one degrees. "We can't let that spread through the staff. Who can we replace her with?" He hesitated, glancing at Lisette from the corner of his eye, but then added, "Would Marcel be interesting in picking up a shift tonight? I would be willing to pay him a little extra, for his trouble. And the short notice."

He looked again at Lisette from the corner of his eye. Was it just his imagination that her fingers seemed stiffer as she counted ten-franc notes?

Dolph looked doubtful. "I can send him a note. He does not have a telephone."

That could be a problem, Oliver realized, glancing at his watch. Still, there was enough time for Marcel to get ready and arrive before the club opened. Just enough time.

"Do that," Oliver said. "But if he's not...available...tonight, what would be the next plan? It's Friday, so we'll be too busy to be short a waiter."

"I could have Armand dress for it," Dolph said. "He has never waited tables, but he knows our business and our regular customers, he would have no trouble. We have extra shirts and trousers in the storeroom that would fit him."

That seemed reasonable enough. Low risk. "Will you have the time to help him if he gets into difficulty?"

"It will not be a problem," Dolph said, with a firm nod.

14

Chez Oliver was packed by nine o'clock, and Oliver grinned at the sight of waiters scurrying around the room carrying trays of drinks. Armand only looked tentative and unsure for the first half-hour after opening, and now hurried about as efficiently as the rest of the staff.

At the end of that musical set, Oliver announced the band's break, and went to the bar. Fabien hurried back and forth from one end to the next, looking calm and efficient; but Oliver saw the faint gleam of sweat on his forehead and knew he was at maximum capacity.

He poured his own gin and tonic from the private stash he still had in one corner cabinet, courtesy of the black market.

"That last song was a new one," Lisette said from her usual chair at the corner of the bar.

Oliver nodded after taking a long drink of the cold cocktail. "Yes, it's the first time we've played that one. I wrote it a while ago, though. I had to keep working on it, and it wasn't ready until this week."

"Everyone seemed to enjoy it." She nodded toward the room at large. "It got big applause."

Oliver beamed at her and put his hand over hers.

Then the sound of shouting from the far side of the room caught his attention.

"I said I want a *French* waiter," a tall man seated at a table shouted at Dolph. A brave thing to do, Oliver mused, walking around the bar and into the room.

"I am a citizen of France," Armand said, raising his chin.

The man ignored him and shouted again at Dolph. "He is not French. I want a *French* waiter."

"All of our waiters are French, sir," Dolph said, clearly struggling to remain patient. Oliver picked up his pace.

"You will give us a *real* French waiter"—a glance at Armand while the man wrinkled his nose—"or we will not stay."

Oliver had reached the table now, and his ire was up. He looked down on the man, who wore a wispy thin mustache. "As you wish, sir. I will see you and your companions out."

The man's eyes narrowed, and he regarded Oliver with undisguised hostility. He sniffed. "*You* are not French, either." He looked at his five companions and sneered, "Three foreigners. What is France coming to?"

They shared a laugh, which made Oliver's stomach clench.

The man looked back at Dolph. "If you are the *manager*," another sneer, "then let me speak to the owner of the establishment. I wish to discuss his insistence on giving French jobs to *foreigners* who do not belong in France."

A hint of amusement cracked Dolph's stern veneer when he nodded at Oliver. The man turned to Oliver, mouth ajar.

"That is me, sir," Oliver said, straightening to his full height. He enjoyed the look of discomfort on the man's face. "I am Oliver Carmichael, owner of Chez Oliver. I accept your offer to leave. This way please." He motioned toward the door with a nod of extreme *politesse*.

The man huffed as he shot up from his chair, and angrily tossed his black linen napkin onto the table. His companions rose, all with their mouths pursed and their noses in the air, and spun away without looking Oliver in the eye. They marched toward the door so fast that Oliver struggled to keep up.

"We will tell *everyone* we know not to come here," a woman with a fox wrap around her shoulders said, only half-looking back as she passed the maître'd station.

Oliver almost laughed out-loud, thinking about how full the club was. "Thank you," he said, unable to keep the amusement from his voice. The woman sniffed and hurried out the door.

"I will make sure they never come back in here, Mr. Oliver," Claude, the maitre'd, said.

Oliver chuckled. "I don't think we'll have to worry about that." He turned back to the room, where several patrons watched him, a full range of expressions on their faces. "My apologies for the disturbance, ladies and gentlemen. There will be no more fascist outbursts tonight. Please, enjoy yourselves, and the music will resume in a few minutes."

The guests at a couple of tables stiffened and looked away, heads huddled together. But most of them resumed the gaiety of a cabaret on Friday night.

Dolph hurried to him while he was on his way back to the bar. "I'm sorry, Oliver."

Oliver patted his arm. "Not your fault, my friend. Let them tell their fascist friends that Chez Oliver is not a good place, and we won't have to worry about their kind disturbing everyone else's good time."

Armand hurried past on his way to another table. "Thanks, Boss," he said with a grin.

Oliver slipped behind the bar and found his cocktail where he had left it by Lisette. She looked at him with an expression of admiration mixed with exasperation. "They could have started a riot." She nodded toward a table of guests who were hurrying out. "They had some sympathizers."

Oliver wasn't surprised at the group that was leaving. Another group quickly followed them out, and he recognized them also as some who had not seemed to appreciate his apology for the racist disturbance.

"Our regulars would have had them beaten into a corner in no time," Oliver said with a show of bravado that he almost felt. He pictured a saloon brawl in an old western, and almost laughed, until he saw her scowling at him and crossing her arms.

"That is not funny, Oliver."

He leaned across the bar to put his hands on her shoulders. "I'm sorry, darling. I meant only that we have the support of a large number of regulars, so those people cannot hurt us."

She arched an eyebrow in apparent doubt, but amusement tugged at the corner of her mouth. "You are impossible. An eternal optimist." She shook her head, but the half-smile on her lips only grew.

"I have to get back to the band. The show must go on." He winked at her and turned away.

**

They were performing the third song of the next set, when a half-dozen gendarmes came in the front door. Ignoring Claude, they fanned out across the room, stopping at tables and addressing the guests.

Oliver saw them, but kept directing the band. Dolph caught his eye and nodded, hurrying toward the one with the insignia of a captain on his arm, who was standing by Claude's station with his hands clasped behind his back, watching.

"Let's take five," Oliver said to the band at the end of the number, using a literal translation of the American idiom. They were used to that, but there were no amused half-smiles this time, all of them watching the room with anxious expressions.

"Is there a problem, sir?" Oliver asked the nearest gendarme, at a table a few yards from the stage.

"May I see your papers, please, sir," the gendarme asked Oliver, not looking at the dark-haired woman to whom he thrust back a set of identity papers.

"Of course." Oliver removed his identity paper and American passport from inside his dinner jacket. Then he also handed over a business card. "I am Oliver Carmichael, the owner of this establishment. May I ask why the police have come here?"

The gendarme didn't answer, only looked toward the front door, and waved the captain over.

"The owner of the cabaret, captain," the gendarme said with a crisp nod. "American." He handed Oliver's papers and passport to the captain and moved on to the next guest at the table.

"Good evening, Mr. Carmichael," the captain said in English, glancing from the photograph on the identity paper to Oliver's face. He opened the passport, but only made a perfunctory glance inside before handing everything back to Oliver. "I am Captain Beauchemin, Lyon Police."

"What is the reason for this?" Oliver asked in French, no longer hiding his irritation.

"Routine identity checks," the police captain said, in English, with an attitude bordering on geniality but not quite succeeding. "Nothing to be concerned about, sir."

Routine, my ass. But Oliver kept his mouth shut.

"As long as everyone's papers are in order, and there are no wanted suspects here, we can leave you to your business," Beauchemin said, still in English.

Wanted suspects. That might cover almost anything. "Are you looking for someone in particular?" he couldn't help asking, in French.

Beauchemin's green eyes grew steely. "Routine, sir," he replied in French, stiff and formal, the almost genial attitude now a memory.

"Of course." Oliver willed himself to be overly polite. "May I offer you something to drink, Captain?" He motioned toward the bar.

"Mineral water would be most excellent, sir," Beauchemin said. Then, switching back to English, "Alas, the police do not take alcoholic drinks while on duty. We must perform at our best, for France."

"Of course," Oliver said, in French, with a polite nod. "I'll get you a glass of our most popular mineral water. One moment, please." He hurried to the bar, where a gendarme was in the process of inspecting Lisette's papers.

Fabien stood near the center of the bar, his posture stiff, arms behind his back, staring ahead. He glanced at Oliver when he came behind the bar.

"Fetch a bottle of Perrier," Oliver said, while he reached for a clean highball glass from the cabinet.

Fabien retrieved a bottle of Perrier from the short cooler and broke the seal. He poured it into the glass Oliver set on the counter. He caught Oliver's eye, made a tiny nod toward the other side of the bar; Captain Beauchemin stood there, watching them. It was unnerving.

"*Voilà*, Captain," Oliver said, handing the glass of Perrier to Beauchemin with his friendliest smile.

The captain's expression remained stoic, and he took a long drink of the mineral water. "Thank you, Mr. Carmichael," he said, stiffly and in English, when he put the half-empty glass back on the bar. "We should be finished with our task soon."

Oliver wondered if the captain's continual use of English was meant to be polite, for his benefit—or to be incomprehensible to most of the people around.

He slipped over to the corner, where Lisette sat with her hands folded in her lap. "Everything go ok?" he asked her, quietly, nodding toward the gendarme who now inspected papers at a nearby table. He'd lost track, but it seemed they had checked almost everyone by now.

"He was professional," Lisette said, and didn't elaborate.

"No extra scrutiny?" Oliver arched an eyebrow and watched her closely.

She shook her head and put her hand on top of his. "It seemed routine, like they have said."

"Hmmm," Oliver said, frowning.

"What?"

"What's routine about barging into a cabaret on Friday night and asking to inspect everyone's papers? Has that ever happened before?"

She shrugged. "How should I know? I've never seen it."

"Certainly not during the Republic," he muttered.

"Shhh!" she hissed, quietly, swatting his hand. Not in front of the police, her eyes said. He didn't care.

"Speaking of extra scrutiny..." he mumbled, and nodded toward Armand. The young Antillean stood next to one of his tables, his back rigidly straight; the gendarme in front of him was holding up his identity papers, quizzing him on every detail, barking out the questions the second Armand answered the previous one, almost talking over him.

Lisette's eyes warned Oliver to stay where he was.

Captain Beauchemin approached a few minutes later. "We are finished, Mr. Carmichael," he said, in French. "As I said, it was routine. You may carry on with your business. Good night, sir." He clicked his heels together and nodded crisply, then spun and marched away. The gendarmes trailed behind him in single file out the door.

A collective exhale seemed to escape everyone in the room when the door closed behind them. Conversations resumed, but sounded somehow tentative.

Oliver raised his hand for attention and shouted across the room. "Please, everyone, enjoy yourselves again. We apologize for the interruption." He paused at the corner of the bar, gave Lisette's hand a quick squeeze, and hurried onto the stage.

*

Dolph waited at the opening to the back hallway, near the bar, and watched Armand finish with a table of guests, then hurry toward the back. He motioned for the young *Martiniquais* to join him.

"Is everything alright, boss?"

"Are you ok?" Dolph asked, looking the biracial young man in the eye.

Armand relaxed. "Yes, I am ok. This is not the first time I have dealt with people like that, who don't consider me 'real French.' It is nothing."

Dolph shook his head, holding Armand's eyes. "It is not nothing, Armand. They called the police to check our papers."

Armand sighed. "It is not new...but they are getting bolder." He shrugged, trying to put it off, but Dolph wasn't buying it.

"They will be dealt with," he said, staring at Armand to make sure he understood.

Armand looked doubtful. "How will you find them?"

Dolph looked away, toward the open room, like a manager surveying the activities of the staff. "Everyone saw their faces. We got a good look. They will not remain anonymous. And then, we will deal with them."

**

Wednesday, March 11

They watched the man leaving an office building on the Place Bellecour, the largest square in Lyon, and the third largest in all of

133

France. Fabien and Simon fell into step behind him, keeping a distance of about ten meters so that they blended in with the end-of-workday crowd.

When the man crossed the square and passed close by the marble pedestal of the giant bronze statue of King Louis XIV on a prancing horse, Dolph and Marcel started to pace alongside him at a distance of about a dozen meters, pretending to converse. Dolph trusted that with a hat pulled low over his brow, and his face turned away from the man, he wouldn't be recognized.

The man continued south through central Lyon, down the Rue Victor-Hugo, striding past the elegant stores and seeming oblivious to the two pairs of men following him—one pair a short distance behind, the other pacing him on the opposite side of the street.

Térèse stepped out of a boutique on the corner of the Rue Sainte-Hélène, where they knew the man would turn east, toward the Rhône. She carried a large shopping bag in each hand and wore a fashionable green skirt that hit above her knees, with a white sweater and matching pillbox hat and lace snood. Her three-inch heels clicked on the sidewalk just ahead of the man. She swayed her hips as she walked, trusting that this would catch his attention.

Just past the Rue de la Charité, a couple of doors before the ritzy apartment building on the Place Gailleton where the man lived, Térèse took a funny step, as she'd practiced for days, and managed to break the heel of her shoe without twisting her ankle. She cried out, dropped her bags, and grabbed at her ankle.

Right at the entrance to a covered alley, one of the few *traboules* left in central Lyon.

She hobbled a couple of steps off the sidewalk, removing her shoe and looking at the broken heel with a heavy sigh, all the while rubbing her ankle.

"Are you alright, miss?" the man asked, putting his hand on the middle of her back, and leaning down to look her in the face.

"Yes, I think so," she said, straightening and picking up one of the shopping bags. Then she sighed again, looking at the broken heel. "These were brand new," she said, melodramatically.

"Is your destination far?"

She gave him a grateful smile and glanced up at the building in front of her. "It is here. I was nearly home."

"Ah, I am in the next building, by the Place Gailleton," the man said. "It is not out of my way to help you into your building. Then the concierge can help you from there, no?"

"Thank you, but it is not necessary," she protested, and then 'accidentally' dropped her broken shoe farther into the *traboule*. "Oh! So clumsy!"

"Allow me," the man said, taking a couple of steps and then leaning down to pick up the errant shoe.

At that moment, Dolph, Marcel, Simon, and Fabien burst into the alley, having just tugged kerchiefs from their necks over their noses. Simon kicked the man's legs out from under him at the same time Dolph shoved him hard with both hands against his back, sending him sprawling deeper into the *traboule*. Within a second, they had him surrounded, kicking him and muttering "Fascist pig."

Armand came sauntering up the Rue Sainte-Hélène from the opposite direction, from the Rhône, and he shifted a utility workers' barricade into place across the sidewalk, then another across the entrance to the *traboule*. He paused at the end of the alley, smoking a cigarette. A few pedestrians hurried home from the work day, and he waved them around the barricade; residents would have to circle around the block to reach their courtyard.

Dolph whistled once, and Armand glanced into the *traboule* to see him wave; then all four of them sprinted toward the interior courtyard, from which a perpendicular *traboule* led back to the Rue de la Charité.

On the stones, half-hidden behind a trash can, lay the man. Bulging eyes stared at the stone archway, unseeing, an ether-soaked rag stuffed in his mouth and purple handprints across his crushed throat.

"You should not have called the police on the Résistance," Armand muttered, and tossed the lit cigarette at the body's feet.

He sauntered back down the Rue Sainte-Hélène toward the Rhône. At the corner, he turned right onto the narrow Rue de Fleurieu, and Térèse hurried across from the little Place Gailleton, where pale green buds colored the ends of the plane trees, and little yellow forsythia blossoms brightened the shrubbery.

"*Vive la France*," she said with an impish smile, slipping her arm through his.

15

Thursday, March 19
Luzinay, Unoccupied France

Matous watched the little farm south of the village of Luzinay for some time before he exited his car. The other three men, plus the four in the car parked behind his on the gravel road, exited at the same time.

"This is the place," he said. The farmer who came in from the field and went to the house for his midday meal matched the description the grocer had provided this morning.

Another transmission using known but undeciphered Free French codes had been sent last night, and the Gestapo listening stations at Brest, Augsburg, and Hamburg had narrowed the location to a fifteen-kilometer radius in the Unoccupied Zone just to the northeast of Vienne.

Matous and his team had spent the overcast morning going from village to village—Serpaize, then Septème, and Saint-Just-Chaleyssin, to Luzinay. And it was there, around eleven o'clock, that they got a solid lead.

Yes, someone new had come to Luzinay recently, the grocer told them, seeming eager to help the SOL men. He had thought there was something suspicious about that man. He'd shown up at the café a week ago Wednesday, wearing a suit and an overcoat, using the name Forgeron. He left the café with that farmer, Florent. Yes, of course he could tell them where Florent lived, he had the farm on the edge of the woods, off the Route des Moillés.

Matous and his men had driven down the Route des Moillés and stopped in front of the last farm before the road began to wind up a wooded hill. A half-dozen horses grazed in a pasture on one side of the house, toward the woods, and on the other side lay an open field where a middle-aged farmer drove a tractor pulling a plow, churning up the black earth in preparation for spring planting.

It was impossible to get a good look at the farmer until he climbed down from the tractor and walked toward the house. But once Matous saw his face, he knew.

He had half of his team circle around the house, while he and three others marched toward the front door.

He could hear the scrambling of footsteps inside the farmhouse after he knocked. Someone was frantically moving across the house and up the stairs; two sets of feet, if Matous's ears did not deceive him. It took nearly a minute before the front door was opened by a plain-looking woman with mousy brown hair in a faded blue gingham dress.

"Mrs. Florent, I presume?" He looked past her, to the dining room table less than four meters away. It was set for three, and all three plates were full; furthermore, the forks sat on the plates, having already been used.

"Yes, what do you want?" Mrs. Florent said, eyes narrowing in suspicion. But Matous recognized fear in her blue eyes; she couldn't mask it with that show of peasant suspicion of strangers.

He pushed past her and marched into the portway to the dining room. "You were in the middle of eating your dinner," he observed, his voice louder than what he would ordinarily use inside. "And yet, it took you a long time to answer our knock." He noted the tremble in her hands, which she folded in front of herself. "And I see that three people were eating—and yet, you are the only one here."

But something else was off...yes, there it was—four chairs sat slightly askew, as if four people had been sitting at the table, not just at the three place settings.

"My husband and my son, they forgot to water the horses. They stepped out five minutes ago."

Matous shook his head and wagged a finger at her in mock scolding. "The food is still hot." He motioned toward the steam rising from the plates. "And from the sounds I heard at your door, it sounded more like the horses were inside the house than out in the pasture."

He glanced at the sink, but it stood empty. He walked to the oven and stooped to open it. A rush of heat hit his face, making him close his eyes for a second; when he opened them, a plate of food sat on the rack, pushed all the way to the back.

He strode toward her and gripped her arm tight enough that she winced. "Where is the traitor you are hiding, ma'am?"

"I don't know what you're talking about." Her voice shook. Then she looked past him in obvious relief, and he turned to see the farmer Florent and a dark-haired boy of about eighteen come into the room from the rear of the house.

"What is the meaning of this?" Florent demanded, in an admirable display of false surprise and outrage. "Unhand my wife, sir!"

Matous released Mrs. Florent's arm, at the same time giving her a hard shove that sent her sprawling onto the floor. Florent raised an arm to stop his son from lurching toward Matous.

Matous motioned toward the open oven door, and enjoyed the look of panic that swept over Florent's face. He blanched and swallowed hard.

Keeping his eyes on the farmer's—staring him down in deliberate intimidation—Matous spoke over his shoulder to his men. "Desai, you stay here with the Florents, and keep them company.

The rest of you, come with me." He broke the stare and marched from the kitchen, SOL men trailing behind him.

They tore through the house room by room, overturning beds and dressers, cutting open the upholstered cushions on the couch.

Then, in the spare bedroom upstairs that sat next to the attic ladder, he noticed something on the back wall of the little closet. The white paint there seemed a little too clean, not faded almost yellow like the other two walls on either side. He put his hands on either side near the corners and pushed upward.

The wall moved away, and a narrow space appeared behind it. With a man crouched in the corner.

The man lunged at Matous, who saw the glint of a knife almost too late. He moved out of the way at the last second, taking a glancing blow to his left side from the man's shoulder, but thankfully missing the knife.

The man performed a controlled roll on the floor and sprang into a fighting position.

Two of Matous's men appeared at the door, both with pistols drawn and aimed at the man with the knife.

The man let the knife fall to the floor, and it clattered under the bed. He raised his hands.

"Search him," Matous ordered, and crouched down to retrieve the knife from where it had slid under the bed. While his men searched the suspect, he began cutting open the quilt.

"No other weapons on him," one of the SOL men said. "Here's his identification—Charles Forgeron, from Vienne."

Matous barely listened, having found a brown paper bag wrapped around a block of something. He opened it and dumped out stacks of cash—thousands of francs. "Very interesting, Mr. Forgeron. This is a lot of money for a simple farmer." Then, to his men, "Hold him here for a moment."

He continued his search, shredding the quilt, but finding nothing else hidden there. He tore open the two pillows, sending goose down flying, but found nothing else.

Then he saw a place on the side of the mattress that had been recently stitched. He cut the stitches and pried apart the seams.

Inside he found another bag, with two sets of passports and identification papers. Both contained photographs matching the man in custody. "Jean Sévenne, and Claude Villette," he read aloud. Then he looked up at their suspect. "Both of these surnames are nearby places, I believe. Villages we passed today. And Forgeron—that is as generic as can be, sir."

The man glared at him with undisguised hate, but his mouth was clamped shut.

Matous stepped right to him, straightened to his full height, and looked down at the man's face. "Illegal radio broadcasts have been made from this vicinity, to the Free French in London. I think we have found that traitor."

"You have no proof," the man said, raising his chin in defiance.

Matous chuckled. "We will find your illegal radio, 'Mr. Forgeron.' You will tell us the names of your accomplices. And then before the week is finished, you will be shot as a spy."

He motioned for his men to bring the spy out, but he went in front of them. As he passed through the doorway, he heard a crunching sound, like someone had stepped on a glass bulb. Panic filled him a second later, and he spun around.

The Free French spy spasmed in the arms of Matous's men, face turning bright red; and within another second he slumped lifelessly, eyes staring blankly at the floor, mouth ajar.

Matous caught the faint whiff of something bitter. *Cyanide*. There would be no interrogation, no finding out who his other contacts were.

Matous stomped down the stairs and out the door.

**

Sunday, March 22

Chaponost, Unoccupied France

The ride from *vieux Lyon* was only eleven kilometers, but it had been a long time since Oliver had ridden a bicycle any distance, and the hilly terrain rising steadily upward out of the Rhône valley made his thighs burn with every turn of the pedals. He had to continuously will himself to keep peddling.

"You are going to be late," Lisette called over her shoulder from ahead of him when they were still nearly a kilometer from the village of Chaponost.

He glanced at his watch. It was ten minutes before one. He could still make it. Just.

Lisette had insisted on coming with him. It would make it more realistic, she said. Just a couple out for a Sunday ride in the springtime. He had to admit it made sense. It hardly looked suspicious. "You can't join me when I meet him, though," he'd warned her, earning him an indifferent shrug.

The forsythia were in full bloom, their happy yellow blossoms lining the side of the road, and the trees dotting the rocky hills had turned that pale shade of green that only appeared in the early spring. The road leveled out as they entered the village, and Oliver's legs relaxed in response. He pushed harder, though, and sped past Lisette into the square at the center of the medieval heart of the village.

The church here had an extra-tall steeple, square with a peaked roof, and the clock was beginning the one o'clock chime when they stopped their bikes in front of the church stairs.

"Why don't I go see the aqueduct while you visit the church?" Oliver said, louder than normal, which got an amused half-smile from Lisette.

"Roman ruins do not interest me as much as they do you," she said, sounding perfectly natural reciting the line he'd given her.

"I will see you in thirty minutes," Oliver said, and sped off toward the west, following the signs for *Le Plat de l'Air* and *Aqueduc du Gier*.

His watch said five minutes past one when he reached the open grassy field, vibrantly green in the sunshine, stretching toward the line of ancient stone arches holding up the aqueduct that had carried water from the low mountains of the *Massif Central* to the ancient city of Lugdunum at Lyon.

He hopped off the bicycle and walked it alongside the giant arches rising fifty feet above him, and stretching almost a half-kilometer in a gentle arc toward Chaponost. A tourism sign informed him that there were 52 arches in this remnant, one of the largest complete sections of Roman aqueduct in France.

There was no sign of Forgeron. That was strange, given how open the area was. There were several clusters of people strolling the grounds, which was hardly surprising given the beautiful weather, but no other lone individuals.

A grove of pine trees stood some distance away, but unless Forgeron were hiding in the trees—which was hardly likely—then he had to be behind one of the ancient columns between the arches. Which seemed more probable once Oliver fully considered it. Still, given the size of the site, he'd expected the Free French agent to be strolling in plain sight.

The stonework was remarkably intact, given that it was nineteen-hundred years old. One of the tourist plaques said that the aqueduct was built in the first century AD. Aside from some chips here and there, and visible cracks in many places hosting small plant life, it was easy to imagine how it might have looked when Roman soldiers guarded its length.

When he reached the end of the remnant, which tumbled down in a jagged-edged ruin, Oliver circled around it and returned the way he'd come, but on the opposite side. Perhaps he'd missed Forgeron at the other end.

Oliver checked his watch when he reached the opposite end, and he had still seen no sign of Forgeron. It was twenty minutes past one. Forgeron had always been on time in the past, usually only waiting a few minutes to make sure Oliver was alone.

A chill ran up Oliver's spine. Had he been followed? Was that why Forgeron remained hidden? He glanced around, but there was no one close, and none of the tourists seemed to be paying any attention to him.

He walked the bike a distance into the field, trying to stay calm and look casual. After about a hundred yards or so, he stopped and turned around, taking in the whole site. He stood there for several minutes. The stones of the aqueduct glowed golden in the sunlight, an almost breathtaking sight to behold. Then he took his camera out of his jacket pocket and snapped a couple of pictures.

One-thirty found him nearing the road back to the village, and with a final look back at the magnificent piece of Roman architecture, he threw his leg over the bicycle seat and peddled toward the church square.

Something had gone wrong. He hoped to God it didn't mean he was in danger.

Part II

16

Monday, April 6
Marseille, Unoccupied France

The sun was hot as it beat down on the Mediterranean city, and the breeze coming in off the harbor was downright balmy. Almost hot, even, in Oliver's opinion. Like May in Indiana, or June in Paris. The streets through the Old Quarter were packed with pedestrians and bicyclists. No one worked on Easter Monday, still a national holiday, and it made for slow going. But it gave him time to take in the sights and smells of the city.

The smooth stone walls of the old buildings, glowing golden in the sunlight, and the black wrought iron railings around the windows, reminded him of the French Quarter in New Orleans, when he had visited there once during the year he lived in New York. He supposed that resemblance wasn't a coincidence.

Marseille certainly felt as hot as New Orleans, but thankfully not as humid.

Reaching the quay in front of the old harbor, he scanned the shore for the harbor ferry, and finally found it around the corner at the far end of the quay. He bought a ticket, and waited at the shore for five minutes, until the ferry returned.

A handful of others boarded the boat at the same time he did, and he scrutinized their faces. They all seemed to be normal day tourists, in pairs and small family groups. No one stood out. No one looked like a secret operative.

He stood at the rail, looking out over the water, and relished the breeze on his face. It smelled of salt and fish, but it felt refreshing against his skin, and he closed his eyes for a moment to enjoy it. The sound of the waves lapping against the side of the ferry, the rumble of boat motors, the shouts of fishermen, and deep bellow of boat horns filled his ears; and above it all, the constant screech of the seagulls overhead.

He turned back to look at the city, its details growing steadily smaller as they moved farther into the harbor. Marseille was an ancient city, founded by the Greeks in the seventh century before Christ. From this angle, it was easy to see why they chose this location for a colony, with the deep and wide harbor opening to the Mediterranean, and the tall, rocky, sun-bleached mountains ringing it from behind like a castle wall.

Looking at the fishermen in the boats around them, with their weathered faces and wind-swept longish hair, he wondered if their ancestors had been plying these waters for the entire twenty-seven centuries. It was certainly possible. He thought of the bouillabaisse stew one found in restaurants during the winters months and realized this was where it came from.

After about five minutes, the ferry passed the ends of the harbor, and entered the open Mediterranean. Less than ten minutes after that, they arrived at the first of a trio of rocky islands called the Frioul Archipelago, but known to locals only as *Les Îles*.

Oliver got off the ferry, noticing with dismay that most of the passengers also exited here. He supposed that was to be expected— this small island was dominated by a well-preserved medieval fortress, the Château d'If.

It was his destination as well—but for an entirely less innocent reason than sightseeing.

He paused just off the pier, waiting for the crowd to scatter among the sun-bleached stone walls of the castle. Looking back at the city, two miles distant, his eye focused on the towering spire of the Basilica Notre Dame de la Garde, high on a hill where the Virgin Mary could look down over the city.

Lisette might be there right now. It was on her itinerary for the day. He imagined her standing at the entrance of the Basilica, looking out toward the sea, staring in his direction.

He wished he could be there with her, instead of here meeting a stranger.

He turned back toward the castle, took a deep breath, and hiked up the rocky trail.

The series of fortifications and towers were extensive, and the trails through them quite rugged, so Oliver was a little breathless before he'd explored half of them. He climbed the steps of a corner tower, and hoped his contact rendezvoused with him soon.

Inside the main tower, he soon noticed a slender man in a gray suit, with black hair combed backward from his long face, slicked with oil, who had come into this room from the last one only a moment after he did. Oliver glanced at him several times and caught the man watching him. He was dark complected, with a prominent nose, and deep-set dark eyes. He looked more Italian or Greek than French.

Was this his contact? If so, why didn't he approach Oliver and use the pre-determined words to identify himself? It must not be him. The thought crossed Oliver's mind that perhaps he was being cruised for sex; it fit the pattern—a single man, alone, following another single man, alone, making regular eye contact, in a place that had many hidden corners.

Then the more nefarious thought jolted into Oliver's brain, that this might be a police informant, hunting spies. His blood ran cold in spite of the heat, made all the more stuffy in the close space of these small castle rooms.

He hurried out of the tower and walked briskly down the rampart.

The man followed a moment later, and he picked up his pace to keep up. Oliver's heart raced.

Play it cool.

He'd be much less suspicious if he didn't act like he was trying to get away. He resolved to let the man catch up to him—and hopefully pass by. If the end result was that he got propositioned instead, well…he would deal with that if it happened.

Oliver stopped at one of the sixteenth century gun embrasures at the next corner, and imagined himself the Count of Monte Cristo.

The man paused a few feet from Oliver, and leaned against one of the crenellations, looking for all the world like someone just casually staring across the crystal blue water.

This was it, Oliver thought. Either the man would say the expected phrase, or perhaps some sort of come-on instead. Or if he remained silent Oliver would leave, go back to the ferry, and return to Marseille.

The man shifted his posture, crossing his ankles and facing toward Oliver. A very open posture; inviting, presenting. More than five years of living in Paris had taught Oliver how to read the body language of invitation. He braced himself for the come-on.

"The gulls are more active than usual today, don't you think?" the man said.

Oliver exhaled in relief. He hadn't realized how shallow his breathing had become. "They are a nuisance," he replied, following the script.

The man slipped a little bit closer. "Cigarette?" He held out a pack of *Gaulois*.

Oliver shook his head, and the man took a cigarette for himself, turning away from the sea breeze and shielding it with his hand while he lit it. He shook out the match and dropped it on the rampart. He turned back toward the sea and put his elbow on the top of the crenellation, blowing out a stream of smoke.

Oliver had always found it odd that with all of the shortages because of the British—now Allied—blockade of the continent, tobacco was never in short supply. How was that possible?

"There are plans being put in place," the man said, quietly, inching even closer to Oliver, so that their arms almost touched.

"What sort of plans?"

The man waited while a middle-aged couple with two school-aged children walked by. He glanced around to make sure no one else was within earshot before he spoke. "Nothing is certain, yet. But it will be more than just anti-Vichy propaganda. Most French still trust Marshal Pétain to lead France, and to maintain the peace. We have swayed few."

His voice sounded bitter on that last part. Oliver felt sorry for him. And for all his friends struggling to restore some semblance of freedom in France. It had to be terribly frustrating for them to see most of their countrymen shrug it all off as if the authoritarianism were nothing.

"What are some of the ideas?" Oliver asked.

The man took a deep drag on his cigarette, and exhaled slowly. The breeze kicked up just then, scattering the smoke and blowing some of it into Oliver's face. He suppressed the urge to cough, but had to clear his throat a couple of seconds later.

"If the Allies invade France, we must be prepared to support them," the man said.

That's nice and vague. "How will you do that?"

The man shrugged, took another pull on his cigarette. "We are collecting guns. We have hired smugglers to bring them in from Spain. And there is talk of how to...incapacitate the police and army when the Allied invasion comes."

Oliver knew he wouldn't get any specifics from this meeting. The man would never bestow that level of trust to someone he'd just met—and an American, at that. But this was plenty, and Dryden would pay him well for this information.

"How many men—and women—do you have?" he hastened to add the second gender to his question, thinking belatedly about Adrienne back in Paris, and Térèse in Lyon.

The man turned toward Oliver—that same open posture that made him a little uncomfortable. "It is difficult to say for certain. Too many different groups, here and down the coast. And different levels of cooperation between these groups."

Oliver took that in for a moment, nodding slowly. "What is your affiliation? Free French? Socialist? Communist?"

The man frowned. "The communists do not work with other groups." He turned back toward the sea.

Oliver took a deep breath. That had not really answered the question. "You are Free French, then?"

The man was silent for a moment, staring across the water at the metropolis climbing up the hills, gleaming in the bright sun.

"It is not a precise thing," he said at length. Oliver stared at his face, waiting for an elaboration. After several uncomfortable seconds, the man glanced sideways at him, then down toward the rocky shore below them. "My compatriots and I, we are not affiliated with a specific political movement. We want to restore the liberties that generations of French have held dear; and to make the country whole again, free from German occupation. And from collaboration. We are practical people, my compatriots and I—if the Free French are the ones the Allies support, then we will support the Free French."

"That is very logical of you," Oliver said, with a smile to let him know that he meant that sincerely.

The man glanced around, then inched closer to Oliver again. Their elbows touched on the stone wall. "Tell me—do the Allies plan to bring the Free French with them when they invade?"

Oliver had no idea. "I'm not told what the plans are. I cannot say."

The man looked disappointed, but he nodded. "I am called Symphonie. If you learn anything more, will you send me a message?"

If Frank Dryden wants me to. Oliver couldn't make promises, but he wasn't sure how to say that in such a way as to keep Symphonie and his group on the line. "I do not know what information will be shared with me. But if I learn anything that you should know, I will send a message to you right away."

"Come in person, if you can," Symphonie said. He looked past Oliver, down the coast toward where the buildings of Marseille tapered off into a rocky scrub land. "There are many secluded places along this coast. Many good places for a private conversation."

Oliver couldn't help wondering if Symphonie wanted more than just a private conversation. Nothing he could put his finger on specifically, just a feeling in his gut.

"If I can," he said, noncommittally.

"Good," Symphonie said, with one firm Gallic nod. He turned toward Oliver and extended his hand—not an easy task in the limited space between them. Oliver had to shuffle backward a few inches to be able to shake hands.

And he felt the slip of paper in his palm. He put his hand in his pocket right away and turned back toward the sea.

Symphonie put his hat on, touched the rim with a nod, and walked away.

**

Oliver waited until he was alone on a path down to the shore from the outer wall, and took the paper out of his pocket.

It was an address in Marseille, typed. Handwritten below it were the words: "Order seventeen kilograms of squid for the traveling symphony."

He refolded the slip of paper and thrust it back in his pocket. Looking around, and finding no one in the general vicinity, he hiked across the rocks toward the pier.

**

He found Lisette at the café they had picked near the basilica, one that was said to have spectacular views of the city.

The guidebook had not lied about that, Oliver mused as he crossed the café's portico toward where Lisette sat. High on the edge of the hill, all of central Marseille spread out below them, and the crystal blue Mediterranean stretched to a hazy horizon. The Old Port, from whence he had just come, looked tiny to their right, and the Frioul islands were little rocky outcroppings to their left. He did a double take when he spotted the Château d'If, appearing the size of a child's toy from here.

He leaned down to kiss Lisette's cheeks, and then took the seat next to her, situated so that they could share the view.

"Your trip was a success?" she asked, outwardly friendly, though he could see in her eyes that she wasn't enthusiastic about it.

"Very successful. Yours?"

She nodded. "You should have seen the Basilica with me. It is beautiful. The view there is like this," she motioned toward the city below them, "But the interior is indescribably beautiful. Very unique, not like anything in Paris."

"I wonder what the Basilica in Lyon is like," he said. "We've never visited it. Perhaps we should. We are Lyonais now."

She shrugged. "I will never truly be Lyonaise. My heart will always be Parisienne."

The waiter came by, and they ordered lunch. They sipped their wine in silence, each alone with their own thoughts while they looked out over the city and the sea.

"This afternoon, would you like to go down the coast a little way?" he suggested when their food arrived.

She looked surprised. "That would be fine. But I thought you wanted to explore the city more."

He shrugged. He did, but that could wait. "We can explore the city tonight. There's plenty of time—it doesn't get dark early anymore."

"Do you have somewhere particular in mind?"

He nodded while he swallowed the bite in his mouth. "I heard there are some inlets about ten or fifteen kilometers down the coast, south of here, which are something to be seen."

"*Les Calanques,*" she said. At his questioning look, she added, "It was in the guidebook. There are dozens of them, all unique, and all striking."

"Then let's check them out," he said, grinning and taking her hand under the table.

**

After lunch, they took a short train ride to the village of Cassis, fifteen kilometers south of Marseille. It was a quaint little fishing village, not tiny by any means, but hardly a town, either. The kind of coastal village on a wide harbor that looked like it might not have changed much in centuries.

After inquiring with a few locals, they took a trail out of the village and uphill into the scrub woods. They passed a handful of men in pairs or trios, recreational fishermen, standing at the edge of the cliffs, casting lines into the sea. Other than that, and one young couple coming the other direction, the trail was practically deserted.

It was a rugged hike, and after about a kilometer, breathless, they reached a peak with a view over the Cassis harbor to their left, the open Mediterranean in front of them, and to their right the first in a series of narrow inlets cut into the rock as if some giant had run his finger through the landscape.

Oliver pointed at the inlet, and they took that fork in the trail. It was slightly downhill here, and it gave them a little breather. Which was a good thing, because the sight of the first *Calanque* took Oliver's breath away.

He had never in his life seen water that color. He stared at it, mouth open, not even caring if he looked dumbstruck. The walls of bare rock rose straight up from the water at a perfect perpendicular angle, except at the very end of the inlet, where a small beach spread out, ringed by steep hillside. The trail led down there, but they stood locked in place for several minutes.

He had no words to describe the color of the water below them. It was almost otherworldly in its beauty. He had to ask Lisette what it was called.

"Aquamarine. They are famous for it."

"I've never seen anything like it." He put his arm around her, and they stared out at the water in silence for a few minutes. The lapping of the waves below, and the birdsong in the brush behind them, were the only sounds.

She leaned her head on his shoulder and whispered, "Is this where the Allies plan to invade?"

He looked at her, eyes wide with surprise. Shock, even. "My God, Lisette! I do not know. What I mean is, they would not tell me that sort of thing."

She shrugged, looked back at the waves lapping at the pebble beach below them. "It would be a good place, I think."

He couldn't disagree with her. He'd have to mention that to Dryden at their next meeting. Probably nothing would come of this observation—but perhaps, just perhaps, Dryden would send that information up the chain, and some general in Washington or London would decide to use it.

Looking out, he could picture waves of United States Marines wading ashore here, from American battleships anchored outside the inlets. It would be an unexpected place.

The Nazis obviously expected an invasion from the north or west, not from the south. It was an open secret that the Germans had heavily fortified the beaches from the Low Countries all the way through Normandy and Brittany, then down the entire Atlantic coast to the Spanish border. There was a reason the Germans only occupied the northern half of France, plus a strip of the southwestern coast. Therein lay the military advantage.

"You want that to happen as much as anyone, don't you?" he asked her, softly, admiring her quiet determination.

She was silent for a few seconds. "You know I do not relish the fighting coming back to France," she said, quietly. "But it is the only way."

He smiled and kissed her on the forehead. "Let's go check out the rest of them."

17

Saturday, April 25

Lyon, Unoccupied France

"That Mr. Dryden is here to see you, Boss," Armand said, poking his head inside Oliver's office door.

That was unexpected. Cécile had just given birth to their baby less than a week ago—what was Dryden doing in Lyon now? "Tell him I'll be with him in a moment." Oliver hurried to finish what he was working on, slipped on his white dinner jacket, and went out into the club.

He found Dryden sitting at the bar. Fabien was in the process of pouring him a glass of wine, and when he'd finished, Oliver motioned with his head for Fabien to split. The bartender lowered his eyes and went to wash some glasses at the far end of the bar.

"I wasn't expecting you. I thought you'd be back in Vichy, enjoying your new baby." *So why aren't you?*

"I wish I were," Dryden said with a chuckle. "I'll be back there tomorrow, though."

"Congratulations, by the way," Oliver said. "Lisette and I sent a gift, but depending on when you left, you might not have seen it."

"Cécile told me," Dryden said. "I called her this afternoon after I checked in at the Hotel Carlton."

If he just arrived today, it wasn't from Vichy.

Dryden seemed to sense the question on Oliver's mind. "I was called away for a couple of days on official business. Geneva. There were a lot of important things discussed there—and some of it

160

impacts you, which is why I had to stop in Lyon and talk with you right away, instead of going back to Vichy."

"Should we go into my office?"

Dryden shook his head. "Let's take a walk. Can you get away for a few minutes?"

Oliver hesitated. He was certain his absence would be longer than a few minutes. But then he nodded. "Let me tell Mr. Hansen. I'll leave him in charge while I'm out."

He found Dolph in the storeroom, counting inventory. "I have to step out for a little while. Can you keep a watch over everything?"

"Of course," Dolph said, putting down his clipboard and leading the way out of the storeroom. "How long will you be out?"

"Twenty, maybe thirty minutes," Oliver said.

Dolph's gaze settled on Frank Dryden at the bar. Dryden was watching them. If it were anyone else, Oliver would be worried about what his manager was thinking; but he trusted Dolph.

"We'll be fine, Boss," Dolph said. "We don't open for another forty minutes, anyway."

Oliver headed toward the door, and Dryden fell into step beside him.

"Dolph Hansen is a leader in a local resistance cell, isn't he?" Dryden asked quietly once they'd gotten out on the street.

"Yes." *You know that already.*

"He'll be curious why you're meeting with me, and not staying in the club."

"Leaving the club was your suggestion."

"Indeed, it was," Dryden said, without a hint of irony. "His speculation about our conversation is a necessary risk. But having him possibly overhear it is not."

This is serious. Oliver's heart quickened. "Should we go where there aren't as many pedestrians?" He nodded toward the crowds strolling around the Old City, out enjoying a gorgeous spring evening.

"Let's go up the hill and back," Dryden suggested.

Oliver led them past the cathedral, and turned onto the Montée du Chemin Neuf, the only perpendicular street in the Saint-Jean Quarter, which was also one of only two roads that wound up the side of the Fourvière Hill from the Old City. It passed through a wooded space for a couple of hundred meters, and it was here that Dryden slowed their pace and began to talk.

"No further contact from Chastain?"

Oliver shook his head. "No."

Dryden didn't comment on that, leaving Oliver wondering what he was thinking. "I'm sure you've noticed all of the war news looks bad for us."

"I assume it's not all as bad as it seems," Oliver said with a shrug. "The censors probably won't let the newspapers print anything favorable to the Allies, so we only see the bad."

"Your thinking is correct, but your conclusion is unfortunately not," Dryden said, sounding terse. "There's been almost no good news. The Japanese have been on an all-out offensive since Pearl Harbor, and our forces in the Pacific keep getting pushed back. In spite of what President Roosevelt promised Mr. Churchill, the United States has had to devote considerable resources to the Pacific Theater—and we haven't even been able to achieve the 'holding action' necessary there in order to implement the 'Europe First' strategy we agreed to."

Oliver took a few seconds to ponder that. "What does that mean for us?"

"It means all grand plans in the European Theater have been delayed, considerably. And it means we're going to have to rely even more on small actions by groups within the Occupied countries—and of course, Unoccupied France as well."

In other words, there would be no rescue from the Germans in the foreseeable future. And therefore, no returning to Paris. Oliver's heart sank.

Dryden fell silent, and Oliver sensed there was more. He waited.

"And it means our need for knowledgeable informants within these territories will be a priority long-term. And also, an expanded propaganda campaign against the Vichy regime."

He added that last almost as an after-thought. But Oliver knew immediately it was the most important element in his role.

"What sort of propaganda campaign? And what is my role in it?"

Dryden chuckled. "Straight to the point. Alright, I'll lay it all out for you—Colonel William Donovan, the Coordinator of Information, has made the destabilization of Pétain's government a key part of our strategy in Europe. We know that Vichy is collaborating with the Nazis, and far more than what the terms of the armistice require of them. There is ample evidence of it, so Colonel Donovan is targeting Vichy for a secret war. And Oliver, you are one of our foot soldiers in that secret war."

A thrill rushed through him, and a small smile spread across his lips. Only then did an image of Lisette's worried face cross his mind.

"This is going to mean more than just propaganda, isn't it?"

Dryden stopped walking and turned to face Oliver. "I can't answer that."

Oliver took a long, slow breath, and considered that. "OK, what's my assignment?"

**

"But you can't!" Lisette said, crossing her arms. "Oliver, you have responsibilities here. You own the club. It might be fine to leave it in Dolph's hands for a night, or perhaps two—but what you are describing is not just one or two nights away at a time."

"I know," Oliver said, letting her vent her frustrations before he responded.

She paced the apartment. "Nice! Corsica, even! Those are not quick trips, Oliver. You might be gone for a week."

"That's true," he agreed. He knew her well enough to know she still had a lot to vent before she'd be ready to listen.

"And what about me? What am I supposed to do while you are crisscrossing the countryside?" She stopped in front of him, and glared up at him. "This is not like Paris, Oliver. I do not have any close friends here. And it is not easy to make them here."

"Everyone in Lyon is very friendly," Oliver pointed out. It was true, but it earned him a scolding scowl.

"Yes, they are friendly—especially to you, an American. But the Lyonais are suspicious of Parisians. They think that we believe ourselves superior to them, and so they maintain a distance."

But Parisians do *consider themselves superior to everyone else in France.* He kept that thought to himself.

She'd been silent for several seconds, so he put his hands on her shoulders, and spoke softly. "It's important work, Lisette. You know that. This is important for my country, and it's important for France. Plus, Mr. Dryden is going to pay me well for it."

She frowned, but didn't immediately respond. He waited.

"But I cannot go with you on these trips."

It wasn't a question, but he shook his head. "I'm afraid not. Mr. Dryden was very clear—the less you know about what I'm doing, the better." He was content to blame that on Dryden and didn't mention that he was in complete agreement.

Her frown turned back into a deep scowl. "It still puts me in danger, either way. I am your fiancée. If you are arrested, they will not believe that I know nothing."

"I'll tell them you know nothing."

She scoffed. "Everyone tells them that. They won't believe you."

He knew she was right. Still, her recalcitrance was starting to irritate him. "I'm not allowed to involve you, Lisette. It is forbidden."

"Forbidden," she said, bitterly, and turned away from him, crossing her arms again. Then she muttered, "Everything is forbidden these days."

His patience snapped. "This is how it's going to be, Lisette." He grabbed his hat from the rack by her door and stormed out of her apartment. He stomped down the hall, wishing for once that his apartment were farther away.

18

Sunday, April 26

Nice, Unoccupied France

The presence of a dozen police gendarmes at various points along the train platform, rifles slung over their shoulders, was a disconcerting sight. Oliver unconsciously tugged the rim of his fedora lower, but then willed himself to act naturally. The extra police presence was probably because the Nice station was the last stop before the new Italian border, that's all.

The old border had stood some fifteen miles to the east; but after France surrendered to Germany, Mussolini had annexed more than three hundred square miles of French territory, moving the border west to the very edge of Nice.

Oliver stifled a yawn as he crossed the station to the little restaurant near the entrance. He'd left Lyon in the wee hours of the morning, and the express train to Nice didn't offer a bed since it was only a seven-hour trip without stops.

He silently cursed Frank Dryden for the short notice.

It was not quite eleven-thirty when he sat at a table near the picture windows looking out over the street, and set his valise under the table. Below him, the street was packed with pedestrians in travel clothes rushing into the station. The train from Marseille would be pulling in any moment. He ordered an ersatz coffee from the waiter.

Symphonie sauntered in ten minutes later, his tall and slender form unmistakable even in a nice suit. He took a seat at the empty table next to Oliver's, tossing his hat onto the table. His movements were fluid, almost languid, giving the appearance that he was completely at ease. In contrast, Oliver's stomach was tying itself in knots.

"Why not meet him in Marseille, like before?" Oliver had asked Frank Dryden when he handed him the ticket to Nice.

"Because you were just there two weeks ago, and it might look suspicious to go back so soon," Dryden had explained. "You've never been to Nice, so you're an American tourist getting a look at the famous French Riviera."

It made a certain amount of sense. *Except that I'm only here for a few hours.*

Symphonie lit a cigarette, and then ordered a Salade Niçoise and a Socca from the waiter. The waiter bobbed his head, and returned a moment later to set a small bowl of olives in front of Symphonie.

Oliver knew he should be hungry, but his stomach refused.

Symphonie opened a newspaper. "There will be only small food on the ferry," he said quietly, not looking away from the paper.

Oliver flagged down the waiter and ordered another ersatz coffee, plus a croissant. The waiter wrinkled his nose in disdain. "We do not have *croissants.*" He said that word with an exaggerated Parisian accent. Oliver ordered a piece of baguette and jam instead, and the waiter sniffed and marched away without a word.

"The Niçois are not like other French," Symphonie said, just above a whisper, still looking at his newspaper. It seemed to Oliver that the waiter's attitude was quintessentially French.

"What is the plan?" Oliver asked out of the side of his mouth.

Symphonie turned the page. "I have been here many times; I know the way to the port. You will follow a moment later. But you must not look like you are following me out. Leave the restaurant before I do, but stop at the newsstand across the street. When I leave, you follow on the opposite sidewalk."

Oliver's heart fluttered with nerves. The restaurant was beginning to fill up, so he kept silent. Then the waiter returned with Symphonie's lunch, so Oliver looked away. *Look like you're minding your own business.*

He tried to remember everything Cécile had taught him in Paris. *I'm not ready for this.*

**

The Promenade des Anglais, the broad boulevard overlooking the Mediterranean shore, looked like something out of a movie. Big bushy palm trees lined the sides, and grand Beaux-Arts façades faced out toward the sea. Gleaming stone staircases at regular intervals led down to the pebble beach stretching along the shore, where dozens of people in bathing suits stretched out on blankets, taking in the sun. Only a few stepped gingerly into the surf

Crowds of well-heeled Niçois couples strolled along the wide path overlooking the shore, and Oliver worried because he was the only one sweating in the summer-like heat, dabbing at his forehead with his handkerchief every block or so. But maybe that made it easier to blend in as a tourist. He kept Symphonie in sight and stayed about twenty or thirty yards behind him.

The boulevard narrowed a bit when they left the city center and passed the *Vieux Quartier*, but the crowds of pedestrians remained full. Here, small pastel-colored buildings faced the sea, with little cobblestone streets branching off the boulevard into the Old City. A wooded hill rose ahead of them, the cathedral spire rising from the top, and the boulevard rounded the edge of the hill.

Then the port opened in front of them, lined with the sleek yachts of the wealthy. This was definitely like something from a movie. The ferries to Corsica docked at the opposite side, forcing them to follow the quay all the way around the long and narrow port.

Cars lined up to enter the hull of the ship, belching black smoke from their charcoal adaptors. A pair of gendarmes searched each one before it drove aboard. Oliver bought a ticket and hurried past the waiting automobiles. He walked onboard, and the smell of car exhaust almost overpowered him. After an attendant tore his ticket, he bounded up the stairs, thankful for a lungful of fresh air.

There were three levels above the hull, and Oliver went to the top, where the interior seating area was relatively small, surrounded by the widest deck. He went out on the deck, and a stiff breeze off the sea cooled his face from the heat of the day. He removed his hat and let the breeze blow through his damp hair. The midday sun gleamed off the water, and he squinted against the glare.

The ferry was pushing away from the dock at twelve-fifty, when Symphonie sauntered toward Oliver, and leaned against the rail a few feet from him.

"I watched for a long time, I do not believe we were followed," he said, and lit a cigarette. "But the SOL are crafty. They blend in. It is six hours to Bastia—be suspicious of everyone onboard."

Oliver frowned. "I've heard that the SOL all have military haircuts and mustaches."

Symphonie exhaled a stream of smoke. "They do not all look the same. They have learned." He pushed back from the rail. "Best if we keep apart for now. When we land in Bastia, go to the bus station and buy a ticket to Calvi. I will take the same bus, but we must not sit together. When we arrive at Calvi, go to the Hotel San Carlu. Someone from the resistance will meet us there."

Trains, ferries, and now buses—Oliver suppressed a groan.

After Symphonie walked away—his slender form moving languidly toward the stairs—Oliver turned back toward Nice, its red-roofed buildings growing smaller as the ferry picked up speed.

The rugged coastline of the French Riviera slipped into the distance, and with it any semblance of safety Oliver had felt.

**

The bus from Bastia to Calvi bounced along mountain roads, cutting across the north of Corsica. With every bump and jolt, the springs of the seats creaked, and Oliver swore he could feel the metal frame of the bus shudder.

The two-hour trip felt endless, and by the time the bus pulled into Calvi, Oliver's butt was so sore he thought he'd not sit again for a week.

The sun was setting across the Mediterranean when they drove into town, a big red disk slipping below the dark watery horizon. Dusk had fallen by the time Oliver stepped off the bus ten minutes later. His stomach growled, reminding him that he hadn't eaten in—how many hours? He glanced at his watch. Almost eight-thirty. He hadn't eaten anything in almost nine hours, and not that much then. Eight-thirty would be prime dinner hour at restaurants—if there were any restaurants open on a Sunday evening in a town this size.

As in Bastia, most of the people around him were speaking something that sounded vaguely Italian—it certainly wasn't French—but when he approached the custodian sweeping the station floor and asked in French how to find the Hotel San Carlu, the man gave him directions in French.

He spotted Symphonie alighting from the bus, but he walked the opposite direction from where Oliver had been told to go. Oliver hesitated, unsure if he should follow—but he decided he'd take the route he'd been told, and trust that Symphonie knew what he was doing.

It was not far—a right turn followed by a pair of lefts—and a pleasant breeze came in from the bay, wafting down the narrow streets and caressing his ears and neck. It was balmy without being hot, and Oliver was glad to have escaped the stuffiness of the bus.

The Hotel San Carlu was a quaint three-story stone building on a corner of two streets lined with quaint stone houses. Every small French town or village was full of stone houses, but somehow these looked different. Oliver couldn't put his finger on what exactly was different about them, but they reminded him of scenes from an Italian postcard.

The front door stood open, and a ceiling fan circulated the air in what looked like a Victorian parlor. Oliver rang the little brass bell on the front desk, and a man with a big bushy old-fashioned mustache came out. He greeted Oliver in French.

"I need a room for one night, please."

"Are you English, sir?" The look on the mustachioed man's face wasn't exactly suspicious, but it wasn't exactly friendly, either.

Mers-el-Kébir. Oliver shook his head. "I'm American."

The man nodded and asked him to sign the registry. Oliver hesitated a second, pen in hand. Mr. Dryden hadn't told him to use a fake name, so he signed his own. He was just a tourist, after all.

The man handed Oliver a big brass key. "Number six, first floor." He pointed toward the staircase on the far side of the parlor.

Oliver thanked him and looked toward the open door. He took his time picking up his valise, and walked slowly across the parlor.

Symphonie strode through the door when Oliver reached the bottom of the stairs. He made a show of spotting Oliver, raised his hand to wave, and then met him in the middle of the parlor. "It is good to see you, my friend. It has been too long." His voice was jovial for the proprietor's benefit. He shook Oliver's hand across the coffee table.

With the proprietor behind him and unable to see, his fingers briefly traced Oliver's palm when they disengaged the handshake, and he held eye contact for a couple of seconds before looking down while lighting a cigarette.

"We were not followed," he whispered, and then took a drag. "Which room are you in?"

"Number six."

"Go get settled, I will come for you soon." He walked to the front desk and asked the mustachioed man for a room.

******

Oliver leaned back on the twin bed, reading the book he'd brought. It was a French novel, not very good, really; too melodramatic for his taste. Then a soft knock on his door pulled him from the story, and he scrambled up and hurried to the door.

Symphonie stood in the hall with a shorter and stockier man, dark with thick black hair and scruff of dark beard. He was dressed in working-man's clothes—faded blue shirt and dark blue trousers, dirt and grime dotted across both.

"This is our contact," Symphonie said, just above a whisper, and came into Oliver's room without waiting for an invitation. "We will call him 'Paoli.'"

Oliver glanced both directions down the empty hallway, and closed the door. "You may call me Candle," he said, and extended his hand. The man eyed him warily while taking his hand in a firm grip.

"Are you English?"

"No, American."

The man relaxed and released Oliver's hand. "We cannot be found working with the English."

"I understand."

Paoli turned back toward Symphonie. "The ship you want, the *Santa Rosa de Velas*, it docked at Ajaccio earlier today. They unloaded their legitimate cargo there and departed an hour ago. It will be here with the night tide."

Symphonie looked at Oliver. "Paoli works at the docks. The local resistance is based there."

"Our men are on the early shift, so that we can unload your crates while it is still dark. We have labels we will put on the lids, to identify them as Corsican wine. I have secured a truck to take them up the coast to your boat."

Symphonie nodded. "How many men?"

"We are a small group," Paoli explained. "Five of us only. Corsica is a conservative island, and we found little sympathy when we tried to organize a union years ago. But those men and I are armed, and prepared to help the uprising when it comes."

"Calvi is not a big town," Symphonie said, apropos of nothing.

Paoli shrugged. "Even in Ajaccio and Bastia, they are not numerous. Perhaps a dozen men, no more. But these men have been ignored for too long, and they are dedicated." He crossed his right arm over his chest, his hand in a fist.

"Five men is enough," Symphonie said. He put his hand on Paoli's shoulder and guided him back to the door. "Candle and I will meet you at the dock at five-thirty."

Paoli gave them a firm nod and slipped out the door.

"That is an hour before sunrise, so we will have perhaps twenty minutes to unload the crates before first light." Symphonie handed a notecard to Oliver. "The visitor pass that Paoli provided. I have one as well. If the harbormaster questions it, allow me to do the talking."

"You don't want him to hear my accent."

"Yes." Symphonie's dark eyes held Oliver's for several seconds. "Be prepared to leave here at five o'clock. I will come get you—or we could stay together." His eyes never wavered from Oliver's.

The intensity of his gaze made Oliver uncomfortable; and yet, a familiar lightness swept through his belly. He ignored it. "I have a fiancée," he said, and didn't elaborate.

Symphonie's narrow shoulders made a tiny shrug. "Then I will see you in eight hours."

Oliver stood beside the door for several moments after closing it, pondering every aspect of that conversation.

19

Monday, April 27
Calvi, Corsica, Unoccupied France

The harbormaster was barely interested in scrutinizing their visitor credentials at five-twenty in the morning. He didn't even ask for their identity papers, just took a cursory glance at the visitor passes and waved them through.

They found Paoli and three other men standing at the entrance of an empty dock. The low rumble of a ship's engine and the blinking of a pair of lights told Oliver their timing was perfect. A moment later, an old freight ship pulled up to the dock. The engine revved momentarily when the captain shifted into reverse to stall their forward drift, and Paoli and his companions sprang into action, tossing thick ropes to sailors along the port rail.

Once the gang walk had been secured, a man in the garb of a sailor—long-sleeved dark blue collarless shirt and dark blue trousers—but with the ungainly gait of one not accustomed to time at sea, came gingerly down to the dock.

"Anyone here speak English?" he asked in a southern drawl. "There's supposed to be an American with you." Oliver detected a touch of twang in that drawl; maybe Texas, or Louisiana.

"I speak English," Oliver said, stepping forward.

The southerner shook Oliver's hand. "You must be Murphy's man."

Indirectly only. He nodded. "Code name Candle."

A faint smile graced the man's lips. "You're the one I'm supposed to ask for. I'm from COI, code name Louis." He didn't even attempt a French accent for the name. But at least he pronounced it 'Louie' and not 'Lewis.'

"Pleased to meet you. You escorted the cargo?" Oliver couldn't remember what 'COI' meant, but it was some sort of government acronym.

"That's right," Louis said in an even tone, but with an unwavering gaze that seemed to scrutinize Oliver. "The COI insisted we keep custody until it gets delivered. You're the one I'm supposed to hand it off to."

Obviously. I shouldn't have asked such a dumb question. "I wasn't told you'd be here." Oliver was glad that only a hint of defensiveness came through in his tone. Louis had been told about him, but not vice versa.

Louis put his arm around Oliver and guided him toward shore, away from the others. "I speak Spanish, so the COI sent me to Madrid to assess the situation there." He kept his voice quiet, little more than a whisper. "Naturally, he's suspicious the Nationalists will back Hitler. I'm pleased to report there's not a chance Franco will toss his hat in the ring with Hitler and Mussolini, no matter how much he lines up with them politically. He's too weak. Even after three years in power, his forces haven't recovered from their civil war. Hitler can bellow all he wants about Franco's ingratitude for all the help he gave him, the Generalissimo's too concerned about his opponents in Spain taking advantage if he sends troops to fight with the Germans."

"But Vichy's another story," Oliver said, filling in the blanks.

"You got it, partner."

Texas. Definitely Texas.

Louis continued. "The Brits have been supplying the resistance in the Occupied Zone, but they've ignored the Unoccupied Zone. The COI aims to close that gap. Unofficially."

The 'secret war' Mr. Dryden mentioned. "What did you bring us?" Oliver assumed the shipment would be guns, but Dryden had declined to specify.

"Five hundred Colt .45s, brand new, plus cartridges."

Oliver nodded as if that answer had been expected, or something similar. "We're taking them to Marseille tonight. I've got a leader of the resistance from there with me."

"I don't need to know who he is," Louis said. Then he made a low whistle and waved to a sailor on deck. The sailor hurried below, and a moment later men emerged carrying wooden crates.

Paoli took over, directing the sailors to stack the crates on a cart one of his men wheeled out. There were big crates that took two men to carry, and smaller crates an individual sailor could haul. About a dozen of each, Oliver estimated. Once they were loaded, the résistants pushed the cart down a gravel lane.

"This is where I leave you," Louis said. "We're pulling out before dawn, heading back to Spain."

Oliver shook his hand and hurried after the shipment of guns. He found Symphonie directing Paoli's men to load them into the back of a truck idling in the shadow of a small warehouse. It only took a few minutes, and then Oliver and Symphonie climbed into the truck and squeezed onto the seat beside the driver.

Paoli gave the driver instructions in the local dialect, and he took them around to a side gate, where he showed a badge to the security guard who waved him through without scrutiny.

"Eight kilometers up the coast road," Symphonie told him in French.

The driver glanced at him in annoyance. "Yes, I know. Paoli told me where to make the delivery." His French carried an almost-Italian accent, but it was good.

The first pre-dawn light started to glow behind the hills to their east as they curved around Calvi's half-moon bay. The road was deserted, and a medieval castle on the far side of the bay was the only thing watching them.

I hope it keeps its secrets, Oliver thought. The sardonic jest kept him from wondering whether the SOL had eyes and ears on Corsica.

The driver turned left off the main road at a sign for Plage de Sant Ambroggio, and the truck bumped down a one-lane dirt road toward a beach circling a crescent-shaped inlet. A boat lay anchored in the inlet, close to the beach. As the truck neared, Oliver realized the boat was a sleek yacht.

An inflatable raft with an outboard motor emerged from the shadow of the yacht when the truck's wheels hit the sand and stopped. It made the short distance to the beach in barely five seconds, and the shape of a man dressed in black jumped out and hauled it onto the sand.

"You'll have to carry them," the driver said as he climbed down from the truck. He unlocked the back, and Symphonie and Oliver took hold of the first crate and lugged it the twenty feet toward where the raft had beached. It was heavy, and sweat pricked from Oliver's forehead by the time he and Symphonie put it on the raft.

"Three of each at a time, no more," the man in black whispered. His French was flawless, sounding Parisian. The familiarity of the accent caused a flutter to run through Oliver.

By the time they'd loaded the third crate, Oliver was winded. He was grateful for the brief rest when the raft sped off to the yacht. Shadowy figures dropped a crane from the yacht's side and hauled the crates up one by one in under a minute. Oliver suppressed a groan when the raft turned around to come back, and Symphonie tapped him on the arm to get the next crate.

It took twenty minutes to finish loading the crates onto the yacht, according to Oliver's watch. The sky had turned a pale rose color in the interim.

"We must be leaving," Symphonie whispered. He turned to wave at the truck driver, who backed the truck into a tight turn, somehow not getting the tires stuck in the sand, and sped back up the dirt road toward the coastal highway.

The raft returned once more, but this time its driver didn't pull onto the sand. Symphonie stepped into the calf-deep seawater and scrambled onto the raft. Oliver followed suit. The water was surprisingly icy, given how warm the night air had been.

Moments later, they climbed a narrow ladder onto the yacht. The raft's driver pulled it onboard, where he and a crewmember deflated it. Then the black-clad raft driver put a hand on each of their shoulders with a grin, turned them toward the cabin door, and led them inside.

Oliver's mouth opened at the sight of the luxuriously appointed living room in front of them. He remembered to close it before the man with his arm around his shoulder noticed.

"Welcome to my home away from home," the man said jovially. "Would you gentlemen care for a cognac? We have something to celebrate, no?" He marched to a wet bar along one side of the room, removed a bottle and three snifters, and poured a short measure in each.

It was barely six AM, and Oliver had never cared for cognac—might as well be lighter fluid, to be honest—but to be polite he put out his hand to accept the glass their host handed him.

And that's when he recognized the face before him. His mouth dropped open again. "You're—"

A wide grin brightened the famous face. "Call me Julien."

Julien Daignault had appeared in at least twenty films over the last decade, and starred in half a dozen. Oliver had seen his face on a silver screen many times, and to see it before him in real-life, natural size, was surreal to say the least. He was probably mid-to-late thirties—little lines around the eyes that movie makeup hid from the camera gave him away—and yet he was every bit as dashing as he was on screen.

Oliver almost said his own name—it quite nearly slipped out while he remained in awe—but he stopped himself just in time. *Code names only*. Not that Julien Daignault could hide his identify with a code name; perhaps that's why he hadn't tried.

Julien raised his glass. "To bringing freedom back to France." They sipped their cognac—it burned Oliver's nose and throat as it went down—and Julien motioned for them to sit. They sat on the plush couches, Oliver and Symphonie facing the movie star, who crossed his legs in a casual manner, and looked at his guests with a faint smile stretching his lips.

"Your friend was not expecting me, Thé—" Julian shook his head and closed his eyes momentarily. "Symphonie."

Symphonie shrugged, and looked at Oliver when he answered Julien. "It was best if he didn't know before."

Just in case, Oliver filled in. Just in case the SOL followed them from Nice. Just in case the harbormaster called the police.

"I haven't seen you in any films in a while," he said to change the subject. "Not since before the occupation."

Julien smiled wistfully. "Like most of my colleagues, I came south ahead of the Germans. Everyone enjoyed an extended holiday at Cannes. At least, until their money ran out, and they had to return to Paris and make collaborationist pictures with Continental Films." He motioned around the room with his right hand. "I am fortunate to own a cottage in Saint-Tropez, plus this boat—so I am not beholden to collaborationists."

If this forty-foot yacht was a 'boat,' Oliver wondered what Julien Daignault's 'cottage' looked like. "And that freedom enables you to help the resistance." He nodded his head sideways toward Symphonie.

Julien made a modest shrug. "I do what I can. My face is recognizable, you see, and that limits what work I can do. But this," he motioned around the room with both hands, "is one way I can help. Giving our patriots the equipment they need to prepare for the Allies' invasion brings France a step closer to liberation."

"And then we can return to Paris," Oliver said. He was unsure why he revealed that detail about himself, but he suspected Julien Daignault shared the sentiment.

"That is so," Julien said with a hint of smile, and raised his glass in Oliver's direction before taking a sip of his cognac.

Oliver raised his glass far enough to hide a yawn he unsuccessfully stifled, but didn't sip the contents.

"You should rest, my friends," Julien said, rising. "You have had an early start, and you will be working late tonight. We have a nine-hour voyage, and you should take advantage. I myself wish to rest an hour or two. My boat has two bedrooms, and I would be delighted if you gentlemen would make use of the guest bed."

Julien put his hand on the small of Symphonie's back as he guided them toward a door off a narrow corridor leading forward from the living room. Oliver's gaze fell to the placement of Julien's fingers, lightly bending into Symphonie's spine, with the pinky resting over the slender man's tailbone below his belt. When he opened the door, those fingers trailed down and grazed the curve of a buttock before falling to Julien's side.

Oliver couldn't help a small smirk. He shouldn't have been surprised. "I am comfortable resting on the couch," he said, and turned back the direction they'd come.

Julien greeted this announcement with an enigmatic smile. "Very well, then we will each have our own space. I'll have Gérard make some coffee and breakfast in two hours. Sleep well, my friends."

**

The yacht anchored near the entrance to the harbor at Cassis an hour before sunset. The inflatable raft sped away a moment later, motoring toward one of the wharfs.

"I have sent Gérard to buy seafood for dinner," Julien said. "Raphael makes excellent Mussels Provençale."

Two hours later, bellies full and dressed all in black, Oliver and Symphonie waited at the rail near the starboard bow as the yacht slipped around the rocky promontory after twilight had faded into night. The waves crashing into the rocks shined in the moonlight. Nosing into the cove, two dark inlets forked to the right and left, and the yacht crept to the entrance of the one on the right.

The Calanque de Port Pin, Symphonie had said earlier, during the passage from Corsica. "Members of my organization will be waiting for us there."

The sea air was still warm, even a little sultry, but the wind had begun to pick up, cooling the sweat on Oliver's brow and leaving a salty taste on his lips.

The yacht had slowed considerably, and now came to a stop barely five hundred feet into the cove. Chains rattled, and the anchor splashed into the water. The rattle of the chains continued for ten or fifteen seconds; the water was deep here.

Julian appeared beside them. "Beyond this point, the calanque is too narrow for us to turn around. You must use the raft to take the cargo to shore."

Butterflies danced in Oliver's stomach. "How far is it?"

Julien shrugged and made that exaggerated frown the French were good at. "Six hundred, six hundred twenty-five meters, perhaps."

About two-thousand feet, roughly. That was over a third of a mile. The butterflies multiplied.

The wind coming in from the sea had increased by the time they finished loading the first round of boxes into the raft, and it whipped up the calanque between the steep cliff sides. Its whistle was soon drowned by the whine of the outboard motor as Symphonie sped up the inlet.

**

"You must get in this time," Symphonie told him after they'd loaded the last crate.

"Will that be too much weight?" Oliver asked, concerned about adding himself to an already full load. The raft already sat low in the water.

"It will be fine. And we have no choice."

That last part did nothing to ease Oliver's nerves. He did some quick mental math. Each gun crate was fifty kilograms—about a hundred and ten pounds. Each smaller crate of cartridges was about half that. That was over five hundred pounds of cargo, plus Symphonie's body weight. He was slender, so probably not much more than a hundred and fifty pounds—but Oliver was closer to one-eighty these days.

"There is no time for another trip. Quickly!" Symphonie motioned impatiently with his hand, and Oliver scrambled into the nose of the raft, wedging his feet into the tiny space in front of a gun crate. They sped away immediately.

The yacht's engine, which had been purring in idle, roared to life a few seconds later, and the boat turned back toward the open sea.

"Don' they want their raft back?" Oliver asked over the whine of the outboard motor.

Symphonie shook his head. "They must not stay here longer than necessary."

The yacht's wake hit them broadside, and rocked them more than Oliver was prepared for. His arms flailed, and his stomach dropped as he imagined the boat overturning; he leaned the opposite direction to counterbalance.

Too far, it turned out. His head and shoulders dipped over the side. His arms wind-milled in the air uselessly, but his right hand managed to grab the corner of the gun crate next to him. That wasn't enough to stop his momentum, and a second later he was enveloped by cold darkness.

He came up a second later, gasping for breath. The raft stood on its side, almost perpendicular, and Symphonie pushed against it to drop it back into place. But even as it fell back, crate after crate tumbled into the water, bobbing on the surface.

The coldness of the water felt like needles in Oliver's skin. His clothes dragged against his arms and legs when he treaded water, and he felt out of breath almost immediately.

His heart sank at the sight of the crates slipping below the waves, bubbles rising. Symphonie pulled the raft around, and Oliver tried to point at the nearest crate before it disappeared, but his chin dipped below the surface and water filled his mouth before he could shout. He began treading again, and spit out the salt water before he inhaled or swallowed any.

The rubber raft bumped his back, and Symphonie's hands gripped him under the armpits. "Kick," he said, tugging upward. "Kick hard."

Oliver rose several inches, but then slid back into the icy water.

"Kick harder!" Symphonie said through clenched teeth, and he pulled upward again. Oliver forced his legs to kick as hard as they could, and he emerged up to his waist before Symphonie's strength gave out, and Oliver slipped back into the water up to his neck.

Symphonie gripped him tighter, and he panted hard next to Oliver's ear. "Rest a moment," he said. Oliver allowed his body to relax back against the boat, only occasionally kicking to keep his head above an incoming swell.

"OK, now—kick as hard as you can, and then bend at the waist." Symphonie tugged him upward again, Oliver kicked with all his might, and then his abdomen contracted with a burn as he pulled his kicking legs up to the surface.

His body broke from the water, and he tumbled backward into the raft, landing on top of Symphonie. The two of them lay still for several seconds, panting hard, while the raft rocked on the waves.

"The guns," Oliver said between pants. "The ammunition. It's lost, all lost."

Symphonie's hand patted his chest, splashing tiny droplets of sea water onto Oliver's face. "It is only ten meters deep here. They can be retrieved at dawn."

Oliver shifted his weight to the side of the raft, keeping low, letting his head rest on the side. The air was warm, and he was shielded from the wind, but he began to shiver.

"We must get to shore immediately," Symphonie said, and revved up the motor.

It likely only took a minute or two to reach the beach, but it felt like an eternity to Oliver, who had started shaking violently by the time the nose of the raft shot onto the pebble beach.

"Where is the rest of the cargo?" a voice behind Oliver demanded in a twangy accent.

"Most of it fell into the water when we nearly capsized," Symphonie said. "Two crates of cartridges remain, but we must recover the rest at dawn."

"Fishermen come to these cliffs at dawn," another voice said, gruff, and also twangy. Oliver almost laughed at the thought of rural southern Frenchmen being like southern rednecks back in the States. But he was shivering too hard to have the energy leftover to laugh.

"My friend also fell in the water," Symphonie said. "He needs a blanket."

"The blankets are to cover the cargo in the back of the truck," someone replied.

"But with some of the cargo resting at the bottom of the calanque, we should have an extra blanket," Symphonie countered, his voice even and calm, but firm.

Oliver's head felt fuzzy, but when he turned it he saw someone with an electric torch hurrying up the steep trail from the beach into the hills. Closer to their left, men were lashing crates onto some sort of pulley system, and unseen résistants above hauled them up.

"We need to start a fire," Symphonie told another résistant.

"A fire will be too visible," the man warned in a gruff voice which seemed so in contrast to the whiny twang of his rural accent.

"We have no choice," Symphonie said, now sounding very insistent. "My friend must be warmed quickly. You will be gone soon, and then we will appear to be two visitors enjoying a campfire at the beach on a warm night."

"It must be twenty degrees this evening. Too warm for a campfire."

"It is believable," Symphonie insisted. "Now go collect driftwood while I build the windbreak."

Twenty degrees—that would be sixty-eight degrees Fahrenheit. Oliver hardly believed it. It felt so much colder than that. *Must be the wind.*

A few moments later, Symphonie lit a twist of paper under a stack of driftwood in the pit he'd dug. He'd piled all of the pebbles he'd dug out on one side, facing toward the water, rising several inches and blocking some of the wind. The flames lapped up, and soon the dry wood began to crack and pop.

"Come closer," Symphonie said, grabbing Oliver by the arm and tugging him a few feet from the fire. He stood behind Oliver, between him and the wind coming up the calanque from the sea, and rubbed his hands hard up and down Oliver's arms and shoulders. "That water is only fifteen degrees. That's much too cold to be submerged."

Oliver did the calculation—fifteen degrees was about fifty-eight or fifty-nine degrees Fahrenheit. That was indeed frigid. "How long was I in the water?" he managed to ask through chattering teeth.

"Perhaps two minutes," Symphonie said. "When the blanket arrives, we must get you out of these wet clothes. You will never warm up otherwise."

The dark figure of a man came hurrying down the trail a moment later. "We have two extra blankets, since we were expecting more crates."

Oliver wasn't sure if he heard a note of reproach in the man's voice. Maybe that was just his imagination. The two men tugged off his shirt, shoes, socks, and trousers, the soaked fabric dragging roughly along his skin. When he was down to only his boxer shorts, they wrapped a blanket around him, and then the other.

"Get the cargo to the safe house, we will meet you there in the morning," Symphonie said, and the other man disappeared up the trail.

Symphonie spread Oliver's sodden clothes across the pebbles, barely two feet from the fire. Then he reached under the blanket and tugged off Oliver's boxer shorts, spreading them on the beach as well. "Sit," he ordered, and helped Oliver onto a stump he'd pulled close to the fire pit.

"Thank you," Oliver croaked between chattering teeth.

"It is nothing," Symphonie said, and pulled his shirt over his head. He dropped his trousers and undershorts, and Oliver averted his eyes. But then Symphonie's naked form blocked the light of the fire, and Oliver looked up.

"Open," Symphonie ordered, and tugged at the end of the blanket Oliver clutched in front of his chest. In one swift move, Symphonie opened the blankets, slipped inside them, and plopped onto the stump next to Oliver, shoulder to shoulder and hip to hip. He pulled the blankets tightly around them, and put his arm around Oliver's shoulder, hugging him to him and rubbing his hands up and down Oliver's arms. "This is the only way you will warm."

Oliver vaguely remembered reading about this in a Boy Scout manual almost twenty years ago. A couple of his fellow scouts had giggled and pointed to the passage for treating hypothermia. "Better hope your friend's not a sissy!" one of them had said, to snickers from their companions.

It would have been a wonder for a bunch of twelve-year-old boys in 1924 to have had more than the vaguest notion of what their friend's joke meant; but they were clear that it was bad, dirty even, and something to be feared.

Oliver seemed to recall fearing it the way one would fear something in a haunted house before Halloween—scary, and yet thrilling. *How bizarre*. He hadn't recalled that in a long time. And so much had changed since then.

Oliver's most violent shaking passed, and though he continued to shiver, the chattering of his teeth subsided. Occasionally a short bout of spasm swept down his jaw, but he felt almost normal again. Chilled, but not cold. And the touch of Symphonie's hands moving up and down his arms had begun to feel warm.

The warmth spread to his cheeks when he noticed blood had started flowing between his legs, making him a bit chubby in an embarrassing place. He shifted his knees away from Symphonie and leaned forward, as if he were leaning toward the fire.

"I am much better now, thank you."

"Do not rush," Symphonie said. "Your clothes are still too wet. Wait an hour until the fire dries them."

Oliver nodded and stared at the flames flickering where the wind blew across the top.

"We have done good work," Symphonie said. "Do not worry about the cargo that sank. The salt water will not damage them for several days, and they will be retrieved before then. Once they are cleaned, they will be as good as new."

"That's a relief." Oliver exhaled hard, and a weight lifted off his chest.

"More shipments will come," Symphonie continued. "The resistance will be prepared when the Allied invasion comes."

"Will we escort them each time, you and I?" Oliver was keenly aware of Symphonie's arm still around his shoulder, his hand now moving more languidly across his upper arm.

"Yes. Paoli's identity must be kept secret, known to only a few. You and I will work with him." He slipped out of the blanket long enough to lean forward and take a pack of cigarettes from his pants pocket. He lit one, and moved back against Oliver, pulling the blanket tight around them. The cigarette remained between his lips, and he spoke around it. "Next time, we will take the ferry from Toulon. Or perhaps Julien can take us from Saint-Tropez. Or maybe from Cannes. Those would be believable for a foreign tourist." He inhaled, then blew out smoke. "There is nothing to see in Toulon."

Except the remainder of the French fleet. Oliver suspected Frank Dryden and Robert Murphy might want him to take a look there.

They stared at the fire in silence for some time. When the flames grew low, Symphonie stood and walked a few steps to the stack of kindling he'd made. Oliver's eyes watched the flickering glow of the firelight on his bare back, as if mesmerized. Symphonie leaned over, and turned to toss a handful of twigs onto the fire, then another. Silhouetted in the firelight, his erection was apparent.

He noticed Oliver looking at it, and the corners of his mouth tugged up in amusement. Oliver looked away. "My clothes might be dry."

"I will check." Symphonie walked around the fire, his erection boldly leading the way, and stooped to feel Oliver's shirt and pants. He shook his head. "Too damp still." He passed in front of Oliver before retaking his seat next to him and pulling the blankets back in place.

His left hand rested on Oliver's thigh. Butterflies flew through Oliver's stomach.

"I have a fiancée," he said, though the words barely croaked out of his dry throat.

Symphonie shrugged. "I have a wife." His hand moved up Oliver's thigh, raising goosebumps all over him. Then it lowered to his groin, and the fingers slowly encircled his swelling member.

**

Tuesday, April 28

It was almost a six-hour trip by truck from Cassis to Lyon. Three hundred and fifty kilometers. Plenty of time for Oliver to stew over what had happened.

He had been tense, that was all. It was a combined effect from the hypothermia, and the anxiety of smuggling illegal arms into France. His body had made a natural reaction to the tension, and his mind had been addled enough to let it happen. It didn't mean he wasn't devoted to Lisette.

And had it really been that bad, after all? It was only a hand jive, for crying out loud, nothing more. It wasn't as if he'd had *actual sex* with anyone. He put it out of his mind.

But the bigger consideration that wouldn't budge from his consciousness was the illegal cargo in the back of this truck. He was bringing half of what they'd brought from Corsica back to Lyon. His heart raced every time he passed through a village or small town and saw a gendarme walking the main street.

Two hours into the trip, he encountered a police roadblock entering Orange, twenty-one kilometers—about thirteen miles—north of Avignon. The traffic was backed up a quarter kilometer, and it took almost ten minutes to creep up to the check-point.

A police sergeant approached his window. "Papers, please." He inspected Oliver's passport and identification card, and handed them back with a tiny frown. "You are American, but living in Lyon?"

"That's right." Oliver's heart pounded, and he hoped he didn't look or sound as nervous as he felt.

"What is the purpose of your journey in this...vehicle." He glanced at the old truck in obvious distaste.

"To purchase wine for my nightclub in Lyon."

"Do they not have wine in Lyon? But yes, they do." The gendarme raised his nose in a haughty expression. "Open the back, please."

Oliver killed the engine and got out of the truck, swallowing down the lump that formed in his throat. It settled into the pit of his stomach while he unlocked the back.

A pair of gendarmes climbed into the truck bed, shining flashlights onto the labels on the crates. "Corsican wine," one of them said to the sergeant.

The sergeant looked at Oliver with arched eyebrows and pursed lips. "*Corsican* wine?"

Oliver forced a shrug. "It is inexpensive."

The sergeant turned back to the gendarmes and gestured toward the crates. "Open one of them."

Oliver's heart jumped into his throat. Panic swept through him, and perspiration soaked the pits of his shirt within seconds. He watched helplessly while one of the gendarmes called to another on the ground for a crowbar.

He wondered how long it would take for them to shoot him if he ran now. He probably wouldn't get twenty feet.

The screech of the nails coming loose from wood echoed in his ears, far louder than was natural. Only the pounding of his heart matched the volume. *Please God, don't let them kill me. I'll plead ignorance, please let them believe me.*

The gendarme held up a bottle of red wine, its green glass plain. Then he held up another with his other hand. "There are no labels on these bottles."

Oliver's jaw nearly came unhinged. He closed his mouth immediately.

"Black market," the sergeant announced with obvious satisfaction. He glared at Oliver. "There are severe penalties for participating in the black market. But, sir, if you were to pay the tax on these items…" he gestured at the crates and waited.

Oliver nearly cried. "How much?" he managed to ask.

The sergeant pretended to look up in thought. "The tax on a case of wine is seventy-five centimes—but with penalties for late payment it is two francs per case. You have six full cases, sir, but it would seem you have small ones as well—special bottles?"

The curve of the police sergeant's mouth told Oliver that he didn't believe it, but they would pretend he did.

"If you give me twenty francs, sir, I will make sure that your tax is paid."

Oliver smiled. Twenty francs was about four dollars—definitely worth it. He only hoped he had that much in his wallet. He counted out the bills with trembling fingers and came up with eighteen francs. He reached into his pocket and pulled out all his coins. Another franc and a half.

"Will you take nineteen fifty?"

The sergeant took the money from Oliver's hand swiftly, gave him a haughty sneer, and waved him along.

Oliver exhaled hard when he restarted the truck. His breathing had been quite shallow during that whole encounter. He needed to add more charcoal to the burner, but first he had to get as far away as possible.

He had almost relaxed by the time he reached the center of Orange and passed the large stone walls and partial columns of the ruined Roman Gymnasium, followed immediately by the massive stone structure of the nearly intact Roman theater, towering over the town at the base of a hill.

His heart raced again. There had been no word from the man called Charles Forgeron in over a month now. He'd definitely been capture. Or killed. A twinge of guilt pinged at Oliver's heart when he hoped Forgeron had been killed; if he were dead, he couldn't be forced to reveal his contacts. He might give up Oliver's name first—better to give up the American foreigner than one of his résistant countrymen.

It's been over a month, they would have come for you already if they knew. He took a deep breath and pulled to the side of the road to restock the charcoal.

20

Wednesday, May 6

Lyon, Unoccupied France

Oliver could sense the tension in the air when he first stepped out of his building that morning to walk to the bakery down the street. At the café along the way, men sat at outside tables, reading newspapers with angry faces.

It was a beautiful, warm and sunny day, so something must have happened. *War news, no doubt.* But with France officially out of the war, he had no idea what it could be that would warrant this reaction.

After buying his croissants—enough for him and Lisette, since she'd stayed over last night—and a baguette, he stopped and picked up a copy of *Le Progrès*. The headline told him exactly why everyone seemed angry this morning:

BRITISH SEIZE FRENCH NAVAL BASE ON MADAGASCAR

Battle for Harbor of Diego Suarez Rages as French Forces Defend French Soil

He folded the paper and put it under his arm until he got home.

Lisette sat at the table in his kitchen, waiting with two steaming cups of ersatz coffee. He leaned down to kiss her, set the croissants next to the coffee cups, and put the baguette on the counter. Then

196

he opened the newspaper and laid it out in between them. "That happened yesterday."

"What?" she asked, knitting her brows together and staring that the paper. "But why?"

Oliver read down the article. The point-of-view was openly hostile to the British action, so there wasn't much of anything to explain their rationale for attacking French Madagascar.

Finally, deep into the article, he found a clue. He read the paragraph aloud to Lisette. "Admiral Darlan also emphatically denies British claims of cooperation with the Japanese in the Indian Ocean. 'It is a ridiculous excuse for the British to seize French territory for their own benefit,' he said."

"Do you suppose it's true?" she asked.

Oliver shrugged. "Hard to say. The Japanese occupy southeast Asia and the East Indies, which gives them access to the Indian Ocean. So I suppose it's possible."

"I would believe that Vichy is cooperating with all the Axis powers," Lisette said with a frown.

"I would, too."

**

He passed his concierge on his way out that afternoon to open the club. She was watering the flower boxes with a metal can, and she frowned when she saw him. Not her usual reaction, and Oliver was a bit bemused. He greeted her as usual.

"The American Chargé d'Affaires told Prime Minister Laval this morning that the United States will consider a French attack against the British as an attack against all of the Allies," she said, crossing her arms and glaring at him. "I heard it on the radio. He said it would mean war. So will the United States attack us next?"

"I don't think so," Oliver said.

"Marshall Pétain said that France will defend herself against any attack." She wagged the watering can Oliver's direction, in scolding motion. "The United States should be wary of supporting the British in their *unlawful* attack against us."

"I'm sure they will." He hurried off before she could say anything else.

**

"All of my neighbors are suddenly patriotic supporters of the regime," Térèse grumbled while she stocked clean glasses under the bar. "You should have heard them today! Pétain, Laval—you'd think they were saints who are saving France. I haven't heard a positive word about either of them since that trial started in Riom. But today..." she rolled her eyes.

"My landlady as well," Oliver said.

"They suspended that trial in Riom weeks ago," Armand said, also stocking glasses under the bar. "Everyone's forgotten about it already."

"I'm sure the newspapers aren't reporting the full truth," Oliver said. "It will take a little while, but we'll see what the American papers are saying soon enough, and then Combat can challenge the misconceptions."

**

Monday, May 11

Oliver left one at the bakery that morning when he bought his croissants. He left more scattered around the train station. Lisette left a couple in front of the flower shop's front door. Marcel left a few on the seats of the tram he rode into the city center before working the lunch shift.

By the middle of the day, the news was spreading across Lyon—the French military authorities on Madagascar had been negotiating with the Japanese Imperial Navy to allow them to use the naval base at Diego Suarez for their submarines; and this would have put the Japanese submarines in the center of British supply lines to India, Burma, and Australia.

It took some time for the shocking news to sink it—it was France that had committed treachery, not the British—but by lunchtime, people were openly arguing *in public*, around lunch tables, about who was at fault for the battle raging in Madagascar, Britain or Vichy.

**

Seditious, traitorous garbage!

Gilles Matous prided himself on the ability to stay dispassionate, calculating. But the sight of the headline on that libelous, traitorous rag made his temples throb. The gall, blaming the French government for the British invasion of Madagascar!

He'd spent hours sitting on a bench at the Place Bellecour, facing toward the giant statue of Louis XIV, pretending to read a book. He kept a close watch on the people passing by, looking for any sign that someone was distributing illegal broadsides.

This was the perfect place to watch, in the largest square in Lyon, in the heart of the city, a place that was busy at all hours of the day. A great many people were reading the seditious trash entitled *Combat*, but he left them alone; it was unwise to get distracted by minor transgressors and miss the opportunity to catch the real criminals.

Shortly after three o'clock, his patience was rewarded. His eye was caught by a brown-skinned young man with coarsely curly dark hair; one of those *mulattoes*, probably from the Antilles. Matous watched him moving across the square from east to west, but in an odd meandering way, not straight across. He passed several benches, but never paused.

Matous watched him in growing frustration, certain he was leaving illegal papers on the benches, but not seeing him do it, no matter how closely he watched. *He's a slick one.*

He kept watch on the young man for a long time, and finally he saw it—an almost imperceptible flick of his arm, and something flat now sat on the bench he had passed.

Matous closed his book and got up, marching toward the spot. When he got to that bench, a large envelope sat on it, closed but not sealed. There was no writing on it, and when Matous looked inside, he saw the illegal *Combat* broadside.

That explained why they didn't fly around the square on the breeze. Matous tossed it into the nearby trash can and stuffed it down inside.

It only took a couple of seconds to spot the brown-skinned young man nearing the far end of the square, and Matous followed him.

From the Place Bellecour, the culprit moved west down Rue Bellecour, no longer meandering. A few blocks later, he began to cross the Pont Tilsitt over the Saône, toward the Old City. The spire of the Saint-Jean Cathedral rose in front of them, and behind it the towering basilica on Fourvière hill dominated the western skyline.

About a quarter of the way across the bridge, the young man glanced backward over his shoulder. Then he picked up his pace, hurrying across the bridge.

Damn! Matous cursed his clumsiness. He hadn't kept enough distance between himself and his quarry, and had made himself too obvious. It was an amateur mistake, allowing himself to get too eager, and he knew better.

But now that he was known, he needed to close that gap. He picked up his own pace, rushing after the young Antillean. By the time they reached the quay on the far side of the Saône, he had closed the gap to perhaps thirty meters.

And here, the young man began to sprint.

Matous took off after him, running full tilt, but the résistant was faster than he. *Damn his youth!* He suddenly veered to the left and disappeared, as if the stone walls had swallowed him.

One of those cursed *traboules* which cut through the old quarters of Lyon. Matous had not yet mastered their intricacies. He tried a couple of locked doors on the left where the fleeing résistant had disappeared, and then found the unlocked door to the *traboule*. His quarry was almost at the end of the long tunnel. He pushed himself to get a little more speed as the young man veered to the right on the next street.

Matous reached that street just in time to see the résistant veer into yet another *traboule* to the left, its door snapping shut. By the time Matous identified the door to that passageway, the only people passing through it were two young women with baskets on their arms, dragging along three small children.

"Out of my way!" Matous shouted, waving his arm furiously. They were slow to react, mouths open in surprise, and he had to slow his gait in order to avoid trampling a child. Once he was past them, he sprinted the remaining distance to the end of the *traboule*.

And found himself in a courtyard, with covered passageways exiting all four corners. A pair of old men sat on a bench in front of a little fountain, and another young woman with two small children emerged from a spiral staircase in the center of one wall—but otherwise, the courtyard was empty.

No sign of that brown-skinned résistant.

Matous cursed this ancient city and stalked back the way he had come.

**

"I had a close call this afternoon," Armand whispered to Dolph when he called at his boss's apartment twenty minutes later. He recounted being followed from the city center, and his escape through the *traboules*.

"Describe the man to me," Dolph said.

Armand described his pursuer as best he could. "I didn't get a good look at him because I was running, and I didn't want to slow myself."

"That is good enough," Dolph said, giving Armand a reassuring pat on the back. He opened his sketchbook, and began drawing with a pencil.

Armand watched over his shoulder. "Yes, that is the man," he said in awe, shaking his head. "But his face is a little bit narrower, and his nose a little longer." Dolph made a few adjustments, and Armand nodded. "That looks just like the man I saw."

Dolph ripped the page from his sketchbook. "I will see that this man's description is circulated. We will watch for him."

21

Annemasse, Unoccupied France

Oliver took the cable car up the side of Mont Salève, a steep slope of bare limestone rising 1,379 meters—about 4,525 feet— above the little market town of Annemasse. The town was just two kilometers from the Swiss border southeast of Geneva, and as the cable car rose into the clear air, the city of Geneva, and the great blue expanse of Lake Geneva, spread out below him. The sun glinted off the deep blue of the long lake, and from the little blue ribbon of the Rhône River flowing from it.

He was alone in the car on this Monday afternoon, while everyone in the cluster of communities in the green valley below him went about their weekday business. The car began to sway gently in the breeze, and he chose to sit down for the second half of the trip.

It was a surprisingly fast climb, not much more than five minutes, and he stepped out in front of an alpine chalet at the top and looked around for the trailhead. The temperature was noticeably cooler here, despite the bright sunshine, and he wished he'd brought a sweater.

He found the trailhead up a slight rise from the chalet, in a scattering of pine trees. In the distance to the south rose the great snow-covered peak of Mont Blanc, appearing almost close enough to touch in the crystal-clear air, and he stared at it for several minutes.

"It is fifty kilometers from here, Mont Blanc," Franz Lemiel said beside him, startling him from his reverie. His heart momentarily raced, and it took a few seconds to catch his breath.

"It looks so close," Oliver said. Franz was dressed for hiking in knee-length leather shorts and white cotton shirt. Thick-soled boots and woolen socks completed the look. "Thank you for meeting me."

"I come to Geneva often these days," Franz said, and cracked a mischievous half-grin that dimpled his perpetual five o'clock shadow. "And I have many unofficial ways of crossing the border here."

That wasn't surprising. "I have a dilemma, and Dolph said you'd be able to help me."

Franz nodded down the trail. "You are not dressed for hiking, my friend, but a short trek won't seem out of the ordinary if anyone is watching."

Oliver followed him. The trail seemed to generally follow the ridgeline, so it wasn't steep or overly rugged, though he did have to step across some rocky outcroppings.

"What is your dilemma?" Franz asked after they were out of sight of the chalet.

"I was transporting some contraband materials from Marseille to Lyon a few weeks ago, in the back of a truck, but I ran into a little trouble outside of Orange. The police had a roadblock, and they were checking every vehicle. They opened one of my crates—but thankfully the supplier had arranged a couple of real bottles of wine at the top. The gendarmes didn't dig any deeper, and their captain let me pass after I paid him a tax for black market wine."

"Mmm," Franz murmured. "That was very wise. But tell me— what would the gendarmes have found if they had dug deeper into the crate?"

Oliver looked around instinctively, though there was no one else in sight. "Guns. From Spain. For the Resistance."

Franz stopped, and turned toward Oliver, his mouth set in a tight line. "I do not run weapons, and I do not get involved in operations that do." His voice carried a bite that startled Oliver. Franz was always so happy-go-lucky, even when talking about serious subjects. "Books? Yes. Newspapers? Yes. People? Of course. But guns, never. I do not involve myself in war things."

"I don't need to involve you," Oliver said, hoping these words were sufficient reassurance. "I only need your advice on other ways to transport the, um, materials. So that they don't get stopped and searched. Dolph says you have more experience moving banned material than anyone he knows."

A faint smile stretched Franz's lips. "He is correct, I have extensive experience." He paused, as if deep in thought. Then after a moment, he nodded his head down the trail and resumed hiking. "I know a man who can help you, but his help will not be cheap."

Oliver took a breath to consider this. He was sure Frank Dryden would approve the expense. But for now, at least, he'd have to operate on that assumption. "That shouldn't be a problem."

"Good," Franz said with one firm nod. "Tomorrow in Lyon, go to the Rhône shipyards south of the confluence. Go to the Commerce de Lyon office on the Quai de Beaucaire, ask for Mr. Georges Morel. Tell him you need to arrange a shipment of Emmentaler. That is my code name, but this is the only association I want it to have with your operation. It is only a key to grant you access, and nothing more. Understand?"

"I understand."

"I do not want my code name associated with gun shipments, so make clear to Mr. Morel that I am only making an introduction. Tell him that I know nothing about your shipment."

I get it. "I'll make sure he understands, I promise."

"Good." Franz's serious tone was followed by a broad grin, which dimpled his stubbled cheek. Then he slapped a hand across Oliver's shoulders. "Now, tell me what is new in your life, my friend."

**

Tuesday, May 12
Lyon, Unoccupied France

Georges Morel's dark eyes narrowed when Oliver mentioned *Emmentaler* the next morning. "When is your shipment required, sir?"

"We'll need to have regular shipments," Oliver said. "The next one should be later this month."

Morel scribbled something on a piece of paper and folded it in half. Looking back at Oliver, he said a touch louder, "Our barges do not run on routine schedules, sir. We can provide route information for the next two weeks, but no more." He slipped the paper across the counter.

Oliver peeked at the message: *"No. 7 Rue de Vercors, 13:00h"*

He pocketed it. "That would be helpful, sir."

Morel went to a wooden table and took hold of the big red leather-bound book sitting open there. He lugged it to the counter and spun it around to face Oliver. "Perhaps one of these will suit your purpose, sir," he said, pointing at a list of handwritten entries on the right.

Oliver perusued the list. There were a couple of arrivals at Marseille or Toulon in the next few days, but that would be too soon for Mr. Dryden to arrange another shipment from Spain. No stops at either port the following week. His heart sank.

But there was a barge returning from Lisbon and Cartagena that was scheduled to stop in Arles on the 25th, before continuing to Lyon on the 28th. That might do.

"That one might possibly work, but I will need to verify," Oliver said, pointing at the entry.

"You will let us know as soon as possible, of course," Morel said, spinning the book back around. "There is limited space."

"Of course. Good day, sir."

**

Number 7 Rue de Vercours was a tavern several blocks north of the port. It wasn't crowded, and about a dozen men with scruffy beards, dressed in the garb of sailors—dark trousers, dirty white shirts—occupied about half the tables. Oliver sat at a back table where he could watch the door, ordered a Croque Monsieur and a beer, and settled in to wait.

The beer was watered down and almost tasteless, but it washed down the food; and the sandwich was good, in any case.

Georges Morel sauntered in precisely at one o'clock. His eyes met Oliver's briefly before looking toward the bartender. He took a seat on a barstool and ordered potato leek soup and a beer.

He never looked Oliver's direction, and Oliver began to wonder if he was supposed to approach Morel at the bar, or if he needed to wait for Morel to come to him.

A group of several sailors left several minutes later, loud with drink, and the interior of the tavern seemed almost silent in their sudden absence. A trio of men near the window spoke quietly amongst themselves, and the bartender ignored everyone, for all appearance concentrating exclusively on his labors.

Oliver took the opportunity to approach Morel at the bar. For realism, he got the bartender's attention and ordered a second beer. He'd manage to drink some of the tasteless swill if it cast off suspicion.

"The cost is two thousand francs," Morel muttered when the bartender moved off to fill Oliver's glass.

About four hundred bucks. Dryden would surely approve that. "And no questions asked?"

Morel frowned. "Of course not."

"Emmentaler doesn't know any details," Oliver said, keeping his promise. "He only meant to introduce you, but he couldn't be here in person."

Morel shrugged with obvious lack of interest.

The bartender brought the glass of beer, and Oliver slid a two-franc coin across the dark and grooved wood. He took a big gulp for appearance's sake, managing not to make a face before the bartender went back to his work at the other end of the room.

"How do I make the connection in Arles?" Oliver asked out the side of his mouth.

Morel glanced around, then tugged a slip of paper from his left sleeve with his right hand and slipped it quickly across the bar to Oliver. "Follow those instructions precisely. And now you must go."

Oliver put the paper in his pocket without looking at it. He took one more drink of the thin beer—God, this stuff really was awful without food—and walked away.

**

Saturday, May 23

Saint-Tropez, Unoccupied France

Oliver circulated through a big and airy room in the most sumptuous villa he'd ever seen, a silver tray of canapés on the upturned palm of his right hand, raised over his shoulder.

It had taken a week for Frank Dryden to arrange the shipment from Spain to Corsica.

"It's not my connection, you understand," he'd told Oliver on Monday the 18th, when Oliver asked about the delay. "Robert Murphy has someone at the office of the COI that he works with on these matters."

There was that acronym again. "Coordinator of Information," Dryden supplied, noticing Oliver's look. "I told you about Colonel Donovan last month, if you'll recall. His office sets these things up. The State Department isn't officially involved."

A message from Dryden on Tuesday morning confirmed his reservation at Calvi, Corsica, on the 24th. Oliver then immediately sent a message to Symphonie in Marseille, ordering seventeen kilograms of squid for the travelling symphony on May 24th. From then it took three agonizing days to get a response, during which time Oliver worried they would miss their window of opportunity to catch the barge at Arles on the 25th.

When the courier finally brought the reply from Symphonie on Friday afternoon, the 22nd, Oliver's relief was palpable. Until he realized he'd have to miss a Saturday night at the club.

> Sir, your seventeen kilograms of squid will be ready for you on 23 May at 17:00h, No. 9 Chemin de Bainier, Saint-Tropez. Thank you for your patronage.

Dolph was agreeable to watch over things in his absence; Lisette met the news with stony silence.

And now Oliver pretended to be an hors d'oeuvre waiter at a ritzy cocktail party on the Rivera. Symphonie circulated with a tray of champagne flutes. Both wore black trousers, white dinner jackets, and black bow ties; while the guests—mostly men, Oliver couldn't help but notice—wore open-collared shirts with colorful scarves tied in artistic ways at their throats, and linen pants cut short enough to reveal colorful socks in shoes that looked like they'd never been worn. The handful of women in attendance wore cocktail dresses, had movie-star good looks, and impeccable hair and makeup.

Julien Daignault moved through the crowd with the careless ease of someone hosting the weekend's premier party. Not at all like someone who might be on-edge about smuggling illegal Spanish guns on his yacht in twelve hours. He chatted and laughed with every cluster of his guests, for only a moment or two before slipping away with the most gracious of exits and attaching to another cluster.

It was something to behold. Oliver was impressed, in many ways.

Giant windows overlooked the bay, dark blue in the soft glow of dusk. The open door next to them led to a large patio of perfectly smooth white stone where other guests mingled, and Oliver took the opportunity to step out into the evening breeze.

"You there, waiter," a man called in a high voice, and motioned Oliver over with a wave of his upturned fingers. Oliver dutifully approached, lowering his tray without a word so that the cluster of middle-aged men could pick an hors d'oeuvre.

"You're a new one," the man observed, looking Oliver up and down. He was probably early or mid-forties, thinning hair barely covering his scalp, slender but with a hint of paunch in front, and the slight droop of his jowls hinted at once full cheeks. "Not one of Julien's regulars."

Oliver hardly wanted to be memorable. If he acknowledged vocally, his accent would make him memorable, so he nodded silently and backed away.

"Well-fed, that one," an older man said as Oliver turned away.

"Not skinny like that other one," another remarked.

"He's one of Julien's regulars, the skinny one," the first one sniffed. "He works all of Julien's parties. Don't you remember him from last year?"

Cold prickles ran down Oliver's back.

**

Oliver followed Symphonie down a path on the side of the bluff, from Julien's patio to the beach below. The light of the half-moon bathed the scrub brush in a silvery hue, but the path was dark, and Oliver placed each step carefully to avoid twisting an ankle.

Julien himself had taken the wooden staircase from his patio, but that would hardly seem out of the ordinary if any of his neighbors happened to be looking out their windows. Seeing two young men accompanying him might raise eyebrows, however, and so Oliver and Symphonie had been relegated to the path instead.

Julien's "cottage" was a half-mile walk from the Old Port in the heart of the village; probably shorter as the crow flies, but the road circled around the medieval citadel perched on a hill overlooking the bay. East of the citadel, at least a dozen villas like Julien's stood atop the bluffs, but separated by wide lawns. The result was that it was quiet and dark here.

The picturesque setting had attracted artists such as Henri Matisse and Paul Signac at the beginning of the 20th Century, and by the Roaring Twenties it had become a favorite vacation spot for Paris icons such as Coco Chanel and others in her circle. This resulted in a stretch of villas lining the bay east of the citadel, with a slope covered in piney woods rising behind them to give the wealthy some privacy from the hoi-polloi during their summer holidays.

At the base of the bluff, the beach was wide—perhaps a hundred feet to the edge of the water, where a low surf crashed onto the sand—and Oliver felt exposed as they hurried across to where the inflatable raft waited. Their dark clothing would mask them in the brush while they descended the bluff, but they contrasted with the sand, shadowy figures rushing toward the water. He silently cursed the moonlight.

Julien waited for them there, and he fired up the motor as soon as they scampered inside and pushed off. He steered them around to his yacht, moored a half-kilometer away. A moment later, Gérard helped them aboard.

"It is six hours to Calvi," Julien told them when they were all seated in his elegant living room. "Get some rest. We arrive at five."

"I'll stay here on the couch," Oliver said, letting Symphonie take the guest bedroom. He ignored the brief look of disappointment that crossed the young man's dark eyes.

Less than six hours of sleep awaited him, and Oliver was exhausted already. And he wouldn't be shocked if Symphonie crept out to the couch in the middle of the night. But at least the nine-hour trip back to Cassis from Corsica would give him time to nap.

**

Monday, May 25

Arles, Unoccupied France

Oliver dozed through much of the two-hour drive from Cassis to Arles. Symphonie nudged him awake shortly before they entered the city.

"Sorry," Oliver said, rubbing his eyes.

"It is fine, but you must be alert when we reach the port."

They drove past a remarkably intact Roman arena, the stones at the top beginning to glow golden with the rising sun. A few minutes later, Symphonie drove the truck onto the quay and parked in the gravel near the end of a wharf.

"Good luck, my friend," Symphonie said, and shook Oliver's hand, letting his fingers trace Oliver's palm when they disengaged.

Oliver stared at their hands for a second. Hands that had, in the privacy of Julien Daignault's yacht, brought each other pleasure in the darkness. Yes, it had been mutual this time, the hand jives, though Oliver wasn't exactly sure why. He'd allowed it to happen again, and had actively participated this time. He looked away, out the window.

The Rhône was nearly half a kilometer wide here, at the top of its delta, and several ocean barges could be seen. Oliver climbed down from the truck and walked to the guard shack nearby. As instructed, he asked for a man named Bisset.

Thirty minutes later, Oliver climbed the gang walk onto a barge, dressed in the grimy shirt, dark trousers, and work boots of a sailor. His crates had already been stowed below.

A big-shouldered man with a full black beard waited for him at the rail. "I am Caron," he said, giving Oliver's hand one firm shake. "You will work for me until we reach Lyon."

Of course he would. It was the only way to avoid suspicion from any members of the crew not privy to his business. But Oliver cringed at the thought of the hard labor that awaited him.

**

Thursday, May 28
Lyon, Unoccupied France

Oliver walked stiff legged down the gang walk from the barge that morning. Every muscle in his body ached. He'd never been so happy to see the red roofs of Lyon.

He found Dolph at the wheel of a bakery truck, and once his cargo had been loaded in the back, he climbed in the passenger seat. Dolph drove them to a warehouse about a kilometer to the north, where several young men unloaded the crates and disappeared into the dark interior.

**

He walked into the flower store on the Rue Boutelle in the Renaissance-era Croix-Rousse district. Lisette was arranging magenta-hued Clematis in a small crystal vase for an old woman with a kerchief on her head; she glanced up from her work, and a wave of relief washed across her warm brown eyes.

"One moment, please," she told him, professional, and finished the arrangement.

After the old woman had departed, Lisette waved Oliver behind the counter. He expected a lecture about his absence, and the danger he'd put himself in. Instead, she threw her arms around his neck and hugged herself tightly to him.

22

Sunday, June 14
Lyon, Unoccupied France

It had been two years that morning since the Germans marched into Paris. The somber anniversary set Oliver in a melancholy mood from the beginning, in spite of the beautiful weather. Sunlight streamed through the window, the air was warm, and a lovely cool breeze wafted the linen curtains and glided across the table where he sipped a steaming cup of bitter ersatz coffee. Lisette sat next to him, having spent the night—as she often did on Saturdays—but none of that assuaged his mood.

He knew she could sense it, as well. She was quiet this morning, eating her bread and jam in silence, sipping her ersatz coffee. Two years ago, they'd still had real coffee—rich, satisfying coffee, not this bitter chicory brew.

But if he were honest, that night before the Germans marched into Paris had been the night he and Lisette put away the bitterness of their broken engagement, had leaned on each other and become friends again. It had ultimately paved the way to the renewal of their love, but that took more than a year, plus other factors pushing them together. If there were a silver lining to this horrid dark cloud, perhaps that was it.

And, for the first time in those dark two years, there was hope that it might soon be over. The Allies would invade, and France would be free again. The timing was undetermined, of course, but it

216

couldn't be too far out. They were laying the groundwork now, and Oliver was part of it.

He looked at her, staring somberly at the middle of the table and slowly chewing her bread, and he reached over to take her hand. She looked at him, head cocked in curiosity. "What is it?"

"I'm just glad you're here." He gave her hand a little squeeze.

She gave him a faint smile, but her eyes remained sad.

Impulsiveness got the better of him. "Why don't we get married? At the earliest possible date."

She looked startled. "We would have to post the wedding banns fourteen days in advance, at the Hôtel de Ville."

Which isn't open on Sundays. "Let's do that first thing tomorrow morning," he said, getting more excited by the idea. "We've been talking about getting married for almost three years now, so let's do it."

She smiled at him, and patted his hand on the table, but her eyes remained sad. "My parents would not be able to come. They couldn't get an *Ausweis*, not for their daughter's wedding. The Germans don't care if the Line of Demarcation divides families."

"My parents wouldn't be able to come, regardless," he said, a touch of irritation rising. "They were never going to be able to attend in the first place."

She sighed and pulled back her hand. "I always pictured my parents there, my father giving me to my husband. It would not be the same without them. I wouldn't be as happy."

That stung, and Oliver pulled back, looked down at his cup. "I would be happy."

He could tell she regretted saying that. Her words became rushed. "I would be happy, too. What I meant was, the day would be more happy with my parents there. And if they weren't there, it would feel that something was missing. That is all."

He nodded, still staring at his half-empty cup.

She stood and walked to the counter, poured herself some more of the bitter concoction that passed for coffee these days. Then she leaned on the counter, staring into the room with the steaming cup suspended in her hand.

He tried a different angle. "It would be safer if we were married."

She frowned and looked at him. "What do you mean?"

"The war is coming back to France, at any time. We don't know what will happen, but it will be safest for both of us if we're married."

Her frown deepened into a scowl. "How will that make us safer?"

He felt awkward, hesitant to raise any hint of pessimism, no matter how realistic. But he was this far down the trail…

"I mean, if something were to happen to me, you would have claim to the club, and to my bank accounts. You would be protected."

"Oh, I see." The words were quiet, but they seemed to echo around the room. "You think that is what I want?"

"No! Of course not. I only mean, it would be something, some little security you would have if I…"

If I'm killed. The words hung in his chest like an anvil tied to his heart. He hated thinking that. But he couldn't avoid it entirely, even if he never spoke it out-loud. It was always there, like a watcher in the night.

If he died single, he really wasn't sure what would happen to any of his assets. He supposed his parents would be able to file a claim—eventually. But the war would complicate everything, and they might never be able to prove their claim. It would all just be lost to the war.

**

That afternoon, as they strolled arm in arm in a park overlooking the confluence of the Saône into the Rhône, Oliver tried again.

"I'd like to have children at some point, wouldn't you?"

She was quiet for several seconds. He held his breath. "I like children," she said at last. He wondered if that was all she was going to say on the subject. "And I want to have children with you, Oliver. Someday."

That last word landed like a brick. *Someday?* He stopped, and put his hands on her shoulders, looking directly into her dark eyes. "Lisette, you're twenty-eight years old, and I'm almost thirty. Don't you think we should get on with it?" *Jesus, I should just like my father.* He put that thought out of his mind in a hurry.

Her lips tightened into a thin line. "Maman was twenty-eight years old when Gaston was born."

"And he was her second child."

Lisette's lips tightened further. "Cécile Fournier just had a baby, and she's forty-one."

Oliver sighed, and nodded. He took her arm again and they resumed strolling down the path between well-manicured hedges. They neared the point and stopped at the end of the walkway. To their right, the dark blue waters of the Saône rushed past, and to their left the muddier blue water of the Rhône carried barges on their way south to the Mediterranean. Ahead of them, the two distinct colors remained separated by an invisible line for a great distance, only slowly churning together in the enlarged Rhône.

They watched the boats in silence for several minutes.

"Why don't you want to marry me?" Oliver asked when they turned around to go back up the promenade.

He felt her arm stiffen. "I do want to marry you—but not now, not when things are...the way they are."

"They may never again be the way they were, Lisette." He sympathized with her concerns. To a point. "And there is no guarantee that they will ever be better than they are now. Waiting for a time when your parents can come here from Paris might mean we wait a very long time."

He glanced at her face, saw her frowning. *She doesn't want to hear that.* Then she seemed to deflate.

"But there is always...hope."

That broke his heart. The last thing he wanted to do was to take away her hope for the future. But neither could he let her put their lives on hold for a future that might not turn out.

"Then let's make a bargain. We wait a few months to see if things get...better. If they do, we get married as soon as we can, and telegram your parents to come down for the wedding. If they don't get...better...then we wait until the end of the year to make up our minds. At the start of the new year, we get married, whether things have improved or not. Deal?"

She considered it for only a couple of seconds before nodding her head one time, firmly, and thrust her hand out at him, sideways. "Deal."

He suppressed a smile while shaking her hand, business-like. But then her face broke into a smile, and she laughed and threw her arms around his neck. He laughed with her, then kissed her on the lips and hugged her tightly to him.

Hutson

23

Thursday, July 2
Vichy, Unoccupied France

Jackpot, Frank Dryden thought when he looked through the stack of papers from the diplomatic pouch.

A week before, Robert Murphy had told him—confidentially—that OSS had broken into the French Embassy in Washington and had stolen and photographed their entire code book before returning it to the safe where it was stored. The French had no idea their codes had been compromised.

And now Dryden was looking at a gold mine of decoded communiqués between Vichy and their embassy in Washington.

He had no doubt that the juiciest information had only been shared with military commanders, and not included in this week's diplomatic pouch—but what he had in front of him painted a picture of collusion with Germany that had only been suspected until now.

Robert Murphy himself had recently been reassigned to the consulate in Algiers as Special Envoy of the President—and Dryden was one of the few people in Vichy who knew that this was at the request of William Donovan, director of the OSS. Dryden had his suspicions as to why, but that information was classified beyond what he had access to.

Still, the information he'd been delivered came with directions from Washington to alter their covert approach to the Vichy regime, if not yet the overt one. This would mean additional work for his informants across the Unoccupied Zone—but most of all for Oliver Carmichael in Lyon.

**

Monday, July 6

Lyon, Unoccupied France

Every inch of Oliver's skin tingled while he sat through the meeting that night. The usual discussions of secret newspapers and circulating banned books faded into background noise in his head while he rehearsed repeatedly what he would say.

"I have new business," Oliver said, raising his hand when Dolph asked if anyone had other business to discuss.

Dolph's eyes registered momentary surprise—Oliver was rarely vocal during these resistance meetings—but he motioned for Oliver to take the floor, and sat down.

Oliver stood, butterflies doing somersaults in his stomach, and cleared his throat. "I have a friend at the American embassy," he began, hoping he was the only one who could hear the tremor in his voice. His friends in Paris had not been pleased when they learned he was working with someone at the embassy. All eyes were on him. "He told me a few days ago that the American government has proof that Vichy is actively tracking down Allied pilots in the Unoccupied Zone, and turning them over to the German occupation authorities in the north. This is an act of treachery for a country that is not at war with the United States."

On the other side of the room, Marcel's eyes darted to Dolph. Oliver looked at Dolph and saw a strange expression on his tall friend's face.

"My friend wants us to begin acts of sabotage against the SOL, the fascist organization which is conducting these treacheries. It will help the Allied war effort against the Nazis, and it fits with our mission to undermine the authorities at Vichy."

"I believe everyone here has suspected that Vichy is doing this," Armand said, clearly unimpressed.

"But it's good to learn that the Americans have proof of it," Térèse said, shooting Armand a look. He feigned indifference and looked away.

"Acts of sabotage?" another man asked, looking skeptical. "If they capture one of us, we'll be tortured to name everyone else."

"That is no different than now," the thin young man standing next to Marcel said. "It is too long overdue for Combat to live up to its name!"

There were murmurs of agreement around the group, and Dolph raised his hands for silence. "I agree that we should be more offensive, and take the fight to the SOL instead of only trying to evade them. Sabotaging their operations will help our missions, as well as the Allies." More words of agreement around the room. "Many of you know our contact in Switzerland, code name Emmentaler. He has worked with many underground groups in Germany who do acts of sabotage against the Gestapo. We should ask him to come and teach us."

**

After the meeting, while everyone was making their way to the door, Dolph took Oliver by the arm. "May I have a word with you in private?"

"Of course." Oliver followed him back into the room, where Marcel stood alone along the back wall. Their eyes met, and as usual Oliver had no idea what was going on behind those dark pools.

Dolph closed the door, silencing the hum of conversation from the front of the house, and the three of them were alone.

"You know that I am part of Sébastien's escape route," Dolph began.

"Yes, of course." Dolph had been the one to meet them last fall when Franz brought them across the Cher from the Occupied Zone.

"We had a safe house raided a few months ago," Dolph said. "Two British pilots were apprehended by the SOL and handed over to the Wehrmacht and the Gestapo."

So they'd known that was happening all along. It also explained something. "That's why Sébastien came here."

"Yes. We had to move our hosts to another city, for their safety, and had to secure another safe house here in Lyon."

Dolph glanced at Marcel, but if something passed between their eyes Oliver wasn't able to see it.

"Marcel and I believe we have identified the man who is leading the SOL's pursuit of résistants in Lyon. We don't know his name, but we know his appearance. Armand was pursued by him a few weeks ago, and he gave us a detailed description. I did a sketch, and Armand confirmed it is the man who chased him. Since then, we have spotted this man all around Lyon; he is everywhere. We've been able to observe him many times, and it is obvious he commands the others."

Oliver nodded, taking a few seconds to absorb this information. "Why haven't you shared the man's description with the rest of us? You should show your sketch to the group, so everyone can watch for him."

"We may need to do that, now," Dolph said. Another glance passed between him and Marcel, and Oliver wondered what unspoken messages they were passing between them.

Marcel said, "Everyone has been told often that the SOL may be watching. We are all of us watchful when we go out on missions. But we decided it was best if our friends are not watching for someone specific; it would make them appear paranoid when they do normal activities, and that would only draw suspicion to them."

That made sense. But Oliver couldn't help but notice Marcel's use of 'we.' Since when was Marcel making decisions with Dolph?

And then he figured out why, and a shock of jealousy stabbed through his chest.

"I think that was wise; but circumstances have now changed." Oliver's tone was brusquer than he would have liked, but at the moment he didn't care. Unwelcome images filled his head, of Marcel doing things with Dolph that he used to do with Oliver.

"Yes, that is so." Dolph nodded, sadness darkening his deep blue eyes. "If we are to begin more dangerous missions, acts of sabotage against the SOL and police, then everyone must be warned to watch for this man; and any who accompany him."

"Better late than never." Oliver hadn't meant the clipped tone, but it came out before he could think.

What on Earth was wrong with him? He'd let Marcel go because he loved Lisette. Why was he now so hurt that Marcel might have moved on with Dolph?

A veil seemed to fall over Dolph's eyes. Marcel continued to watch Oliver with his unreadable expression. An uncomfortable silence gripped them for several seconds.

"We should go," Dolph said, straightening his shoulders and motioning toward the door with a stiff arm. "It is not long until curfew. We will continue this discussion at the club tomorrow."

**

Tuesday, July 14

Oliver closed his office door after Lisette sat at her desk with the tills to count out the night's cash.

"I'm glad you're here, I've been eager to tell you something since last night." He couldn't keep the excitement from his voice, or the smile from his lips. "You left for work early this morning, or I would have told you then."

"What is it?" her eyes sparkled, catching his excitement.

"Our old friend Franz from Switzerland was at our meeting last night. He taught us some tricks to sabotage the SOL and the police."

Oliver's grin stretched wider. The thought of dumping a gallon of sand into a gasoline tank alone sent a wave of glee through him, and the image of confused gendarmes unable to get a phone connection after the lines to the building were cut almost made him laugh. Throw in some slashed tires and he felt almost giddy.

The look of wide-eyed shock on Lisette's face didn't seem as excited as he would have hoped.

"Oliver! What are you all thinking?" the sharpness of her tone caught him by surprise, and it stung.

"This will help us disrupt their operations," he said, and cringed at how meek his voice sounded. He squared his shoulders. "This is war, Lisette. And for too long we've been on the defensive. It is time the Resistance took the war to the fascists."

Lisette looked down, shaking her head, and he couldn't comprehend the muttered words coming from her mouth. But he might have heard "stupid" somewhere in there.

"What was that, dear?"

Her face snapped his direction, and she glared at him. "Don't use that tone with me, Oliver Carmichael." She looked away and started counting stacks of cash into the nearest till, snapping the metal clasps shut harder than needed.

He crossed his arms. "I don't understand your reaction. I thought you would be excited. This is the next step toward winning the war. Toward freeing France."

She glared up at him for the barest of seconds before returning to her work in stony silence.

He marched from the office and slammed the door, ignoring the startled looks from Armand and Fabien. He grabbed his hat from the stand and thrust it on his head before bolting out the front door.

**

Friday, July 17
Aigues Mortes, Unoccupied France

The third mission to retrieve smuggled Spanish guns, Oliver finally felt like a pro who knew what he was doing. The well-preserved medieval town of Aigues Mortes, near the Mediterranean coast of the Camargue—the proper name of the flat and marshy Rhône delta—was an ideal place to pose as a tourist. He even visited its famous tower, built by Louis IX—Saint Louis—on his way to the Crusades in the 13th century, and later used as a prison for Protestant women in the 17th and 18th centuries.

But his nerves still made butterflies tumble around his stomach at dusk when he strolled along the sand between the intact medieval walls and the shallow brackish lake called the Étang de la Ville. The day's earlier crowds had thinned, but the shore wasn't entirely empty. Symphonie approached from the opposite end of the walls, and by the time they met in the middle the rose hues in the western sky had faded into the deep blue of a long summer twilight, and they were alone.

Symphonie followed the script and asked him for a light, though there was no one around to hear. Oliver dutifully struck a match. The other man's fingers caressed the back of his hand while inhaling his cigarette to life, but then took several steps away before leaning against the old stones to smoke.

"I do not see anyone above," he said, barely loud enough for Oliver to hear. "But just in case, it will appear I am only enjoying a cigarette. Do not worry, you blend into the shadows."

Oliver had chosen a dark blue outfit, which wouldn't seem as conspicuous as black during the daylight, but would still disappear in the dark of night.

**

They stood in silence for several minutes. When Symphonie got to the end of his cigarette, he held his watch up in the glow of his last drag on it, and then stubbed it out.

"Five minutes."

Oliver nodded, though his companion wouldn't be able to see it.

Soon the honk of a flamingo rang across the sand, and Symphonie touched Oliver's arm. They hurried toward the sound, and found a fishing boat at the edge of the water. The shadowy figures of two men in dark clothing faced them.

"Fishing for Zander?" Symphonie asked.

"Pikeperch," the man closest to him said.

Symphonie patted Oliver's shoulder and then scrambled onto the boat. Oliver hurried to follow, assuming that was some script he hadn't been told. But that was part of their bargain—Oliver didn't disclose how he worked with Dryden on the timing of the gun shipments, and Symphonie didn't disclose how he arranged their transportation to Corsica.

"Those are two names for the same fish," Symphonie whispered in Oliver's ear after he sat.

The two fishermen adjusted a sail, and the breeze sped them across the étang, then down the canal between patches of sand and marsh grass. The crash of waves grew louder, and when the boat began to bob on the swell it pulled onto the edge of a wide beach.

"Good luck," one of the fishermen said as Oliver and Symphonie stepped out of the boat.

A light flashed three times, about a hundred meters down the beach. They ran toward it—not an easy jog in the sand—and found Gérard in Julien Daignault's inflatable raft. He fired up the motor the moment they climbed aboard, and ran them out to the yacht.

**

The yacht ran dark that night, with no lights and only a few candles to illuminate the interior. The crescent moon was just rising, and Oliver sat alone in the darkness on the stern deck, watching the silvery glint shine across the swells.

He hadn't asked Julien why the extra caution this voyage, afraid to hear the movie star was being watched. He'd rather not know, honestly. Even so, he sat in the deck chair with his heart beating in his throat.

24

Wednesday, July 22

Lyon, Unoccupied France

Oliver waited across the street from the café on Rue de Savoie for quite some time before he screwed up the courage to approach it.

Marcel worked here. Oliver had followed him this morning. Testing his skills, that's what he would have said if Marcel had caught him following. But if Marcel knew he was being followed, he gave no indication of it.

That in and of itself might speak to Marcel's skill, Oliver realized after he watched the young man walk into the café. He felt foolish loitering on the corner, waiting for the café to open; and then waiting until he had enough courage to go inside.

He couldn't put into words the reason for the sudden impulse to see Marcel, to talk to him, to reignite some spark of relationship beyond the occasional small-talk before Resistance meetings. But there was no denying Marcel had been on his mind more and more lately. Perhaps it was because Symphonie was tall and slender like Marcel, though his build was hardly as androgynous. No, if Oliver was honest, it was because Symphonie had kissed him a few nights ago, when he slipped out onto the stern deck in the middle of the night and awakened Oliver in his deck chair. Oliver hadn't kissed a man since Marcel. He broke off Symphonie's kiss immediately—no need to inject any intimacy into a mere hand jive, and the kiss felt like cheating on Lisette. But he and Marcel had once shared intimacy, even if Oliver had kept it at arm's length. Of course he came to mind.

It was definitely *not* because Marcel was involved with Dolph now. Oliver banished that thought. How ridiculous. He wasn't the jealous type, damn it.

It would have been better to visit Lisette at the flower shop after he got off the barge this morning. But instead his feet had taken him to Marcel's building in time to spot him leaving for work.

And now the café was busy, every sidewalk table full. Oliver had waited too long. He should just turn around and go to the flower shop. Lisette's anger from last week would be forgotten when she saw him enter. Just like last week. They would go home and make love, and all would be as it was before.

He crossed the street and walked into the café.

Only about half of the tables inside were occupied, in contrast to the ones on the sidewalk. The summer weather was too beautiful to spend lunch inside. Marcel had his back to the door, in the middle of delivering sandwiches to a table near the big front window. But in the back corner table, with a view of the entire room as well as the sidewalk tables outside, sat a tall thin man in a dark suit, his ears a little too big for his head. His brown hair was buzzed unusually short, and his rigidly-straight posture immediately put Oliver on alert.

Former military, clearly. And quite possibly an SOL man.

Oliver hesitated, not sure what to do. Then Marcel turned around, and his dark eyes caught Oliver's. He thought he detected a hint of annoyance for a second, before Marcel's expression went placid again.

"You may sit over there, sir." Marcel nodded at a table along the wall, and hurried through the kitchen door.

Oliver took a seat facing the room. And kept his eyes on the suspected SOL man.

The man's gaze moved from table to table. He might have only been engaging in that favorite of French pastimes, people watching. Except that Oliver knew better.

Marcel rushed through a moment later, carrying a demi-carafe of red wine, which he took to a table outside.

And the big-eared man's eyes followed him the entire way. Nerves prickled Oliver's arms, and he watched the man from the corner of his eye. The man's gaze definitely followed Marcel back to the kitchen before resuming its casual wander around the room.

Shit! The SOL was onto Marcel.

Oliver swallowed down the panic, telling himself that he couldn't be certain what was happening. He couldn't even be certain the big-eared man was actually SOL, let alone that Marcel was under surveillance.

Still, he was going to keep his eye on this one.

Marcel came through two more times, carrying plates of sandwiches or salads to outside tables. He didn't so much as glance at Oliver. And the big-eared crew-cut man in the corner watched Marcel come and go both times.

The next time Marcel came from the kitchen, he stopped at Oliver's table. "Are you ready to order, sir?"

Oliver could have almost laughed at Marcel's professional demeanor, were he not on-edge over the man in the corner. "You know what I always have for lunch." In Paris, at Chez Marius, Marcel had always just brought him his croque monsieur without asking.

"I don't believe you have ever been here before, sir." Marcel's expression was unreadable.

"I'll have a croque monsieur." Oliver couldn't keep the annoyance from his tone.

Marcel gave him a crisp nod and hurried away.

The big-eared man in the corner, who had been watching the interaction, resumed casually looking through the front window.

Marcel continued scurrying in and out of the kitchen, never glancing at Oliver until he brought his sandwich ten minutes later.

"Thank you, Marcel," Oliver said, smiling. "I wonder if we could talk—"

"I am very busy," Marcel interrupted, and hurried off.

The big-eared man got up just then, laying some coins and ration coupons on the table, and strode stiff-backed toward the door, putting on his hat as he exited.

Oliver relaxed, feeling the tension leave his shoulders. Marcel's attitude still vexed him, but he ate quickly and didn't bother him again until after he'd finished. He laid three franc coins next to his empty plate, along with one ration coupon each for bread, meat, and cheese.

Marcel was on his way back inside from the sidewalk when Oliver walked out the door, and he stood aside. "Thank you, sir. Good day."

Now that the lunch rush had subsided, and several outside tables stood empty, Oliver took a chance. "Marcel, we should talk. Would you listen to me for a few minutes, please? There are things I need to say."

"Not here," Marcel said, quietly, but through gritted teeth, his lips not moving. Then he nodded his head and added at normal volume, "Good day, sir."

"Another time, then," Oliver said, putting on his hat and walking away.

A few steps down the sidewalk, something caught Oliver's eye and almost made him stop in his tracks. In the window of the bookstore across the street, the big-eared man stood behind a chest-high bookshelf, an open book obscuring the bottom of his face, but his eyes staring over the top of the book at the café.

Oliver crossed the street at the next intersection. He bought a magazine at the newsstand, and then stood behind the corner of the building, peeking around at the café.

**

It was almost an hour later when Marcel left for his break, and headed down Rue de Savoie toward the Saône. Oliver inched back from the corner, raising his magazine over his face, peeking over the top.

A moment later, the big-eared man passed the corner just feet from where Oliver stood. He was also headed toward the Saône, on the opposite side of the street from Marcel.

Oliver waited a moment, and then closed his magazine and followed the man.

They crossed at the Pont Exchange to the Saint-Paul quarter in *Vieux Lyon*. Marcel passed through a door to a *traboule*, and a moment later the big-eared man followed. Oliver reached the door, glanced up and down the narrow street, and slipped through after them.

At the end of the covered passageway, Marcel turned into the spiral staircase at the corner. The big-eared man went into the staircase a moment later. Oliver lingered at the edge of the courtyard, looking up at the long narrow openings rising along the curved stone wall, catching glimpses of Marcel on his way up.

When the big-eared man passed the narrow window, he was looking down at Oliver.

Oliver inched back into the shadow of the *trabloule*. A moment later, not long after Marcel passed the window on the next flight up, the big-eared man went by. Staring down at where Oliver stood.

Shit! Oliver hurried back down the *traboule* and exited onto the street. As he suspected, the door a few feet down opened onto another spiral staircase for this building, and Oliver sprinted up the stairs two at a time. Perhaps he could reach the top floor in time to warn Marcel that he was being followed.

At the top of the stairs, he bolted around the corner into the hall—and stopped in his tracks.

At the far end, near the opposite stairs, Dolph conversed with the big-eared man.

Oliver slipped back into the shadows and stood on the top step, peeking around the corner. Dolph and the SOL man stood close together, talking quietly. Oliver couldn't make out any of their words, but the tones of their voices sounded tense.

The conversation continued for several minutes. Oliver's pulse raced for far longer than it would have from the sprint up the stairs. A vein on his left temple throbbed.

This didn't make sense. It was obvious Dolph was not merely confronting the man who had followed Marcel. They were *talking about something*, damn it. What the hell did that mean?

When the big-eared man finally left, Dolph went through Marcel's door. Oliver considered creeping down the hall and putting his ear to the doorframe, but his heart was pounding and his breath coming short and fast, and he wasn't sure how silent he could be.

He backed down a couple of steps, collapsed back against the cool stones, and beat his fists against the wall.

**

Oliver half-walked half-ran across central Lyon to the train station. He hurried to the ticket windows, fingers twitching while he waited in the short line. He rushed to the open window the moment his turn came.

"One for Vichy, please."

**

Frank Dryden's eyes widened in surprise. "Oliver! I wasn't expecting you." Then he smiled—that smile that never reached his eyes—and motioned toward the chair in front of his desk. "To what do I owe the pleasure?"

Oliver had rushed to the embassy directly from the train, and hurried past the French receptionist and up the stairs, ignoring her calls to check in. He remembered where Dryden's office was from his visit last October, the day after they escaped from the Occupied Zone. He was still breathless when he plopped onto the wooden chair.

"Why do we always go to Corsica to get the guns?"

Dryden cocked his head ever-so-slightly, the only hint of his curiosity. "As I understand it, the Spanish merchantman Louis prefers to deal with has a relationship with the dock workers at Calvi. Paoli's men. Why do you ask?"

Oliver took a second to catch his breath.

"Now that I have a contact at the Commerce de Lyon office who arranges barges up the Rhône-- Georges Morel—why can't we cut out the middle step of bringing the guns from Corsica to the Mediterranean coast? Why not have Louis send them directly to Arles from Spain? The fewer steps involved, the fewer people in the know."

He hated how untrusting he'd become. He hoped to God he was wrong about Dolph. But he couldn't take the chance.

Dryden nodded slowly. He was silent for several seconds. "You suspect a breach in security."

Oliver took a deep breath and told him what he'd seen.

25

Friday, August 28

Lyon, Unoccupied France

"That's out of the question!" Oliver's mouth hung open. He couldn't believe Frank Dryden would ask such a thing of him.

"We need for you to do this, Oliver," Dryden said. His tone said he wasn't going to take no for an answer. "It's important."

Oliver shook his head emphatically. "I have a say in my own life," he said, bolting from his office chair.

Dryden grabbed his wrist, stopping him from turning away. "If you lived in the States, you would have already been drafted into the army by now. Your life is *not* your own when your country is at war. And at this moment, your country needs you."

Oliver seethed. He knew he couldn't argue with Dryden's reasoning. But it made him furious nonetheless. "Two months? Why so long?"

Dryden scowled. "Like I said, the timing is not definite. We don't know for certain when the action will take place—but it should be within the next two months, if all goes well. And your role there will help us ensure that it goes well."

Oliver wrenched his arm away from Dryden and paced the room. "But I own a business! I can't just leave it in someone else's hands for two months—*possibly* for two months," he added that last part when Dryden opened his mouth to correct him. "I can't expect someone else to run the club for me while I'm away, not for that long."

"You're sounding very selfish, Oliver," Dryden said, and the icy tone of his words cut like glass. "How many American men do you think have left businesses behind to join their country's armed forces because of this war? Thousands. Tens of thousands. And they've left those businesses in the hands of someone else while they're away, *indefinitely*. And do you think many of them have complained about it like this?"

I bet they have, just not in public.

"You have a duty to your country, Oliver. I'm asking you to do your duty and answer your country's call."

Oliver stopped pacing, and stood in front of his desk. He stared at Dryden for several seconds, and then looked down at the floor. He had worked so hard for this, to be his own boss, to call his own shots—and the idea of possibly throwing it away made his stomach tie itself in knots.

He closed his eyes, swallowed hard. He knew Dryden was right—duty was duty, no matter how much he hated it. The word itself made his skin crawl. But if there was ever a time when the word duty actually had real meaning, this was one of those times.

An image of his father's scowling face, arms crossed disapprovingly, lurched into his consciousness. *Damn it all to hell!*

He opened his eyes, looked back up at Dryden, and sighed. "When do I leave?"

Dryden stood, looked him in the eye. "Tonight."

**

Oliver rushed home right after telling Dolph he had something to do and wouldn't be there that night. He didn't offer an explanation, and Dolph didn't ask for one.

Lisette was the one he dreaded telling.

Instead of thinking about that, he replayed the conversation with Frank Dryden while he threw clothes into his steamer trunk.

"You're going in an auxiliary role," Dryden had said. "Robert Murphy's main objective is convincing French military forces in Algeria and Morocco to not resist the Allied invasion when it comes. We don't want to start a war with France. He's got five agents working across the region—and between managing them, and liaising with General Eisenhower in London, and Colonel Donovan in the OSS, he hasn't had time to devote to the local Resistance. You're going to help him with that."

"I'm reporting to him now?"

Dryden shook his head, a hint of frown on his lips. "No, you're still my agent. You're just on loan to Bob Murphy for two or three months."

That was a relief. Dryden was a known entity, and they worked well together. "Are there any differences I should know about between the Resistance in Algiers, and the Resistance across the south of France?"

"We don't really know. We haven't had enough contact to get a feel. We're pretty sure Combat doesn't have any affiliates down there, but our general feeling is that you'll still find most of the *résistants* are either Gaullist or communist, with maybe a few socialist groups occupying the space in between."

So, not much different, then.

Dryden smiled, one of his trademark smiles that didn't extend to his eyes. "Naturally, we want you to avoid the communist groups—but as for the others, use your discretion. The idea is for them to support the invasion when it comes, just in case the French military decides to fight our landing force."

"But surely Mr. Murphy will have that all figured out before we invade, right?"

Frank Dryden's expression was enigmatic. "Absolutely. Think of yourself as an insurance agent."

The knocking at his apartment door jolted him like a flash of lightning, and he spun from where he'd laid his open trunk atop his bed.

"Oliver?" Lisette's voice called, muffled by the door. "Are you ill? Dolph said you came home."

He walked from the bedroom toward his front door, each step painfully slow, his feet like cement blocks. His stomach dropped to the pit of his belly, and his heart rose into his throat, leaving a void in between.

**

"Tonight?" Lisette's jaw dropped, and she let her mouth hang open for a while.

Oliver thrust stacks of folded shirts into a suitcase on his bed. He'd been dreading this conversation.

"I take the eleven o'clock train to Marseille. I'll board a freight ship tomorrow night, and it will depart from Marseille on Sunday morning, arriving at Algiers on Monday. I have to take my trumpet," he added, almost absently. He'd have to remember to fetch it from the club tonight.

"I'm going with you," Lisette announced, and spun on her heels.

He caught her arm in the bedroom doorway. "You can't, Lisette. It's not allowed."

She glared at him, fierce Gallic defiance setting in. "If you are going to be away for two months, I am going with you."

"No!" he said, harsher than he intended, but not actually regretting that. "It is not allowed. In fact, it's expressly forbidden. You must stay here, and help Dolph run the club while I'm away."

She folded her arms across her chest. "Is this because I haven't married you yet? Is it punishment?"

The accusation stunned him, coming from left field as it did. "No, of course not. That has nothing to do with it. My assignment is top secret—more secret than my previous assignments. Dolph and the others cannot know where I've gone. You are the only one who knows I'm going to Algiers, and you cannot say a word to anyone, understand?"

Technically, he wasn't supposed to tell her even that much, but he'd had to give her *something*.

Her arms stayed folded, and she continued to glare at him, but a flicker of hesitation crossed her stern dark eyes.

"This is serious, Lisette," he said, gripping her shoulders and staring into her eyes. "It could endanger a lot of people if the fascists find out that we're mobilizing the Resistance in Algeria. You must keep silent."

Her eyes widened a little, and her mouth opened just a bit. After a couple of seconds, she said, "The Allies aren't going to invade the south of France after all, are they? They're going to invade Algeria instead."

"Shhh," he said, quietly, never breaking the stare.

She looked off across the room, shaking her head slowly, lost in thought for a moment. "But that does not make any sense, Oliver! Why would they do that? It is so far away."

Oliver had wondered the same thing when Dryden told him. Dryden had been a bit cryptic in his response, but he said that German ships used Vichy-controlled Algerian and Moroccan ports for refueling on their missions to attack British ships resupplying Gibraltar, Malta, and Egypt. U-boats prowled the Mediterranean with impunity. He'd also mentioned massive numbers of German and Italian troops in Libya, the Italian colony between French Tunisia and British Egypt.

"We have to trust that the strategists in Washington and London know what they're doing," Oliver said, without getting into anything that Dryden had told him. Best if she didn't know much.

She slipped from his grip, sort of meandered across his apartment, and sat on the couch, looking a bit dazed. He took a seat next to her.

"You have to take your trumpet?" she looked confused.

He nodded. "Yes. I'm going to play in a band at a nightclub in Algiers. I'm pretending to be an itinerant musician—since that's an easy role for me to play." He smiled at the humor, but she didn't return the smile. Her eyes looked calculating.

"But I don't understand why I can't go with you," she said. "Wouldn't it look more convincing if you had your 'wife' with you? Won't a single man your age be more suspicious? Spies are always men travelling by themselves."

She had a point—but Dryden said she'd be a needless distraction, and Oliver needed to have his focus solely on the mission.

"Itinerant musicians don't usually have wives in tow," he said with a shrug. He knew that wasn't always true; but it was true enough, anyway.

She was quiet for a long time, and he took her hands and held them tightly in both of his, in the hopes that it would show how much he was going to miss her.

"Can I at least see you off at the train station?" she asked, finally looking at him again.

His heart wrenched inside his chest. His voice cracked when he said, "No. We'll say goodbye here. If anyone is watching, they will see me leave alone. That way, you won't be involved."

She nodded, then walked out of his apartment without another word.

Oliver stared after her as his door closed. A chord wrapped around his heart and squeezed it so tightly he could barely breathe.

Part III

26

Monday, August 31
Algiers, Algeria – Unoccupied France

Oliver's legs felt wobbly when he walked down the gangplank at the Port of Algiers. Sweat ran down the side of his face and stung his eyes. The sun glaring off the white buildings made him squint, even after he tugged the rim of his hat low over his brow. He lowered his eyes.

After twenty-six hours at sea, the solid ground under his feet was a blessing. Oddly, he still felt as if his body were rocking with the waves. The freight ship from Marseille rocked quite a bit more than the giant ocean liner from New York to Le Havre seven years before. And the sailors said it was a smooth sea!

His senses went on overload the moment he stepped off the freighter. The sights, sounds, and smells of Algeria were like nothing he had ever experienced. Cars competed with donkey-drawn carts for space. Europeans in western attire mingled with Arabs, some in western attire, some in traditional robes, and others in various combinations of both. Sheep and goats bleated, car horns blared, vendors shouted in Arabic and French. The scent of spices wafting on the breeze enticed his nose one second, only to be replaced with the stench of donkey manure the next.

Over the cacophony, he heard his name shouted somewhere to his left, and his eyes scanned the crowd until he spotted the figure of Robert Murphy towering over everyone else, pushing his way toward Oliver. He looked comfortable in a white linen suit, and his face was shielded by a wide-brimmed white straw hat with a navy-blue band. Oliver resolved to find one of those hats for himself as soon as he could.

"I see you made it in one piece," Murphy said in English, in his flat nasal Wisconsin accent.

"Yes, sir," Oliver said, and shook Murphy's hand.

"Glad to have you, son. Welcome to Algeria."

"Thank you. Glad to be here." Oliver almost cringed the moment the words escaped his lips.

"I've got a car waiting, over this way," Murphy said, and cut a path through the crowd toward a waiting Packard Touring Car. An Arab driver in a chauffer's uniform opened the back door, and Oliver got in. Murphy slid in after him, and the chauffer closed the door and got in behind the wheel.

Murphy tapped his cane against the ceiling, and the driver pulled out slowly into the densely packed street.

"We've got an apartment for you in the colonial district. European settlers are about half the population of Algiers, and they have their own communities, distinct from the Arab districts."

Come wiz me to ze Casbah. Oliver heard the satirical line about the movie *Algiers* in his head, and smiled. It hadn't actually been in the film, which he'd seen in a cinema in Paris four years before with Lisette and most of their friends. It had been a surreal experience watching the film's French characters speak English, mostly with bad accents, while French subtitles flashed below them.

Serge had hated the film. Adrienne gushed about Hedy Lamarr. Sébastien had been more equivocal, but upon a challenge from Serge he had agreed that the previous year's French film *Pépé le Moko* had been a better version of the story.

Looking out the window at the activity around them, Oliver wondered if the real Casbah was anything like its depiction in the movie. He'd have to find out for himself.

The car accelerated once they exited the packed Port and sped off toward the southeast. Out Oliver's window, on a hill above the city stood a huge church with a Byzantine dome, but it didn't look old enough to actually be Byzantine.

"*Le Basilique Notre Dame d'Afrique*," Robert Murphy said, following Oliver's gaze. His accent in French was excellent. "It's meant to mirror the basilica in Marseille, *Notre Dame de la Garde*, opposite us across the Mediterranean."

Oliver noticed the resemblance, minus the towering spire of the one in Marseille.

The car turned several times, ascending from the city center and winding through streets between white-walled buildings.

"The cabaret where we secured your employment is down that way," Murphy said, pointing toward the left. "You'll be able to walk there. While you're here, your cover is that you're a musician who's played at several clubs across France. Use your real name—just be stingy with specifics. Don't share too much, and you'll do fine."

That would be easy enough. Hopefully.

The car turned right, went a couple of blocks, and stopped in front of a four-story building with extra wide windows across the front.

"Let's get you set up," Murphy said before exiting the car after the chauffer opened the door. "You start work at the cabaret tonight."

The immediacy surprised Oliver. "What time?"

"You report for duty at six o'clock," Murphy said. "Now come along, I only have a short time to get you settled."

The interior of the building was blessedly cool compared to the blazing heat outside. They climbed two flights of stairs to the second floor, and Murphy unlocked a door before handing the key to Oliver.

It was a simple, two-room space, sparsely furnished. The wide front window was open, and lace curtains fluttered in the breeze coming off the bay. Oliver set his suitcase down in the middle of the room.

"The rent is paid through the end of October," Murphy said. "The concierge is Monsieur Laufin. There's a shared bathroom down the hall, typical stuff. I'm sure you're used to that kind of arrangement, after all your years in France."

He handed Oliver a business card. The name on the front was Joseph Garnier, and the French word for "Manager" was printed in smaller letters underneath. On the back was the name of a cabaret in bold, exotic lettering, with an address in fine print near the bottom.

"That's about four or five blocks from here," Murphy said. "To the south on Rue Amirouche, and then a right on Rue Lamaraz. You'll see the marquis. He's expecting you at six. Any questions?"

Lots. "Mr. Dryden said you'd give me more details about my mission here."

"What do you need to know?" Murphy asked, glancing at his wristwatch.

Oliver resisted the urge to frown, but Murphy's impatience bothered him. "I know that I'm supposed to contact the local resistance, gain their confidence, and then recruit them to aid with the invasion when it comes. I don't know any other details, though."

Murphy scowled. "What details do you need? I assume you know how to gain their confidence—you've been doing that all across Unoccupied France for the last six months. This is just one more city, same deal."

This time, Oliver allowed his irritation to show. "In those other cities, I was told where to meet with the resistance leaders."

Murphy pointed to the business care in Oliver's hand. "There you go, right there in your hand. I'm told the place is crawling with *résistants*." His eyes narrowed a little. "Much like your own cabaret in Lyon, I understand."

Oliver stopped himself from sighing in frustration. "Are these *résistants* expecting me?"

"No," Murphy said, his tone saying this was the end of the conversation. He thrust his hat on his head and nodded at the card in Oliver's hand. "See that you're there promptly at six. Good day." He spun on his heel and let himself out.

Oliver exhaled hard in frustration, and plopped onto a chair, shaking his head.

Hutson

27

Oliver was shown into the office by an Arab doorman in a Fez hat, who spoke better French than he did. "The new musician you're expecting, Boss," the man said to Joseph Garnier, bowed, and backed out.

"Close the door," the manager instructed, and Oliver complied. "You're the one Mr. Murphy sent, yes? The American."

Oliver nodded.

"We already have a trumpet player, but I told Mr. Murphy that you could play back-up."

Oliver's heart sank. He'd gone from directing his own band, to playing back-up in a band in a third-tier provincial city. *It's only short-term.*

"You have your own horn?"

Oliver held up his trumpet case. "Yes, I brought it with me from France."

"This *is* France," Garnier said, scowling, his brow furrowing with three deep lines. "Algeria is France, it is not a colony. Tunisia is a colony. Morocco is a colony. Algeria is as French as Corsica."

Oliver lowered his head in a show of contrition. "Of course, my apologies. I should have said that I brought it with me from Lyon."

"Good," the manager said, curt, formal. "I'm going to pair you up with our trombonist, Vincent. He will go over the music with you."

Oliver cocked his head. "Why the trombonist?" *Why not the other trumpet player?*

The manager stared back at him for a couple of seconds. He evidently didn't like being questioned. "Your part will be similar to his. We haven't had time to translate the sheet music from C Key for Trombone to B Flat Key for your trumpet. Can you translate in your head? Or will you need to sit out tonight?"

"I can transcribe the part into B Flat," Oliver said. After a second's hesitation, he added, "I write music."

The manager grunted. "I'll have Vincent get you some staff paper and set you to work. Come!" He made a quick motion with his hand and strode from the room. Oliver hurried to follow him.

A cacophony of sound greeted them backstage, where a dozen musicians scattered around the small space warmed up their instruments in front of music stands. Oliver noticed immediately that all of them were European—not a single Arab or Berber to be found.

The trumpet player in particular was quite fair; he was a short and slightly-built little fellow, and young—couldn't be more than twenty-five at most. His light brown hair was fine, and though parted on the side, still hung low over his forehead.

The closest candidate would have been the trombonist, with his dark hair and full dark beard, and deep tan; but he just didn't look Arab. And when he looked up at the manager and Oliver striding toward him, his pale blue eyes were striking in their contrast to his dark looks.

"Vincent Montagano, this is Oliver Carmichael, the new second trumpet," Garner said, his introduction perfunctory, even a touch gruff.

"Welcome," Vincent said, shaking Oliver's hand. His hand was thick, and his grip firm. His eyes held Oliver's for several seconds, and his handshake held on a second too long. He was as tall as Oliver, but stockier. He didn't look fat, really, but his midsection wasn't slim, and he had broad shoulders and a barrel chest that looked muscular in the way it stretched the fabric of his white shirt.

"See that he finds some staff paper, so that he can transcribe your music into his key," the manager said, and marched back toward his office.

"Don't mind Mr. Garnier," Vincent said with a crooked grin that made an unexpected dimple in his round cheek, at the top of his beard. "He's always like that. You'll get used to him."

"I hope so." Unofficial cover or not, this job could be miserable for the next several weeks if he didn't tolerate the management well. *Remember, it's only temporary.*

"Come with me, I'll introduce you to the others." Vincent led him around the backstage area, introducing him to the musicians one by one. They acknowledged him with a polite but cool nod and quick handshake, before returning to their practicing.

"I'll show you where we keep the blank music paper," Vincent said, and put his big hand on Oliver's shoulder to lead him down the hall to the storeroom. "Take a pencil, and an eraser. And you can take this stand with you. Are you familiar with Django Reinhardt's music?"

Oliver almost laughed but stopped himself at just an amused smile. "Yes, but it's been a while."

"Good then, you'll probably pick it right up. That's mostly what we play here," Vincent said, then shrugged. "Plus a few other things from time to time. But mostly Django Reinhardt."

Not a bad choice, if a bit cliché and predictable. At least it was still jazz.

"Mr. Garnier said I'd be paired up with you," Oliver said. "I suppose that to mean I'll sit with you onstage?"

"I suppose so," Vincent said, brightening. "I'm in the back row, and there's room in the back for another man. You can take the spot next to me." They walked toward the backstage area where the others continued to practice on their own. "And don't worry if you don't have time to transcribe it all into your key tonight. The good thing about being in the back row is how easy it will be to slip behind the curtain for any song you can't play yet."

"I'll be alright, thanks," Oliver said. He was grateful for the kindness after the chilly reception from Garnier.

"Can you work on that while I play?" Vincent asked when they reached his music stand.

"Yes, of course," Oliver said. Vincent began to practice the song on top, and Oliver set about transcribing the notes onto the blank staff paper, translating from C to B Flat. It wasn't hard, and he was able to do the entire page while Vincent practiced it.

"You're very quick at that," Vincent said when he paused for a breather, and nodded toward the page of penciled-in musical notes Oliver had made.

"I have some experience writing my own music," Oliver admitted, but then his cheeks heated. Why should he be embarrassed about that?

Vincent's eyebrows shot up in surprise. "That's fantastic. I wish I could do that." Then he glanced around, and leaned close to whisper, "I wouldn't tell Mr. Garnier, though—he'll think you're too ambitious, and he'll fire you."

Too late. Somehow, that didn't surprise Oliver; he wouldn't be fired, though, due to Robert Murphy's influence. Not that he could admit that. "Thanks for the warning."

**

The night seemed to drag. Even though he picked up the music right away—there wasn't anything he hadn't played before, at one time or another—Oliver still felt like a fish out of water here.

The club drew a decent crowd for a Monday night. He wished Chez Oliver had this much business in the middle of the week.

Of course, his place was closed on Mondays, so Oliver could have two days off. He was the boss, so he called the shots. Obviously, Garnier had taken advantage of the abolition of the forty-hour work week a couple of years before. Five to midnight, six nights a week.

During the two ten-minute breaks between sets, the other musicians shuffled off in small groups, and Oliver was left by himself. After a moment's hesitation, he screwed up the courage to follow the largest group outside.

The night air was surprisingly cool for August. *We're at the edge of the desert*, Oliver realized belatedly, stopping himself right before asking about it. He nodded at the group of musicians standing in a cluster, staring at him, and said *"Salut"* with a tentative smile, hoping the informal greeting would put them at ease.

"Salut," a few of them said in return, raising their chins in cool acknowledgement, and continued to stare at him.

"Is this a typical Monday night here?" He edged closer to the group.

One man nodded, the clarinetist. "Yes, it is typical."

They all continued to stare, and Oliver felt the urge to squirm under their scrutiny. He held his place, keeping his feet rooted in the dust.

"You are American," Patrice, the little trumpet player said. He was the only one not smoking a cigarette. "But you came here from Lyon. How did you come to be in France?"

"I lived in Paris for six years," Oliver said, pleased to be able to offer his bona fides, as it were. "And then Lyon for the last ten months."

The little trumpet player seemed to consider this for a few seconds. "I have never been to metropolitan France," he said, with an almost dismissive air, and turned back to his companions.

The others chuckled, and voiced agreement.

So not a well-travelled bunch. The word 'provincial' just kept repeating in his head this evening. He told himself not to be so judgmental—he remembered plenty of New Yorkers looking down their noses at the boy ingénue from Indiana when he first left home.

He wandered back inside. In the hall, not far from the men's room, he found Vincent Montagano chatting with the bassist and the cellist.

"You're doing well tonight," Vincent said.

"Thank you, Vincent." The bassist and cellist took the opportunity to nod at Oliver and depart. Vincent seemed not to notice.

"Your family name, it's Italian?" Oliver asked, curious about that, but making small talk more than anything.

"Yes, my father's parents were from Italy." Vincent didn't elaborate. A typical French reluctance to discuss anything too personal.

"And you are from Algiers?" Oliver asked, trying to sound friendly.

"No, I am from Bône."

"Oh? Where is that?" Oliver had never heard of it.

"It is east of here, five hundred fifty kilometers. Near the border with Tunisia. In Roman times it was called Hippo."

It took Oliver a few seconds to place it. "St. Augustine," he said at last, grinning in satisfaction.

Vincent's eyes lit up. "Yes, that's it."

"My father is a pastor," Oliver said, for some reason feeling the need to offer that explanation for his familiarity with the most influential theologian of western Christianity.

A look of curiosity passed across Vincent Montagano's face, but then he looked away suddenly. "It's almost time for the next set. We should get ready." He hurried backstage.

**

Saturday, September 5

Oliver worked the entire week with barely any interaction with his bandmates, and even less with customers. It became increasingly apparent that the people of Algiers were more cliquish than he was used to.

Then just before midnight on Saturday when they were closing for the week, the little trumpet player sidled up to him when he was ready to walk out the back door.

"You left Paris in October," Patrice said, quietly, head leaned close. "That was before America entered the war. Why would you leave Paris before you had to? Unless, perhaps, you had to?" He glanced sideways at Oliver, one questioning eyebrow raised.

Oliver looked around, but no one else appeared to be listening. He nodded without speaking.

"Let me see your trumpet," the young man said at a normal volume. Oliver set his case on the ground and opened the clasps. The little man slipped a small sliver of paper between the valves, and then closed the case. "Very nice. You must be proud of it. Good night."

He walked away at a brisk pace. Oliver picked up his trumpet case and walked home, anticipation gnawing at his gut, wanting to know what Patrice had put inside his case. He bounded up the steps of his building and hurried inside his apartment.

He set the case on his table and opened it right away. He pulled the sliver of paper from where it lay between the first and second valves, and opened it.

It bore an address and the words "One AM."

Well after curfew. It must be a Resistance meeting. A thrill rushed through him.

28

Sunday, September 6

Oliver paced his apartment for the next thirty minutes, a bundle of nervous energy. At the last moment, he changed into black clothing, complete with black leather gloves that were entirely too hot for the weather, and crept out of his apartment and down the stairs. He gingerly took the last few steps across the foyer in front of the concierge's door and slipped out the front door undetected.

It was more than a kilometer to the address on the paper, past the club, and several turns on side streets. The skinny crescent moon only gave off a little light, but even so he kept to the shadows of awnings, creeping along as close to the buildings as he could.

He arrived at two minutes before one o'clock. No one answered his knock, and it occurred to him that there was probably some sort of secret knock, in a certain rhythm. He looked around to see if someone else was coming, someone in the know who might allow him in. He felt exposed standing on the street, alone, after curfew.

No, fool, they won't know who you are. Someone might well be watching from a dark corner, concerned about the stranger standing outside their meeting spot. He wondered if he should leave. Standing here too long might get him arrested; or it might get him beaten up by suspicious *résistants*.

A couple of minutes later—when the bells of the basilica on the hill tolled one o'clock—he spotted a slightly-built figure in black creeping toward him. A few seconds later, he recognized Patrice's face.

"I wondered if you would come," the young man whispered. Then he knocked at the door in a complicated rhythm.

The door opened half-way, and the little trumpet player pointed back at Oliver while slipping inside. "I brought someone with me."

The door closed so quickly after Oliver entered that he was surprised it didn't hit him in the shoulder.

"Who is this?" the scruffy-faced man in front of him asked, eyeing Oliver with narrowed, suspicious eyes.

"He's an American who had to flee Paris last fall, for reasons he won't say," Patrice said, a suggestive expression on his face. "Then he left Lyon last week and came to Algiers, also for mysterious reasons."

The scruffy-faced man didn't look convinced. "How do we know he's not an informant?"

"Why would the police use an American informant?" The little trumpet player looked and sounded exasperated with his compatriot's suspicion.

"I was with the Resistance in Lyon," Oliver said.

The scruffy-faced man folded his arms and glared at Oliver. "Prove it."

Oliver wasn't at liberty to reveal much, so he said, "I don't have proof, but I was with the group called Combat. I have passed messages for Free French agents who came back to France from London, but I cannot say anything more about that."

The scruffy-faced man didn't look convinced. "And why did you leave Paris? Were you in the Resistance there, also?"

His smirk said that he was being sarcastic. But Oliver shook his head as if he hadn't noticed. "No, I was not. But I did kidnap a police captain who had detained one of my friends who was in the Resistance. I am a wanted man in Paris, which is why I had to leave."

A flicker of doubt crossed the man's hazel eyes. Oliver suspected his story carried the ring of truth, but the man didn't look quite convinced. "Then, why did you go to Lyon? Weren't the police looking for you everywhere? You wouldn't have been safe there."

"A certain government official in Paris with influence in Vichy did not want me arrested. You can imagine why for yourself." Oliver hoped the vague insinuation would suffice.

A brief look of amusement flitted across the man's eyes. Then he looked back at Patrice and pointed at his face. "You had better keep an eye on this one. You are responsible."

Patrice ignored him and took Oliver's arm. "Come." He led Oliver toward the next room. "I thought you might be one of us. When I saw you waiting outside, I knew for certain."

About twenty men crowded in the room—no women, Oliver noted. These provincials were more socially conservative than Parisians or Lyonais about the role of women, he supposed.

The room was stuffy, with the large window closed and the shutter beyond it locked, and the accumulated body heat was barely circulated by a slow-moving ceiling fan. Sweat gathered on Oliver's forehead, and dampened the hair at the back of his neck.

**

The bells of the basilica chimed two o'clock when everyone filed out the front door. The cool night air blasted against Oliver's face, a welcome relief from the stuffiness of the house. He was glad he'd come, even though he'd stayed quiet while they discussed ways to undermine the police and the pro-Vichy local officials. Nothing terribly advanced.

Patrice clapped him on the shoulder. "Which direction are you?" he whispered.

Oliver pointed toward the club.

"Me also," Patrice whispered.

The bright light of two electric torches suddenly bathed the dark street in white. Oliver's hand rose to shield his eyes. Police whistles pierced the night.

"Stop! You are in violation of curfew, and you are all under arrest!"

"Go! Run!" Patrice shouted, shoving Oliver in the center of the back. He started running a split second before Oliver did, but with his longer legs Oliver passed him within seconds. "Split up!" the little trumpet player hissed, and suddenly veered to the right down a heretofore hidden alley.

Oliver took the next left, not entirely sure where he was going, but vaguely aware that this street led generally toward the Bay of Algiers. The sound of police whistles was multiplying, and they were clearly spreading out. They'd been lying in wait.

He edged closer to the buildings, hoping the shadows of the awnings would help hide him from the little bit of moonlight that shone between the buildings.

A dark figure emerged from a doorway right in front of him, and Oliver tried to skid to a stop. An arm grabbed him and pulled him into the darkened doorway.

He was about to shout, but a big hand covered his mouth.

"Shhh...be quiet," a husky male voice whispered in his ear. The voice sounded familiar, but was obscured by the whisper, and Oliver couldn't quite place it. The hand over Oliver's mouth was loose, and a second later it slipped down to his chest.

The large man pulled him backward, through the half-open door. "Don't fight, you're safe," the voice whispered, and Oliver allowed the man to pull him into a ground floor apartment.

The big shadow figure closed the door quietly, and the locked clicked. The lights remained off, however, and Oliver could see nothing at all until the curtain parted an inch or two, and the man peeked around the edge into the street.

A moment later, a pair of police gendarmes ran past the building, one blasting his whistle. The heavy curtain fell back into place, eliminating the tiny sliver of dim light, and the room went black again.

Oliver stood rock still and listened as the sound of the police whistle grew fainter.

To his right, a match was struck, casting a warm yellow glow around the room. In the flicker, he saw Vincent Montagano's face, and his big hand held the match to the wick of a candle, then shook it out.

Oliver exhaled hard in relief. "Vincent!"

"Shhh." Vincent held a finger to his mouth.

Oliver nodded. "Thank you for rescuing me," he said, quieter.

Vincent shrugged. "It is nothing."

Oliver thought about it for a moment. This seemed too fantastic to be real. He wanted to pinch himself. "But, how did you know?"

Vincent was quiet for a moment. If the light had been brighter, Oliver would have sworn he looked a little sheepish; but with only a single candle flickering, he couldn't be certain. "I was still awake, and I heard the police whistles. Knowing the hour, I suspected they were after résistants."

Oliver watched his face closely. "Are you sympathetic to the cause?"

"Yes, I am." Vincent reached inside his jacket—and Oliver noticed for the first time that he was dressed in dark clothing. Vincent pulled out a short stack of small pieces of paper and set them on the table next to the candle.

Oliver moved closer, craning his neck to read the handwriting on them.

"The idea that the French are a free people is stronger than the will of Vichy to suppress it. Alexandre the Great."

He looked at the stocky trombonist next to him, mouth open in awe. "You're the one who leaves these notes around town?"

A proud smile tugged up the corners of Vincent's mouth. "For almost a year now. I write them to remind the French of who they are. This one was inspired by Victor Hugo: 'There is one thing stronger than all the armies in the world, and that is an idea whose time has come.'"

Oliver shook his head in wonder. "You're 'Alexandre the Great?' Why that name?"

Vincent's smile widened, and he patted his chest with a flat palm. "I am Vincent Alexandre Montagano. Alexandre the Great, at your service, sir." He made a half bow in Oliver's direction.

"Are you part of the Resistance?" Oliver couldn't imagine doing that kind of thing all by oneself. But Vincent hadn't been at the meeting, nor had there been any mention of him.

Vincent shrugged with a false modesty that Oliver found endearing. "I think these qualify as resistance, no?"

Oliver laughed a little. "What I meant is, are you part of a Resistance group? Surely you have help with these."

Vincent shook his head with great solemnity. "No, I work alone. I do not belong to any group."

Oliver was certain there was a note of melancholy in his tone, perhaps a vague longing to belong, but not belonging. He wondered about that.

The look in Vincent's eyes made him uncomfortable, so he glanced back at the little slips of paper on the table. "You were out tonight, weren't you? That's why you heard the police whistles—and why you were in your doorway when I ran down this street."

Vincent nodded. "I was almost home when I heard them. I hurried to reach my building's doorway, but I stayed there to watch. I knew I could slip inside if the police came down this street—but before then I might rescue some hunted résistant." He paused, staring at Oliver for a few seconds. "I am glad I waited. I recognized you from twenty meters away. I was surprised it was you." His tone didn't sound displeased.

"Thank you," Oliver repeated. "I am grateful for your help. Do you mind if I stay here a little while longer? Only until it is safe from the police."

A startled look briefly crossed Vincent's face. "You should not leave until dawn," he said. "The night patrols will be alerted, and they will remain vigilant. You should stay here until the curfew lifts."

That caught Oliver by surprise. The curfew wouldn't life until six AM—almost four hours from now. He shook his head. "I can't impose on you all night."

"It is not an imposition."

Oliver felt embarrassed, but he knew better than to argue with an offer of hospitality. "Well, thank you, again."

Vincent motioned toward a couch on the far wall. "Why don't we sit for a while?"

Oliver agreed, and sat beside Vincent, who half-turned toward him. Oliver watched the candlelight dancing across the opposite wall, which was bare, with no photos or other wall hangings to decorate it.

"Would you want to join a Resistance group?" Oliver asked after a moment.

Vincent shrugged at the question. "Perhaps. I don't know."

This piqued Oliver's curiosity. "Why don't you know? Are you afraid of getting caught?"

Vincent shrugged again. "Perhaps, I suppose—but that is not the reason I do not know if I should join a resistance group."

"Then what *is* the reason?"

Vincent was silent for a moment, and from the look on his face he appeared to be deep in thought. "I suspect that several musicians at the club are part of a resistance group. And I suspect that this is the meeting you attended tonight."

Oliver nodded slowly, considering this statement. "But they have never asked you to join—is that it?"

Vincent looked at him and held his gaze. "That is one reason."

Oliver wondered what the other reasons might be, but decided to let that part go for now. "If they asked you, then—would you join them? The work is important, and it can use all the hands it can get."

He briefly thought about the total absence of women in the group, but put that out of his mind for now. That was a fight for another day.

Vincent continued to hold Oliver's gaze, and Oliver watched the flicker of candlelight reflect in the pale irises. "I would join if *you* asked me to," Vincent said at length, his voice strong and steady. A promise.

Oliver hesitated—it wasn't his place to ask someone new to join the group, not after one meeting. He wasn't sure if they had a formal induction process, but if they did, then he wasn't a member of the group anyway.

He put those concerns out of his mind. The cause needed recruits, period. He would deal with the consequences later.

"I would like for you to join us, Vincent." He grinned then, and added, "Alexandre the Great."

Vincent laughed at that, a hearty, genuine laugh that shook his shoulders. It was contagious, and Oliver laughed with him, even though it had only been a mediocre joke.

When the laughter subsided a moment later, Vincent put a hand on Oliver's arm. Oliver looked down at the big hand for a second, before looking back up at the smiling eyes that stared at him. "Very well, then. I will join your group. *Vive la France!*"

Oliver had to grin. "*Vive la France!*"

**

Oliver awoke to the sound of the basilica's bells tolling eight o'clock. He opened his eyes slowly and saw bright sunlight streaming into the room around the edges of the curtains. It took him a few seconds to remember where he was.

He threw the blanket off and sat up on the couch, rubbing his eyes. He grabbed his shirt and pants from where they sat folded on the floor at the end of the couch and dressed quickly.

The door at the opposite end of the room stood slightly ajar, and it was dark in the room beyond. Oliver crept to the half-open doorway, and softly knocked against the door. Peering into the room, he could just make out the figure of Vincent Montagano sprawled in bed, a white cotton sheet pulled up only to the waist. His slow, rhythmic breathing indicated he was still asleep.

Oliver hesitated, unsure what to do. He didn't want to wake him. And he looked so peaceful. Though his midsection appeared soft, like a pillow, his chest and shoulders bulged muscles, as did his arms. Black hair covered the pectoral muscles, and collected in a trail down the soft belly, disappearing beneath the sheet...

Oliver realized with a start that he was staring. He turned away from the door, and his cheeks burned hot. He wasn't sure what had gotten into him. Maybe it was just the confusion from the sudden twist of last night's events.

A big stack of little slips of paper sat at the corner of a roll-top desk. Destined to become 'Alexandre the Great' notes. Oliver couldn't help but smile at that. He took the top slip, and the nearby fountain pen, and wrote a quick note:

Vincent,

I've gone home. Thank you for the hospitality. And for everything else.

Oliver

He left the note in the middle of the kitchen table, next to the burnt-out remains of the candle. He unlocked the apartment door, and slipped into the hall, closing the door carefully with a quiet click.

The morning air was already sultry, and the sun beat down hot even at this early hour. There were a few people out, all dressed up for church, and they gave him strange looks as he passed them. It was only after he reached his own building that he realized it was because he was wearing black clothing.

"Damn!" he muttered under his breath, angry at his own foolishness. Hopefully, no one thought too much of it.

Upstairs in his own apartment, he stripped off the dark clothing and tossed it into the hamper, cursing again that he had allowed himself to be seen in it in the daylight. He should have left at six AM, as soon as curfew lifted.

He wouldn't make that mistake again.

29

Monday, September 7

Apprehension tingled Oliver' spine when he showed up to work. All day yesterday, and all day today, he'd worried that someone from the band had been arrested after the meeting, and that his presence there had been mentioned to the police. He half expected to see the police in the club when he arrived at five o'clock, ready to question everyone.

All of the members of the band showed up, though, and no one acted as if anything were amiss. They tuned up and practiced on their own, as usual, scattered around the room.

Only Vincent seemed a little bit different—though that was subtle enough that Oliver supposed he was the only one who would notice. Vincent's eyes seemed to hold his a second or two longer, and those pale blue eyes always seemed to be smiling at him, even when the rest of the face wasn't. It was like a secret shared.

Oliver cautiously approached Patrice at the start of their first break. "You got away?" he whispered.

"Yes, of course," Patrice said with a nonchalant shrug.

"Was anyone caught?"

The little trumpet player looked back at him with an unreadable expression, and Oliver wondered what he was thinking. "A couple of men were arrested—but no one you would know. The police did them over pretty well, but they didn't crack. They had to let them go yesterday. It was only a curfew violation."

Oliver breathed a little easier. "But they'll be watching us, the police."

The little trumpet player shrugged again. "No one from the club was caught, so do not fear."

"May I come to your next meeting?" Oliver ventured to ask, but stopped himself from asking if Vincent could be included.

"Of course," the little trumpet player replied, giving Oliver a bemused look. "You are one of us now."

**

Saturday, September 12

"Tonight, one o'clock," Patrice whispered to Oliver when he passed him backstage after the show.

Oliver hurried to catch up to the little trumpet player. "Where?" he asked quietly. He couldn't imagine they'd risk meeting at the same place, not after the police were waiting for them last Saturday.

"The address is in your pocket," Patrice whispered, and walked another direction.

Oliver put his hand into his pants pocket and was surprised to feel a slip of paper there. He had no idea when Patrice would have slipped it in, but he knew enough not to take it out here, where anyone might see.

Oliver found Vincent waiting for him outside the back door. He raised his eyebrows in expectation. Oliver nodded. An excited smile cracked Vincent's expression. "Where?"

"I don't know yet," Oliver said. "Patrice gave me the address, but I haven't looked at it. It's at one o'clock."

"Come to my home first. Then we will go there together." Vincent touched the rim of his hat in silent salute, and impish grin on his lips, and turned toward his neighborhood.

**

Sunday, September 13

273

Oliver hurried home. He fretted a little bit about bringing Vincent to the meeting unannounced; but Patrice had brought him unannounced last week, and that had only been a problem to the sentry answering the door.

He changed into his black clothes as soon as he got home, waited a few minutes to calm his nerves, and then snuck out of the building. He crept through the streets toward Vincent's neighborhood. The moon was only a sliver tonight, even tinier than last week, and the sky was dark.

He reached Vincent's apartment at twelve-thirty. He knocked very quietly, worried about the concierge hearing; but then he worried he hadn't knocked loudly enough for Vincent to hear it. He was about to knock again a little louder, when the door opened, and Vincent motioned him in.

The room was lit only by a pair of candles on the table, and their competing flickers danced across the walls and ceiling. Two glasses of red wine sat beside the candles, and Vincent handed one to Oliver. "I assumed you might need to relax before we leave," he said, with the impish half-smile that was becoming familiar.

"Thank you," Oliver said, and took a long drink of the wine. It had an interesting spicy note to it, something he wasn't familiar with.

Vincent must have seen the surprised look on his face, and he chuckled. "Cinsaut—the biggest grape crop in Algeria, plus a bit of Grenache like what they use in the Rhône."

"You know wine?" Oliver asked, intrigued. He wouldn't have expected that kind of expertise from a musician.

Vincent's pale eyes clouded. "My ex-lover was a vintner," he said, and took a big swallow.

It took a couple of seconds for the implication to settle into Oliver's brain. A vintner, not a vintner's wife or daughter. He couldn't help the surprise.

Vincent must have noticed—he looked down, sheepish. "That bothers you?" It was barely voiced as a question.

"No," Oliver hurried to say, and took a step closer to Vincent to illustrate the point. "Not even a little bit." He wanted to explain that he himself had an ex-boyfriend, but the admission might lead to a conversation he wasn't comfortable having right now. He kept it to himself.

"I thought, perhaps, that it might not. But I couldn't be certain." Vincent was staring at him now, and Oliver looked away, embarrassed. His cheeks flushed hot, and he hadn't had enough wine for that.

"We should leave soon," he said, hurriedly, and fished the address out of his pocket.

Vincent came up behind him—Oliver was uncomfortably aware of the warmth of his proximity—and looked over Oliver's shoulder at the unfolded slip of paper. "That is nearby. Just two blocks from here. It will take five minutes to walk there. We have plenty of time. Let's sit, and finish the wine."

He sat on the couch, and Oliver took a seat at the opposite end.

"You were in the Resistance in Lyon, weren't you?" Vincent asked.

"Yes," Oliver said, but opted not to reveal anything else just yet.

"Were they after you?" Vincent looked concerned. "Is that why you had to come to Algiers?"

That was a question without easy answers. Oliver took a deep breath, considering how to answer it as minimally as possible without sounding evasive.

"No, I don't think they were after me," he said, with just enough hesitancy to seem like he was thinking it through and coming to a conclusion on the spot. "But the surveillance in Lyon is getting very heavy. Very dangerous. I have heard it is the same in Marseille. So, I came here." He shrugged, hoping it looked like a semi-casual decision.

"I have been to Marseille," Vincent said, brightening a little from the gloomy topic. "My family went there on vacation twice, in the twenties. My mother's parents were from Marseille and Toulon, respectively, and so we have a lot of family on the coast of Provence."

"Oh, yeah?" Oliver said, smiling a little. "I've been there a few times. It's an interesting city. Very beautiful there." He leaned toward Vincent a little, and added more quietly, "A lot of *résistants* in Marseille, I think. But, like I said, the surveillance there is getting bad; or so I hear."

Vincent looked thoughtful. "I do not know how my relatives there would feel about the regime," he said. "About Vichy. There are a lot of conservative people in Provence. I think that Marseille is a liberal city, overall, but it is still Provençal, no?"

"I know what you mean," Oliver said. "I found Lyon to be a very liberal city, a lot of quiet opposition to the Vichy regime—but there are always plenty of Pétainistes. The Riom trial made a big impact, and it shook a lot of people's faith in the old Marshal. But even so, there is still sympathy for him personally."

Vincent made a little grunt. "We heard little about that trial. There were rumors that it did not go well for the government—but who can say, really? The newspapers did not write much about it."

Oliver laughed. "They weren't allowed to." He hesitated, unsure how much to say. *Oh, what the hell.* He scooted closer to Vincent and leaned toward him. "The group I belonged to in Lyon, called Combat—it put out an opposition newspaper, several issues each week, using reports from American and British newspapers that were smuggled from Switzerland. It was distributed widely around the south of France, and its reports did not earn the regime any friends."

Vincent looked back at Oliver with undisguised admiration. "I wish that we had this in Algeria." He patted Oliver's knee. "I wish you had come to Algeria sooner, my friend."

Oliver ignored the flash of electricity that ran up his leg and spine. But his heart skipped a beat, nonetheless.

He glanced at his watch. "I think it's time to go." He downed the last of the wine in his glass.

**

Patrice was waiting for Oliver in the shadows of a plane tree beside the house bearing the address he'd given. When he stepped out to meet Oliver by the door, his eyes widened in surprise at the sight of Vincent Montagano walking behind Oliver.

"I recruited another," Oliver said, quietly, but with a chipper tone and smile.

Patrice's eyes remained wary, watching Vincent. "I did not realize that you were friends." There was an edge to his tone that Oliver found odd.

"Vincent wants to help the cause. He's been passing opposition notes all around the city. The ones signed 'Alexandre the Great.' I think he'll be a big help to the group and our mission."

A flicker of uncertainty crossed Patrice's eyes. He continued looking at Vincent with a strange expression that Oliver couldn't interpret. "I have seen them. They are very clever. But I do not think this is your kind of meeting." Then he looked at Oliver, and there was an odd note of hostility in his posture. "Are you the same sort, then?"

Oliver was taken aback. "Pardon?"

"Like him," he pointed his thumb at Vincent. "A faggot. We are not like that in this group, and we do not want that reputation."

Panic raced through Oliver. He took a step back, an involuntary reaction. The little trumpet player couldn't hurt him, but rationality had already fled into the night.

"No! My God! Of course not."

From the corner of his eye, he saw Vincent deflate. Oliver's stomach dropped, and his belly filled with shame.

Patrice was eyeing him closely, appraising him. Oliver swallowed and waited for some sort of reaction. Finally, Patrice snorted a sort of laugh, turned his back on Vincent, and put his hand on Oliver's shoulder, steering him toward the door. "Come, then. You are welcome here with us. That one must go."

Oliver looked back at Vincent, whose eyes seemed to plead with him not to leave him alone in the street. He stopped short of the door.

"I think that's a mistake. Vincent can be a help to the cause, and only a fool would ignore his potential contribution because of prejudice over something that doesn't matter." Seeing the flash of anger crossing Patrice's face, Oliver hurried to add, "Doesn't matter to the cause, that is."

Patrice gave him a withering look. "You don't understand the rules here. Maybe things are different in Paris, different in Lyon—but in Algiers, no one will take us seriously if they associate us with that sort. They will believe we are like that, too. It will undermine the cause."

Oliver put on his most condescending smirk—learned over years of living in Paris—crossed his arms, and looked down on the little trumpet player from his full height. "How will people know, if we don't say anything?"

Patrice puffed out his lips in that peculiarly French way, a nonverbalized "*Bof*." He looked at Vincent and scoffed. "We could all tell soon enough. How can we be the only ones?"

Oliver played his last card. He had hoped to hold onto this one until he'd gotten to know the group better, but it was the only hope for including Vincent.

"I have information about the Allied invasion," he announced, louder than he'd intended, and he almost cringed. Instead, he glared down at the little trumpet player like a disapproving parent. "If you don't include Vincent, I won't include you when the invasion comes, and you will be on the outside."

Patrice looked around, almost panicked. "Get inside, quickly." He grabbed them both by the arm, and tugged them into the doorway. He was stronger than he looked, Oliver mused.

**

They were a few minutes late, and the others inside the house had already begun the meeting when Patrice led Oliver and Vincent into the room. He clapped his hands for attention.

"Silence, please, compatriots! I have an important announcement." Patrice looked back at Oliver, and a cold sweat broke out on Oliver's back and forehead. "The American I brought last week, Mr. Carmichael, he is working for the Allies. He knows about the Allied invasion, and he wants to include us in the plans."

That was hardly how Oliver wanted to introduce the idea, but the cat was out of the bag now. All eyes were on him, electric with excitement.

"First, let me say that I don't know exactly when, or exactly where, the Allied invasion will be. I won't be told specific details until just before it happens. I am in Algeria to prepare the local Resistance, so that French Resistance fighters can support the Allied forces when they arrive."

A chorus of questions arose, and it was almost impossible to pick out what anyone was saying in the din. He looked over at Patrice, who stood against the wall, ankles crossed and hands in his pockets, looking quite proud of himself. *He'll get all the credit for bringing me to them.*

He looked back at Vincent. His friend's pale blue eyes twinkled, and a crooked smile pulled up one side of his mouth, bringing the dimple to his cheek right at the line of his beard.

My friend. Yes, he supposed Vincent was his friend. He had saved him from the police last week, at risk to himself. He'd put him up for the night to keep him safe, given him his couch, and he didn't have to do that, either.

**

Once the chaos had simmered down, Patrice led the discussion of how to prepare for the arrival of the Allied invasion.

"My cousin is in the Foreign Legion, stationed at Lake Tchad, in the Sahara. Their garrison has declared their loyalty to General de Gaulle. All of the troops in the Central Africa colonies are Free French, not taking orders from Vichy."

"But they could not come to Algeria without passing through the West Africa colonies," one of the others pointed out. "Those garrisons still report to Vichy, I think."

Patrice shrugged. "They could be turned, especially if General de Gaulle lands in Algeria."

Oliver held up his hands. "Whoa, whoa. First, I don't know if General de Gaulle himself will come to Algeria. I believe that Free French troops will be part of the invasion, but I cannot say who will lead them."

Several looks of disappointment greeted Oliver's words, but Patrice shrugged nonchalantly. "Still, if Free French troops come into Algeria from the sea, and we attack the Vichy garrisons from the rear—would it not also be good for Free French troops from Central Africa to attack Vichy garrisons in West Africa?"

That was military strategy, and it was beyond Oliver's abilities. But he didn't want to seem weak or ineffectual, so he just nodded.

He did wonder about Patrice's communications with his cousin in a Free French garrison in the Sahara, though. He'd have to ask Patrice about that sometime. Privately.

**

After the meeting, Oliver said goodnight to Vincent on the way out the door and held back for Patrice. He ignored the strange look that momentarily crossed his friend's eyes.

Patrice was one of the last to leave, and Oliver asked him if they could go somewhere private to talk. Patrice nodded for Oliver to follow him down the street, and then he slipped into an alley. There were no windows over this alley, and it was nearly pitch black, the buildings on either side blocking out the little moonlight.

"How do you communicate with your cousin? The one in the Foreign Legion at Lake Tchad."

"It is not often," Patrice said, blasé about the whole thing. "He wrote to me more than a year ago, asking me to come to Lake Tchad and enlist in the Legion. I wrote back that I did not want to commit to the Legion—but that did not mean that I was not committed to France and her ideals. I knew that would be enough clue for him to understand, he is a smart fellow."

"And you think he deduced that you belong to the Resistance?"

"Yes, of course," Patrice said. "We are careful what we write in letters, since they will go through the Post and be inspected—but we can both read between the lines. And lately, he has sent me messages through other channels."

That got Oliver's heart racing. "What other channels?"

Patrice was quiet for a few seconds, and Oliver wished he could see the little trumpet player's expression.

"How do you get your information about the Allied invasion?" Patrice asked.

So that's how it's going to be. Tit for tat. Oliver wasn't about to give any names, though. "I have someone at the American consulate."

Patrice grunted. "That much is obvious. If you won't tell me more, then why should I tell you how my cousin in the Legion gets information to me?"

It was a fair point, but it still aggravated Oliver. His reply was a little testy. "I can't tell you the person's name, or how they get the information. I don't know the latter, and I won't betray the former, no matter how hard you try."

To his surprise, Patrice chuckled, and then he patted Oliver's arm. "That is good. You are better at this than I thought an American would be. You learn fast, no?"

"Yes." *Because we have to.*

"Alright, then," Patrice said. "The concierge of my building has a servant man, an Arab who speaks good French, and he came to me a few weeks ago with a message hidden inside a book that he said he would loan to me because I would like it. It was from my cousin. I asked the man where he got this message, and he said only that he knows a man in the caravan. I asked if I could send a message back that way, and he said 'Of course, but it will cost you fifty francs.' Fifty francs does not seem like too much, so I agreed."

About ten dollars. A sizable sum, but Oliver supposed that was more than reasonable, considering it would be split amongst at least two couriers, and possibly more.

"Do not tell them about the Allied invasion," Oliver said. "Secrecy is of the utmost importance for that. If word of it gets to the wrong people, it will endanger the operations, and possibly cost thousands of lives. You *must* keep it to yourself, Patrice. But perhaps you could ask him what his garrison would do if the Free French tried to wrest the remaining African colonies from Vichy."

Patrice clasped Oliver's arm firmly, an unexpected move in the dark that startled him. "Yes, I will be glad to do that."

"Good, thank you. Mention only the Free French, and do not use the word invasion—is that clear?"

"Absolutely," Patrice said, and his tone was resolute. Oliver could imagine the firm nod his head must have made.

"How long does it take for a message to get to him?"

He heard Patrice exhale. "A long time. It is twenty-five hundred kilometers, across the desert. For much of it, there are no roads, and the Berbers still lead trains of camels."

About fifteen hundred miles, Oliver calculated. Even if there were roads the entire way, it would still take a car or truck two full days of travel to traverse. He couldn't begin to guess how long it would take camels.

"But it's not done by camel the entire way, is it?"

Patrice laughed. "No, not anymore. They take a caravan of trucks to the Salah oasis, about nine hundred and seventy kilometers."

About six hundred miles—so ten or twelve hours, Oliver calculated quickly.

"From Salah, they must proceed by camel, and they cross the desert for eleven hundred kilometers, until they reach Agadès. From Agadès, there are roads, and a caravan of trucks can reach Lake Tchad in less than a day."

That was a lot of detail, that didn't solve Oliver's problem of how long it would take. He sighed in frustration. "I think that is probably too slow to be practical for us."

"Do not dismiss the Free French garrisons in the colonies," Patrice said. "General de Gaulle sends them information regularly, by ship from England. If he needs for them to move west into the Niger while he invades Algeria, they will know it. And they have airplanes that can cross the Sahara in a day, but they will only use them if they must."

Comprehension dawned on Oliver. "But if they move west into the Niger valley, and they expect forces loyal to de Gaulle are invading Algeria, then they might send word by airplane. Is that it?"

"Exactly. Coordination with them may be possible, my friend."

Oliver wasn't entirely convinced of it, but this gave him some ideas. "When the invasion comes—and I don't know when that will be—we will need as many men as possible to keep Vichy's forces occupied inside the city. But we will also need to keep reinforcements from coming into Algiers, and that is where you can help us, Patrice."

"I am ready," Patrice declared, and Oliver heard the thud of him smacking his chest. "Tell me what you want me to do, my captain."

30

Monday, September 14

Oliver walked into the American consulate at eleven o'clock in the morning and asked to see Robert Murphy. The Arab receptionist asked him his name, and when he provided it, he saw the spark of recognition in her dark eyes.

"Yes, you are expected, Mr. Carmichael," she said in an accent that was an interesting blend of Arabic and French. "Mr. Murphy is not in, but someone will see you very soon. Please take a seat."

And she wasn't kidding. He'd barely had time to relax in the lobby chair before a man about his age, in an expensive blue suit, came hurrying down the stairs.

"Mr. Carmichael? I'm Jack Archer. I work with Mr. Murphy. I know he was expecting you, but he asked me to meet with you in his stead if he happened to be away. Which in fact he is. He's a very busy man, Mr. Murphy, and he's away quite a lot, I'm afraid. Won't you come with me, please?" He motioned toward the stairs, oozing friendliness, and Oliver followed him to the next floor.

He ushered Oliver into a small office that was overcrowded with a desk, two chairs, and a filing cabinet. The latter seemed to have exploded all over the room, judging by the minimum of free space on top of Archer's desk.

Archer's diction was crisp and precise, probably Ivy League. That also jived with the expensive suit he wore, and the silk handkerchief in the pocket—and so the untidiness of the office came as a shock.

"How much do you know about the project I'm working on for Mr. Murphy?" Oliver asked when Archer directed him to the chair in front of the desk.

"Oh, don't worry—it's all on a need-to-know basis."

Oliver frowned. "That didn't answer my question."

The friendly smile on Archer's face wavered. "No, I suppose it didn't. You're right to be cautious. But I assure you I have clearance to discuss the matter with you, and to take updates from you on Mr. Murphy's behalf."

"And I'm sure you have documentation of this?" Oliver said, arching an eyebrow. He hoped he wasn't pushing it too hard, but Archer just responded with a smile that didn't reach his eyes.

"Of course." He opened a drawer, fished out a manila folder, and took a piece of paper on U.S. State Department letterhead and handed it to Oliver. "Well done, by the way, insisting on my bona fides. I can see why Frank Dryden recommended you."

The letter was brief and to the point, but Oliver read through it anyway. It gave him a moment to breathe. It was from Robert Daniel Murphy, special envoy of the Coordinator of Information, deputizing Mr. Jonathan Fitzhugh Archer, United States Department of State, into the OSS, and authorizing all agents of Operation Torch to speak with Mr. Archer in his absence.

"All in order, then?" Archer asked with a wry smile when Oliver handed the letter back to him.

Oliver only nodded.

"Well, then—what news do you have for us?"

"I've made contact with a Resistance cell in Algiers, about two dozen men. They are prepared to assist the Allies in whatever way we ask."

"Excellent news," Archer said. "And you believe they are reliable?"

Oliver nodded. "Yes, I do. They've been laboring in isolation for two years, trying to undermine local support for the Vichy regime. Among the settlers, that is."

"Of course," Archer said. "I don't think we have to worry about the natives lifting a finger to help Vichy. This is a fight among the French."

Oliver didn't respond to that. He supposed it was true, but something about it rubbed him the wrong way. Too dismissive.

"What stores do they have, these resistors?" Archer asked. At Oliver's questioning look, he elaborated. "Weapons. Do they have stores of weapons in the ready?"

"I don't know yet," Oliver said. He should have known to ask that, though he assumed the way they'd spoken of fighting from the rear that they did.

"Have you made any promises to these men?"

This surprised Oliver. "Promises? No, no promises. Why?"

Archer gave him a disarming smile and spread his hands wide. "Of course we'll show our appreciation to those who stand with us when this is all said and done. But none of us are authorized to make any specific promises on behalf of the United States government. We wouldn't want to promise anything we couldn't deliver, would we?"

"No, we wouldn't," Oliver said, cautiously. It was a reasonable enough statement, but there was still something about it that didn't sit well. He couldn't put his finger on it, though.

Oliver decided he didn't like Jack Archer very much.

"Oh, before I forget," Archer said, and opened another drawer, withdrawing an envelope and handing it across to Oliver. "This came for you in the diplomatic pouch from Vichy a few days ago."

The envelope was printed with "The Office of Frank Dryden" in the upper left corner, and it bore his name in Dryden's handwriting. It was also stamped "CONFIDENTIAL" in red ink.

Oliver slipped it into his jacket.

"Is there anything else you'd like Mr. Murphy to know?" Archer asked, the pseudo-friendly smile plastered on his face.

Something told him not to reveal Patrice's contacts in the French Foreign Legion. Not until he could speak with Mr. Murphy directly. "No, I think that's everything." Oliver rose from the chair.

"Let me show you out," Archer said, and accompanied him downstairs. "If there's anything you need while you're here in the field, you can send me a message. Unlike Mr. Murphy, I'm here at the consulate every day."

"In other words, you're my handler now?" Oliver asked, quietly since other consulate staff were moving around the building.

"Not officially, no," Archer said. "That would still be Robert Murphy. But I'm his right-hand man here. And as I said, he's often out."

"Understood," Oliver said as they reached the bottom of the stairs. He shook Archer's hand and said goodbye, then walked out without looking back.

On his way home, Oliver stopped in the Jardin d'Essais, the sprawling public park overlooking the port. He strode down the central promenade, between towering palm trees and thick stands of cypress, and took one of the side paths through the woods, where there were fewer people, toward a pond. Tropical trees of varieties he couldn't identify grew out of the water along the edges of the pond, some sending down shoots like a Florida mangrove. He found a bench in the shade of a cypress tree and sat.

He removed the envelope from inside his jacket and tore it open. It was dated last Wednesday.

September 9, 1942

Dear Oliver,

I've been to your club recently, and met with Lisette and Mr. Hansen. You'll be happy to know that everything here is proceeding as before. You needn't worry about Lisette or your friends, all are quite well.

Mr. Hansen has a source within the SOL, of which I was not aware. However, through this source we have learned that you may have been followed to Marseille. From there, it is possible that they learned of your destination. Be watchful. The SOL has not had a presence in Algeria to now, but they have been expanding throughout the Unoccupied Zone, so we cannot say they won't continue to reach new territories.

Cécile sends her best wishes. And you always have mine.

Yours,

Frank Dryden.

Oliver folded the letter and put it back in the envelope before slipping it back inside his jacket. This was unexpected, and unwelcome news. *As if the police weren't enough to worry about.* "Damn!"

**

Patrice sat in the warm water of the bathtub, enjoying the ministrations of Madame Astruc's sponge. For three years, he'd spent his Sundays and Mondays at the widow Astruc's townhouse in the old Jewish Quarter, happily being her plaything. But this weekend, he'd been on edge, and she could sense it. When he needed to get cleaned up for work that evening, she had suggested giving him a bath. How could he refuse such an offer?

"You are still so tense, my dear," she said, dropping the sponge down his front, and kneading his wet shoulders with her fingers.

"That feels wonderful," he moaned. Her fingers were quite strong for a woman her age—she never said what that was exactly, but he knew she had children older than he, and so he guessed her to be mid-fifties. And yet, after a few seconds of enjoyment, his worries came right back to the front of his mind.

"Hmmm," she murmured, a note of doubt in it. She reached between his legs to retrieve the sponge, and in the process brushed her fingers against his scrotum. He smiled, doubting it was accidental.

She began to move the sponge slowly up and down the inside of his thigh, an incredibly erotic feeling; then quickly across his genitals—a tease—and down the inside of the opposite thigh, before coming back up again and slowly rubbing across his penis. It sprang to attention.

"I will not let you leave here so tense," she murmured in his ear, and nibbled on the lobe with her lips. Her hand wrapped around him and the sponge simultaneously and moved them up and down in the soapy water.

It didn't take long, and then he stood up from the water, his smooth body covered in soap bubbles, and grabbed the big luxurious towel she had folded on the stand next to the tub.

"Allow me, my dear," the widow Astruc said, and rubbed the soapy water from his skin in a languid motion.

Her ministrations were enjoyable, as ever, and yet his mind was still preoccupied.

"What has you so worried, my dear?" she asked, and he broke from his reverie to see her staring into his eyes. Her face was careworn, but kind, and he could hardly resist such a sincere and caring inquiry.

He took her hands in his and stared back into her eyes. "I worry for you, darling. Vichy is coming for the Jews, everyone knows it.

They took away your citizenship, so they can do anything they please to you from now on."

A sad sort of smile creased her face, and she placed the palm of her hand against his cheek. He leaned into it.

"My sweet boy, you need not worry about me. I have plenty of money to keep up the bribes for years to come. They have always worked so far, as I am unmolested in my home, and in the market. Others from the synagogue have not been so lucky—many have been harassed in the streets, in stores, even in their own businesses. But the police look out for me when my driver takes me out. They do not want to risk the steady income I provide them."

Patrice shook his head. "There were many wealthy Jews in Germany who thought they could always bribe their way to safety. It ended."

Her dark eyes clouded, and she looked away.

He reached for her hand. "I am sorry, darling. I do not mean to upset you."

"It is not your fault," she said, almost absently, and patted his bare, damp chest as she turned away. She took a seat at the vanity, appearing lost in thought.

He wrapped the towel around his waist and stepped out of the tub. He hurried across the room and knelt in front of her. "I promise you, darling, that I will do everything in *my* power to stop the fascist thugs. But there is only so much that can be done—and that is what has worried me these last days."

To his surprise, that didn't seem to affect her. She looked indecisive, staring at her wrinkled hands in her lap, playing with the long fingernail on her thumb. "Would it shock you to learn that I have also contributed much money to buy illegal weapons for Jews who have organized underground?"

It did, slightly, though not in the way she thought. "Shock? No. Only surprise. *Pleasant* surprise."

She looked at him, head cocked in curiosity. "You are pleased, then." It was not a question.

He grinned, relief washing through him like a wave on the beach. "Since we are sharing secrets, I have also organized underground—though there are no Jews in our little group." He hesitated a second before adding, "And our group is making plans for the imminent overthrow of the Fascists who govern Algeria in the name of Vichy. But we need others—many, many others."

She put her palm against his cheek again and beamed at him. "It is as if God has sent me an angel."

He grinned back at her, his pulse quickening. "We are a good team, you and I. We should join forces."

She looked away in thought for a couple of seconds, and then smiled back at him. "Next Saturday morning, you will go with me to the synagogue. I want to introduce you to some men there."

31

Tuesday, September 15

Oliver hesitated outside of his building door that morning when he left to pick up his daily croissant from the bakery down the street. He'd slept poorly, worried by what Frank Dryden had written; and what sleep he did get was punctuated by dreams of a sinister villain in a black cape following him through his neighborhood. It was ridiculous, of course, but he'd awoken deeply shaken.

Just act natural, damn it. And what could be more natural than a morning routine, going to the bakery and fetching his breakfast roll and ersatz coffee?

But the thought of someone following him through his usual routine felt like a bigger violation than if they followed him doing something unusual. He wanted to explore more of Algiers, so why not do that now? What could be more natural than a newcomer to the city exploring its ancient byways? Today seemed as good a day as any to check out the Casbah.

He turned west and descended the slope from his neighborhood into the fashionable *Quartier Belcourt*, south of the port. The sidewalks here were crowded with white businessmen in expensive European suits scurrying between offices in modern buildings of concrete and glass.

The Jardin d'Essais appeared on his right, stretching toward the port, and he paused on the Avenue Belcourt to get his bearings. Behind the buildings opposite the park rose wooded hills, and a sign in French identified it as the Bois des Arcades. Another sign pointed down the avenue toward the northwest, indicating the Port of Algiers was a kilometer that direction, and the University of Algiers was two kilometers. He saw nothing indicating where to find the Casbah.

A bus stopped a short distance away, and several young men and women descended the steps; secretaries and clerical workers, he surmised from their outfits—clean and crisp, but not fancy. He raised his hand as they passed and got the attention of a couple of them.

"Where would I find the Casbah?"

A young woman in a navy-blue dress with a white lace collar frowned, and glanced at the young man in a white shirt and black necktie who had stopped behind her.

"I don't know why you'd want to go there, sir," the young man said, looking bemused.

"I've never seen it," Oliver said. He noticed the young woman had hurried off, disinterested.

"You're going there alone?" the young man said, frowning.

Oliver shrugged. "Why not?"

The young man pointed northwest around the bend in the avenue. "It is that way, perhaps three kilometers. Somewhere on the other side of the university." And then he scurried off, in a hurry to get to some office nearby.

Oliver hailed a taxi, and ignored the way the driver stiffened when he asked to be taken to the Casbah.

"I will take you as far as the Port Square, sir," he said in a harsh and twangy sort of working-class accent. Looking at Oliver through the rear-view mirror, he added, "That is where most of the black-market traders are located, if that is what you seek." He hit the gas hard and swerved into traffic.

The avenue followed the port around the curve of the Bay of Algiers, first northwest, and then veering north. The traffic thinned somewhat after they passed the University on the left, and was now mostly trucks leaving the port and going south toward the city center.

The taxi jolted to a halt in front of a small square filled with tall palm trees. On the opposite side of the street to their right, the wharves were smaller and closer together than other sections of the port that lay nearer to the city center, and the freighters docked here were old and rusty. Sailors of every size, shape, and nationality roamed around in filthy clothing, faces and arms covered in grit and oil.

The taxi driver quoted the fare, and Oliver counted out the coins. As he opened the door to exit, the driver said to him, "Most of the merchants around the square are connected to the black market, so you will not have to search long for what you want. For an extra twenty-five francs, I can wait here until you are finished, and I will see nothing."

It was a tempting offer, Oliver thought, looking around in trepidation at the rough-looking men meandering between the port and the square. But no, he had come to see the old Arab citadel, and he'd be damned if he'd let irrational fear keep him from that. He thanked the driver and declined.

At first glance, the white-walled buildings encircling the square on three sides didn't look much different from the rest of Algiers, though perhaps a bit shabbier; but the ground floor entrances were all a series of tall arches. He stood in the middle of the parklike square for a minute to get his bearings.

Besides the sailors, obvious by their manner and attire, there were also plenty of Arab men in loose-fitting clothing and fez caps, and some Arab women in veils and long robes moving around the perimeter of the square. A few moments observation told Oliver that most of them were entering the square from the northwest corner. He headed that direction.

The street here was narrower than the streets in the European section of the city, and was lined with large awnings of every color imaginable. Shopkeepers set up their wares along the side of the street under their awnings, and shouted overtures in Arabic at passersby, lending the whole place a bazaar-like quality.

Most of the vendors glanced past him, concentrating on their own people; a few frowned when they noticed him, and then looked away. But a couple of them shouted at him in halting, deeply accented French.

"Hey, sir, you interest in cheap cigarettes? Very good price, only five francs for pack."

Oliver had to smile at that. He didn't smoke and even he knew that five francs—about a dollar—was way too expensive for a pack of cigarettes. He knew he was supposed to counter with an offer of one franc, and then barter from there, but he just waved his hand and shook his head, continuing down the narrow street.

A Moorish mosque came into view at the end of the street, with tall key-hole shaped arches through an outer wall decorated with squares of color in alternating russet reds, yellows, and sandy browns, supported by Roman-looking columns. Beyond the key-hole shaped arches were smaller, pointed arches of an inner wall leading inside, surrounded by bands of red and yellow.

As he drew closer to the mosque, a familiar but almost-forgotten smell assaulted his nostrils, and he almost stopped in his tracks.

Coffee! Real coffee!

His nose led him to a little coffee shop around the corner, with large open windows along the street, and—he soon discovered—also in the back leading to a courtyard garden. Four ceiling fans rotated on moving bands of leather, and his eyes followed these through a series of pullies that lead to a fountain beside the backdoor that turned a wheel.

Eight small tables filled the little room. Only two of them were occupied—one by a trio of old men around a water pipe, with cups of coffee, who stopped their conversation the moment Oliver entered; and the other by a lone man in a western-style linen suit, eating an artichoke by dipping its leaves in a plate of olive oil and black pepper, a newspaper on the table beside him, who paid no attention to Oliver.

The thin Arab man with a scraggly beard behind the counter stared at Oliver for several seconds after he came in, and Oliver asked in French if he could sit and have a cup of coffee.

After a few more seconds of staring, the man nodded and motioned to a table in the middle of the room without a word. Oliver wondered if perhaps the man could understand a little French but couldn't really speak it.

The wall above the windows was decorated in an elaborate geometrical pattern of yellow, indigo, pale blue, and the occasional green tile. An entirely different geometric pattern of bronze overlaid on the wall behind the counter.

The thin man from behind the counter brought him a steaming cup of coffee, and the smell was so intoxicating that Oliver couldn't help but grin as it was set before him. He blew across it for several seconds before venturing a sip. It was still too hot, but he hardly cared—the flavor was so rich he closed his eyes and savored it for a second before swallowing.

He hadn't had real coffee in two years, and he couldn't believe how luxurious it seemed.

The man returned and set a bowl of olives and a bowl of dates in front of Oliver, then bowed and backed away. Oliver thanked him in French, and the man nodded in silence.

Another Arab man came out from a door behind the counter, and the thin man nodded toward Oliver. The second man, who was broader and barrel-chested, wearing a plain linen tunic over baggy pantaloons, approached Oliver's table and stood quite close to him.

"Welcome, sir," he said in heavily accented French. "What brings you to our establishment today?"

"The smell of your coffee." Oliver raised his cup in silent toast. "It is quite good."

The man nodded in acknowledgement, and continued in a quiet voice. "And what else might we interest you in, sir?"

"This is exactly what I came for, thank you," Oliver said, hoping it wasn't too disappointing to them that he hadn't ordered more food. He wasn't sure of the etiquette here.

A strange look crossed the man's eyes, and Oliver worried that he'd offended him somehow. But he nodded and bowed, and took a couple of steps back. "Thank you, sir. Enjoy the coffee."

After he'd walked away, Oliver ate a couple of olives, and put the pits back in the bowl. He looked out at the lush greenery of the courtyard. *What a lucky discovery.*

"He thought you were here for the black market," a man said in excellent French with only a slight Arabic accent, and Oliver looked at the man in the linen suit, the one who was eating the artichoke. The man gave him an apologetic half-smile. "Forgive me, I am Doctor Khalil Hassan. I come here often, as it reminds me of my youth. You must forgive Hakim his assumption—most white men who come here are looking for something on the black market. Things that they cannot find elsewhere."

Oliver caught his drift. "I wasn't aware of that," he said, letting his voice trail off in such a way that he hoped conveyed possible interest. Perhaps that would get Dr. Hassan to elaborate.

Hassan cast him a curious glance. "Please forgive my impudence—but your accent, I cannot place it. You are not French, certainly, nor are you Spanish or Italian. May I ask where you are from, sir?"

Oliver smiled at Hassan's *politesse* before he could help himself, but quickly remembered that smiling at a stranger was not considered polite. "I am American," he said, resuming a serious expression and tone. "My name is Oliver Carmichael."

"I am pleased to make your acquaintance, Mr. Carmichael," Hassan said with a nod. Then he rattled off a string of Arabic to the thin man behind the counter. Turning back to Oliver, he said in French, "Mustafa will bring you more coffee, as my gift."

Oliver almost said that it wasn't necessary—but curbed his Midwestern manners in time and just nodded and thanked Hassan.

"While we wait for Mustafa to bring the coffee, I will show you the courtyard."

Oliver followed Hassan through an open portal in the plaster wall, and his eye was caught by a chipped stone column on one side. It looked Greco-Roman, with part of a face visible at the jagged top where it met the plaster, and out-of-place in the Moorish architecture all around.

"Yes, that column is from the Roman period," Hassan said, noticing Oliver's gaze. "The Casbah is built on the ruins of the Roman town, Icosium. There are columns like that one, and pieces of walls, all over the Casbah. The people built their houses around the old ruins, incorporating them. The Romans themselves built part of their town on the ruins of the Phoenician colony, Ikosim—its name meant 'twenty,' because that was the number of Phoenician men who founded the colony. They took wives from the local Berber tribes, and that was the origin of the Moorish people."

Hassan paused to light a self-rolled cigarette, and Oliver took the moment to look around the courtyard. It was small, centered around a fountain that took up half of the space, with lush palm shrubs all around.

"You are an American, so I can only assume that you are here to buy guns for the Resistance," Hassan said, so matter-of-factly that it startled Oliver. He chuckled at Oliver's obvious surprise. "That is the only reason someone like you would come to the Casbah, Mr. Carmichael. But do not worry—I am sympathetic to your cause."

Oliver took a moment to contemplate this. "How can you help us?"

32

Sunday, September 20

"I have made contact with other résistants who are arming themselves with guns smuggled from Spain," Patrice announced as soon as the meeting began at one AM. "They are a much larger group than our own. I propose an alliance."

Excited murmurs filled the room, but Oliver's stomach fluttered and dropped. *He* was supposed to help the resistance organize against Vichy's administration in Algeria. *He* was supposed to help them find arms. He scolded himself for the reaction, but couldn't help feeling that Patrice has stolen his thunder.

"How much larger?" one of the men asked.

"They have two hundred men," Patrice continued, his chest puffing up noticeably at the murmurs of appreciation that swept the group. "And they are on the opposite side of the city, between the university and the Casbah—so between us, we can surround the regime's headquarters when the time comes."

"Isn't that the Jewish Quarter?" another man asked, tone pointed, eyes narrowing. Oliver couldn't remember his name, but he had the gravelly voice of a long-time smoker.

"Yes," Patrice replied, staring back at the questioner. "It is a Jewish group, based out of the Great Synagogue. I spoke with its leaders this morning. They are eager to replace the Vichy administrators in this city with others who are sympathetic with the Free French. It makes sense that we should work together toward our common goal, so that we are not working at cross purposes."

"If we ally ourselves with *Jews*,"—the questioner's expression of distaste at even saying the word spoke volumes—"won't that harm our recruitment of real Frenchmen to the cause?"

A couple of the men expressed agreement, and Oliver shook his head in disbelief. That earned a glare from the original questioner.

"If every man here recruited another to the cause, we would still be fewer than forty-five men," Patrice said, squaring his shoulders. "If our recruitment worked beyond our biggest dreams, and every man here brought in three more, we would still be smaller than the Jewish resistance group I have met with. We would be foolish not to ally ourselves with them."

Oliver raised his arm. "And this way, we can tell potential recruits that we are more than two hundred strong. That strength in numbers will recruit more to our cause." *No one wants to join a suicide mission.*

The questioner glared at him again. He raised his voice to address the group, while keeping his eyes locked on Oliver's. "What does an *American* know of how to recruit the French?"

Oliver stiffened. "I have lived in France for seven years. I know the French."

"Enough foolishness!" Vincent's sharp tone startled Oliver. "We French will not win the war acting on our own. As a nation we must work with our allies against the Boche and their puppets at Vichy. Patrice has found us allies here in Algiers, and we must work with them or we are lost."

"Let us vote," Patrice said. "All in favor—"

"One moment, please, Patrice," Oliver said, holding up his hand again. "Can we vote to ally with the Jewish group, but not to merge our operations? You see, I also have news, which may affect the relationship." He described his discussion with Dr. Hassan on Tuesday. "We can use their guns to arm ourselves, as long as we are still our own operation."

"The Arabs will not sell guns to *Jews*," the questioner interjected.

"That is precisely why I propose an alliance, but not a merger," Oliver said, not hiding his irritation.

"A *secret* alliance," someone else said, and this was greeted with a chorus of agreement.

"It is *all* secret," Patrice said, scowling. "Very well. Let us vote. All in favor of an alliance with the Jewish resistance group at the Great Synagogue, raise your voice."

The room echoed with enthusiastic "Yes!"

A hint of smile stretched Patrice's lips. "All opposed to the alliance, raise your voice."

Three men shouted "No!"

Patrice's thin smile stretched wider. "The alliance is approved. I will work with them to coordinate our operations. And I propose that Oliver work with the Arabs to bring us guns for our own work. Let us vote."

That proposal passed unanimously, though Oliver couldn't help but notice that the original questioner sat in stony silence, neither voting for nor against. He stood a moment later and stormed out of the room. A door slam announced his departure from the building.

"We must keep a watch on Marchand," Patrice said. "He must not be allowed to go to the authorities."

**

Monday, September 21

Police Headquarters, central Algiers

The intercom buzzed on Matous's desk.

"There's an informant on the line with credible information about a resistance group in Kouba," his assistant's voice crackled. "You should speak with this one, sir."

Matous looked up at the map of Algiers he'd tacked to the wall beside his desk. He hadn't had time yet to memorize all of the districts of this God-awful city. He found Kouba just to the southeast of the city center. Only four kilometers from where he sat.

"Put him through." The receiver rang, and Matous's hand shot out to pick up the receiver. "This is Matous. What information do you have?"

"I know a group of résistants in Kouba, about two dozen men, who are conspiring with Jews—hundreds of them—to overthrow the authorities in Algiers and support De Gaulle."

Matous's lips tightened. "How do you know this? Are you part of the group?"

"They think I am," the gravelly voice replied. "I am leaving the group. I want no part in their treason. And I do not want to defile myself with Jews."

"That is a wise choice," Matous said. "Where does this group meet, and when?"

There was a brief pause on the line. "That is valuable information, is it not, sir?"

Matous knew where this was leading. "What do you want for the information?"

"Information that stops a treasonous uprising must be worth at least five thousand francs."

Matous scowled. "That is out of the question."

"How badly do you want to protect the government from traitors, sir? They are armed, you see."

Matous exhaled hard through the nose. Five thousand francs was an outrageous sum—but in the end, this informant had them over a barrel. If the information proved reliable, of course.

"We are prepared to pay you five hundred francs upon receipt of the information; plus two thousand if it prevents an uprising."

A bark of a laugh sounded over the line, hurting Matous's ear. "One thousand francs up front, plus four thousand more when you see that I'm telling the truth."

"We will pay no more than five hundred before we have verified your information, sir," Matous said through gritted teeth. "But we will pay you the rest of the five thousand if it proves decisive at stopping a credible uprising. Those are the terms."

The line was silent for several seconds. Finally, the gravelly voice replied, "We have an agreement. Meet me at the Café Etoile on Rue Garidi in thirty minutes. I am the one with the yellow ruffled shirt. Bring the five hundred francs with you."

Matous took a gamble. "Tell me something now, something useful in good faith, or I will not meet you."

The voice on the other end grunted, but relented sooner than Matous expected. "One of the conspirators is an American, who has promised the group support from the Allies if they overthrow the authorities here."

**

Matous got to the Café Etoile ten minutes early. After first stepping inside to see if the man in the yellow shirt was already there, he pretended to change his mind with an apologetic shrug to the waiter and went back outside.

He'd brought a newspaper, and stood at the corner and opened it, keeping his eye on the café door.

Fifteen minutes passed. Matous folded the newspaper and walked down the sidewalk, past the café—with a quick glance inside to be sure the man in the yellow shirt hadn't entered some other way—to the end of the block. No sign of him anywhere.

In Matous's experience, someone expecting to receive five hundred francs would not be late.

He picked up his pace and looped around the block to the entrance of a narrow alley that ran behind the row of buildings that included the café.

A man lay sprawled face down in the alley midway down the block, wearing black pants and a yellow shirt. A pool of blood was spreading from his body, and a hint of ruffles was visible at the man's throat.

Four men with their backs to Matous exited the far end of the alley and turned onto the sidewalk beyond.

A police gendarme would have shouted for them to stop, but that would only ensure they would begin to run. And with quite a head start already, Matous would never catch them. No, he was much smarter than a simple gendarme, and he waited a second for them to disappear around the corner—having not seen him, he was certain—and then he sprinted after them.

He reached the end of the alley and looked down the sidewalk in the direction the men had gone. They'd disappeared.

He hurried down the street, looking in every storefront he passed. He grew frantic after the first dozen lacked anyone resembling the men he'd seen. He hadn't gotten a good look at them, since they were some distance away with their backs to him, but he was certain he'd recognize them if he spotted them.

Three of them were of medium height and build, with dark hair. Not easy to put such a description on an alert and expect to get results. But the fourth one was shorter, and slighter of build, with lighter brown hair. Not much more specific, but it could possibly yield a lead.

Even as Matous thought it, he knew it was unlikely. He cursed under his breath and stormed back toward his office.

CONFIDENTIAL

21 September 1942
Algiers

To Lt. Joseph Darnand:

Honorable sir,

My mission in Algeria has borne fruit. We know that an American diplomat has been cozying up to military commanders in Algeria and Morocco, with the goal of obtaining promises of cooperation for Allied maneuvers in the Mediterranean. We have no details about these maneuvers.

While we can take no action against the diplomat, my office has made plain to the French officers involved that the State is watching. I am confident our forces will remain true to the mission of the French State, as illuminated by Marshall Pétain, to pursue collaboration with Germany, and they will not be wooed by the Allies.

More recently I have obtained information that there is also at least one American in Algiers with unofficial cover who is working with local résistants, encouraging and aiding their treason against the French State. I will bring the full force of my office to bear in identifying this treacherous American, and he will be eliminated by any means necessary.

I remained respectfully yours,

Gilles Matous

33

Friday, October 23

Oliver was ushered upstairs to Robert Murphy's office the moment he gave his name to the Arab receptionist at the American consulate. The red-haired middle-aged diplomat-cum-spy master was seated at his desk, talking to Jack Archer seated opposite him. The conversation stopped the second Oliver appeared at the door, and both men shot up from their chairs.

"Mr. Carmichael, have a seat," Murphy said, brusque as usual, motioning stiffly toward a second chair next to Archer.

Oliver sat without a word and waited to be told what this was about. He'd been summoned that morning when an American courier brought him a note at his apartment, telling him to come to the consulate in an hour. Why the rush? Whatever the reason, it made butterflies tumble in his stomach the moment he arrived.

"This is all highly classified, so neither of you may repeat anything said here today. To *anyone*. Is that understood?" Murphy's eyes narrowed into a stern expression, like a father warning a teenage boy about to take his daughter out to the movies.

"Yes, sir," Oliver said. Archer nodded without a word.

"I had a meeting yesterday at a secret location outside of the city, with a member of the Army's command center. I won't tell you who, but he's a general, and he was smuggled in and out on a British submarine." Murphy sat back in his chair, took a breath, and folded his hands on the desk. "The invasion has been delayed, again. The president had been pushing for it to happen no later than the end of this month, but Generals Eisenhower and Marshall have convinced him that the army needs more time to prepare. This mission is critical to the future outcome of the war, and it can't be rushed.

"For our part here, there is still much more work to be done with the French forces in this area that are loyal to Vichy, to ensure their neutrality when our men come ashore. Carmichael, this gives you more time to arm the local resistance, and rehearse the coup to coincide with the landings. We need things to run like clockwork, and that can't be rushed, either."

Oliver's heart sank into the pit of his stomach. While part of him was terrified at the thought of fighting should the Vichy forces decide to resist the Allied invasion, to the point of keeping him up at night, the rest of him wanted desperately to put it all behind them so he could return to Lyon.

Lisette was expecting him soon. He'd told her it would be two months. Possibly sooner. Now he looked like a liar. "When do you expect it to happen now, sir?"

Murphy frowned, looking at his hands folded on his desk. "The president wanted the invasion well before election day—but that's just not possible. Based on the conversations I had yesterday, I'd expect it to be mid-November. Once we have a firm date, I'll send you a message to prepare for our guests. The number of guests will correspond to the date. Understand?"

Oliver nodded, though he doubted Murphy would send that message as soon as he had the date. It would probably come last minute. "I do, sir."

"Good. Now tell me about your work with the Resistance the last few weeks."

**

Oliver's mind was pulled a million different directions when he exited the consulate a half-hour later and turned toward home. He hardly noticed the man on the park bench reading a newspaper, until the man spoke, startling him from his thoughts.

"Excuse me, sir. I am without matches. Do you have one I could use?"

The man held an unlit cigarette in his right hand, and arched one eyebrow as he looked at Oliver, waiting for a response.

Oliver could barely breathe for a second. He'd seen that face. But not in person. The man sitting on the bench staring at him now was the SOL leader Dolph had sketched that summer from Armand's description. Prickles of nerves ran up his arms and legs, raising gooseflesh under his suit and causing a sudden sweat on his brow. He recalled Frank Dryden's warning letter a few weeks ago.

He silently cursed himself for not paying attention to his surroundings.

"Sir?"

"Yes, of course," Oliver said, shaking himself from his momentary freeze and reaching into his jacket pocket for the matchbook he always carried. It was a habit he'd learned early when he opened his club at the start of the year.

He struck a match, and the man leaned forward with his cigarette and puffed it into life.

"Thank you, sir." The man blew a puff of smoke into the air, took another drag, and blew it out.

The smoke came out in puffs, not a thin stream. The man hadn't inhaled. He wasn't a smoker.

Oliver nodded and hurried away, not daring to look behind him until he got to the end of the block.

The man was not following him, but his eyes were.

**

Saturday, October 31

It was only a few seconds after the curtain opened that Oliver saw the man sitting alone at a table in the middle of Garnier's club. He seized with nerves, and almost missed the start of the first song.

For eight days, he'd been even more cautious than usual, hyper aware of his surroundings wherever he went. He varied his routes more than ever. And there had been no sign of this man who had chased Armand through Old Lyon months ago. Oliver had begun to hope the SOL's interest in him had waned.

But here that man was tonight. And his eyes never wavered from Oliver.

As soon as the curtain closed for their first break, Oliver motioned for Vincent and Patrice to join him in a corner.

"The man I told you about at last week's meeting, he's here tonight," Oliver whispered.

Vincent stiffened. Patrice's eyes narrowed. "Are you certain?" the little trumpet player asked.

"Absolutely certain."

Patrice inhaled hard through his nose. "Then you must not come to tonight's meeting." He held up his hand when Oliver's mouth opened to protest, silencing him. "It might endanger the rest of us. If this man is following you, let him see you go home and stay there. Let them lose interest, and you may rejoin us in a few weeks."

Oliver's whole body itched with anxiety. Patrice was right, of course. "But what if I get word that the invasion is coming?"

Patrice frowned. "That is a concern. If you learn it is imminent, you can tell me here, while we practice before the show. I will make sure everyone else knows." He reached up to put his hand on Oliver's shoulder—but didn't touch Vincent, Oliver couldn't help noticing—and gave it a friendly little shake. "Do not worry, we know our roles. When the time comes, we will be ready."

*

When the curtain opened for their next set, Oliver's gaze was on the place where the man had sat, watching. The table now stood empty. Oliver scanned the room, but the man was nowhere in sight.

******

Thursday, November 5

Oliver sat at his table drinking his morning coffee—real coffee, thanks to Dr. Hassan—and reading the local French newspaper. A short article on page seven detailed, in somewhat glowing language, the set-back that week's American elections had delivered to President Roosevelt. The opposition Republicans had gained seats in both houses of Congress, trimming the ruling Democrats' majority to the slimmest of margins.

The speculation that the American public was weary of how poorly the war was going for the Allies hinted at the paper's editorial slant.

The knock at his door interrupted him before he reached the end of the article, but he gladly set the paper down—damned Vichy propaganda, practically—and got up to answer the door.

A young man in the uniform of an American consular employee—white shirt, no jacket, black necktie, black pants—stood on the other side. "Message for Mr. Oliver Carmichael."

"I'm Mr. Carmichael."

"Can I see your identification first, sir?" the consular employee said, and couldn't quite conceal the hint of amusement—or self-important pride—tugging at one corner of his mouth. "I've been instructed to be certain I only hand it over to Oliver Carmichael himself."

Of course. "Just a moment." Oliver walked a few steps to where his jacket hung on a coat rack in the corner and fished his passport from the pocket. He opened it to the picture and held it toward the young American.

The young man glanced from the photo to Oliver's face, and then handed over a small, sealed envelope. "Have a good morning, Mr. Carmichael."

Oliver nodded without a word and closed the door. He tore open the envelope, his pulse accelerating. His skin tingled as he read the words on the tiny slip of paper.

> My dear Mr. Carmichael,
>
> Thank you for offering your hospitality. Please prepare for eight guests. They will arrive at three o'clock.
> Sincerely,
>
> RDM

That meant it would be on the eighth. That was this Sunday. And it would be at three AM.

Oliver plopped into his armchair, the breath exploding from his lungs, a strange mixture of excitement and fear washing over him.

34

Saturday, November 7

A breathless American consular officer handed Oliver a sealed envelope and waited in his doorway while he opened it.

University Library, English and American Literature section, two-thirty.
-RDM

Oliver glanced at his wristwatch; that was only thirty-five minutes from now.

"I was told to tell you to burn that as soon as you've read it, Mr. Carmichael," the young consular officer said, and removed a pack of matches from his pocket.

Oliver let him strike a match, and held the note over the flame until it licked at his fingertips. He dropped the corner of the paper and stamped it out the second it hit his floor.

He'd have to wash away the black ash later, there was no time now.

**

Oliver hurried to the nearest tram stop, but had to wait almost ten minutes for the next one. By the time it got him through the city center and to the university, he had to run to reach the library in time.

It was two-twenty-nine when he walked through the front door, out of breath.

It took a couple of minutes to find the English and American literature section, but when he got there at two-thirty-one, there was no sign of Robert Murphy.

He spent the next ten minutes pretending to peruse the titles up and down the aisle, but all the time glancing around for Murphy.

Finally, at almost two-forty-five, Jack Archer came walking up, and stopped about ten feet from Oliver.

"Mr. Murphy was planning to meet you himself, but he's been detained," Archer said, in a library-appropriate hush.

Oliver glanced around, ensuring that they were the only two within earshot. He'd done this routine with Frank Dryden at the American Library in Paris a few times, almost two years ago. "What's the rush?"

"We have a small problem," Archer said, and took one step closer. "Admiral François Darlan, the Minister of National Defense in Vichy, has arrived in Algiers unexpectedly."

A chill ran up Oliver's spine, and his stomach jumped with sudden butterflies. "Do you think they know?" *About the invasion tonight.*

"We don't think so," Archer said.

Oliver noticed his use of 'we,' but it really meant Murphy didn't think so.

"Darlan's son has been in the hospital here," Archer continued. "Tuberculosis. Sources tell us he's critical, probably dying. That's why Darlan came to Algiers. He's at the hospital right now."

Oliver nodded, taking a minute to digest this information. "But if he's here, what does that mean for our plans?"

Archer glanced around, and then came up close to Oliver. "The invasion can't be rescheduled. Everything's in motion already. But Mr. Murphy's worried that Darlan might leave his son's bedside to rally the local French forces against our troops. He's working channels as we speak, trying to head off that possibility."

He took a step away, but whispered out the side of his mouth, "It's imperative that your group seizes control quickly, before Darlan has a chance to act. We also need for them to try capturing Darlan himself."

Oliver wondered how in the hell they were supposed to do that, but Archer had already walked away.

**

Oliver called in sick to work that night. Mr. Garnier was furious, shouting into the phone that Patrice had also called in sick, and so now he was stuck without a trumpet player.

"The only reason to have a second trumpet player at all is for when Patrice is ill! You are useless, sir!"

Oliver replied with a half-hearted "Sorry," and hung up. With any luck, he wouldn't be returning to that club, and this was the last he'd speak to the ill-tempered manager.

In the early evening, as dusk was settling over the city, he went into the Casbah and picked up the pair of bicycles he'd ordered from Omar Saidit. They were dark brown, which on a moonless night should be as invisible as black. At least, Oliver hoped so.

He pedaled one of the bikes and pulled the other one beside him—not an easy task, he discovered—through the crowded city center, and reached the botanical gardens in the Jardin d'Essais shortly after dark.

Patrice was there waiting for him, along with a tall and swarthy man that Oliver didn't recognize. He didn't ask the man's name. Together, the three of them dug up the two crates of guns that had been buried there two weeks before. It took all three of them to lug each crate the fifty-meter distance to where the tall swarthy man had parked a truck on the Rue Belcourt, under the overhang of several large trees.

That distance hadn't seemed far when they planned this, but with a heavy crate in their arms and only being able to take short steps in tandem, it felt like forever. And then they had to do it a second time.

"Everyone is clear on their instructions?" Oliver whispered to Patrice after they'd loaded the second crate onto the back of the truck.

"Yes, everyone will rendezvous in the Bois des Arcades at ten o'clock. We will wait there until ten-thirty. And then we will move into our positions. I will lead the group surrounding the police prefecture. At eleven o'clock precisely, we strike." The little trumpet player held up his wrist. "Let us synchronize."

Oliver compared his watch to Patrice's, suppressing a smile as he adjusted his by forty seconds so that they were exactly in sync.

"Very good," Oliver said, patting Patrice on the shoulder. "Vincent and I will meet the Allied troops at the secret landing spot, between three and four o'clock, and we will guide them into Algiers."

Patrice shook Oliver's hand in both of his. He looked solemn. "Go with God, my friend."

"You as well," Oliver said. "If any of the other groups run into trouble with their assignments, I'm counting on you to assist as best you can. We'll adapt as needed, and the rest is up to God."

**

Vincent left the club early, complaining of a stomachache at eleven, and slipped through the quiet streets to Oliver's building.

Once upstairs, they changed into black clothing without a word, and Oliver pulled a bag from under his bed. He removed two pistols, Colt .45s, and handed one to Vincent. He shoved the other into the back of his pants and hid it under his jacket. He threw the bag over his shoulder. "Let's go."

They slipped out the back door of the building into a dark alley, where Oliver had stashed the bicycles. They pedaled east, and

Oliver's heart was in his throat as he constantly looked around, vigilant for any sign of police.

**

Sunday, November 8

It took thirty minutes to reach the edge of the city by bicycle, and beyond that the road was truly dark. They could hear the waves crashing a short distance to their left, but the dunes that rose between them and the beach were black in the darkness. There was no moon tonight—the date had been chosen for that reason—and so Oliver reached inside the bag on his shoulder and removed the large flashlight. An 'electric torch' it was called, and Oliver found that amusing. Tonight was called Operation Torch. Holding it to the handlebars, he switched it on, and a bright beam of light illuminated the road in front of them.

After another thirty minutes they passed a directional sign for Aïn Taya, pointing right down a side road that teed onto the coastal road. *Not far now.* Oliver counted one hundred turns of the pedals, and then hit the brakes. "It's here," he called over his shoulder to Vincent.

They walked the bikes off the road into the sand and hid them in a thicket of grass some twenty feet off the road, at the base of a dune.

Oliver looked at Vincent, a hulky shadow in the darkness. "Are you ready?"

"Ready."

They trudged up the sandy dune, following a narrow trail through the tall grass, which just barely reflected the tiny bit of light from the stars in its flecks of quartz.

At the crest of the dune, some twenty-five feet above the road, they saw the black mass of the sea in front of them, punctuated by little white lines of breaking surf. They descended the dune, which sloped more gradually on this side, stopping at the edge of the beach.

Oliver checked his watch in the beam of his flashlight. Almost one thirty. He looked at Vincent, standing a few feet from him. "And now we wait."

*

"We used to come to the beach often when I was a child," Vincent said while they sat on the sand in the dark. "My father insisted, every weekend in the summer. He loved the beach. My mother, she didn't like it much. She did not like the sand, and complained every time about having to wash the sand out of our clothes, having to wash the sand out of our hair before bed.

"My father never paid her any mind. He would play with us on the beach. It was the only time he ever played with us children. We built sandcastles with him, big elaborate fortresses formed from buckets. My brothers and I would dig moats around them—but not too close, or the castle would collapse, and Papa would be cross. But he was never cross for long on the beach. He would take us into the water, and we would ride the waves on our bellies. Those were good days."

Oliver was surprised at the wistful tone in Vincent's voice.

"What was your family like at home?"

Vincent shrugged, barely visible in the darkness. "My father worked hard, six days every week, and he came home tired and grumpy. He wanted to be left alone until dinner. My mother had her hands full at home, with seven children. She expected the older ones to look after the younger ones for her." Another shrug. "My older brothers could be cruel. But my sister Marlène always looked after me."

"I had an older brother, too," Oliver said. "Paul wasn't cruel, but sometimes he'd smack me upside the head if I got on his nerves."

"That is not so bad," Vincent said, a tone of levity in his voice. Oliver was relieved the melancholy had passed.

They continued to talk into the night, with only the sound of the waves crashing onto the beach accompanying their conversation, which meandered from topic to topic. The temperature continued to drop, and Oliver began to shiver.

"Here," Vincent said, slipping off his coat and then scooting across the sand to sit right up next to Oliver. "Give me your coat." Oliver slipped it off—reluctantly—and handed it over. Vincent draped it across their legs. Then he draped his larger coat across both of their backs and put his arm around Oliver's shoulder under the coat, tugging him close.

Oliver tensed at first, but then he relaxed into the warmth accumulating between them. It was a relief. But there was also a familiar lightness in his belly at the proximity. He ignored that.

*

They sat in silence for some time. After a while, Oliver checked his watch again, switching on the flashlight for a second. "They're late."

"What time is it?" Vincent asked, concerned.

"After four o'clock."

"They're probably only a little bit behind schedule," Vincent said, sounding reassuring. "Ships navigating unfamiliar waters in the dark, it can be tricky."

Oliver nodded in silence. But his mind filled with worry. *What if they ran aground somewhere? What if German U-boats found them somewhere off the coast?* Any number of things could go wrong.

Vincent seemed to sense his tension and hugged him closer. Oliver let him, and even relaxed against his side.

**

Oliver awoke with a start, realized he'd fallen asleep with his head on Vincent's shoulder.

"Shit!" he cursed under his breath, and lifted his wrist in front of his face. He fumbled with the switch on his flashlight, and Vincent stirred.

"Are you alright, Oliver?"

"Just trying to see what time it is," he muttered, and finally got the flashlight turned on. He shined it on his watch, and then cursed as he turned it back off. "Damn! It's almost six o'clock. Where are they?"

"Perhaps we should go back to Algiers?" Vincent ventured. "It could be that they landed somewhere else by mistake. Or maybe a last-minute change of plans."

Oliver was torn. One of those things had probably happened. But if the invasion force was only delayed, maybe even almost here…

"No, let's stay here, at least until dawn."

Vincent nodded and snuggled close again. "If you think that's best, then we'll wait."

**

The screeching of seagulls roused Oliver to find that dawn had broken across the beach.

The empty beach, he realized, lifting his head to look around. He was lying on the ground on his side under a pile of their coats. Vincent's body was pressed up close against him from behind, spooned around him. His big arm was wrapped around Oliver's waist and hugged him tightly to him.

Oliver could feel Vincent pressed against his buttocks, and panic raced through him. What if someone saw them? What if the American marines had seen two queers snuggled together in the sand and passed on by in disgust?

He threw the coats aside and jumped to his feet, brushing sand from his clothes. The chill morning air made the hairs on his arms stand up under his sleeves. Rationality crept back into his brain slowly, telling him that the marines would have awakened them with their landing, no matter how quiet they were trying to be.

And there would be signs of their passing, he realized, pausing long enough to gaze across the unbroken sand as far as he could see.

Vincent had stirred when Oliver jumped up, and now propped himself on his elbows and looked at Oliver through half-open eyes. "What is it?"

Oliver knelt next to him. "It's after seven-thirty. Either the invasion force didn't arrive, or they landed at the wrong beach." He tugged on his coat, almost frantic.

Vincent scrambled up from the sand and stood in front of Oliver. "We should go back to the city. Now."

Oliver's mind raced. Vincent was right, there was no use staying where they were any longer. They had to get back. But if the 34th Infantry had landed somewhere else, it would have had to be between here and Algiers—otherwise, they would see evidence of their passing by on the way to the city.

"We'll take the beach," Oliver said. "We might find the missing American forces that way. And we should stay off of the road, in case Vichy's troops launch a counterattack."

"And the bikes?"

"Forget them," Oliver said. "They're hidden, we can come back for them if we decide to." It wasn't *his* money that had paid for them, anyway.

"Then let's go," Vincent said.

*

They jogged west across the sand at the border of the beach and the grassy dune—a difficult thing—for a little over a mile, a process that took more than thirty increasingly breathless minutes.

And then Oliver saw them.

The beach a short distance ahead of them was crawling with American G.I.s in green fatigues, with dozens of landing craft grounded just offshore.

Oliver picked up speed, doing his best to achieve a full run, and motioned with his arm for Vincent to hurry with him.

A handful of G.I.s raised their rifles as the pair approached, so Oliver raised his hands in the air and shouted, "American! Don't shoot!"

The G.I.s looked at him in confusion, and only half-lowered their rifles. "You're American? Out here?"

Oliver ignored the question. "Is this the 34th Infantry?" He barely got the words out, out of breath from the run in the sand.

"That's right," one of the G.I.s said, cautiously, eyes narrowing. Oliver noticed for the first time that he had three stripes on his shoulder.

"They're armed, Sarge," said another G.I. who had slipped around behind them.

"We were supposed to meet your landing this morning, Sergeant," Oliver said, still panting hard. He leaned forward and put his hands on his knees, trying to catch his breath. "You were supposed to land about a mile and a half that way." He pointed back toward the east.

"I don't know about all that," the sergeant said, still eyeing Oliver and Vincent with deep suspicion. "What's your name, mister?"

"Oliver Carmichael." He pointed over his shoulder at Vincent. "And this is my liaison with the French Resistance in Algiers. We're supposed to meet with General Ryder."

The look in the sergeant's eyes was disbelieving, but he called over his shoulder, "Lieutenant! Got a couple of civilians here who want to see the general."

The officer who approached was younger than Oliver expected—he couldn't be more than twenty-five, and he kept his right hand on the hip holster of his pistol as he eyed them. "Yeah? Which general?"

"General Ryder," Oliver said, still a bit breathless.

The young lieutenant snorted. "Major General Ryder? The commander of the division?"

"That's right," Oliver said, straightening. "We're expected."

"Oh yeah?" the lieutenant said, taking on a bit of swagger.

"I'm the OSS agent who was supposed to meet your division this morning, but about a mile and a half to the east of here."

The lieutenant's smug smile widened. "Really, now? I'm supposed to believe it took you two hours to come a mile and a half?"

Oliver's face flushed hot. "We initially went looking the other direction," he lied.

"And who's this fella?" The lieutenant pointed at Vincent.

"He's my liaison with the local French Resistance," Oliver said, resisting the urge to add that he'd already been over this with the sergeant.

"Does he speak English?"

"A little bit," Vincent said, holding his fingers close together.

Oliver shook his head. "Not really."

The lieutenant widened his stance, hooked his fingers through his belt loop. "And why should I believe you?"

Oliver's patience snapped. "Because if you don't, you'll make a serious fuck up." He blushed at using the most taboo of swear words, but soldiers and sailors spoke that way. And this was urgent. "If you believe me and you're wrong, you'll only get yelled at. If you don't and you're wrong, they might court martial you."

This clearly made an impact. The lieutenant hesitated a couple of seconds, and then motioned them to join him. "Come with me."

*

The lieutenant took them to his regimental colonel, who believed Oliver without question. He personally took them in a strange box-like open vehicle with massive tires—the colonel's driver called it a "Jeep"—to General Ryder's headquarters another mile west, and over the dune.

The headquarters, located in the largest tent Oliver had ever laid eyes on, was a scene of controlled chaos. The captain whom the colonel introduced as General Ryder's Aide-de-camp knew immediately who they were.

"We wondered what happened to you," the captain said. "The general's already sent most of the division into Algiers to capture the port. They should have arrived there at oh-eight-hundred."

Oliver's heart sank. His job this morning was to guide them into Algiers. And he'd slept right through it. *Damn it!*

He turned to Vincent, who had been following him in silent bemusement. He felt bad for his friend, who couldn't understand what was being said around him. "We're too late," Oliver told him in French. "Most of the division has already gone into the city, and they're capturing the port right now."

"Then we should get back to Algiers ourselves, and help the others complete the coup."

Oliver agreed. He turned back to the captain. "We need to get back to Algiers PDQ, to check on the status of the coup d'état the Resistance staged this morning. Can someone take us in one of those Jeeps?"

"Let me see if someone's going, and has room. Give me a minute." He hurried off.

Oliver translated for Vincent. A moment later, the captain motioned for them from an open tent flap, and they jogged to him. He pointed toward a jeep with a single driver, a young-looking toe-headed lieutenant with an enormous expandable folder on the seat beside him, held closed with a pair of rubber bands.

"Get in the back, sirs," the lieutenant said. "My name's Dykstra, and I've gotta get some status reports to a Brigadier General stat. I can drop you off once that's done."

"Where are we headed?" Oliver leaned forward to ask, but fell back against the seat when the lieutenant gunned the engine, sending them hurtling forward onto the coastal highway.

"Just this side of the port," Lieutenant Dykstra yelled over the rush of wind. "And hold on, sirs—this is gonna be a bumpy ride if you're not used to it."

He wasn't kidding. Oliver was almost dizzy by the time they reached the city. They sped through the neighborhoods of the east side, and around the curve of the Bay of Algiers.

And that's when they heard the sharp crack of gunfire ahead of them.

Dykstra slammed on the brakes. Oliver and Vincent slammed into the back of the front seats.

"Take cover, sirs!" Dykstra yelled, and grabbed the expandable folder from the floor of the jeep, tucking it tight under his left arm, while unholstering his pistol with his right hand.

"What's going on?" Oliver asked, taking cover behind the jeep. Vincent crouched beside him, head down. He put his big hand on the back of Oliver's head and pushed it lower.

"There's a fire fight up ahead, at the port," Dykstra said.

Oliver's heart plummeted. That meant French troops firing on the American invasion force. Robert Murphy's secret contacts in the local garrison must not have been as solid as Mr. Murphy thought they were.

A platoon of American troops came running up from the port, and Dykstra flagged down the platoon's lieutenant.

"We're circling around," the platoon lieutenant shouted. "The whole division's moving inland, gonna surround the defenders at the port."

"I can guide you!" Oliver heard himself shouting before he really thought it through, head popping above the back of the jeep.

"Sir?" the platoon lieutenant replied. Lieutenant Dykstra looked at him open-mouthed. Vincent just looked at him in confusion.

"I live near here," Oliver explained. "My friend and I know these streets. I can guide you through them, save you some trouble."

The platoon lieutenant only hesitated a second. "Come on." He turned to Dykstra and said, "You might as well tag along, too. You ain't gettin' where you were goin' anyway."

"Get in the front seat with me," Dykstra told Oliver.

Oliver turned to Vincent and gave him a hand getting off the ground. He quickly explained what had been discussed, and as Vincent scrambled into the back seat, Oliver said, "I'll have them drop you off by your home. You can take shelter and wait there. I'll come find you later."

But Vincent shook his head ferociously. "No, I am coming with you."

Oliver climbed into the front next to Dykstra, who slammed on the accelerator before Oliver's backside hit the seat. Once they'd reached the front of the platoon, Dykstra slowed to keep pace with the running G.I.s. Oliver directed Dykstra where to turn, and took them through the neighborhood and around behind where Garnier's club was located, keeping the sounds of the battle to their right.

Once, Vincent disagreed with one of Oliver's instructions. "No, not here," he shouted, tapping Oliver on the shoulder. "Go onto the Rue Laveran instead. It connects all the way to the Avenue Miguel de Cervantes, which will take us toward the far side of the port."

He was right, of course. Oliver translated for Dykstra, and once they'd made that turn instead, Oliver glanced back at Vincent with a grateful smile, and mouthed "Thank you" in French.

They passed a party of police gendarmes, who all four dropped their pistols and raised their hands at the sight of the American platoon. "Smart frogs!" Dykstra yelled, grinning as the jeep sped past them.

Below the wooded hillside of the Bois des Arcades, south of the port, they encountered another platoon of American troops. Dykstra stopped the Jeep, and the three lieutenants conferred for a few minutes.

That gave Oliver a chance to catch his breath. He turned toward Vincent, heart racing, and laughed out loud as the relief flooded through him. He hadn't had time to be scared, but now that they'd stopped, his head was buzzing from the adrenaline.

Vincent laughed with him.

**

Sitting on a cold metal bench in a jail cell on the other side of the city center, Patrice listened to the crack of gunfire—like a never-ending strand of firecrackers—growing steadily louder. The battle was getting closer.

"The Americans are coming, my friends," he said to his comrades. Four others crowded in the little cell with him, plus more than a dozen others in the cells around and across from his. Their eyes, so recently downcast with disappointment, now glowed with anticipation.

From time to time, one of the guards would rush down the corridor, face strained. Their words to one another were clipped and hushed, and Patrice struggled to make out what they were saying.

But they were frightened, that much was clear. He took heart from that.

He and his companions had taken the police by surprise last night, and locked them in these very cells with the criminals. Then they hunkered down to wait for the invasion. But the Allies had been late, and by five AM the French army had retaken everything the résistants had captured. With soldiers surrounding the prefecture, they'd had no choice but to surrender. Their guns were taken, the police beat them, and then shoved them in these cells with the vilest of epithets.

But the ever-increasing gunfire, closer and closer, told him the Allies were taking the city. Soon they would be freed. And then they would take their revenge on the gendarmes who had abused them so egregiously.

"The Americans are coming," Patrice repeated, more to himself than anyone, and a smile slowly spread across his lips.

**

More platoons of American troops arrived, and the area was soon full of G.I.s in battle formation. Troops scaled telephone poles with wires in-hand, and tapped field telephones into the local lines. They gave thumbs-up to lieutenants on the ground, who turned the hand cranks, and began shouting their positions into the receivers.

Oliver watched in awe.

Lieutenant Dykstra returned to the Jeep a few minutes later. "The Regimental commander says they don't need any more scouting help right now, and it's about to get hairy around here. He says he doesn't want to be responsible for the safety of a couple of civilians, so I'm to take you home."

"Thank you, lieutenant," Oliver said.

Dykstra shrugged. "Don't mention it. Brigade HQ has set up back that direction, so it's on my way. I'd keep your heads down, though, in case we encounter any enemy fire."

They sped back towards the east, keeping close to the American military formations.

"Wouldn't it be safest to move farther inland, away from the battle?" Oliver asked over the whine of the Jeep's engine.

"Allied personnel have been ordered to stick close together, and to not fan out through the city unless ordered to do so as part of a counter-attack," Dykstra shouted back.

That made a certain amount of sense, though it was hardly comforting.

They were passing along the western edge of Oliver's neighborhood when they crossed a street and suddenly found themselves under fire from the direction of the port.

"Shit! Get down!" Dykstra yelled and veered the wheel hard to the right. The Jeep briefly turned on two wheels before the left side of the vehicle slammed back onto the ground. A loud report made Oliver drop his head to his knees, but then the wobble of the slowing vehicle told him they'd popped a tire.

"Damn!" Dykstra slammed the brakes. "Take cover behind the Jeep!" But Oliver and Vincent were already scrambling behind the vehicle, crouching shoulder-to-shoulder and peeping over the top of the hood.

A battalion of American troops a block down the street were taking fire from a group of French troops a few blocks farther down. Bullets whined overhead, and chipped bits of plaster from the sides of the neighboring buildings.

Vincent threw his arm around Oliver's shoulder and tugged him closer, and downward at the same time. Oliver stared at the surface of the street, close enough he could see the individual pebbles embedded in the asphalt. Vincent's breath was hot against his cheek, coming hard and fast.

His heart raced like a Kentucky thoroughbred, and each clink of a bullet in plaster above them sent a fresh wave of fear through his belly. An image of Lisette crossed his mind's eye. Would he live to see her again? Then he thought of Marcel, and of all the things he should have said to him. He prayed he'd get the chance.

He had no idea how long they crouched there—long enough his legs began to cramp—but the sounds of the gunfire gradually grew farther away. Then Dykstra crawled around to them, and clapped Oliver on the back.

"The frogs have pulled back a few blocks, toward the port," he said. "We can change the tire and move on, but keep your heads down, just in case."

**

They had nearly finished tightening the lug nuts onto the new tire when a loud voice behind them made Oliver jump.

"Stand up, all of you," it said in French. "Drop your weapons. Put your hands up."

Oliver and Vincent stood, raised their hands. Lt. Dykstra looked at them in confusion, but followed their lead and stood.

The man standing in front of them with a pistol aimed at Oliver's chest was the SOL leader from Dolph's sketch. "I said drop your weapons." He wagged his pistol at Dykstra, but then pointed it squarely back at Oliver.

Oliver translated, and Dykstra unstrapped his pistol harness slowly from his hip, and let it drop to the ground at his feet. Oliver pulled his from his belt, and tossed it next to Dykstra's.

*

Matous stepped forward and kicked the Americans' pistols to the side, out of reach. He was a fast shot if someone were foolish enough to reach for the guns, but there were three of them, and he was alone.

"You, Mr. Carmichael, come with me."

The American musician stayed where he was. *The arrogance!*

"I know you understand French, Mr. Carmichael. Yes, I know your name. You think me a fool? The SOL knows all about you, and what you have been doing. Now, you will come with me."

The American raised his chin. "If I don't?"

Matous chuckled. He saw the fear in Oliver Carmichael's eyes, though his face tried to look unafraid. Typical American bluster.

"Then I will shoot you where you stand. And your companions, too. Now, act like a man instead of a boy and come with me."

*

"What's he saying?" Dykstra whispered out of the corner of his mouth.

"He wants me to come with him, alone," Oliver said. He hesitated to reveal too much, but made the snap decision that Lt. Dykstra deserved an explanation. "I've been working with the Resistance. He's with Vichy's secret police, and he's been after me for months."

"Holy shit," Dykstra muttered.

His tone sounded impressed, though Oliver wasn't sure why that pleased him right at this moment.

"He's probably not alone," Oliver muttered as he took his first step forward, hands still raised by his ears. Then he half-turned his face toward Vincent and said in French, "Back away slowly. It's me he wants."

He took a few more slow steps toward SOL man, staring him in the eyes. "The Allies are taking over the city. You should surrender while you have the chance. If you shoot me, they will pursue you as a murderer."

An angry puff of air escaped the man's lips. "The Americans will never defeat French soldiers on French soil. Your troops will be driven back into the sea, and spies will be shot. And anyone who aided them."

Oliver took a side-step to place himself between the armed man and Vincent. The man's gun followed him.

*

From the corner of his eye, Matous saw the American lieutenant nod toward the heavier-set bearded man—a résistant, Matous knew, from that same club where Oliver Carmichael had sown his treachery—and his lips moved, but at that moment Carmichael chose to step sideways, and Matous was forced to keep his attention on him.

"Yes, I know you are a spy for the American secret services," Matous told him. "Do not deny it. We have evidence. Now, we will go back to my office, and you will answer my questions, or you will experience pain such as you've never felt in your pampered American life. If you are cooperative enough, perhaps we will choose to spare your life."

Sudden movement from two sides caught Matous by surprise, and in a flash, he detected two objects hurtling at him from different angles.

*

The jeep's blown tire flew past Oliver's face on the right, while at the same moment the flash of the tire iron swept past him on the left.

The SOL man's arms came up to deflect both objects, but he was too slow. The tire iron clanged against the bone of his right wrist, and the sickening crack it made was soon drowned by the man's cry of pain. The tire thudded into his left side, silencing his scream by forcing the air from his lungs, and knocking him sideways, off balance.

His gun clattered on the pavement between them. The tire iron clattered off to the right. Oliver's reflexes were slowed by his surprise, but a half-second later he lunged for the gun. He landed on his knees, and shots of pain ripped up his legs from the pavement, but he threw himself forward, arm outstretched, and his fingers touched the handle.

The man landed shoulder-first on the pavement a couple of yards in front of him. He cried out, and rolled over, clutching his shoulder, which seemed to come from his torso at a wrong angle.

Oliver flexed his fingers, over and over, willing them to scoot the handle of the pistol inches closer. It seemed to take forever, sound and motion ceased, all save the thunderous scrape of the gun on the pavement as it came closer, millimeter by millimeter.

Finally, its corner touched his palm, and he wrapped his fingers around the handle, bringing it up just in time to see the man scrambling up on his knees, that right arm still dangling at an unnatural angle. But from the fist of his left hand a knife blade glinted in the sunlight.

Oliver's finger felt for the trigger, but panic swept through him when the man launched to his feet, waving the knife forward in Oliver's direction.

A flash of movement to his right caught Oliver's attention, and the SOL man's, too. Vincent swung the tire iron downward, and its blunt end struck the man on the temple, sending a spray of blood into the air.

The man's knife hand had already begun to swing toward Vincent's thigh. Again, the world moved in slow motion, and though Vincent was already moving backward Oliver could see that the SOL man's knife would still swipe across before he could get away.

His finger found the trigger and pulled it.

The force of the gunshot sent him backward, and the wind rushed from his lungs when his back hit the pavement. Somehow, he had the presence of mind to raise his head when his shoulder blades struck. Even so, a stab of pain ran up his spine to his brain, flying to the front and crashing into his forehead.

He lay motionless, time suspended.

Then Vincent's face was above his, close, his pale blue eyes wide, the pupils shrunk into tiny black dots from worry.

"Oliver! Oliver!" Vincent's voice sounded muffled, and his hand smacked Oliver's cheek three times, but somehow gently. Then Oliver's ears popped, and sound rushed in like thunder.

"Jesus, man! Are you alright?" Lt. Dykstra stood over them, leaning forward, hands holding his gun holster.

Oliver managed a nod. "I'm fine," he said in English. He raised himself onto his elbows, then pushed up into a sitting position. His back was sore, but everything seemed to work.

On the pavement a few feet away, the SOL man lay with his body twisted. A massive hole in his chest bled onto the pavement, the pool spreading toward Oliver's hand.

"Holy fuckin' hell, man!" Dykstra said, strapping on his holster.

The pains in Oliver's back and knees slipped away, and within seconds he felt nothing at all. Only numbness.

"Let's get out of here, man," Dykstra said, slapping Oliver on the shoulder. He grabbed the tire iron, tightened the last two lug nuts, and hopped in the jeep. "C'mon, let's go!"

Vincent gave Oliver his hand and pulled him to his feet. "I'm ok," Oliver said. The numbness was swept away by a wave of euphoria, and a huge grin broke across his face. "Let's go."

**

It was only a few blocks to Oliver's building, which the jeep traversed in barely a minute, and Oliver had Dykstra drop them at the corner. The lieutenant gave them a quick salute and sped off.

Random bursts of gunfire echoed off the buildings, an indeterminate distance from them. "Let's get inside!" Oliver shouted to Vincent and ran full-tilt toward his building.

35

Oliver and Vincent sprinted up the stairs. They might be safely inside the building, but the adrenaline coursing through Oliver's veins had his heart pumping, and he took the stairs two at a time.

Once inside his apartment, Oliver threw the deadbolt, and then collapsed against the door. Vincent stood in the middle of the room, wiping his brow with his sleeve. They looked at one another and laughed in relief.

Oliver would never be able to explain what happened next. It must have been the adrenaline, but for some reason as he leaned back against his door, laughing, head buzzing, he sprang the hardest erection of his life. He saw something in Vincent's eyes, and he lunged himself across the room.

Their torsos crashed together, mouths met. Arms wrapped around each other, hugging tightly. Hands moved under shirts while tongues did a dance between their locked lips.

When they finally broke the kiss after a couple of minutes, they both looked down and unbuttoned the other's shirt, fingers flying. Short, fast breaths were the only sound in the room. Oliver's heart thudded against his chest. Shirts were tugged off shoulders, and their fingers flew down the buttons of the other's pants fly.

Trousers and boxer shorts dropped to their ankles, and their bodies pressed together again, mouths locked, hands caressing bare backs and then groping buttocks. Oliver was momentarily surprised that Vincent's buttocks were covered in hair, but he put that from his mind and gripped the firm muscles in both hands.

Then Vincent broke the kiss, locked eyes with him, and grabbed his hand, leading him toward the bedroom in an awkward waddle with his pants bunched at his ankles. Oliver tripped himself trying to kick off his pants, which tangled in his shoes; Vincent's arms caught him before his knees could hit the floor, but his face crashed against Vincent's belly.

For some reason, he wasn't the least bit sorry about that. It was soft like a pillow, and yet firm underneath. And the smell was…intoxicating. He started kissing. The coarse black hair tickled his nose in a not unpleasing way, and he let his mouth roam.

He stopped just shy of doing something he'd never done, never even considered doing. And for a second he sat as if in suspended animation, staring at it; torn.

Vincent's strong arms pulled him up, and then pulled him into the bedroom. They tumbled sideways onto the bed, and they both laughed. Oliver worked his feet back and forth in a furious effort to kick his shoes and pants off, and finally succeeded.

And then their bodies were pressed together again, hands roaming backs and backsides, hips grinding and erections rubbing together across sweat-soaked bellies.

Oliver had only ever done this one time, more than two years ago, and he'd been completely drunk at the time. Marcel and Sébastien had been as drunk as he. Not that Oliver regretted it, mind—but he'd been too inhibited to ever try it again.

Over the course of his two-year affair with Marcel, Oliver had always exclusively taken the dominant and masculine role. Marcel took him in his mouth, in his ass; Oliver took pleasure from Marcel's body. But this—like that once with Sébastien and Marcel—this was more mutual. And satisfying in a way he hadn't felt in a long time. There was no taking. He abandoned himself to the moment, and to the fierce emotions coursing through him so fast he could hardly process them.

Moments later they held each other, spent and panting, foreheads together, sweat and semen mingled between their bellies. An overwhelming euphoria swept through Oliver, and he laughed again, collapsing back against the mattress and placing a palm on his forehead. "That was—unexpected."

"You surprise me, Oliver," Vincent said, quietly. He leaned against Oliver's side, tracing a finger languidly up and down Oliver's sternum while staring into his eyes. "It was unexpected, and wonderful."

Oliver's pulse and breathing slowly returned to normal, but his head still buzzed a little. He reflected on his time with Marcel, and the unresolved feelings that had been dredged up by seeing him again in Lyon last winter.

"What is on your mind?" Vincent asked, softly, circling one of Oliver's nipples with his finger. The motion sent a pleasant shiver down Oliver's spine.

Oliver realized he'd been staring at the ceiling. He looked at Vincent, met his pale blue eyes, and smiled sadly. "I never told you, I had a boyfriend once. But I never really allowed myself to appreciate it."

"I suspected this wasn't your first time." Vincent grinned.

Oliver shook his head. "No, not my first time. But I always kept it distant, not emotional. Just something to do." He sighed. "It wasn't fair to him, but I didn't see that for a long time."

Vincent's finger rose to stroke his throat, and then across his chin to caress his cheek. "It is dangerous to love a man," he said, almost a whisper. "If we act like it is only sex, if we keep it in the shadows, we stay safe. But danger leads to exhilaration."

He kissed Oliver on the mouth, but slowly now, tenderly. It was a nice contrast to the urgency of before, and Oliver sank into it in spite of himself.

Vincent rolled completely off him then, and propped himself on his elbow beside him, only his leg wrapped around Oliver's. "You are going back to Lyon once this operation is finished, aren't you?"

Oliver nodded. *Lyon. Back home.* Then an image of Lisette crashed into this head for the first time since they were crouched behind the Jeep, under fire.

His insides turned ice cold.

Vincent put his palm flat in the center of Oliver's chest. "I could go to Lyon with you, if you would like that."

Oliver didn't reply, only stared at the ceiling, a vice seeming to clamp onto his heart as he pictured Lisette's face.

"There is nothing keeping me in Algiers," Vincent added. Then, more quietly, "I would go to Lyon with you. I would go anywhere to be with you, Oliver."

Oliver squeezed his eyes shut, trying to shut out the images. Trying to shut out Vincent's voice.

"We can't." Then he opened his eyes and looked at Vincent—though it pained him to do so. "I haven't told you something. I have a fiancée. Her name is Lisette. We're getting married in January."

A hint of sorrow clouded Vincent's pale eyes. He glanced away, and his face fell almost imperceptibly. But he kept his palm on Oliver's chest.

"I understand," he said, his voice sounding heavy now. "It is the way of the world. We are safer if we take a wife, no? That is what is expected."

Oliver shifted away slightly, turned on his side to face Vincent, and propped his head on his elbow. "Why have you never taken a wife?"

A sad half-smile creased the right side of Vincent's face. "That is why I came to Algiers. My family expected me to marry the daughter of their friends. There was so much pressure to marry her—from my parents, from her parents, from the priest, from everyone who knew us—but I could not do it. I could not see myself in that life. And so I left Bône six years ago, when I was twenty-three."

Oliver thought of his own flight from Indiana when he was twenty, first to New York, and a couple of years later to Paris. He, too, had rejected the expectations of his parents, and chosen his own path.

Perhaps he and Vincent were kindred spirits, after all.

He laid back and closed his eyes. He would think about all of that later.

36

Shortly after four-thirty in the afternoon, Oliver was roused from a light sleep by the sound of a commanding voice over a loudspeaker drawing near.

He had an instant flashback to the day the Germans marched into Paris, and the new Occupation Authority had commanded everyone to come to the Champs-Elysees for the Wehrmacht's victory parade. He bolted from his bed, not even pausing to put on a robe, and hurried to the front window. He pulled back the curtain to look down on the street.

A police car was moving slowly, and a loudspeaker attached to the roof blared the words of a gendarme inside. "General Juin has surrendered the City of Algiers to the Allied forces. Further violence will not be tolerated, and violators will be arrested. The city's nightly curfew remains in place."

Vincent slipped up behind Oliver and wrapped both arms around him—one hand on his belly, and the other on his chest. He laid his chin on Oliver's shoulder, his bearded cheek to Oliver's cheek.

"That's good news," he murmured, and turned his face briefly to kiss Oliver's cheek.

Vincent hugged him tighter, his warm hands sending waves through Oliver's midsection. And Oliver could feel the soft mass of Vincent's penis resting in the crack of his buttocks, the coarseness of Vincent's pubic hair against his tailbone, and his insides suddenly felt light as air. His own penis twitched involuntarily and started to fatten.

He tried to inch back from the window, but only succeeded in pressing himself more firmly against Vincent's front. "If the police see us at the window this way, they'll arrest us for certain."

"They cannot see us," Vincent said, placing gentle kisses on the back of Oliver's neck. The feel of his lips sent shivers down Oliver's spine. His right hand slid lower on Oliver's belly, resting now just above the groin.

It was an incredibly erotic feeling, having Vincent's hand that low on his belly, with the pinky finger tangling in the top of his pubic hair, and Oliver grew aroused again. Vincent chuckled in his ear while he took an earlobe between his lips.

"See, Oliver? You want me in Lyon with you."

**

Patrice was livid.

As soon as the cease-fire was announced at four-thirty, the police released the résistants at the prefecture.

It was then that Patrice and the others learned that General Juin had announced the ceasefire on the orders of Admiral Darlan—whom the Americans had just installed as supreme commander of French forces in North Africa.

"Darlan? *Darlan*?" Patrice had spat out. "He's a Pétainist! He is not Free French! Are the Americans siding with Vichy now?" If so, the whole operation last night had been a colossal waste.

His fellow résistants grumbled, but Patrice wanted answers. He wanted satisfaction.

And he knew just the American he needed to confront.

**

Dusk had settled over Algiers, and Oliver's bedroom was cast in deep blue shadow. Vincent dozed next to him on the bed, naked; Oliver lay awake, one arm behind his head, staring at the ceiling.

He berated himself for letting it happen, again. He should have resisted the urge, should have told Vincent no. He didn't want to admit that in the moment he hadn't wanted to say no. In the moment, it had felt right.

I'm leading him on. Just like Marcel. The thought tied his stomach in knots.

Negative thoughts whirled through his head like a cyclone. He'd done wrong by Lisette. That thought more than the others made his stomach turn sour, and bile rose in his throat. What kind of man had he become? *Unfaithful, that's what kind, idiot. A cheater.* He didn't understand how he'd come to this.

Sure, he'd carried on an affair with Hélène for over a year, knowing full well she was married, and he hadn't felt guilty. But that was different. It was Hélène's decision to seek pleasure outside of her marriage, so the guilt was on her.

But it was also on you, a tiny voice in the back of his head whispered. He realized with a start that the voice sounded like his father.

No. That was different—it was Hélène's relationship that was wronged, not his. When Oliver had been with Lisette the first time, he'd never once stepped out on her, the whole three years they'd been together. And even after they got back together more than a year ago, he hadn't been with anyone but her...until today, anyway.

Twice, damn it.

Then he thought of Symphonie. No, that didn't count. It was only hands, for crying out loud, not actual sex. But this...

It was the separation, that was the reason; he hadn't seen Lisette, or heard from her, in over two months. But the argument rang hollow as soon as he made it. *Loneliness is no excuse.* It aggravated him to hear these words in his father's voice, but they were true.

He was jolted from his self-rebuke by pounding at his door. He glanced at the little clock on the bedside table. Five minutes to six. He wasn't expecting anyone.

The pounding grew more insistent. He sprang from bed, tugged on his boxer shorts, and slipped into his bathrobe. He pulled his bedroom door closed and tied his robe tightly while crossing the living room.

Patrice pushed his way inside the second Oliver opened the door. Then he spun on Oliver, grabbing a fistful of his robe, and tugging him down toward his face. "Why have the Americans sided with Vichy?"

"What?" Oliver asked, confused.

"The Americans have left the Pétainistes in charge," Patrice snarled. "Why did we fight to take over the city if the Allies then hand it back to Vichy's authorities?"

A sinking feeling spread through Oliver's gut. "I don't know what's happened. I've been here all afternoon."

Patrice scowled. "Here? Doing what?"

Oliver stiffened. He also blushed, but he covered it up with a show of bravado. "After guiding some American troops who were encircling the port, we came under fire from French troops. I was not far from here, so I took cover and came home. I slept this afternoon because I was awake all night."

"We took the prefecture last night," Patrice hissed, tightening his grip on Oliver's robe and giving it a tug for emphasis. "We succeeded in our task. Others took the Summer Palace, the arsenal, the telephone exchange, and the radio station. Government officials were arrested. All was going according to plan—except that the Army repelled the attack on their barracks. The coup could still have succeeded, but the Allies did not arrive, and the Army retook everything we had captured, one by one. Many résistants were killed. We were arrested at the prefecture at four o'clock, and still the Allies had not arrived. We despaired that all was lost.

"After dawn, we heard the battle recommence outside, and we overheard some of the gendarmes saying that the Americans had invaded. We took hope. But after the Americans took the city, we found out that they put Admiral Darlan in charge. *Darlan*! He is one of Pétain's leading supporters. Vichy is still in control, and our comrades fought and died for *nothing*!"

Spittle flew from Patrice's mouth, and droplets of it hit Oliver's cheek and chin. He recoiled, but the little trumpet player held a firm grip on his robe.

"I have nothing to do with any of that," Oliver said. But Patrice tugged him down toward his face.

"You are American. *You* convinced us to fight for the Americans. And the Americans have betrayed us."

A floorboard creaked behind the bedroom door, and Patrice's face snapped that direction. His scowl deepened into a frown, and he stormed toward the door before Oliver could react. He was at the door by the time Oliver managed to shout, "No!"

Patrice threw open the door, and Oliver rushed to stand between the little resistant and the bedroom. But by the time he reached it a second later, Patrice was already staring in narrow-eyed fury at Vincent standing next to the bed, clad only in his boxer shorts.

At least Vincent wasn't still naked, Oliver thought, momentarily relieved, but then immediately realized that made little difference. Panic swept through his belly.

Patrice turned toward Oliver with a look of such hatred it made Oliver's breath catch. A chill ran up his back. Then Patrice slapped him across the face. Hard.

"I see what you were doing while French patriots were fighting in the streets!" Then he stormed across the living room. "We do not need anything from you faggots. This will be reported." He flung open the door and stormed out, leaving the door wide open.

Panic swept through Oliver again, and then mixed with a sinking feeling of dread. "Shit!" he muttered under his breath, smacking his forehead.

Vincent's hand cupped his shoulder. "I am sorry, Oliver," he said, almost a whisper. "I was trying to be quiet, but I knew I needed to get dressed. I did not expect the floor to creak."

Oliver resisted the urge to bat Vincent's hand away. He took a deep breath instead. It wasn't Vincent's fault, and he shouldn't blame him.

This was all my fault.

37

Monday, November 9

Oliver checked in at the American consulate at nine o'clock—officially to report his safety as an American citizen after yesterday's "activity;" but unofficially to report on his role in those activities.

Robert Murphy took the meeting personally. Oliver assumed, correctly as it turned out, that he'd be in the office that day. He gave Murphy a thorough and detailed report of what transpired.

"Yes, several of the landing forces went off-course. You weren't the only agent who had trouble making contact," Murphy said while Oliver described the morning at the beach.

Oliver continued, telling Murphy everything about their arrival back in Algiers, and guiding troops in their encircling maneuver through the neighborhoods.

"Excellent!" Murphy said, looking pleased.

Oliver's face heated and his heart rate increased when he described the encounter with Matous. It made his stomach tie in knots just thinking through it. He finished with Matous's death, and his own flight away from the scene.

"I wouldn't worry about it," Murphy said. "The body's doubtless been taken to the morgue. They'll see it was a gunshot wound and write it off as wrong place at the wrong time. There won't even be any investigation. Is that it, then?"

Oliver had more he wanted to say, and went right into Patrice's words. "I believe this is a common feeling among the *résistants* who fought behind the lines for us. They feel betrayed by the United States—and I can't say I blame them. I'd feel the same way if I were in their shoes."

Murphy frowned. "Our primary objective was always to reduce American casualties, and we succeeded in that goal. By negotiating with Admiral Darlan, we were able to convince the French forces in Algiers to lay down their arms, thus saving American lives. Darlan is currently negotiating a cease-fire in Morocco, so that we can stop the bloodshed there, as well."

Oliver's cheeks flushed hot. He should have figured that out for himself. But he was also conflicted—he could see Patrice's point-of-view, and what he'd said about feeling the same way in their shoes was still true.

"I understand, and I agree—mostly." He ignored the way Murphy's lips tightened and plunged ahead. "Hundreds of *résistants* fought for us, at great risk; some died, even. If we leave them out in the cold, they'll never support us again. Won't we need the support of the Resistance when we invade France?"

"You don't need to worry about that, Carmichael," Murphy said. Seeing Oliver's frown, he added, "Yes, the Allies will need the support of the French Resistance when we invade France sometime in the future—but we'll have it. You can rest assured of that."

Murphy's tone told Oliver that there wouldn't be any further discussion. "Thank you, sir."

"I'm sure you're eager to return home to Lyon now," Murphy said, taking on a friendlier tone, and wearing one of those smiles that didn't extend to his eyes, that these diplomats were so good at. "Mr. Archer can arrange for your passage back to Marseille in the next couple of days, on a neutral freighter. I'll write to Frank Dryden and let him know what an invaluable asset you were to our team."

"I appreciate that, sir," Oliver said. It was over, and he could finally go home.

So why did he feel conflicted about that?

**

A courier from the consulate knocked on his door a few hours later, and the young man handed him an envelope with his name handwritten on the front. The young man waved off a tip, touched the rim of his hat, and left.

Oliver tore open the envelope and removed the single sheet of paper.

Dear Mr. Carmichael,

I'm writing to confirm that your package has been accepted for transport on the Spanish freighter Caridad. The ship's itinerary is as follows:

Depart Algiers on Thurs, Nov 12th at 17:45, arrive at Palma on Majorca at 03:25 Friday.

Depart Palma at 07:35 on Fri, Nov 13th, arrive at Barcelona at 13:50.

Depart Barcelona at 20:05 on Friday, arrive at Marseille at 05:40 on Saturday.

Your package will be retrieved from the port of Marseille and delivered to Symphonie on Saturday morning.

If you have any concerns about the shipment, please let my office know by Wednesday so that other arrangements can be made. I am, sir,

Very cordially yours,

Jack Archer

Three days. That wasn't so long to wait. He briefly wondered if he could write a short letter to Lisette, letting her know he'd be home by Sunday, or Monday at the latest. But he figured he'd need to get Robert Murphy's permission to do that, and it wasn't worth the trouble. Besides, he liked the idea of surprising her.

He sat back in his chair and pictured the look on her face when she opened her door and saw it was him, and he grinned from ear to ear.

**

Oliver answered a knock at his door that evening around six o'clock and was surprised to see Vincent standing there.

"I thought you would be at work tonight," Oliver said, then stood aside and motioned his friend in. "Did the club not open tonight?"

"Mr. Garnier told me I no longer have a job there," Vincent said, matter-of fact.

"Why?"

"You can guess why." Vincent's steady gaze made Oliver uncomfortable, and he looked away.

"Patrice?" From the corner of his eye, he saw Vincent nod.

"He was there, and he would not look at me, no matter how long I watched him. Mr. Garnier barely looked at me when he fired me, and so I knew." He shrugged then. "There was no one else warming up a trombone, so I know they have not hired a replacement. My dismissal was not planned. It was because of Patrice, and what he saw."

He shrugged again, but there was sadness in his pale blue eyes. Intense guilt swept through Oliver. "I'm so sorry, Vincent."

A faint smile crossed Vincent's lips, and he put his hand on Oliver's upper arm, leaving it there. "It is not your fault. And perhaps it is for the best, no? Now, there is no reason for me to stay here. I would like to go to Lyon with you, Oliver. Perhaps you could put me in your band?"

Oliver's stomach flipped. He pictured the look on Lisette's face when she figured out what had happened between them—and she would figure it out, somehow. "I don't know..." He looked away.

"Why not?" Vincent asked, his grip on Oliver's arm tightening a little, and he put a hand on Oliver's other arm. "I would like to see other parts of France. And the way you describe Lyon, it sounds like a wonderful place. I think I could be happy there." He paused, and in the one-second silence Oliver heard volumes. "I would be happy to be where you are, Oliver."

It felt like a vice was closing around Oliver's heart. He squeezed his eyes shut. *Not again.* It was like with Marcel, barely more than a year ago. He could still picture the sorrow in Marcel's dark eyes.

"Tell me why not." Vincent's voice rang firm and a little bit loud.

Oliver looked back at him, but focused on his chin instead of those pale blue eyes. "I told you that I'm getting married in January. I think for us to see one another often would be—uncomfortable."

He could feel the intensity of Vincent's deep sigh through his arms.

"That is always the way, Oliver," he said, quieter, with a hint of resignation in his voice. "Every lover I have had since I was twenty-two years old has been married. The vintner I told you about, who was my boyfriend for four years—he was married with three teenage sons. But he still found time to commit to me. And I was happy with our arrangement, until he found someone else, someone younger and handsomer—an apprentice at his cave."

He put his hand on Oliver's chin and raised it up so that Oliver had no choice but to look in his eyes. "I understand how the world works. This is the way of things. I know I would rather share you with your wife than to not see you again."

Oliver tensed and pulled away from him. He went into the little kitchen to pour a glass of wine. Yes, he was sure what Vincent said was true; instead of a mistress, most men like Vincent—or Dolph, or Marcel—had wives but gave their hearts to a male lover. He had probably met dozens of such men without ever knowing it. Their wives were a cover.

Like spies had a cover.

The realization smacked him in the face. He'd been living the same way, essentially, for the last few months, his outward life a cover for his spy activities.

But he didn't have the strength to keep that up forever, let alone the double dose of it should Vincent follow him to Lyon, and they were to continue a liaison…

"I can't," he said, head down.

It was quiet for almost a full minute. He stood there, hands on the counter, staring at the base of the wine bottle. Vincent didn't move from his place in the middle of the apartment, watching him.

Then Vincent's voice made Oliver jump. It was loud, almost accusatory, and he spun toward it.

"You speak often of wanting to live your own life, Oliver. But then you are afraid to live it."

The look in Vincent's eyes was so sad it almost broke Oliver's heart. Might have, even, if he weren't stung by the rebuke.

He looked down at the counter again. "Maybe what I want, and what is right, are not the same thing."

He saw his father's disapproving face in his mind's eye, and he squeezed his eyes shut again, trying to banish the image. Damn it, this wasn't about the church, or people's judgments, or any of his father's commandments. He'd flaunted those for over a decade, for Christ's sake. No, this was only about Lisette, and his obligation to her.

Obligation. That most dreaded word.

And then Vincent was next to him, his warmth radiating like a furnace inches from his arm. He put his hand in the small of Oliver's back, and it burned like fire.

"What is right is being true to your own self, Oliver—like that Hamlet said in the English play. You will see, someday. I hope it is soon—and I hope I am there to see it."

He leaned forward and kissed Oliver's temple. It was an unexpected and tender gesture. Oliver looked up, stunned.

And then Vincent was gone, out the door. The apartment was silent. And empty.

Oliver stood rooted in place, staring at the closed door, for almost a full minute. And then a shock wave rushed through him out of nowhere, and he couldn't control the tears that poured forth.

38

Tuesday, November 10

Chéragas, Algeria, Unoccupied France

It was a rugged seven-kilometer hike through the hills west of Algiers, and it took more than two hours to come within sight of the barbed wire fence surrounding the internment camp a couple of kilometers south of the coastal town of Chéragas. Patrice held up his hand for the others to stop, and then motioned for everyone to take cover in the scrub brush beside the dusty trail.

From behind a scraggly bush, he put a pair of binoculars to his eyes, and scanned the perimeter of the camp, counting guards and guard towers.

Ten guard towers, each with two armed guards, plus one guard patrolling the perimeter between each tower. And he could see other guards standing around the prisoner barracks, or lounging near the other buildings, an unknown number who kept coming and going between buildings.

Patrice had only been able to round up seventeen other résistants last night; he made eighteen. So they were seriously outnumbered. They could only hope that the prisoners would take the opportunity to revolt against their captors. There was a chance makeshift weapons were hidden in the floorboards of those prisoner barracks.

The internment camp outside of Chéragas had been built to house political dissidents, those whom Vichy found dangerous—but within months it had become home to hundreds of French soldiers whose only crime was being born Jewish. They were kicked out of the army when their citizenship was stolen from them in October 1940; but on account of their military training local authorities deemed them too dangerous to simply be allowed to return to civilian life, and so they were locked up here and at six other camps across Algeria.

With any luck, that military training would compel them to attack their captors as soon as they realized liberation was at hand.

Patrice raised the sixty-year-old rifle and aimed it at one of the guards standing in the nearest guard tower. He motioned for the others to do the same, and heard them cock the iron hammers behind him. He waited until he had a perfect shot—the guard facing fully toward him, chest exposed—and pulled the trigger.

**

Algiers, Unoccupied France

The afternoon newspaper made Oliver's heart race.

The top headline announced that General Eisenhower had named Admiral Darlan as French High Commissioner in North Africa. In return, Darlan had ordered all French forces to cease combat against the Allies—and so the fighting had stopped at Casablanca and Oran.

Oliver sighed. It was the expedient move, and ended the fighting after just three days, but his heart ached at the thought of Vichy's reactionaries remaining in charge here. And he could imagine how Patrice and the others would react to the news.

He didn't have to imagine the Axis reaction, it was spelled out in the second main story below the first one:

German and Italian Forces Cross Libyan Frontier Into Tunisia

Oliver shook his head and grumbled when he read that Pétain had ordered General Barré in Tunisia to not resist the Axis entry into Tunisia—and Barré had complied, pulling his forces back from Tunis and allowing the Germans to take all of the airfields.

In case the world had any doubts whose side Pétain is on, he's made it clear.

But then one of the other front-page stories caught his attention, farther down the page:

Guards at Chéragas Internment Facility Repulse Attack

Oliver read the opening paragraphs of the story, and he knew that Patrice was behind that attack. He'd always been passionate about that internment camp. And then Oliver's heart sank when he read how it concluded:

"One guard was killed, and three wounded. All of the résistants were apprehended and executed by firing squad."

His stomach sank into the pit of his belly, and a wave of guilt washed through him. "Shit!"

39

Wednesday, November 11
Lyon, France

It was mid-morning, and Lisette was arranging flowers in a vase for the gray-haired woman at the counter when the sound of sirens split the air. More sirens joined the first, and she stopped what she was doing to join the older woman at the shop window.

The people in the streets all stopped to listen. Apprehension showed on every face.

"I haven't heard sirens like that in two-and-a-half years," the old woman said. "But it can't be an air raid, not here in the Free Zone."

Lisette hurried to the back of the shop. "Turn on the radio," she said to Mr. Moreau. He turned to the radio cabinet behind him, opened the doors, and turned the power dial.

"...has ordered French troops not to resist the German columns. All citizens are commanded to not interfere, under penalty of law. Repeating: German infantry and armored divisions have crossed the Line of Demarcation into the Free Zone. Marshall Pétain, head of the State of France, has ordered French troops not to resist the German columns. All citizens are commanded..."

Mr. Moreau switched off the radio. His face was heavy when he turned back toward Lisette. "Please mind the front of the store, Miss Rousseau. I believe you have a customer."

**

Dolph watched in tight-lipped silence as columns of Daimler trucks barreled into the square and vomited out squadrons of

Wehrmacht soldiers in field gray. The sense of dread that weighed down his belly grew into visceral terror when he saw open-topped black Citroen convertibles depositing officers in the familiar black uniforms and caps of the Waffen SS.

His mind flooded with memories of SS officers dragging away his friends while he hid in a shed, peeking through a crack in the clapboards. That had been more than eight years ago, and so much had happened in the interim—but at this moment it felt as if it had just happened yesterday.

He walked past without looking directly at them, tugging the rim of his fedora lower to hide his features, but otherwise acting nonchalant, unhurried. It was only a couple of blocks to the restaurant where Marcel worked, and he tried to calm his nerves.

Marcel met his eye when he entered, and nodded toward the kitchen door. Dolph looked around to make sure none of the lunchtime patrons were watching—fortunately, they were all engrossed in hushed conversations, heads down—and he slipped through the swinging door after Marcel.

"Are they coming for you?" Marcel whispered once they were alone in the dry storeroom. His eyes were wide, and there was a slight tremble in his lower lip.

"Not yet," Dolph said. "They don't know I'm here to look for. But they'll set up check points before the end of the day, and sooner or later I'll have to show my papers. Once they see I'm German, they'll check my name against the wanted lists. Even if I use false identification, they'll hear my accent and know I'm from Germany, and I'll be kept for 'questioning.' It's not safe for me to stay."

"But how?" Marcel asked, his voice rising a half-octave.

Dolph put his hands on Marcel's arms, stared directly into his dark eyes. "I need for you to get a message to Franz in Switzerland, right away. Can you leave work early to send it?"

"I think so," Marcel said. Then he squared his slender shoulders and raised his chin. "Yes, I will do it."

"Good. Thank you." Dolph took a second to stroke the young man's cheek. "I must hide until Franz can arrange for my departure. I'll go home, collect what I need, and go to your apartment. Meet me there as soon as you've sent the message."

**

Thursday, November 12
Algiers, Algeria, Unoccupied France
The newspaper headline made Oliver's heart stop for a second.

German Military Occupies All Of Metropolitan France

Lisette. His heart pounded. He couldn't get home to her, not now. He would be an enemy alien, and the Germans would send him to an internment camp for the rest of the war. However long that lasted.

Frank Dryden and the rest of the Americans at the embassy in Vichy would be detained by the Germans, but at least their detainment would only be temporary. They would be repatriated in a diplomatic exchange soon enough. But any other Americans in Lyon—or Marseille, or anywhere else in the south of France—would be rounded up and detained until the end of the war.

He thought of all their friends in Lyon. Their resistance work would continue, he was certain, but now they would be hunted by the Gestapo. The danger had just increased exponentially.

And what of Dolph? He had fled Paris ahead of the occupation in June 1940 because the Gestapo would send him to a concentration camp if they discovered him. Oliver could only assume the same thing applied now—but the surprise action meant he wouldn't have had time to get away. He was in the most immediate danger.

And there was nothing Oliver could do, for any of them. He couldn't even get word to Lisette.

**

The American consulate was a zoo when Oliver arrived forty minutes later. The poor receptionist looked frazzled, trying to calm irritated middle-aged American businessmen who wanted to speak with a consular officer right away.

She recognized Oliver, and looked away from the stocky, roughly forty-five-year-old man in the pinstriped suit. "Mr. Carmichael, I will tell Mr. Murphy you're here." Then to the man in front of her, "One moment, please, sir."

"Why does he get to speak to someone before me?" the man demanded.

"He's expected, sir. Just one moment, please." She picked up the phone receiver and dialed an extension. "Mr. Carmichael to see you, sir."

It amused Oliver that he was 'expected' today. But of course he was.

"Mr. Murphy will see you right away, Mr. Carmichael. He said to go right up."

Oliver enjoyed the look of consternation on the stocky businessman's face as he passed. He smiled at the receptionist and thanked her more enthusiastically than usual, just to see the man turn red.

Telephones seemed to be ringing in every office he passed on the way down the hall to Robert Murphy's office. Consular staff scurried from one office to another.

He found Robert Murphy speaking into a Dictaphone, but he stopped and hung up the receiver when Oliver appeared in his doorway.

"Carmichael, come on in. Have a seat."

"Thank you, sir." Oliver took one of the wooden chairs in front of Murphy's desk.

"Seems you're not going back to metropolitan France today after all."

"No, sir, I guess not." Oliver tried to sound nonchalant about it, but he could hear a hint of his own agitation in his tone.

"It's a lousy mess, and we weren't prepared for it," Murphy said, gruff. "Obviously, Frank Dryden is going to be indisposed for a little while, until they can arrange a diplomatic exchange through the Swiss. After that, we can't say where he'll end up. That leaves you unassigned. Fortunately, we've got plenty of work that needs done right here."

Right here. "Then I'll be staying in Algiers?"

"For the moment," Murphy said. "As the army moves east into Tunisia, we might have to send you there."

"'We,' sir?"

Murphy chuckled. "OSS. I'm not officially working for them, of course, but everyone here knows it. Now that you're not going back to Dryden, I think it's time we made your role with OSS official. What do you say, Carmichael?"

**

Vincent wore a strange expression when Oliver went to his apartment to ask him to lunch. It was more than just anger over the expanded German occupation in France, Oliver could see that in his eyes—there was a coldness, a distance there.

"You saw the news," Oliver said after his friend sat across from him on the couch.

Vincent nodded. "The newspaper said the Germans were acting in retaliation for Darlan's surrender. Because he is a representative of Vichy. They saw it as official treachery."

His words had a bite that surprised Oliver, and also made him uncomfortable. It felt as if Vincent were directing that ire at *him.*

"We didn't need any more proof that Hitler can't be trusted to keep his promises," Oliver said. Keeping the focus on whose fault this really was.

Vincent's lips tightened into a thin line. "Perhaps if the Resistance had been allowed to take over the administration in Algeria and Morocco, instead of Vichy's own people, Hitler would have honored the agreement with Pétain. He would not use betrayal as an excuse."

Oliver's cheeks heated. This argument again. It wasn't as if he disagreed with Vincent and the others, not really, but it wasn't *his* fault.

"Well, obviously we can't go to Lyon now," he said, trying to shift the conversation. "That's the bad news. The good news is that the American consulate wants me to stay here for a while."

"How is that good news?" Vincent said, crossing his arms. "I don't have a job anymore. And no other club here will hire me now."

Now that they know. It shouldn't surprise him that Garnier would have told every other club in the city. Vincent was blackballed. A dirty queer. Oliver tried not to think about that.

"What if I could get you a job? One in which you'd be working with me."

Vincent leaned back, arms still crossed. "Working for the Americans? Why would I want to do that?"

Oliver leaned forward to counteract Vincent's leaning back. "You'll be helping to defeat the Nazis. And we can continue to work together. We make a good team, you and I."

"Defeating the Nazis," Vincent said, slowly, in an odd tone.

"Yes," Oliver said, confused by Vincent's tone, and the strange expression on his face.

It was quiet for a moment, and then his friend leaned forward, close to him. "What do you really believe, Oliver?"

Oliver's mind went blank. He wasn't sure what kind of answer Vincent was looking for. He looked back dumbly and could only shrug.

"Why do you do what you do?" Vincent pressed.

Oliver frowned in confusion. "Music?"

Vincent shook his head, not breaking eye contact.

So you mean the spy stuff. Thinking over the recent weeks, Oliver shrugged and said, "Because I love my country." Wasn't that obvious?

Vincent looked sad. "I love my country, too. That is why I work to make her better. I cannot accept that the autocrats at Vichy are the best that France can be. We can make her better, but only if we challenge her. When will you challenge your country's missteps, Oliver?"

Oliver scowled, leaned away, and crossed his arms. "What makes you think I haven't?"

"Have you?"

The intensity of Vincent's blue eyes made Oliver look away. "Yes. The day after the invasion, I passed along Patrice's criticism. I even told them I agreed with his point of view. But when they told me that cooperating with Darlan had stopped the fighting and saved American lives, I couldn't disagree with that." He looked at Vincent then, staring right back at him, challenging. "How could I?"

Vincent looked very sad. He seemed to deflate before Oliver's eyes, and made a little shrug. "I suppose you could not."

They sat in silence for a moment. Oliver slowly relaxed, the tension of the disagreement seeping out of his shoulders. "Will you consider coming to work with me?"

Vincent sighed, and then shook his head. "How can I work in cooperation with the Vichy authorities?"

Oliver took a deep breath, resigned that he would never change Vincent's mind about that. "It won't always be that way," he said, quietly; but he barely believed that himself.

"You cannot promise that."

Oliver nodded and stood. "Let me know if you change your mind. I'll be leaving for the east in a couple of days. I don't know when I'll be back in Algiers after that."

**

Saturday, November 14

A lieutenant in khaki fatigues parked a Jeep in front of Oliver's building at noon. Oliver was waiting, and he threw his luggage in the back. He paused before climbing into the passenger seat, taking one last look around.

Hoping to see Vincent walking toward them.

He knew he wouldn't, but even so a wave of disappointment weighed on his chest when he climbed into the Jeep.

This chapter of his life was ending. He had to keep facing forward, toward the future.

"It's a six-hour drive to Bône, sir," the lieutenant said. "It could get a little rough in spots, after last night's rain. But this baby can handle any terrain. Just hold on tight."

Hold on tight. He kept repeating that to himself as the jeep sped off toward the coastal highway and headed east.

Toward an uncertain future.

EPILOGUE

Friday, December 25

Bône, Algeria, Unoccupied France

The soldiers of the 34th Infantry grew increasingly raucous as the afternoon progressed, and Christmas songs got rewritten on the spot with bawdier lyrics by the more poetic of them, to uproarious laughter. Others took turns dancing with the hundred or so unattached French girls who had been brought to the empty hangar outside of town off the coastal highway, which had been decorated for the dance by the U.S.O. Dozens of men danced with each other, hamming it up as they did.

Oliver sat at a table with a glass of Christmas punch, watching the goings-on with detached amusement. He'd grown friendly with several of the G.I.s in his barracks over the last six weeks, but he remained an outsider.

And he'd made up his mind to leave, anyway.

In the footlocker at the end of his cot back at barracks, stashed between folded shirts, sat the Christmas card he'd received a few days ago from Frank and Cécile Dryden—postmarked from Beirut, Lebanon.

For the last six weeks, he'd been liaising with the French military forces guarding the mountain passes from Algeria into Tunisia, some fifty-five miles to the east of here. They were stubbornly refusing to take *any* side in the ongoing battle between the Allies and the Germans in northwestern Tunisia.

Oliver had no military expertise, but he was teamed up with a trio of Army Intelligence Analysts from MID—Military Intelligence Division—as the OSS representative. He provided the cultural and linguistic expertise that was supposed to help them persuade the French forces to join the Free French and fight alongside the Allies.

It wasn't the kind of work he would have chosen, but it was important—and it might have been satisfying, even, had they had a smidgeon of success. Instead, all he felt was frustration.

The division's HQ was increasingly impatient, and Oliver was getting tired of getting yelled at by generals because the French were being so damned stubborn.

Robert Murphy had come to see Oliver a couple of weeks ago, suggesting he could reach out to the local Resistance in Bône, to recruit scouts and guerilla fighters for the Allies.

He'd quietly ignored that directive. What had happened in Algiers still tasted sour in his mouth.

The news given to the G.I.s was censored, but Oliver got off-base every day, and he read the local French-language newspaper. So he knew that a few weeks ago, Admiral Darlan had ordered the arrest of the résistants who participated in the attempted coup d'état the night of November 7th through 8th to support the Allied Invasion.

The American government had said nothing. Oliver seethed.

And so, it had seemed like a sign from God when he received the note from Frank Dryden on Monday, tucked into an innocuous-looking Christmas card.

> *Monday, December 14, 1942*
> *Dearest Oliver,*
> *Greetings from Beirut! I'm sure you're wondering how I came to be here.*

After a brief internment with the Germans, the embassy staff was put under the custody of the Swiss ambassador, who had us transported to Geneva. Cécile and Justin met me there. It took a little time for Washington to send everyone new orders, so my family enjoyed some time off at St. Moritz.

I got my assignment to the American consulate in Beirut at the beginning of December. It was a little tricky getting here, since Switzerland is now 100% surrounded by Axis-controlled territory. We had to fly on a Swiss commercial airplane to Istanbul, and that took a lot of preparation. But once in Istanbul, we took an overnight train to Beirut, and got here safe and sound on the 10th.

It's been a long time since I had to start from scratch at a new place. I wish I had a trusted lieutenant with me to help get the ball rolling.

Cécile sends her love. I'm sure you are quite busy in Algeria these days, but we would both love to see you the next time you have leave to travel. I think you would really like Beirut. It's called

> *"the Paris of the Near East" for good*
> *reason.*
>   *Write to us when you get the chance.*
> *I hope you are well. Merry Christmas!*
>   *Your friend,*
>
>   *Frank Dryden*

Oliver had made up his mind on the spot. He was leaving for Beirut, as soon as he could arrange it.

But that was tricky business. For starters, he couldn't simply walk away. He didn't know if he could resign, since he was not *officially* employed by the OSS—he was a sort of independent contractor—but he did know that if he turned in his resignation, he would be tossed off base within an hour. Don't let the door hit you on the way out, mister.

No, what he needed to do was use the relative independence of his role here to get away, if he could find the means. Then once he was in Beirut, Frank Dryden could make his reassignment official.

But that lead to his second dilemma—how to get there. There was no going by land, since Axis-controlled Tunisia and Libya stood between here and British-controlled Egypt. But going by ship would be dangerous, given the German U-boat activity in the Mediterranean. Even neutral Spanish ships could be mistakenly torpedoed if the German captain weren't careful enough.

He had to be cautious about asking around at the port, but on Thursday morning—Christmas Eve—he found a Spanish ship that was leaving for Beirut on Saturday, after letting her crew rest in Bône a couple of days for Christmas.

Spur of the moment, he dashed off a short telegram to Vincent in Algiers, asking him to come see him in Bône before the holiday.

There might be a chance that Vincent would visit his family for Christmas, so Oliver took a chance that his friend might like to see him.

He never heard back. And Vincent hadn't come.

Oliver sighed while he watched the American G.I.s dance around the hangar with French girls, doing the wild new Swing moves. He envied them, their faces alight with the possibility of romance, and the joy of the moment. He'd lost Lisette, he'd lost Marcel, and he'd lost Vincent.

He took a flask from his jacket pocket and poured a glug of the gin into his punch glass, then stirred it with his finger. He raised his glass in a solo toast. "Here's to being on my own." He downed it in three gulps.

**

Oliver had gotten up and was about to leave when he was approached by a helmeted soldier with an MP armband. "Mr. Carmichael?" he asked with an arched brow.

"Yes, I'm Oliver Carmichael." Oliver recognized many of the MPs who stood guard at the gate to the base, but he didn't recognize this one.

"There's a visitor to see you at the gate. A civilian. French."

Oliver thought he detected a note of disapproval on that last fact, and he couldn't help a tiny smile that tugged at the corners of his mouth. "I'll follow you, sergeant."

The last red vestiges of dusk on the western horizon were fading into a deep blue twilight, and the temperature was dropping. Oliver could see wisps of his breath while they walked across the base.

They were still twenty yards from the gate when he recognized Vincent's shape, facing away from him, unaware of his approach.

His heart soared. His feet became light, and his steps quickened.

"Thank you, sergeant," Oliver said, quietly, when they were still a few yards from the gate. The MP sergeant nodded and turned back toward the guard shack.

Vincent turned toward Oliver when the pair of MPs standing on either side of the gate stepped aside to let him out.

"I'd started to think you weren't going to come," Oliver said in French, grinning. He wanted to throw his arms around Vincent and squeeze him tight, but he stopped a few feet in front of him, conscious of the MPs watching their every move.

"I got your note," Vincent said, and Oliver grinned wider at the obviousness of that statement.

"I'm glad to see you," Oliver said, quietly. Then, after only a second's hesitation and a quick glance at the MPs, he added even more quietly, "I've missed you."

The look in Vincent's eyes echoed the statement. He took a step closer to Oliver, face lowered to speak intimately. "I've missed you, too. I was glad to get your note." His face screwed up with effort, as if he were struggling with what to say. Then the words poured out quickly. "I was stupid to blame you for things that weren't your fault. I'm sorry. I should not have done that. I should have trusted you. Then, when I read that you're leaving…" His voice trailed off.

Oliver desperately wanted to reach out, to touch Vincent's arm, but a quick sideways glance confirmed the MPs were still watching. His hand stayed at his side.

"Will you come with me?" he whispered, and held his breath, watching Vincent's pale eyes that reflected the electric light from the guard shack.

A tiny smile stretched Vincent's lips, and a hint of his dimple appeared above his dark beard. He nodded, almost imperceptibly. "Yes."

A thrill rushed through Oliver, and he was afraid he was about to start laughing and crying at the same time. He tamped down his emotions with great effort, keeping his expression as passive as he could manage.

He didn't know for certain if any of the MPs understood French, so he stepped as close to Vincent as he dared, and whispered, "Meet me tomorrow morning, eleven o'clock, at the north end of the port. The *Ensanche*, Spanish cargo ship, leaves at noon."

Vincent's face glowed with excitement. "I will be there."

**

Saturday, December 26

Oliver waited until the last moment to hand the envelope to the Jeep driver who had brought him to the port from base. It was addressed to Robert Murphy at the American Consulate in Algiers, and Oliver asked the driver to have that mailed as soon as he got back to base. By the time it arrived on Monday, he would already be in Beirut.

It was almost quarter to noon, so Oliver hurried down the concrete wharf that jutted out into the port, angled toward the light house guarding the entrance from the Mediterranean. He found the *Ensanche* near the end. He rounded the corner of their pier, and Vincent stood at the bottom of the gang walk with a suitcase at his feet. Oliver smiled in relief.

Part of him had wondered if Vincent would change his mind. But now the obvious glint of joy in his friend's pale eyes sent a familiar lightness through his belly. He put his arm around his friend's shoulder, and they walked onboard.

**

Twenty minutes later, they stood at the bow of the freighter, arms on the top of the railing, leaning forward, watching Bône shrink into the distance.

"They speak French in Beirut," Oliver said, nudging Vincent's elbow. "And Lebanon's administration is in the hands of the Free French, not Vichy. We'll be safe there."

"I have always wanted to go there," Vincent said, wistful. "People say it is one of the most beautiful places. The 'Paris of the Near East.' I am glad to go there, at last." He turned his head and looked at Oliver. "And I am glad to go with you. Beirut is a cosmopolitan city, very modern. If we rent a two-bedroom apartment, no one would question it. We would not have to use the second bedroom."

His pale blue eyes held Oliver's for a moment, and the gleam in them was unmistakable.

Why the hell not? "We could do that." Oliver's stomach went light, and a tingle rushed forward to his groin. His cheeks flushed, and he grinned in spite of himself. He looked down at his hands in embarrassment. "I would like that."

Vincent's grin stretched from ear to ear, and his cheek dimples were pronounced above the top of his dark beard. He bumped his shoulder against Oliver's in a chummy sort of way. But the tone of his near-whisper was more intense. "I love you, Oliver."

Love? A moment of panic swept through Oliver. He pictured Marcel in the loft of that church in Vierzon, where Oliver had told him he couldn't love him the way he wanted. Because of Lisette. Marcel's sorrow had broken his heart.

But Vincent was not Marcel. This felt more...what, exactly? He supposed he could love Vincent, in time. But it was dangerous to love a man.

Oliver hesitated only a second, watching the coast of North Africa slip into the haze.

"I love you, too."

THE END

Thank you for reading Each Hidden Passage! If you enjoyed this book, please tell a friend, update your social media, and/or write a review on Amazon, Goodreads, or other forum.

To find out about my other books, get reading recommendations, and to receive notifications when new books are available, <u>sign up for my newsletter</u>.

Questions or comments? Feel free to contact me or sign up for my newsletter at <u>www.garretthutson.com</u>

Also by Garrett Hutson:

Gray Paree (Tales of the Bohemian Resistance, book 1)

In A Safe Town

The Jade Dragon (Death in Shanghai, Book 1)

Assassin's Hood (Death in Shanghai, Book 2)

No Accidental Death (Death in Shanghai, Book 3)

Hidden Among Us (Martin Schuller Spy Catcher, Book 1)

Spy Tango (Martin Schuller Spy Catcher, Book 2)

The Swiss Conspiracy (Martin Schuller Spy Catcher, Book 3)

About the Author

Garrett Hutson writes upmarket mysteries and historical spy fiction. He lives in Indianapolis with his husband, three adorable dogs, an oddball cats, and more fish that you can count. He has one grown daughter. You may contact him at his website, www.garretthutson.com.

Historical Note

This is a work of fiction. All characters, with the exception of a few historical figures noted below, are fictional.

Among the historical figures included in reference only are Henri Frenay, leader of the resistance group Combat; French premier Marshal Phillippe Pétain; American President Franklin Roosevelt; British Prime Minister Winston Churchill; German chancellor Adolf Hitler; song-writers Cole Porter, Irving Berlin, and Hoagy Carmichael; Colonel William Donovan; Vichy French military leaders Admiral Darlan and General Juin; and General Charles De Gaulle.

I try to avoid casting real people as characters, but on occasion it is necessary for the story—some historical figures that appear briefly in the narrative include American *Chargé d'affaires* Robert Murphy; and Joseph Darnand, head of the SOL.

Most of the events I've written are fictional, products of my imagination—however, I have included some real historical events for context. The big snow storm in the far south of France in the winter of 1942 was real, and really did strand a passenger train just north of Avignon; though I have been unable to confirm the exact dates, so I made them up to fit the narrative. The trial at Riom was a real event, and transpired pretty much as described. William Donovan did use the phrase "secret war" to describe his organization's attitude toward Vichy. American intelligence really did break into the French embassy in Washington D.C., stole their codes, and copied and replaced them before dawn. This did enable the U.S. to decode French communiques and determine that Vichy was cooperating with Nazi Germany far more than previously known. Operation Torch, the Allied invasion of North Africa, happened as described in this book. The German occupation of the *Zone Libre* in response was also a real event, and I have attempted to describe it as it actually happened.

The year 1942 was a big one for American intelligence. Colonel William Donovan, the Coordinator of Information, was actively growing a first-rate intelligence organization that he wanted to be on par with much older established organizations in Europe and Japan. America's entry into World War 2 just months after Donovan's installation meant that he and his staff around the world had to make things up as they went along, and fast. In June 1942, Donovan's organization adopted the name Office of Strategic Services (OSS for short).

This learn fast and act fast reality left me plenty of room to use my imagination in regards to Frank Dryden's activities collecting intel on Vichy, and on the anti-Vichy resistance in the Unoccupied Zone. Oliver's assignments are entirely a creation of my imagination, and to my knowledge do not resemble any real events or people. I tried to stay consistent with the general build-up of U.S. involvement in Axis-dominated Europe during this time, however, which focused on quietly subverting both Vichy's collaboration with Germany, and its popular support in France.

I've endeavored to be as accurate as possible in describing the political and social environment of the story, and the complicated interlocking games of diplomacy and espionage in the early years of World War Two. I have taken only a few liberties, such as the American agent escorting Spanish guns to Corsica for the French Resistance in the Unoccupied Zone. I have found no documentation of any specific operations like this, though it is clear that the U.S. supplied fire-arms to the Resistance in the Unoccupied Zone, which had been ignored by

Hutson

British intelligence (which focused on the Occupied Zone). This allowed me to use my imagination when writing these scenes, while keeping with the overall spirit of the American strategy.

The bohemian subculture of Paris and other cities is well-documented, though many writers have straight-washed out the prevalent gay and bisexual nature of many bohemians. While it's no secret that bohemian subcultures around the world challenge established mores, little fiction has focused on the well-documented bisexual undercurrent of bohemian communities. While perhaps not as visible to the world at-large as the more routine bohemian flouting of social conventions, these militantly individualistic communities were home to many gay and bisexual men and women who were relatively open about their orientation—at least, among themselves. I have attempted to depict them as they would have been in 1942. Throughout the 19th and 20th centuries, bohemian subcultures tended to accept alternatives to heteronormative sexuality regardless of the attitude of the larger culture, a fact which is not often well-known among cishet people.

That said, French mores in general might seem scandalous to many Anglophone readers—especially its relative ambivalence to marital fidelity. French love affairs have become a staple in film, and for good reason. This is why I felt comfortable writing Sébastien's relationship with the Verlacs, and Oliver's interactions with Symphonie and Vincent, respectively.

As always, I have done my best to be as historically accurate as possible, except where noted above. Any errors are mine alone.

Hutson

Acknowledgements

Contrary to appearances, writing and publishing a novel is never a solitary endeavor, and I have many people to thank for their contributions.

First, my thanks go to the talented writers in the IndyScribes critique group—Laura VanArondonk Baugh, Stephanie Cain, Peggy Larkin, Stephanie Ferguson, Jim Meeks-Johnson, Jim Thompson, and Chelsea Sanders—who patiently read and critiqued many sections of the early drafts, and provided excellent feedback. They've had a hand in improving every book I've published. You all are the best!

Sincere thanks to my beta readers—Jessi Rauh and Stephanie Cain—who took the time to read the entire manuscript and provided valuable insights and feedback. You helped to bring out the best in this story, and I can't thank you enough.

Many thanks to Stuart Bache for another incredible cover. It really captures the essence and feel of the story.

And last, but never least, my deepest gratitude, love, and devotion to my husband David Lee. I can't say how much your support means to me. For years you've put up with countless hours during which I immerse myself in my stories. You give me the freedom to live this amazing and sometimes infuriating life of a fiction writer, and you're always supportive through all of its ups and downs. I am incredibly lucky, and I know it. I love you more than words can express.

-Garrett B. Hutson, August 2022

www.ingramcontent.com/pod-product-compliance
Lightning Source LLC
Chambersburg PA
CBHW061039190726
48286CB00006B/1521